EASY PREY

Also by John Sandford
in Large Print:

Winter Prey
Sudden Prey
Certain Prey

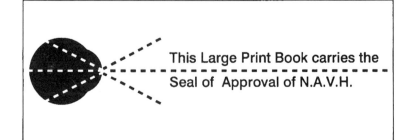

This Large Print Book carries the
Seal of Approval of N.A.V.H.

EASY PREY

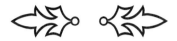

JOHN SANDFORD

G.K. Hall & Co. • Thorndike, Maine

Published in 2000 by arrangement with G. P. Putnam's Sons, a member of Penguin Putnam Inc.

G.K. Hall Large Print Core Series.

The text of this Large Print edition is unabridged.
Other aspects of the book may vary from the original edition.

Set in 16 pt. Plantin by Elena Picard.

Printed in the United States on permanent paper.

Library of Congress Cataloging-in-Publication Data

Sandford, John, 1944 Feb. 23–
    Easy prey / John Sandford.
      p. (large print) cm.
    ISBN 0-7838-9074-5 (lg. print : hc : alk. paper)
    ISBN 0-7838-9073-7 (lg. print : sc : alk. paper)
    1. Davenport, Lucas (Fictitious character) — Fiction.
 2. Private investigators — Minnesota — Minneapolis — Fiction.
 3. Minneapolis (Minn.) — Fiction. 4. Large type books. I. Title.
PS3569.A516 E27 2000b
 813′.54—dc21   00-039650

FOR STEPHEN AND COLLEEN CAMP

1

When the first man woke up that morning, he wasn't thinking about killing anyone. He woke up with a head full of blues, a brain that was too big for his skull, and a bladder about to burst. He lay with his eyes closed, breathing across a tongue that tasted like burnt chicken feathers. The blues rolled in through the bedroom door.

Coming down hard.

He had been flying on cocaine for three days, getting everything done, *everything*. Then last night, coming down, he'd stopped at a liquor store for a bottle of Stolichnaya. His bleeding brain retained a picture of himself lifting the bottle off the shelf, and another picture of an argument with the counterman, who didn't want to break a hundred-dollar bill.

By that time, the coke high had become unsustainable; and the Stoli had been a bad idea. There was no smooth landing after a three-day toot, but the vodka turned a wheels-up belly landing into a full crash-and-burn. Now he'd pay. If you peeled open his skull and dumped it, he thought, his brain would look like a coagulated lump of Campbell's bean soup.

He cracked his eyes, lifted his head, and looked at the clock. A few minutes past seven. He'd gotten four hours of sleep. Par for the course with coke, and the Stoli hadn't helped. If he'd stayed down for ten hours, or twelve — he needed about sixteen to catch up — he might have been past the worst of it. Now he was just gonna have to suck it up.

He turned to his left, where a woman, a dishwater blonde, lay facedown in her pillow. He could only see about half of her head; the rest was buried by a red fleece blanket. She lay without moving, like a dead woman — but no such luck. He closed his eyes again, and there was nothing left in the world but the blues music bumping in from the next room, from the all-blues channel, nine-hundred-and-something on the TV dial. Must've left it on last night. . . .

Gotta move, he thought. Gotta pee. Gotta take twenty aspirins and go down to Country Kitchen and get some pancakes and link sausages. . . .

The man didn't wake up thinking about murder. He woke up thinking about his head and his bladder and a stack of pancakes. Funny how things work out.

That night, when he killed two people, he was a little shocked.

Green-eyed Alie'e Maison stood in the hulk of a rust-colored Mississippi River barge. She was wrapped in a designer dress that looked like froth over a reef in the Caribbean Sea — an an-

8

kle-length dress the exact faded-jade color of her eyes, low-cut and sheer, hugging her hips, flaring at her ankles. She was large-eyed, barefoot, elfin, fleeing down a pale yellow two-by-twelve-inch pine plank, which stretched like a line of fire out of the purple gloom of the barge's interior.

Behind her, a huge man in a sleeveless white T-shirt, filthy Sears, Roebuck work pants, and ten-inch work boots blew sparks off a piece of wrought iron with an acetylene torch. He was wearing a black dome-shaped welding helmet, and acrid gray smoke curled around his heavy, tense legs. The blank robotic faceplate, in combination with his hairy arms, the dirty shirt, the smoke, and the squat legs, gave him the grotesque crouching power of a gargoyle.

A fantasy at three thousand dollars an hour.

And not quite right.

"That's no fucking good. NO FUCKING GOOD!"

Amnon Plain moved through the bank of strobes, his thick black hair falling over his forehead, his narrow glasses glittering in the set lights, his voice cutting like a piece of broken glass: "Alie'e, you're freezing up at the line. I want you *blowing out* of the place. I want you moving *faster* when you come up to the line, not slower. You're slowing down. And I want you to look *pissed*. You look annoyed, you look *petulant* —"

"I *am* annoyed — I'm freezing," Alie'e snapped. "I've got goose bumps the size of oranges."

Plain turned to an assistant: "Larry, move the heater into the back. You gotta get some heat on her."

"We'll get the fumes," Larry said, arms akimbo, a deliberately effeminate pose. Larry wasn't gay, just ironic.

"We'll deal with the fucking fumes. Huh? Okay? We'll deal with the fucking fumes."

"You gotta do something. I'm really cold," Alie'e said. She clasped her arms around herself and shivered for effect. A man dressed in black walked out from behind the lights, peeling off his cashmere sport coat. He was tall, thin, his over-the-shoulder brunette hair worn loose and back. He had a thick hammered-silver loop earring in his left ear and a dark soul-patch under his lower lip. "Take this until they're ready again," he said to Alie'e. She huddled in the coat. Turning away from them, Plain rolled his eyes. "Larry — move the fuckin' heater."

Larry shrugged and began wheeling the propane heater farther into the barge. If they all died of carbon monoxide poisoning, it wouldn't be his fault.

Plain turned back to Alie'e. "Jax, take a hike, and take your coat with you. . . ."

"Hey —" the man in black said, but nobody was looking at him, or paying attention.

Plain continued: "Alie'e, I want you pissed.

Don't do that thing with your lips. You're sticking your lips out, like this." Plain pursed his lips. "That's a pout. I don't want a pout. Do it like this. . . ." He grimaced, and Alie'e tried to imitate him. This was one of her talents: the ability to imitate expression, the way a dancer could imitate motion.

"That's better," Plain said to Alie'e. "But make your mouth longer, turn it down, and get it set that way while you're *moving*. Do it again." She did it again, making the changes. "That's good, but now you need some mouth."

He turned back to the line of lights and the small crowd gathered behind them — an account executive, a creative director, a makeup artist, a hairdresser, a couture rep, a second photo assistant, and Alie'e's parents, Lynn and Lil. Plain did not provide chairs, and the inside of the barge was not a place you'd want to sit down, not if your hand-tailored jeans cost four hundred and fifty dollars. To the makeup artist, Plain said, "Fix her mouth." And to the second assistant: "Jimmy, where's the fucking Polaroid? You got the Polaroid?"

Jimmy was fanning a six-by-seven-centimeter Polaroid color print, which was used to check exposure. He glanced at the print and said, "It's coming up."

Behind him, the creative director whispered to the account executive, "Says 'fuck' a lot," and the account executive muttered, "They all do."

Plain peered at the Polaroid, looked up at an

overhead softbox. "Move that box. About two feet to the right, that way." Jimmy moved it, and Plain looked around. "Everybody ready? Alie'e, remember the line. Clark, are you ready?"

The welder said, "Yeah, I'm ready. Was that enough sparks?"

"Sparks were fine, sparks were good," Plain said. "You're the only fucking professional working here this morning." He looked back at Alie'e. "Now, *don't* fucking pout — blow right *through* the line. . . ."

Alie'e waited patiently until her mouth was fixed, staring blankly past the makeup artist's ear as a bit of color was patched into the left corner of her lower lip; Jax said into her ear, "Love you. You're doing great, you look great." Alie'e barely heard him. She was *seeing* herself walking the plank, the vision of herself that came from Plain's mind.

When her mouth was done, she stepped back to her starting mark. Jax got out of the way, and when Plain said, "Go," Alie'e got her expression right, started down the plank with a lanky, hip-swinging stride, and *blew* past the exposure line, the green dress swirling about her hips, the or-ange-yellow welder's sparks flashing in the back-ground. The stink and smoke of the burning metal curled around her as Plain, standing be-hind the camera, fired the bank of strobes.

"Better," Plain said, stepping toward her. "A little fuckin' better."

They'd been working for two hours in the belly of the grain barge. The barge was a gift: a pilot on the Greek-owned Mississippi towboat *Treponema* had driven it into a protective abutment around a bridge piling. The damaged barge had been floated to the Anshiser repair yard in St. Paul, where welders cut away the buckled hull plates and prepared to burn on new ones. Plain spotted the disemboweled hulk while scouting for photo locations. He made a deal with Archer Daniels Midland, the barge owner: Delay repairs for a week, and ADM would make *Vogue*. The people who ran ADM couldn't think of a good reason why the company would worry about *Vogue*, but their publicity ladies were wetting their pants, so they said okay and the deal was made.

They were still working with the green dress when a team from TV3 showed up, and they all took a break. Alie'e goofed around, for the camera, with Jax, showing a little skin, doing a long, slow, rolling tongue-kiss, which the camera crew asked them to redo twice, once as a silhouette. The interviewer for TV3, a square-jawed ex-jock with bleached teeth and a smile he'd perfected in his bathroom mirror, said, after the cameras shut down, "It's a slow day. I think we'll lead the news with this."

Nobody asked why it was news: they all lived with cameras, and assumed that it was.

Two hours for four different shots, with and without fans, two rolls of high-saturation Fujichrome film for each of the shots. The Fuji would make the colors pop. Plain pronounced himself satisfied with the green dress, and they moved on.

The next pose involved a torn T-shirt and a pair of male-look women's briefs, complete with the vented front. Alie'e and Jax moved against the far hull and a little shadow, and Alie'e turned her back to the photo crowd and peeled off the green dress. She'd been nude beneath the dress; anything else would ruin the line.

She was aware of her nudity but not self-conscious about it, as she had been at first. Her first jobs had been as one model in a group, and they usually changed all at once; she was simply one naked woman among several. By the time she started up the ladder to stardom, to individual attention, she'd become as conditioned to public nudity as a striptease dancer.

Even more than that. She'd worked in Europe, with the Germans, and total nudity wasn't uncommon in fashion work. She remembered the first time she'd had her pubic hair brushed out, fluffed up. The brusher had been a thirty-something guy who'd squatted in front of her, smoking a cigarette while he brushed her, and then did a quick trim with a pair of barber scissors, all with the emotional neutrality of a postman sorting letters. Then the photographer came over to take a look, suggested a couple of extra snips. Her body might as well have been an apple. . . .

You want privacy? You turn your back. . . .

Alie'e Maison — "Ah-Lee-Ay May-Sone" — had been born Sharon Olson in Burnt River, Minnesota. Until she was seventeen, she'd lived with her parents and her brother, Tom, in a robin's-egg-blue rambler just off Highway 54, fourteen miles south of the Canadian line. She was a beautiful-baby. She won a beautiful-baby prize when she was a year old — she'd been born just before Halloween, and her costume was a pumpkin that her mother made on her Singer. A year later, Sharon toddled away with a statewide beautiful-toddler trophy. In that one, she'd been dressed as a lightning bug, in a suit of black and gold.

Dance and comportment lessons began when she was three, singing lessons when she was four. At five, she won the North Central Tap-Fairies contest for children five and younger. That was the pattern: Miss Junior North Country, International Miss Snow (International Falls and Fort Francis, Canada), Miss Border Lakes. She sang and danced through her school days. Miss Minnesota and even — her parents, Lynn and Lil, barely dared to dream it — Miss America was possible. Until she was fourteen, anyway.

When the breast genes were passed out in heaven, Alie'e had been in line for an extra helping of eyes instead. That became obvious in junior high when her friends began to complain about bra straps cutting into their necks. Not Alie'e. As the Olsons' best friends, Ellen and Bud Benton, said — Bud said it, anyway — "Ain't no Miss Minnesota without the big bumpers, y'know."

As it happened, the breasts didn't matter. In the summer of her sixteenth year, Lynn and Lil took her to a model agency in Minneapolis, and the agent liked what she saw. Alie'e had knife-edge cheekbones and those jade-green eyes. They came straight from God in a perfect package with white-blond hair, a flawless complexion, delicate fuck-me shoulder blades, and hips so narrow she'd have trouble giving birth to a baling wire.

Between Minneapolis and New York, Sharon Olson vanished and Alie'e Maison stepped into her size-six dress. She was so famous that the second-most-famous person in Burnt River was a lawn-care service operator named Louis Friar. Friar, one night in tenth grade, nailed Alie'e in the short grass beside the first-base line of the American Legion baseball diamond on Bergholm Road, on an air mattress that he'd brought along for that express purpose.

Louis never talked about it. He never even confirmed that it happened. He held the memory of the event in a beery reverence. Alie'e, on the other hand, talked to everyone; so everyone in Burnt River knew about it, and how, at

16

the critical moment, Louis had cried out, "Oh God oh God oh God oh God," which was why everybody in town called him Reverend. Friar himself thought the nickname was based on his last name, as if the residents of Burnt River were universally fond of puns; nobody ever told him different.

"You don't think they're getting too close to porno?" Lil now asked, under her breath to Lynn, as they watched Amnon Plain push their daughter around the set. "I don't want any god-damned porno." Lil had a thing about porno.

"You know they're not going to do any porno," Lynn said placatingly. He was wearing black-on-black, with wraparound Blades.

"They better not. That'll kill you in a minute." She refocused. "Look at Jax. I think he's so good for her."

Jax — he had no last name — was peering around the set through the viewfinder of a Nikon F5. He thought of himself as a photographer, although he hadn't yet taken many photographs. But how hard could it be? You look through the hole, you push the button. When Alie'e said, "You got anything?" Jax let the camera drop to his side, tipped his head, and they moved together against the hull of the barge. Jax took a plastic nose-drop bottle from his pocket and passed it to her. Alie'e unscrewed the top, slipped the end into a nostril, and squeezed the bottle once, twice. "Whoa, whoa," Jax muttered. "Not too much, it'll kill the eyes." If you had eyes as green and large as Alie'e's, you didn't want them dilated.

Amnon Plain was moving lights around as his assistants refilled the camera backs with Kodachrome. Alie'e would be wearing a torn pale-blue T-shirt that was meant to show just a hint of rouged nipple within the tear, and the film had to hold the subtlety of the pink-against-blue. With the Kodachrome, the flare of the torch behind her wouldn't pop as it would on the Fuji, but that wasn't so important in this shot.

Plain was juggling the color equities in his mind when Alie'e said, past his head, "Hello, Jael."

Plain turned. His sister was standing in the gash in the barge's hull, just inside the line of lights. "What do you want?" he snapped.

Jael Corbeau — she'd changed her name with her mother, after their parents split up — was light where Plain was dark, blond against Plain's deep brunette. Despite their coloring differences, they had faces that were astonishingly alike, wedge-shaped, edgy, big-eyed.

Jael had once been a model herself; didn't need the money, found the life boring, and moved on. Although the two of them looked alike, there was a singular difference in their faces. Three long pale lines slashed across Jael's face: scars. She was a lovely woman to begin with, but the scars made her something else. Striking. Beautiful. Erotic. Exotic. *Something.*

"I came to see Alie'e," she said sullenly.

18

"See her someplace else," Plain said. "We're trying to work here."

"Don't give me a hard time, Plain."

"Get the fuck off my shoot," Plain said, walking toward her. All other talk stopped, and Clark, the welder, stood up, uncertainly, and pushed his mask back. Plain's voice vibrated with violence.

From behind him, Alie'e said, "There's a party at Silly's tonight, nine o'clock."

Jael had taken a step back, away from her brother. There was no fear in her, but she didn't doubt that Plain would physically throw her off the barge. He was bigger. "Silly's at nine," she said, and left.

Plain watched her go, watched until she was out of sight, turned back to Alie'e, took a breath, saw Clark hovering in the background like a sumo wrestler. He turned to the couture rep and said, "I've got your key shot."

The couture rep was a thin-faced German named Dieter Kopp. He had a stubble-cut skull, two-day beard, and gaunt, pale face; his cheeks were lightly pitted, as though he might once have suffered from smallpox. He was the only one not wearing jeans. Instead, he wore a pale gray Italian suit with an open-necked black dress shirt, and a gold tennis bracelet.

Kopp didn't want to be in St. Paul, didn't want to be in America. He wanted to be in Vienna, or Berlin, but he was condemned to this: to sell seventy-dollar male-look underpants, complete with front vent, to American women.

Like a good German, he would do what was necessary to carry out his orders; but at the moment, he was still vibrating with the possibility of violence against the striking blonde who'd just walked off the barge. He knew her face. She'd been a model, he knew that, but she'd been out of it for a few years. She looked better now; she was stunning, he thought. . . .

"What?" he asked. He'd missed what Plain said to him.

"I've got your key shot. We move Clark around back and we put Alie'e dead center — Alie'e, come over here." Alie'e walked toward them, along the plank, as Plain continued: "We light them separately and then jam them together with the long lens. Clark will look like the fuckin' moon coming over the horizon, and Alie'e will be there in the foreground."

"We still need the nipple for the punch," said the German. "We could lose it with a long lens."

"Gotta lose it anyway for the Americans," said the creative director, a man with a red beard and a bald, freckled head.

"We can do it both ways," Plain said. "For the Europeans, we'll hold it. We'll stick a snoot over on the left and light it. Alie'e . . ." Alie'e stepped closer, and Plain slipped his fingers into the torn slit in the T-shirt and pulled it wider, to expose her nipple. "We'll have to tape this back, we'll have to bring it out a little more. Maybe touch it with a little more makeup."

"Not too much. She's really pale, and too much would look artificial," the art director said nervously.

"Artificial would be all right," Plain said. "What could be sexier than rouged nipples?"

"In Germany, yes, I think," Kopp said. "In America . . ."

"Sexy in America, too, but it'd be too much for the mainline magazines," Plain said. "For the American shot, we'll ice her nipple to bring it up, so you can see it through the T-shirt, put a little shading on the side to emphasize it, but we re-layer the rip so there's more coverage, and drop the snoot. But you'll still be able to feel it there — there'll be like a mental tit behind the T-shirt."

"You're gonna ice me?" Alie'e asked. "You're gonna fucking ice me? It's twelve degrees in here."

The German had closed his eyes. After a moment, he nodded. Plain had worked for eight years in Miami, where he'd developed a reputation for a decadent, sexually charged fashion art, juxtaposing outlandishly disparate characters in variations of the Beauty and the Beast theme. Anyone could do that, and many tried, but Plain had something different, something that nobody else could quite get. Something straight out of Grimm's Fairy Tales. Like this shot.

The German could *see* it in his mind's eye, now

that all the characters were assembled in this ridiculous hulk, with the lights, the smell of the welder, the roaring propane heater . . . but never could have thought of it. This was why he traveled to Minneapolis and paid Plain as much as he did.

Plain had vision.

They worked the rest of the morning: hard work, done over and over. Plain had a color card in his brain, and a drama chip. He knew what he was getting, and he pushed it. Shredded the T-shirt, exposed one breast completely. Clark watched from the background, a burning torch in his hand, his cement-block sausage lover's face fixed by the vision of the woman's body. Lynn and Lil watched from behind the lights: "You don't think that's getting toward the porno . . . ?"

When they were done, and while Jax was collecting her dressing bags, one of Plain's assistants walked Alie'e back to a rented Lincoln Towncar. She recovered her purse and the stash of cocaine, caught a little dust under a fingernail, and inhaled.

"What do you think of that Clark guy?" the assistant asked.

Alie'e, whose eyes had been closed, the better to experience the rush, now opened one eye, cocked her head, and thought about it: "He's not bad, for a pickup."

"What I meant was, he looked like he had a

zucchini stuffed in his pants during that last sequence."

Alie'e smiled her wan, coked-up smile and said, "Then it must have been a good sequence."

Dieter Kopp had seen it; so had Plain.

"I was afraid I'd lose it." Plain laughed, brushing the hair back from his eyes. "I was over there waggling that snoot around, trying to get some light on him, hoping it wouldn't go away, hoping he wouldn't figure out what I was doing."

"Not for the American magazines, I don't think?" Kopp said. But it was a question.

"Oh, I think so," Plain said. "You couldn't *say* anything about it. You couldn't make it too obvious. But a little work on the computer, taking it up or down. We'll get it in. And people *will* notice. . . ."

Kopp bobbed his head, flashed his thin, hard grin. At another time, he might've been driving a tank into Russia instead of selling underwear. But that was then, and this was now. He was in underwear.

They all went to the party that night, at Silly Hanson's home: Alie'e, Jax, Plain, Kopp, Corbeau, the photo assistants, Alie'e's parents, even Clark the welder. Alie'e looked spectacular. She wore the green dress from the photo shoot, and hung with Jael Corbeau and Catherine Kinsley, the heiress, the three women like the three fates in the Renaissance paintings, all tangled together.

Techno-pop rolled from small black speakers spotted around Silly Hanson's public rooms and Alie'e images flashed across movie-aspect flatscreen monitors. The crowd danced and sweated and drank martinis and Rob Roys and came and went.

Silly herself got drunk and physical with Dieter Kopp, who left thumb bruises on her breasts and ass. A gambler drifted through the crowd, and met a cop who was astonished to see him.

And the killer was there. In the corner, watching.

2

Lucas Davenport got up that morning at five o'clock, long before the sun had come over the treetops. He ate a bowl of oatmeal, drank a cup of coffee, filled a Thermos with the rest of the coffee, and drove into Hayward. His friend had the boat loaded. Lucas left his Tahoe on the street, and they'd drove together out to Round Lake on the year's last muskie-fishing trip.

Cold weather; no wind, but cold. They had to break through a fifteen-foot line of quarter-inch ice at the landing. In another day, the ice would be an inch thick, and out fifty or eighty feet. All along the country roads, guys were pulling ice-fishing houses out of their backyards, getting ready for winter.

On this day, though, most of the water was still soft. They found a spot off a sunken bar and dropped their baited sucker hooks off the side and waited. Lucas's friend didn't talk much, just stood like a moron and bounced a lure called a Fuzzy Duzzit off the bottom, and kept one eye on the sucker rods. Lucas dozed — a quiet, peaceful, unstressed sleep that always left him oddly refreshed.

They didn't catch anything — they rarely did, although Lucas's friend was an authority on muskie fishing — and by noon, stiff with the cold, they headed back to town. Lucas pulled the battery out of the boat, for winter storage in his friend's basement, while his friend carried nets, oars, a cooler, a pissjug, and other gear into the garage. When it was all done, Lucas said, "See you in the spring, fat boy," and headed back to his cabin.

He could have taken a nap. He'd had only four hours of sleep the night before. But he'd been drinking coffee to keep warm, and the caffeine had him jangled; and the nap in the boat had helped. Instead of sleeping, he got tools out of the truck and started working on his new steel boat shed.

The previous shed had been wired for electricity, and the contractor who built the new shed had left the underground cable coiled next to the foundation. The day before, Lucas had bought four fluorescent shop lights, four outlets, and a wall-mounted junction box, and now started putting them up and wiring them in.

The job went slowly. He had to run into town for more wire, and he stopped for a late lunch and more coffee. By the time he was finished, the sun was dropping over the lake. He flipped on the lights, spent a few seconds admiring their pink glow — he'd gotten the natural fluorescents — and started filling the place up.

He backed in two small aluminum boats on

their trailers, put a utility trailer in the far corner, a John Deere Gator sideways in front of the trailer, and finally, a Kubota tractor. The Kubota belonged to a neighbor who found he couldn't fit it in his garage. It wouldn't start right away, so Lucas had to bleed the fuel line before it would kick over.

A little after six o'clock, he walked in the dark back to the cabin. Just beyond, down at the lake, a merganser squawked. The edge of ice around the lake had disappeared during the day, but the temperature dropped quickly after sundown. Unless a wind came up to roil the water, the lake should ice over during the night.

He spent two hours picking up the cabin, vacuuming, collecting garbage and old summer magazines, washing and drying sheets, cleaning out the refrigerator, wiping down the kitchen. Then a shower, with a beer sitting on the toilet stool. Dressed again, he turned off the water heater and water pump, and pushed the thermostat down to fifty. After a last check, he dragged the trash out to the Tahoe and threw it in the back.

At eight o'clock, he locked the cabin and walked out to the truck. A red and silver Lund fishing boat was parked just beyond the new shed, dropped by another guy the week before. He'd be dragging it back to the Cities. He hooked it up, double-checked the safety chains, checked the trailer lights. Good: They worked, even the turn signals.

All right. Ready for winter, he thought. A merganser squawked again, and then another: some kind of duck fistfight down at the lake. Or somebody rolling over in bed. And a million stars looking down at him on a moonless night; he looked up through the treetops at the Milky Way, a billion stars like bubbles . . .

Davenport was a tall man; he drove a Porsche day-to-day, but fit better in the big Tahoe. He had black hair shot through with vagrant strands of gray; he was as dark as a Sicilian, with a permanent outdoor tan. The tan made his eyes seem bluer and brighter, and his smile whiter. Women had told him that his eyes seemed kindly, even priestly, but his smile made them nervous. He had the smile, one of them told him, of a predator about to eat something nasty.

His face was touched with scars. A long thin line crossed his eyebrow into his cheek, like a knife cut, but it wasn't. Another that looked like an exclamation mark — a thin line from a knife, a round O from a bullet wound — marked the front of his neck, along his windpipe. He'd been shot, and had almost died, but a surgeon had opened his throat with a jackknife and kept him breathing long enough to get him to an operating table. A plastic surgeon had offered to revise the scars, but he kept them, absently traced them with his fingers when he was thinking; personal history, not to be forgotten.

The road out was narrow and dark, and he was in no hurry. He took Highway 77 into Hayward, dropped down to 70 in Spooner, headed west, across the border into Minnesota, out to I-35. By ten o'clock he was on the far northern rim of the Cities, pulling the boat. The owner of the Lund was a guy named Herb Clay who owned the remnants of a farm south of Forest Lake, not far off the interstate.

Lucas pulled into Clay's driveway, bounced past the house to the barnyard, and turned a tight circle. He left the engine running and climbed out of the truck as a porch light came on. A moment later, Clay stepped out on the porch, supporting himself on crutches. "That you?"

"It's me," Lucas said. He started unhitching the trailer. "How're the legs?"

"Itch like hell," Clay said.

"Got a coat hanger to scratch with?"

"Yeah, but there's always a spot that you can't reach." Clay's wife came out on the porch, pulling on a quilted jacket. She hurried across the yard.

"Let me get the door," she said. She pulled open a lower-level door on the barn, which led into what at the turn of the century would have been a milking chamber, but was now a garage. She turned on lights and Lucas got in the truck and backed the boat into the barn.

"Stop," she yelled when the boat was far enough back. He stopped, and they unhitched the trailer and dropped it. The interior of the barn, years past the last bovine occupant, still smelled slightly of hay and what might have been manure; a thoroughly pleasant smell. Clay's wife closed the door and came out to stand by Lucas, and they both looked up at the sky.

"Pretty night," she said. She was a small, slender woman with dark hair and a square face. She and Lucas had always liked each other, and if things had been different, if the Clays hadn't been quite so happy with each other . . . She smelled good, like some kind of faintly perfumed soap.

"Pretty night," he repeated.

"Thanks for helping out with the boat," she said quietly.

"Thanks for bringing it," Clay called from the porch.

"Yup." Lucas got back in the truck. "Talk to ya."

At ten minutes after eleven o'clock, he rolled up his driveway, punched the garage-door opener, and eased the Tahoe in next to the Porsche. A new car, the Porsche; about time.

Clean, mellow, starting to fade, the memory of Verna Clay's scent still on his mind, he dropped into bed. He was asleep in five minutes, a small easy smile on his face.

He got three hours and forty-five minutes of sleep. The phone rang, the unlisted line. Groggy, he pushed himself up in bed, picked it up.

"Yeah?"

Swanson, one of the old-time guys:

"Goddamnit, you're *home.* You know who Alie'e Maison is, the famous model?"

"Yeah?"

"Somebody strangled her in a rich lady's house. We need some political shit over here: This is gonna be a screamer."

3

Saturday. The first day of the Alie'e Maison case.

The morning was cold, even for mid-November. The lake, a hundred miles north, would have frozen over for sure, Lucas thought. He stood at a gas pump, trickling fifteen gallons of premium into the tank of the Porsche. Two blocks out of his driveway, running for the Alie'e Maison scene, he remembered about the gas — he didn't have any. Now, at the least convenient moment, he'd had to stop.

He yawned, and peered around. The gas station attendant sat in an armored-glass booth, punching with his thumbs at a Game Boy, like a figure in an Edward Hopper tableau. Lucas didn't register Hopper; instead, he wondered idly why gas pumps no longer dinged. They used to ding with every gallon or so, he thought, and now they just rattled off yellow electronic digits, gallons and dollars, silent as the night.

Another car, a small Lincoln, the one that shared its frame with a Jaguar — Lucas knew about the Jaguar, but could never remember the Lincoln's name — pulled into the second set of gas pumps. Lucas yawned again and watched as a woman got out.

And stopped yawning. Something familiar about her, from a long time ago. He couldn't see her face, and it wasn't her face that sparked the memory — it was the way she moved, something about the movement and the stature and the hair.

Her face was turned away from him as she opened the gas flap on the car, unscrewed the cap, and maneuvered the nozzle into the mouth of the tank. She was wearing a suit and dark low heels and a dark blouse. She turned toward him to drag her credit card through the pump's card reader, but he caught only a flash of her face. A square chin, tennis-blond hair. He thought of Weather, the woman he'd almost married — should have married, a woman he still thought about — but this wasn't Weather. Weather was smaller, and he'd know her a mile away, whether her back was turned or not.

The pump handle jumped under his hand, and clanked. Filled up. He turned off the pump and walked over to the station, got a bottle of Diet Coke out of a cooler, and pushed a twenty and a ten through the cash window. The attendant, barely able to tear himself away from the game, sullenly made change one-handed. A college algebra book sat on the counter next to him.

"You go to St. Thomas?" Lucas asked.

"Yeah."

"Bad hours."

"Life sucks and then you die," the kid said. He didn't smile; he seemed to mean it. His eyes flicked past Lucas's shoulder and a light soprano voice asked, "Lucas? Is that you?"

He turned, but he didn't have to know who it was. Everything came back with the voice. "Catrin," he said, and turned.

She was smiling, and the smile nearly knocked him off his feet. She was forty-four, ten pounds heavier than in college, a little rounder in the face, but with that fine Welsh skin and wild reddish-blond hair. The last time he'd seen her . . .

"Must be twenty-five years," she said. She reached out and took his hand, then looked at the attendant and said, "I paid outside."

They stepped toward the door, then outside, and Catrin said, "I've seen you on television."

Lucas was trying to recover, but recovery was difficult. The last time he'd seen her . . . "What, uh, what're you doing? Now?"

"I live down in Lake City," she said. "You know, on Lake Pepin . . ."

"Married with kids?"

She grinned at him. "Of course. To a doctor, a family practitioner. Two kids, one of each. James is a sophomore at St. Olaf; Maria's a senior in high school."

"I've got one, a daughter," Lucas said. "Still in elementary school. Her mother and I . . . aren't together anymore." Never married; no need to make a point of it. A thought occurred to him, and he looked at his watch. "It's not four o'clock yet. What are you doing out here?"

"A friend died this morning," she said. Her

smile had gone wistful; he thought, for a moment, that she might break down. "I knew she was going. Tonight. I sort of dressed up for it."

"Jesus."

"It was not good. Lung cancer," she said. "She never quit smoking. I'm just so, just so . . ."

He patted her on the back. "Yeah."

"And where are you going? I don't remember you as an early riser."

"Got a murder," he said. He felt that he was staring at her, and that she knew it and was amused. Back when, she'd know exactly what she did to him. The effect, he thought, must have been wired in, because it hadn't changed in twenty-five years.

"Ah."

"You know the model, Alie'e Maison?"

Her hand went to her mouth in astonishment. "She was murdered?"

"Strangled."

"Oh, my God. Here?"

"Minneapolis."

Catrin looked around the empty gas station pad. "You're not exactly rushing to the scene of the crime."

"Five minutes ain't gonna make any difference," Lucas said. "She's dead."

She seemed to step back, though she hadn't moved. She looked up and said, "You always had a harsh line in you. The cold breath of reality."

And she'd just seen a friend die, Lucas thought. "I'm sorry, I didn't mean . . ."

"No, that's okay. That's just . . . Lucas." She smiled again, took one of his hands in hers, and patted it. "You better go. Take care of her."

"Yeah." He stepped away, stopped. "You're absolutely gorgeous," he said. "You're one of those women who'll be gorgeous when she's ninety."

"Nice to think so, when you feel the age coming," she said. She crossed her arms, hugged herself. "When your friends are dying, and you feel the age coming on."

He left, reluctantly, turning his head to watch her walk to her car. The Lincoln. Conservative, upper crust. Well-tended.

Jesus. The last time he'd seen her . . .

His body ran the Porsche through the gears, out to the interstate ramp, down onto I-94 toward the lights of Minneapolis, his eyes intent on the road and the traffic, his mind stuck with Catrin.

The last time he'd seen her she'd been both angry and buck naked, just out of a hot shower, rubbing her hair with a ratty brown bath towel that he'd had stolen from his mother's linen closet. The trouble had started two weeks earlier, at a pickup hockey game on an outdoor rink. Lucas had caught a deliberate elbow in the face, and with blood pouring out of his nose, had gone after the other guy — and hadn't stopped quite soon enough. The other guy's friends had taken him to a local hospital for some emergency dental work.

36

Then he'd caught a stick in a regular game, against Duluth. Nothing serious, just a cut and a few stitches. After the match, at an off-campus party, a hassle erupted between a couple of the players and a defensive end from the football team. The hassle had cooled quickly enough — no fight — but Lucas had been ready to jump in, Catrin clutching at him, pulling him off.

She started getting on him: He liked to fight, he enjoyed fighting, he had to look at himself, at what he was doing. Did he think fighting was right? Why'd he hang around with all those silly fuckin' jocks who'd be working down at the car wash as soon as their eligibility ran out? He was smarter than they were, why couldn't he . . .

They'd gone around a few times, and she started again as she got out of the shower. He'd finally had enough and shouted at her: *Shut the fuck up.* She'd flinched away — she'd thought he might hit her. That was a shock: He *never* would have hit her. He said so. Then she got on him again.

He walked out of the apartment. Stayed out. Went down and got some ice time. When he came back, a sheet of notebook paper lay on his kitchen counter. She'd scribbled on it, "Fuck you."

When he'd tried to call, her roommate said she didn't want to hear from him. He didn't push it: He was practicing all the time, playing, trying to keep his head above water in school. Never went after her. But always remembered her. They'd dated from October through February of his sophomore year. He'd slept with a half-dozen women in his life, but she'd been the first one who seemed to match his interest in sex. They *studied* it together.

Still remembered . . .

He smiled at the thought — and noticed that the concrete walls of the interstate were a little too blurred. He looked down at the speedometer: one-oh-four. He backed off a bit.

Catrin . . .

Silly Hanson lived in a white-stuccoed house with an orange-tiled roof, across the street from Lake of the Isles, a rich neighborhood of professionally tended landscapes and architect-designed houses from the first half of the twentieth century. A half-dozen police vehicles were piled up at the curb outside Hanson's house. An early-morning blader, who looked too old and bald and fat and way too rich for his skater gear, went by on the lakeside skateway, his face turned toward the cluster of cops. The word about the murder would be getting out very soon now. Lucas found a spot by a fire hydrant, parked, nodded at a cop standing by the stoop.

"Beautiful morning," he said.

"Fuckin' A," said the cop.

"If I get a ticket . . ."

"You won't get a ticket."

Lucas went up the steps. A sloppy, overweight homicide cop, wearing an insulated nylon baseball jacket over a white shirt and necktie, was waiting on the porch. His face was tired, but he smiled in relief when he saw Lucas. "Man, I'm glad you're here."

"So what happened?" Lucas asked. Two more uniformed cops were standing just inside the door, looking out at them.

"You ain't gonna believe it." The fat cop's name was Swanson.

"Alie'e Maison got killed," Lucas said. "I believe it. Where's the body?"

"It's worse than that," Swanson said. "We tried to call you again, but you were out of touch."

Lucas stopped. "What happened?"

"When're you gonna start turning on your cell phone?" Swanson was reluctant.

"If I turn on my cell phone, people call on it," Lucas said. "So what happened?"

"We were just doing the routine, checking the house, opening doors. You know." They both knew. Lucas had been on more murder scenes than he could remember, and Swanson had been to more than Lucas had; he'd been a homicide cop when Lucas was still in uniform.

"Yeah?"

"We found another body," Swanson said. "Stuffed in a closet. Another woman."

Lucas looked at him for a long moment, then shook his head. "That's a *lot* worse."

"Yeah. I thought so." Bad as it was, it *was* something new. They'd both been to multiple murders, but never to one where the cops had already gotten the coffee hot, sent somebody out for donuts, started the routine, then opened a closet door and had another body drop out like a dislodged sock monkey.

"Why'd it take so long to find her?" Lucas asked.

"She was in a closet, the door was locked. Nobody unlocked it right away."

"Jesus, I hope the papers don't get that," Lucas said. "Or maybe we ought to give it to them. You know, our way."

"This woman who lives here, Hanson — she was there when we found the second one, and she's gonna talk about it. She lives for the media. You know what she told me when I was talking to her about it?"

Lucas shook his head.

"She said her only good black dresses were too short for this. For the murders. She sees this as a photo op and she's already figuring out her wardrobe for the cameras."

"All right." That happens.

"There's one other thing." Swanson glanced down at the uniformed cops. Lucas got the idea, and they both turned sideways, and Swanson dropped his breath. "Hanson says there was a strange guy wandering through the place. About the time Maison disappeared out of the crowd. Hanson thinks he did it. She didn't know him, but he was talking to everybody. She said he was like a street guy. Too thin, yellow teeth, and he was wearing this T-shirt that said, 'I'm with Stupid,' and had this arrow that pointed down at his dick. And he had this weird dog-shit-brown sport coat."

Lucas stared at Swanson for a moment, then said, "Huh."

"That's what I thought," Swanson said. "You want to call him?"

"Yeah, I'll call him. Let me look at the scene first."

Hanson's home was elegant but sterile. Lucas recalled another case, a couple of months before, when he'd entered an apartment and found the same high-style sterility. Like a picture on the cover of *Architectural Digest*: Pretty, but not lived-in. Eggshell walls with contemporary graphics — wrenches and hammers and gestures and angst — and then, around the corner, the interjected English country scene, in oil colors, with cows, spotted perfectly to connect with the graphics. Somebody else's sense of humor; a humor spoiled by the underlying scent of alcohol and smoke, the smell of a well-kept motel.

The house seemed divided into two parts — an open plan public area, and a conventional series of bedroom suites at the back. Swanson led the way into the back. Two plainclothes cops were standing in a long central hallway, looking down at the thick gray hair of an assistant medical examiner, who was crouched over a body on the floor. The dead woman was facedown; she wore a reddish-brown party dress. The AME was dabbing at her mouth with an absorbent tissue.

"Name is Sandy Lansing," Swanson said as they walked back. "She's a hostess of some kind, at Brown's Hotel." Brown's was expensive, a hotel where poised young blond women in pearl-gray suits took the guests to their suites, while bellhops in red-and-black monkey suits toted the luggage and kept their mouths shut.

Lucas squatted beside the body; one knee cracked. "Know what did it?" Lucas asked the AME.

The AME was older, like Swanson, with the same tired hound-dog eyes. He had a pack of Marlboros in his shirt pocket, and a black medical bag, which was open on the rug behind him. "I think her skull is cracked," he said. "That's the only trauma I can find, but that was probably enough. There's a cleft, looks like a V-shaped cleft. She could have been hit by something with a narrow edge on it, a board, maybe the end of a cane — a walking stick. Not a pipe, nothing round."

"A cane? Did somebody have a cane?" Lucas asked, looking up at Swanson. Swanson shrugged.

"But could have been a doorjamb, or something like that," the AME continued. "Here . . ." He picked up the woman's head, gently, as though he might have had a daughter of his own, and turned it. A small indentation marked the back of the woman's head, near the top; there was a smear of blood, enough to show the line of the injury.

"We think she might have walked in on the murder, by accident, and the killer went after her. Hit her with anything he had," Swanson said. "Maybe banged her head against the wall."

"Why would he stuff her in the closet?" Lucas objected, but the AME interrupted: "Look at this."

"What?"

He was peering closely at the woman's scalp, then reached back, felt in his bag, and took out a hand lens. "I think, uh, it looks like a little flake of paint in her hair. . . ." He looked up at Swanson. "Don't let anybody touch the doorjambs or any of the wooden trim. Anywhere she could whack her head. You might find an impact mark and maybe a hair or two." That could make the difference between murder and manslaughter, or even an accident.

"All right," Swanson said. He looked up and down the hall at all the doorjambs; there seemed to be dozens.

Lucas went back to his first thought. "Why couldn't this one have been killed first, and then —"

" 'Cause Maison was strangled and she wasn't wearing any underpants, and the condition of her vulva and her pubic hair would suggest that she'd very recently been engaged in sex," Swanson said. "If somebody had killed Lansing first, we thought it was pretty unlikely that he'd stop off to bang Maison and then strangle her."

"Okay." Made sense.

"She's got something written on her wrist in ballpoint, but it's kinda smeared, so it probably didn't happen right at the time she was killed," the AME said. He turned a wrist, and Lucas looked at the smear of blue ink.

"Looks like . . . Ella? Fella? Della?"

"Probably not fella," Swanson said. "Why would anybody write 'fella' on their wrist?"

"Could be a name," the AME suggested.

"Strange name," Swanson said.

"See what you can do to bring it up," Lucas said. "Get some photos over to homicide."

"Okay."

Lucas stood. "Let's see the other one."

The door to the guest bedroom was another six feet down the hall, and Lucas stepped over Lansing's body, Swanson following along behind. Two crime-scene guys stepped out of the room just as Lucas came up. "Video," one of them said. "Crying goddamned shame," said the other.

Inside, a photographer lit up, and began taping the crime scene, while a second guy maneuvered a light. All Lucas could see of Alie'e Maison was one bare foot, sticking out from behind the bed; the body was lodged in the space between the bed and the wall.

He waited until the video guy was finished, then looked over the edge of the bed. Maison was lying faceup, one hand over her head, one trapped beneath her back. Her filmy green dress had been pulled up under her arms, exposing her body from the navel down. Her hips were canted toward the wall, and her ankles were crossed, but the wrong way: The one that should have been on the bottom was on the top.

"Looks like she was thrown in there," Lucas said.

One of the cops nodded. "That's what we think. Tried to hide her."

"But not too hard. You can see her feet."

"But if you just poked your head in, from the door, you probably wouldn't."

"Who found her?" Lucas asked.

"One of the people at the party." He looked at a notebook. "A woman named Rowena Cooper. Cooper knew Maison was back here, supposedly sleeping, and hadn't come out. She went back to see if she was awake. She says she opened the door but couldn't see anything, so she turned on the lights. She was just turning around to go back out when she saw the underpants. She went over to pick them up, and she saw the feet. Started screaming."

"Where's Cooper now?"

The cop tipped his head toward the other end of the house. "The library. We called Sloan, he's coming in to talk to her."

"Good." Sloan was the best interrogator in the department. Lucas took a last look around the room. The bedspreads coordinated with the window treatments and the carpet. He asked, "The windows were locked?"

"In this room, yeah. But we got an open window down the hall," one of the cops said.

"Let me see."

"Check this first," the cop said. He leaned forward, hovering an index finger over the inside of Alie'e's left elbow.

Lucas would have known what that meant even if he couldn't see the BB-sized bruise. A needle user. He sighed, nodded at the cop, said, "Swanson," and stepped back into the hallway. Swanson was a step behind.

"Look, you know what's gonna happen, so we've got to nail everything down," Lucas said. "Everything. I want everything sampled, swept, vacuumed. I want every test there is, on both women. I want interviews with everyone at the party — ask everybody for a list of names, and make sure you get every goddamn last one."

"Sure."

"Who takes over when you get off?"

"I think . . . Thompson."

"Brief him. Do everything. We'll pay for every bit of science anybody can think of." He looked back at the room. "Did you look at her fingernails?"

"Yeah. They're clean. We'll get her vagina swabbed and get a rush on the semen."

"And blood, we need blood right away. I want to know what kind of shit she was shooting."

"Heroin."

"Yeah, I know, but I wanna *know*."

"You gonna call Del?"

"In a minute."

"There's a phone in the office. I was keeping it clear for incomings," Swanson said.

"Show me the unlocked window. . . . This place doesn't look like the windows should be unlocked."

"Hanson says they never are," Swanson said. "But she got them washed a couple of weeks ago, and they were all opened then — they're some kind of tilt thing, so you can wash both sides from the inside."

"I dunno."

"Yeah, well, the window could have been un-locked then. Hanson says she never went around and checked them. She assumed they were all locked."

The unlocked window was in another guest room, one door down the hall; this room had a different set of coordinated bedspreads, window treatments, and carpet. Lucas looked out through the window glass. Nothing but lawn and shrubs. "Any muddy footprints outside the window, with a unique brand-logo impressed in the mud?"

"No fuckin' mud. It ain't rained in two weeks."

"I was joking," Lucas said.

"I wasn't. I went out and looked," Swanson said. "The grass ain't even crinkled."

"All right. Where's that phone?"

Hanson's home office was a small, purpose-built cubicle with cherry-wood shelves at one end for phone books, references, and a compact stereo. The cherry desk had four drawers, filing drawers to the left, envelope drawers to the right. A wooden Rolodex sat on the right side of the desk, a telephone on the left. A Dell laptop computer sat on a pull-out typing shelf, the wiring dropping out of sight, to appear behind a laser printer that sat on a two-drawer wooden filing cabinet beside the desk.

"Hanson still in the living room?" Lucas asked Swanson.

"Yeah."

"Go talk to her. Keep her entertained. . . . Ask her questions, start the witness list."

"You got it." Swanson glanced at the laptop, nodded, and headed toward the living room.

When he was gone, Lucas shut the office door and turned on the computer. Windows 98 came up, and he clicked Programs — Accessories — Address Book. The address book was empty. He jumped back to the opening page and clicked on Microsoft Outlook. When it came up, he checked the Inbox and Sent folders and found that Hanson had a small e-mail correspondence.

He picked up the phone and dialed Del's number from memory, and as the phone began ringing, clicked on the Inbox folder again, clicked again on Find, and typed in "Alie'e."

He was still typing when Del's wife answered the phone. The answer was more like a groan than a word: "Hello?"

"Cheryl, this is Lucas. Is Del there?"

"He's asleep, Lucas. He was trying to get you all night, but he couldn't find you." She was crabby. "What time is it, anyway?"

"Sorry. Wake him up, we gotta talk."

"Just a minute. . . ."

After a few seconds of background mumbling, Del came on the line. "You heard?"

"Yeah, just now. What were you doing here?"

After a moment's silence, Del said, "What?" He sounded only semiconscious. Then, "Where's *here?*"

"Sallance Hanson's. You were at the party last night, right?" Lucas asked.

"Yeah, but what're you doing there?"

"The Maison thing," Lucas said.

"What?"

Lucas looked at the phone and then said, "You don't know?"

"Yeah, I called in," Del said. "I called all over, looking for you. I even had your neighbor up north go look in your cabin, but you'd gone."

"You called in that somebody strangled Alie'e Maison?"

Longer silence. Then, "What the fuck are you talking about?"

"Somebody strangled Alie'e Maison and threw her body behind a bed in a guest bedroom," Lucas said. "Another woman was killed and stuffed in a closet. Hanson thinks a street guy did it — said he was wearing an 'I'm with Stupid' shirt."

49

After a moment of silence, Del said, "You're not joking."

"I'm not joking."

"Jesus Christ." Del was awake now. And again, "Jesus Christ."

Behind him, Cheryl asked, "What happened?"

"That was me, all right," Del said. "I was there until one o'clock. I didn't see Maison there after midnight or so."

"What were you doing?"

"Runnin' drugs, man. That goddamn place was an ocean of shit."

"Maison's got fresh tracks on her arm."

"Yeah, they were all doing a little something," Del said. "I was trying to figure out where it was coming from."

"Figure it out?"

"No."

"You better get over here. I'm gonna have to talk to Hanson pretty quick."

"On my way."

When Del had hung up, Lucas clicked on the Find Now button. The computer thought about it for a moment, then kicked out fifteen or twenty messages. He went through them as quickly as he could: Most of them were "Did you see" or "Did you hear about" Alie'e in a magazine spread. Two of them seemed relevant: Three months earlier, according to the date stamp, Hanson's correspondent, a woman named Martha Carter, had seen Alie'e at a party and she'd been flying on c — cocaine.

Lucas switched to the Sent folder, scanned it until he found Carter's name and the right date. Hanson had replied to the cocaine comment, with the observation that friends told her that Alie'e had started using heroin.

Lucas sent both letters to the printer, then went back to the Inbox, and the Find function, and typed in "Maison." He got two letters he'd already seen. He tried "Aliee," without the apostrophe between the *e*'s, and found only one new letter, about a dress.

He quickly typed in "Sandy Lansing" and found only one letter, in which Lansing was mentioned only in passing. He tried "Sandy" alone, and "Lansing" alone, and found only the one letter. He switched back the Sent folder, and repeated himself. He found nine references to Alie'e and none to Lansing; one letter from Hanson confided to a woman named Ardis — there was no last name — that Alie'e was definitely having an affair with somebody named Jael, and that somebody else, an Amnon, was wildly jealous.

I think Amnon would kill Jael, if she said just the right thing to him. . . .

Lucas sent the letter to the printer, and noted the e-mail address on it.

Sallance Hanson was sitting on her couch, wrapped in a black dress, a black hat beside her, when Lucas wandered into the room. Swanson, who'd been sitting in an easy chair, facing her, stood up and said, "Miz Hanson, this is Deputy Chief Davenport."

Hanson turned on the couch and extended her hand without getting up. She was a pretty blond woman in her forties, with a tight, willful mouth and tough blue eyes. She'd used black eye liner under her eyes, and just touched her eyelids with a gray tone; the combination gave her a played-out, dying-puppy look. "When do we go downtown?"

"I beg your pardon?" Lucas asked.

"To make my statement?"

"Oh, yeah. Detective Swanson will make the arrangements. Actually, we can probably take it right here. . . . But I want to talk to you about another matter."

"Have you found that street person? I identified him," Hanson said.

"That's what I want to talk to you about."

Her eyebrows rose. "You *found* him? Nobody notified *me*. Why didn't anybody tell me?"

Swanson said, "Um, you're more of a . . . witness or bystander . . . than anything else, Miz Hanson. You're not really part of the investigation."

"That's not the way I see it," she snapped.

"That's the way it is," Lucas said.

"I could talk to the mayor, and he might inform you differently," she said. "The mayor's a friend of mine."

"He's a friend of mine, too," Lucas said. "He

appointed me to my job. He'd tell you the same thing we're telling you. You're not part of the investigation. You're being investigated."

"*What?*"

"Two murders were committed in your house, Miz Hanson. You were on the scene when the killings took place. We know nothing about you or your relationship with the dead women." He smiled at her, softening it up. "No politician, the mayor included, would go on the record defending somebody who might later be charged with murdering Alie'e Maison. I'm sure you can see that."

She said, "Oh," tipped her head from side to side, thinking about it, bounced once on the couch, brightened, and said, "That's not bad — being a suspect. But I didn't do it. Either one. That street person . . . is he in jail, or are you bringing him here, or what?"

Lucas felt awkward looking down at her; he took a step away and settled into a leather easy chair, steepling his fingers in front of his face. "The street person's name is Del Capslock," he said. "He's an undercover police officer. One of our *best* undercover people."

"Uh-oh," she said, looking from Lucas to Swanson. "This could cause you problems." Then she frowned. "What was he doing at my party, anyway?"

"That's the other thing," Lucas said. "Del was . . . researching drugs. Miz Maison showed signs of heroin use. She had needle marks on her arm."

"No." Hanson registered shock — something she was good at, Lucas thought. One hand went artfully to her face. "She was using *drugs?*"

A cop stepped into the room, said, "TV's here. They all got here in a bunch."

Lucas nodded, said, "Okay, keep them back." Then, to Hanson: "Miz Hanson, everybody at your party was using drugs."

"I wasn't," she said. Her face darkened. "I think that's an outrageous thing to say."

"Miz Hanson, the officer in question is a drug specialist," Lucas said. "He said an ocean of drugs was flowing through your apartment. He knows what he's talking about. The thing is, there's no way that there could be that much junk around without your knowing about it."

"That's bullshit," she said. Now she was getting angry, and a little fearful. "I don't know anything about it. Maybe my attorney should hear this."

Lucas didn't want to mention the e-mail until they'd taken the computer with a warrant. He put his hands up, palms out. "So you call your attorney and talk it over. The point is, it won't help our investigation if *any* of this is alluded to. If you allow yourself to be interviewed by the press or television, and you talk about our man being at your party . . . we're going to have to explain why he was there."

"You're blackmailing me," she said.

She was quick enough, Lucas thought. "No, no. You can say anything you want to anybody.

Your attorney will tell you that. The First Amendment gives you that right, and all Minneapolis police officers support that right." He flicked his eyes sideways at Swanson. "Don't we?"

"Absolutely," Swanson said piously. "That's why I served in the Marine Corps."

Lucas continued. "I'm suggesting that you . . . understand the consequences before you take a self-destructive position. If you understand what I mean."

"You want me to shut up," she said.

"About our man. He's an undercover officer. If his face were made public, he would lose his effectiveness and might even be endangered."

"What if he did it?" Hanson asked. "Cops do that sort of thing from time to time. I've read about it. Rogue cops."

"This guy doesn't," Lucas said. "Besides, we're detailing a special squad out of Internal Affairs to pull him apart, everything he did last night. When we're done, we'll know every step he took."

"Well . . . I think I could leave him out of my statement," she said. "To the press."

"Excellent," Lucas said. "One more question. This will be covered when you make your formal statement, but I'm just curious. Alie'e Maison is pretty famous. Probably the most famous person at your party?"

Hanson rolled her eyes up and waggled her head from side to side, as if balancing all the equities of fame, or celebrity, and finally decided, "Probably. In that world. We also had some very well-known financial people here, but that's another world."

"If she was so famous, how could she disappear into a bedroom and nobody was curious about her, what had happened to her?" Lucas asked.

"Well, I mentioned this to Officer Swanson . . . she seemed very sleepy, and just wanted to take a nap. So we accommodated her and shooed people away if they asked about her. She was on a very rigorous schedule, early-morning photo shoots and all. She was exhausted."

"So nobody went back and looked at her."

"Oh, I don't know. Maybe some of her friends did." Hanson's eyes slid away from Lucas; she might not be lying, he thought, but she was skating. "Probably some of her friends did. We were just keeping the sightseers away."

"Let me tell you something," Lucas said, "I can't read you well enough to know if you're lying to us, but if you are, you're committing a crime."

He turned to Swanson and asked, "Have you read her her rights?"

"Not yet."

"Do it," he said. He turned back to Hanson, "You don't have to talk to us at all, or you can have an attorney, but if you *do* talk to us, it better be the truth. We can get pretty goddamn cranky about obstruction of justice in a double-murder case."

From the front hall, a man called, "Hello?"

Lucas recognized the voice. "Sloan. In here."

A moment later, Sloan appeared, cleaned up and ready for the day in a fresh brown suit, white shirt, and blue-and-gold-striped necktie. "Lucas . . ."

"This is Miz Hanson, owner of the house," Lucas said. "We need an interview with her, and with the lady who found Miz Maison's body."

"I can take Miz Hanson's statement now," Sloan said. He held up a tape recorder and looked down at Hanson. "If we can find some place quiet and comfortable?"

She flipped a hand, to say, *whatever,* and turned back to Lucas. "Before you go, let me get something straight. You're not telling me that I *can't* speak to the media, you're just saying . . ."

"That you should edit what you say. Carefully. I'm perfectly happy to see you on TV, I *expect* to see you on TV. There's almost no way you could avoid it — but there are aspects of the investigation that we really don't want made public."

"Like this undercover man."

"Who?" Sloan asked, looking at Lucas.

"Del was here last night," Lucas said.

"Ah. Chasing dope?"

Hanson looked from Sloan to Lucas and back to Sloan, and shook her head. "There *was* no dope."

Swanson and Lucas quickly briefed Sloan on what they knew. While they were talking,

Hanson stood up and said, "I'll be back in a sec. I gotta pee."

"Meet you in the kitchen," Sloan said.

"Who's got the list of the people at the party?" Lucas asked Swanson.

Swanson took a notebook out of his pocket. "I've got most of it."

"You got anyone on there named Amnon? Or Jael?"

Swanson said, "Yeah, somewhere. I remember the names. They're brother and sister." He flipped through his notebook, found the names. "Amnon Plain and a Jael Corbeau. Why?"

"There's a rumor that Alie'e jilted Amnon and went off with Jael, and this Amnon guy was pretty pissed about it. So let's get them downtown." He looked at Sloan. "Why don't you fix it? Call me when you get them: I want to sit in."

"Okay."

"Those are both Bible names," Swanson said. "Amnon and Jael."

"Yeah? What'd they do in the Bible?"

"Fuck if I know," Swanson said. "I just remember them from Sunday school."

"Let's get them downtown. We can ask them about it," Lucas said.

Lucas looked in on Rowena Cooper, the woman who'd found Alie'e's body. Cooper was a thin, morose woman with dark hair and red-rimmed eyes; she was sitting with a chubby baby-sitter cop named Dorothy Shaw. "I just

58

wanted to say hello," Cooper said. "The last time Alie'e came to town, we went to a movie together. I just wanted to see how she was doing."

"You didn't have a chance to talk to her earlier?" Lucas asked.

"No, no, I didn't get here until midnight. She'd already gone back to take her nap by then."

She really knew nothing else: She'd hung around the party for better than two hours, mostly because she wanted to talk to Alie'e, if only for a moment. "We shared some concerns about current fashion, and where it's going. . . ."

She seemed genuinely upset about the murder, without Hanson's undertone of excitement. Lucas tried to reassure her, without much luck, and left her with Shaw.

"Del's on the porch," Swanson said when Lucas wandered back into the living room.

Del had taken the time to dress up; he was wearing clean jeans, sneakers without holes, and a gray sweatshirt with the sleeves pulled up over the elbows. He smelled vaguely of musk-scented deodorant, and his long hair was still damp.

"We're gonna have to talk to Internal Affairs. You're gonna have to meet with them," Lucas said. "Just to keep the record straight."

Del nodded. "No problem. I picked up on this party yesterday afternoon, and told Lane where I was going. So I'm covered."

"Good." Lane was the other man in Lucas's

two-man Strategic Studies and Planning Group.

Del said, "But I never told you why I was calling you . . . why I was looking for you. Did anybody tell you about Trick? Anybody call you from downtown?"

"What trick?"

"Trick Bentoin. He was at the party last night. He just got back from Panama," Del said.

Lucas took a long look at him and finally showed a small smile. "You gotta be bullshitting me."

"I'm not, man," Del said, his eyes round. "I talked to him. He thought it was funnier than hell. He hardly ever laughs; he goddamn near fell down in the hallway."

"Ah, fuck." Then Lucas started to laugh, and a minute later Del joined in. A uniformed cop with a solemn murder-scene face poked his head around the corner, saw who it was, and pulled back.

"That's gonna be a little hard to explain," Lucas said finally.

Narcotics and Homicide had worked together, with the county attorney's investigators, for more than four months to build a murder case against Rashid Al-Balah. Al-Balah had killed Trick Bentoin, and had thrown his body in a bog at the Carlos Avery Wildlife Area, the traditional murdered-body-disposal area for the Twin Cities, the state claimed. The case had been a jigsaw puzzle of evidence: weed seeds in the backseat of the Cadillac, identified by a University of Minnesota botanist and unique to the bog; traces of blood in the trunk of the car, confirmed as the same blood type as Bentoin's; a history of death threats by Al-Balah against Bentoin; a lack of any alibi . . .

Al-Balah had been in prison for a little more than a month, looking at a life sentence for first-degree murder.

"What about the blood in the car?" Lucas asked.

"Trick didn't know about any blood," Del said. "He said he had a deal going in Panama, this rich guy who thought he could play gin rummy, so he took off. He never heard anything about the trial. Wasn't that big a deal in Panama."

Lucas scratched his head. "Well, shit. I'll call the county attorney. He ain't gonna be happy. He got a lot of good ink out of that trial."

"You know what's worse? That asshole Al-Balah is gonna be back on the street."

"What'd Trick think about that?"

"He said, 'Leave him in there. You *know* he's killed somebody.' "

"Got that right," Lucas said.

Down the street, TV lights came up, and Lucas peeked: Silly Hanson was being interviewed, posed in her black dress against her expansive lawn. After a second, the lights went down again, and a couple of different cameramen began scrambling around with portable lights. They'd have a roadside studio set up in a moment.

"Goddamnit," Lucas said.

"Gonna be a circus," Del said.

"I know it. . . . Hanson told me she didn't know about any drugs."

"What'd you expect?" Del said. "But the only guy who wasn't putting something up his nose or into his arm was too drunk to do it."

"You know any of the people at the party?"

"Only by sight. None of them knew me, of course."

Swanson stuck his head out on the porch, looking for Lucas. "Rose Marie called," he said. "You got a meeting at six-thirty, her office."

"Okay." Lucas turned back to Del.

"You gotta talk to Internal Affairs right away," he said. "When you get clear, talk to the dope guys and nail down every dealer who might have been selling to Maison or her friends. Find out where she got the shit she put in her arm last night. Did she buy it here, or did she bring it with her?"

Del nodded. "Okay."

"The real problem for us is, if the media finds out you were at the party, they're gonna want to break you out," he said. "You get your face on the nightly news, you'll have to find a new job. Giving out tickets for illegal lane changes."

"No, no, no. I ain't going on TV," Del said. "I gotta stay out of this."

"I'll do what I can, but if the word leaks, we

might need a major plane crash. And you know how the goddamn department leaks."

"Plane crash wouldn't do it," Del said gloomily, looking at the lights down the street. "Not with Alie'e Maison dead. Beautiful, rich, famous, and strangled. It's a CNN wet dream. They're gonna run down everybody who had anything to do with her. Once my cat gets outa the bag . . . shit. We got to find this guy." He nodded toward the house, meaning the killer. "We got to find him quick."

4

Rose Marie Roux had lost thirty pounds on a new all-protein diet and now was thinking about a face-lift. "Just a couple of snips, to pull me up around the sides," she told Lucas. Rose Marie was the chief of police. She put her fingertips on her face just below her cheekbones and pushed the skin back until it began pulling on her lips. The mayor stepped into her office, looked at her and said, "What?"

She let go of the skin, and her face slid back to its usual shape. "Face-lift," Lucas said. He yawned; he liked late nights, but not early mornings.

"I been thinking about getting some hair," the mayor said. He was balding, but still had the remnants of a hairline. "Think anyone would notice?"

"They look like little bushes planted into the side of a grassy hill, the hair plugs do," Rose Marie said. "You don't ever want anybody on a staircase above you, looking down."

"Ah, that's the old-style plugs," the mayor said. "I'm thinking about micro-implants — they're supposed to be really natural." They chatted about plastic surgery and micro-implants for a few minutes, aging politicians doing what they did best — schmoozing — until Lucas yawned again. The mayor stopped the chitchat in the middle of a sentence and asked, "How dead is she?"

"Pretty dead," Lucas said, sitting up. "Strangled. Maybe raped. Did Rose Marie tell you about the second woman?"

The mayor's head went back, and he gave Lucas a startled-deer look, as much as a short, barrel-chested, balding, former personal-injury attorney can have a startled-deer look. "A second woman?"

He turned to Rose Marie, who shrugged and said, "Not my fault. A second body turned up, stuffed in a closet. I just found out."

"Another model?" Swiveling to Lucas.

"No," Lucas said. He gave the mayor a short rundown on the double murder. "Your friend Sallance Hanson says if we give her any trouble, she's gonna call you."

"Fuck her," the mayor said. "Chain-whip her if you want."

"Really?" Rose Marie's eyebrows went up.

"She gave me two hundred bucks," the mayor said. "For that much, she gets a signed photograph. I sure as shit don't run interference on a murder." He looked back at Lucas. "Do we have any leads?"

"Probably, but not that I know of," Lucas said. "We're still processing the scene. Maison had been putting some dope in her arm, heroin probably. The other woman was red around the nose, like she'd seen a lot of coke."

"Chamber of Commerce is gonna love that, coke and heroin," the mayor said. "What do we tell the movie people?" The movie people were television reporters.

"We tell them it's probably a dope-related murder," Lucas said.

The mayor frowned. "Dope-related sounds bad."

"*Everything* sounds bad," Lucas said. "But saying that it's dope makes it simple to understand. And that's what we need. Simple. Boring. Understandable. Nothing exotic. No orgies, no weird sex, no big money or jealous lovers, no scandal. Just a bad guy somewhere. And the movie people'll believe heroin. There's so much heroin in the fashion business that it was a *look* not very long ago. All the models had this fagged-out doper look. It won't surprise anybody."

"We don't want it to drag out: We don't want it to become some culture thing for the movie intellectuals to get onto."

"That's what I'm saying," Lucas said. "We don't want anything mysterious or exotic. A dope-related killing fits."

"Tell him about the window," Rose Marie said.

"Window?"

"A bedroom down from the murder room — the room where Maison's body was, if that was the murder room, and it probably was — had an unlocked window. Somebody could have gone out that way. Or, more to the point, might have come in. A cat burglar."

"With all the people in there? There must've been lights."

"Lights seem to pull cat burglars in," Lucas said. "They get a buzz from going into a house where people are — 'cause they're nuts. Generally, you get a cat burglar, you get a guy who's gonna start raping the victims. Or killing them. They're thrill freaks."

"Ah, man." The mayor shook his head.

"It's better to stay with the dope story," Lucas said. "If a dealer killed her, or she was killed because of dope, everybody understands. It's a one-time thing and she's partially at fault. If she hadn't been using dope, she'd still be alive. But if it's a cat burglar, then we've got a serial killer on the loose, and the worst kind of serial killer — the kind who'll come creeping into your bedroom and strangle you, even with other people in the house."

"Like one of those horror movies. *Halloween,* or the one with the guy with the fingers that are knives," Rose Marie said.

"No, no, no, we don't want that," the mayor said, waving off the idea.

"That's what we thought," Rose Marie said wryly.

"So it's dope," the mayor said. "Who's running the show?"

"Frank Lester," said Rose Marie. "Lucas and his group will fit in sideways, like we did before. Everybody's comfortable with that."

"Good. It's Strategic Planning —"

"Strategic Studies and Planning," Lucas said. "And I need a woman in the group. Marcy Sherrill wants to come over from Homicide."

Rose Marie shook her head. "Then I got to give Homicide somebody else. Everything is too tight."

"We're paying for ourselves about twenty times over," Lucas said patiently. "And I need a woman if I'm going to operate."

"There's politics. . . ."

"Murder is down fourteen percent, and a lot of it's because of my guys — three guys, including me — spotting the assholes," Lucas said. "That's politics."

The mayor held up his hands to stop the argument. To Rose Marie he said, "Half the people in Homicide are going to be working on this anyway, so why don't you give him Marcy for the duration of the Maison case? When that's done, we'll figure something out."

Rose Marie sighed and said, "All right. But I want some more money."

The mayor rolled his eyes, then said, "Yeah, who doesn't?" Then: "You'll do the media?"

Rose Marie nodded. "But you'll have to be there, too, the first time. This is gonna be large, media-wise."

"Who do you think'll come in?"

"Everybody," she said. "Four locals and a freelancer for CNN are already outside the house. All the other networks are on the way. And most of the picture-and-gossip magazines. *People. The Star.*"

"Then we're gonna need something more than just saying it's a 'dope-related killing.' " He looked at Lucas. "Do we have somebody we can throw to them? Some doper asshole they can chase for a couple of days?"

"I can ask," Lucas said.

"Do that. The more they've got to occupy them, the less time they're gonna spend asking why nothing's been done yet." The mayor touched his forehead. "Wish I'd gotten the new hair, though, you know? Like last year."

Rose Marie stretched the skin back from her nose. "Never too late," she said.

The meeting lasted fifteen minutes. As Lucas was leaving, Rose Marie said, "Hey — turn on your cell phone, okay? For the duration."

Lucas shrugged noncommittally. On the way back to his office, he poked Del's number on his phone's speed-dial. Del was in the middle of the Internal Affairs interview, and when Lucas passed on the mayor's request, he said, "I'll see what we got, as soon as I get out of here."

"How's it going?"

"Fine. They're a lovely bunch of people."

Lucas punched off, dropped the phone back in his coat pocket. Del could take care of himself.

At his office, he yawned, peeled off his jacket, and locked himself in, leaving the lights off. He pulled open a desk drawer, dropped into his chair, and put his feet on the drawer. Not quite seven o'clock: He'd gone to bed a little after two, and normally wouldn't have gotten up until ten.

Years before — before he'd inadvertently gotten rich — he'd invented board games as a way of supplementing his police salary. The games were created in all-night sessions that now, in memory, seemed to merge with his time of running the streets. The games eventually became computer-based, with Lucas writing the story and a hired programmer from the University of Minnesota writing the computer code.

That work led to Davenport Simulations, a small software company that specialized in computer-based simulations of law-enforcement crises, intended to train police communications personnel in fast-moving crisis management. By the time the company's management bought him out, Davenport Simulations were running on most of the nation's 911 equipment.

The simulations hadn't much interested him. They'd simply been an obvious and logical way to make money, more of it than he'd ever expected to make. And while games still interested him, he'd lost his place in the gaming world. The new three-dimensional computer-based action/strategy games were far beyond anything he'd been able to do as recently as five years before.

When he'd gotten rich, when he'd gotten political, he'd stepped off the streets. But in the past six months, his life had begun to shift again. He was wandering the Cities at night. Looking into places he hadn't seen in years: taverns, a couple of bowling alleys, barbershops, a candy store that fronted for a sports book. Strip joints, now masquerading as gentlemen clubs. Putting together rusty connections.

And he was talking to old gaming friends. He began to consider a new kind of game, a game set in the real world, with real victories to win, and a real treasure at the end, maybe using palm computers and cell phones. He'd been staying up late again, working on it. He was still in the pencil-twiddling stage, but now had a block of scratchy flow charts pinned to his drafting table. One idea a night, that's all he wanted. Something he could use. But an idea a night was a lot of ideas.

He leaned back in the chair, yawned, closed his eyes. In his mind's eye, he saw Maison on the floor, her foot sticking out from behind the bed, and the woman crumpled on the floor below the closet. Maison and her friends were dopers, and dopers got killed; it happened forty or fifty times a year in Minneapolis, thousands of times a year across the country.

As far as he was concerned, dopers were crap, and if they died, well, that's what dopers did. That Alie'e was famous cut no ice with Lucas. Her fame was entirely ephemeral, not the result of hard work, or intellectual or moral superiority, but simply a by-product of her appearance.

He felt no impulse to revenge; he did feel the first tingles of the hunt. That was something else altogether. That had nothing to do with Alie'e, but was purely between his guys and the other guys.

Then he saw, in his mind's eye, the image of Catrin as a young woman. Man, the last time he saw her . . .

Lucas's eyes were closed, and the corners of his mouth turned up. A small smile, and not a particularly attractive one. Feeling a little wasted; feeling some pressure from the politicals; feeling a killer out there, somewhere, maybe running, maybe not. And a woman on the mind, somebody to wonder about.

This was how life was supposed to be. Propped up in a chair, wishing you still smoked, worried about twenty-four things at the same time. Not that laid-back, going nowhere slowly feeling . . . that prosperous, rich-guy, hand-shaking shit.

Like *this.*

He was sleeping like a baby when the phone rang.

5

Dark. Bad taste. Lucas pushed himself up in the chair, the phone still ringing. Confused for a moment, he realized he was in his office, that he'd dozed off. He sighed and fumbled for the phone. "Yeah?"

Sloan: "I got this Amnon kid coming down here. And his sister, uh, Jail, however you pronounce it. Ya-el, whatever."

"Yeah. Jael." Lucas rubbed his eyes, held on to the phone and stumbled to the light switch, and then looked at his watch. Seven-fifteen. "When are they due in?"

"Amnon's in St. Paul. He said he was in the middle of something, but he could leave there in ten minutes or so. He ought to be here in a half an hour. The sister said she'd be here about nine. She sounded pretty freaked out. I could hear somebody crying in the background. Anyway, you said you might want to sit in."

"Yeah, I would. Are they bringing lawyers?"

"I don't know. I do know that they moved Maison to the ME's, and he was coming in to take a look. I'm going over."

"Wait for me — I'll walk along."

73

The ME was a middle-sized man with long graying hair tied in a neat ponytail, gold-rimmed glasses, and a distracted air. They talked in his office, a routine government cubicle with no bodies in sight. "I've taken a preliminary look, is all I've done — we'll get right on the full autopsy. I'll do it myself. We'll start getting some chemistry back by late afternoon. But I can tell you three things," he said. "Your guys told me that she was strangled, and I can confirm that that's almost certainly the case. This wasn't accidental sexual asphyxiation or anything like that. Her hyoid bone's broken, and that takes direct pressure, probably with the thumbs, from a pair of strong hands."

"A man, then," Sloan said.

Lucas frowned. "Why wouldn't it be?"

"There are some rumors that she swung the other way," Sloan said. "Really, that she swung both ways, but recently, mostly with women."

The ME shook his head. "I can't tell you that it was a man, for sure. Just that it was somebody with strong hands. The second thing is this: The crime-scene people say that her condition suggested sexual activity before her death. And I can tell you that she *did* engage in sexual activity, not long before her death, but at least *some* time before. An hour, maybe as many as two hours. There are two or three small scratches and some light bruising next to her vulva. Fingernails, I think, just enough to draw a little blood — but the bruises had time to develop before she was killed. And it appears — I'll tell you for sure after the autopsy — that while there is light bruising suggestive of rough sexual play, she was not fully penetrated. Not by a penis, anyway. It appears that the sexual play was primarily manual and oral. There's no semen."

Lucas looked at Sloan, who asked, "Is that two things or three things?"

"Two things," the ME said.

"What's the third thing?" Lucas said.

"There are no defensive wounds. No other bruises, no indications of a struggle, no sign that the killer had to fight to hold his grip. She didn't scratch him — her fingernails are clean. I couldn't even find any signs that she thrashed around. She just . . . let herself go. For whoever did it, she was an easy kill."

"Dope," Sloan said. "She might not even have known she was dying."

"Oh, yeah, that's a fourth thing," the ME said. "That *is* a needle stick on her arm, and there are more between her toes. She was taking a lot of sticks."

"An addict?"

"Tell you later. None of this is final. I'll have some definitive stuff this afternoon."

Lucas stopped at the chief's office, gave her a quick capsule of what the ME had said. She made a few notes and said, "So it really *could* be drug-related."

"Yeah. Maybe even *probably.*"

"We got half an hour before the press conference," she said. "I've promised everybody that you'll drag the killer in and hurl him to the floor in front of the microphones."

"Or her," Lucas said.

"Yeah?"

"Maybe."

The chief turned to her window, squinted out at the empty sidewalk, then shook her head. "Nope. It's a man. A woman didn't kill Alie'e Maison."

"You're sure?"

"Yup. And seriously, Lucas . . ."

"Mmmm?"

"We'd look really good if we caught this guy quick."

The chief's secretary stuck her head in. "Lucas, Sloan says a Mr. Plain is here."

"Gotta go," Lucas said. "Good luck with the movie people."

Sloan was waiting in the back of the Homicide office, talking with a tall dark-haired man with black eyes, who might have been called slender except that he had a square-shouldered heft that made him too tough for the word; he could have played a dissolute biker in a rock 'n' roll movie. He was wearing a black leather jacket, black slacks, and a plain black T-shirt. Another man, fleshy, brown-haired, freckled, wearing a Star Wars Crew baseball hat and a single silver earring, sat sideways in a hard-back chair a few feet away.

Sloan saw Lucas coming and said, "Chief Davenport, this is Amnon Plain. He was at the party last night and agreed to come to talk with us."

The dark-haired man nodded at Lucas and the brown-haired man said, "Get a lawyer, dude."

Plain asked Lucas, "Do I need one? A lawyer?"

Lucas shrugged. "I don't know. Did you kill Alie'e?"

"No." Nothing more; no explanation of why he wouldn't have, or couldn't have, or a protest at the question.

Lucas said, "If you've got a simple and convincing story, then there shouldn't be a problem. If there are ambiguities to your statement . . . then maybe you ought to get a lawyer."

Plain looked at the brown-haired man, who said, "Do what the dude says. Get a lawyer."

Plain looked back at Lucas, then at Sloan, then back to Lucas, and said, "Fuck a lawyer. But I want to make my own tape of the statement. I brought a recorder."

"No problem," Lucas said.

Plain asked if the brown-haired man could come along, and Lucas, looked at Sloan, who shrugged. "I'd rather not . . ."

"Get a lawyer," said the brown-haired man.

". . . but if he doesn't get involved . . ." Sloan continued.

"Come on along," Lucas said.

They took the statement in an interview room,

with three tape recorders on the table: two police recorders, backing each other up, and Plain's hand-sized Sony.

Sloan had gone into good-cop mode, and said, pleasantly, "If you'll just tell us where you were and what you did, and who you saw last night."

Plain dipped into a jacket pocket and took out an orange-covered notebook and flipped it open. "I got to the party a little after ten o'clock — as close as I can put it, about ten minutes after ten. Before that, starting at about eight o'clock, I'd been at the New French Café with friends. The friends were . . ."

He listed the friends. In the next five minutes, he gave a nearly minute-by-minute account of his evening, with each friend he encountered along the way.

What about Sandy Lansing?

Plain shook his head. "I don't know. If I saw a picture of her, maybe I'd recognize her, but I don't recognize the name. The party was open . . . to a particular crowd."

"What crowd?"

"The art-money hip crowd," Plain said.

"Any dope around?"

"All over the goddamn place."

"You use drugs?" Sloan asked it mildly enough, but there was a snake in the question, which everyone could see. Plain did not hesitate.

"No. I don't use any chemicals. I did, for two years, when I was a teenager. I used cocaine, heroin, methamphetamine, ecstasy, LSD, peyote, marijuana, alcohol, nicotine, and a couple of other things. Hypnotics. Quaaludes. I found out that each and every one of them made me stupider than I already was, and I decided I couldn't afford that. So, eleven years ago, I stopped."

"Aspirin?" Lucas asked. A little sarcasm.

"I still use aspirin and ibuprofen. I'm not a moron." His tone of voice showed no reaction to the sarcasm, and somehow left Lucas feeling that the sarcasm had been juvenile. Plain was ahead on points.

"So what happened next?" Sloan asked.

At about midnight, Plain said, he left the party at Sallance Hanson's and went back to his studio in St. Paul's Lowertown with a friend, Sandy Smith, where they met an employee, James Graf, to look at scanned negatives from that morning's photo shoot. After half an hour of looking at the negs, Smith left for his home while Plain and Graf continued to work with the negatives.

"What were the pictures of?" Lucas asked.

Plain tilted his head. "You don't know?"

"No."

"Some investigation," he said to the brown-haired man. Then: "I spent all yesterday morning and the early part of the afternoon doing a fashion shoot with Alie'e."

"Did you have a personal relationship with Alie'e?" Sloan asked.

"What do you mean, personal? You mean, was I fucking her?"

79

"Or anything else," Lucas said.

"No. I wasn't fucking her. I wasn't interested in her. She was a dummy. She was like a toy that you plugged your dick into. Or, if you were a woman, that you stuck your tongue into. She was interested in feeling good, and that was about it," he said.

"Your sister was involved with her?" Lucas asked.

"Yeah. They were gobbling each other, or whatever women do. Sticking heroin in their arms, putting coke up their noses."

Sloan said, "Hmph," and Lucas asked, "I was talking to some woman who was at the party, and she said you were so jealous of the relationship between Alie'e and your sister that you might kill Jael if you had the chance. Which suggests that Alie'e was more to you than just another model."

Plain tipped his head, regarding Lucas with some curiosity, and said, "You're lying. Nobody told you that. But that's interesting. You apparently got hold of something, somewhere, and you don't know quite what it is."

"Get a lawyer," his friend said from the corner.

Lucas grinned involuntarily. He'd been caught — and that made *him* curious. "Tell me why you think I'm lying."

"Because you got it just backwards," Plain said.

"What?"

"I wasn't jealous because my sister took Alie'e away from me. I'm a little jealous — I admit it —

because Alie'e took *Jael* away from me."

In the immediate silence, the brown-haired friend said, "Oh shit," and Lucas and Sloan looked at each other, trying to figure out what Plain had just said. Plain, picking on Sloan because he was the straighter-looking of the two cops, leaned toward him and said, "Yup. I was fucking my sister."

"Now, *that* was an interview and a half," Sloan said when they'd finished and Plain and his friend had gone. They had an hour of tape.

Lucas rubbed his forehead. "I was feeling almost sympathetic there, toward the end. Two arty parents, rich dipshits, get divorced. Each one takes a kid. The kids don't see or speak to each other for fifteen years, then they run into each other, virtual strangers, good-looking, one is a model and the other one is working in photography, both running with the same crowd. If they hadn't been brother and sister, you'd *expect* them to fall in bed."

"Yeah, but . . ."

Lucas nodded. "Then there's the other thing."

"What's that?"

"He says his sister quit modeling and now is a professional potter, big in the art world. I've met a couple of potters."

"I wouldn't doubt it," Sloan said. He had an exaggerated idea of Lucas's love life.

"I'll tell you one thing about potters," Lucas continued. "They pick up this clay, and they throw it around, and they beat it and twist it and turn it. . . . a few years of that, and they've got arms and hands like wrestlers."

"Alie'e was strangled," Sloan said. "Be interesting to talk to the sister."

Alie'e's boyfriend, a guy who insisted his only name was Jax, came through Homicide's front door a few steps before Jael Corbeau came in with her lawyer. Lucas had to decide which interview to watch, and he went with Corbeau.

Sloan took the statement, with Lucas and Swanson sitting in; Lucas tried not to stare, but Jael Corbeau was somebody to stare at. Not immediately — not a flash thing — but after a minute or so, he found it hard to stop looking at her. She had the same angular face as her brother, but was blond. And she had tracks on her face, scars; they did something unnatural: made it hard to breathe.

After the preliminaries — Sloan read her the Miranda warning, and the lawyer said that he might ask his client not to reply to certain questions, and that was not to be taken as an indication of guilt — Sloan said, "Tell us about your relationship with Alie'e Maison."

Jael looked at her lawyer, who nodded, and she said, "Well, I didn't kill her. Or the other woman."

"I'm happy to hear that," Sloan said, smiling at her. "Do you have any idea who might have?"

"No. Really. I've been going over and over it in

my head, and I can't figure out who would." Her eyes drifted away from Sloan and stopped at Lucas. "Nobody disliked her enough. I mean, I don't know about the other woman, but Alie'e — some people probably disliked her, but not enough to hurt her."

"How about in New York? Anybody there?" Sloan asked.

"No." She was talking to Lucas now. "Of the top ten or fifteen models that you hear about, you know, the supermodels, she's like number seven or eight. She was very close to the top — maybe she would have become number one, she had the look for it — but there are other people who really are bigger. Who would be more like to attract a crazy person, if that's what you're thinking."

"We don't know quite what to think yet," Sloan said. "So you don't —"

Jael leaned forward, interrupting: "But you know, she had a big following on the Internet. A lot of the . . . you know, engineer-type people were interested in her. They put up Internet pages, or whatever you call them, Websites, with her pictures. Some of them grafted porno pictures on her, so you'd see a woman fucking somebody, and the face would be Alie'e's. . . . there are quite a few of those."

"Hmm. Interesting," Sloan said. He looked at Lucas, then back at Jael, and asked, "Did she ever do any porn?"

"No. Of course not. Aside from everything

else, she couldn't afford to. If she'd done any porn, the big courtiers would have dropped her like a hot rock."

"Okay. . . . How about Lansing? Was she a friend of yours?" Sloan asked.

"No. I knew her — she came to parties — but she really wasn't part of the . . . I don't know what you'd call it. The art scene? That sounds pretentious and stupid at the same time."

"So she wasn't a friend, but you sort of knew her," Lucas said.

"Yes. She was some kind of hotel executive."

Sloan nodded. "Okay. Let me ask you about your personal relationship with Miz Maison. You were . . . what?"

He let the question hang there, unfinished. Corbeau hesitated for a moment, then said, "We had both a friendship and a sexual relationship. I originally met her in New York. We were both working as models — this was before she became as famous as she is . . . was. We were both from Minnesota — that brought us together, and we became friends."

"The relationship continued even after you moved back here? I understand you live here now."

"Yes, although I go to New York every few weeks, to talk with dealers. I represent both myself and several other potters to the New York galleries. I'd usually stay at Alie'e's apartment."

"Not always?"

"Not always. We both continued to have other

relationships — with men as well as women." She was looking at Lucas again. "Neither one of us thought of ourselves as primarily lesbian; we were just very good friends and our friendship had a physical component to it. If she had a man over, then I would stay someplace else. Usually up on Central Park South, so I could walk to the galleries on Fifty-seventh Street and over on Madison Avenue."

"Did you have a sexual encounter with Miz Maison last night at the party?" Sloan asked.

Another quick glance at the lawyer. "Yes."

"You were alone with her?"

"No. There were three of us. The other woman is Catherine Kinsley, who I believe is up north at her cabin with her husband. I haven't been able to reach her." She flushed for the first time. "This is not heavy duty masculine-style sexuality. This is more like . . . cuddling, kissing, talking with each other."

"But there was a physical component."

"Yes."

"What happened . . . afterwards? How was she when you left?"

"Sleepy. We were all sleepy, but she'd gotten up very early for her photo shoot, and had to get up the next day, and Silly — Silly Hanson — said she could sleep there, and so we left her. She was okay."

"And neither you nor Miz Kinsley saw her again."

"No. Well, I don't know if Catherine saw her,

because, like I said, I haven't been able to reach her this morning. I couldn't find her number, and I don't know exactly where the cabin is. Anyway, I don't think she saw her. We walked out to our cars together, said good-bye, and I went home. Your police people woke me up."

"Miz Maison injected heroin around the time of your encounter. Were you present for that?"

"No." Quick and definite, Lucas thought. She'd known the question was coming.

Sloan continued. "You didn't know that she was using heroin?"

A slight hesitation, another glance at the attorney, and, "I thought she might be tripping when we met in the bedroom. She was . . . languid. She was the way you get when you're using. But I wasn't there when she injected, and I don't think she had much, because she didn't fall asleep or anything, not while we were there. It was more like a . . . a . . . party favor."

"A party favor," Lucas said.

"Yeah. That's what people call them. Some people call them short pops — you know, if you want the effect but don't want to get addicted."

"You get addicted anyway," Sloan said.

Corbeau flipped her head. "You know that's not true. That's just a political position."

Sloan looked at Lucas, who raised his eyebrows, and Sloan said, "I'm not here to argue with you, but just for the record, Miz Corbeau: Short pops will addict you as fast as anything.

Believe me or don't believe me. But that's the way it is."

She shook her head, and Sloan said, "I don't want to embarrass you, but I've got to ask this question. The medical examiner tells us that Miz Maison has small light scratches around her vulva, and light bruising, as if she'd been involved in a fairly active sexual encounter involving manual stimulation and perhaps oral stimulation. . . . Would that have characterized your encounter?"

She flushed again, looked at them quickly, one at a time, taking them in. Lucas, still feeling the effect she had on his breathing, squirmed; he felt like a pervert. She didn't help; she asked, "Do you guys get off on this sort of thing?"

Sloan, his face a monk's stolid mask, shook his head. "Sitting in a room like this, full of metal tables and tile floors, this is not very sexual, Miz Corbeau. We need to know, because we need to know if she had another sexual contact after yours, or if yours was most likely the cause of the scratching and bruising. Miz Maison was strangled, which frequently is associated with sexual activity."

"Okay," she said. "Yes, it's possible that she was scratched. Especially by Catherine. Catherine can be a little rough, and she had long nails. I keep mine very short because of my job."

"You're a potter."

"Yes."

"And you had nothing to do with the death of Alie'e Maison?"

87

"No, I did not." She bit her lip as the words came out, and her chin trembled. To Lucas, she seemed shaken.

"Do you think your brother might have?" Lucas interjected.

She looked at him, a frown flickering across her face, and then said, "No. If Amnon was going to go after somebody, it'd be me."

"Why you?"

"We have a personal problem."

"He told us about your relationship," Lucas said. "You think that could turn to violence? The breakup?"

She turned away, looking at the floor, twisting her fingers together. "Amnon has violence in him. He wouldn't have killed Alie'e, because he had no . . . regard for her. He didn't care about her. You'd have to have some feeling for a person before you killed her, wouldn't you?"

"No," Lucas said. "Not if you're psychologically disturbed. People who are disturbed may kill to change the way they feel about something. The person killed may be a complete stranger, if the killing somehow . . . medicates . . . the disturbed person."

"God, that's awful."

"Yes. Your brother?"

"No. He's not disturbed that way. I know him well enough to say that."

"How did you get your names?" Swanson asked.

"Our parents were hippies, they went from one

thing to another, and they eventually tried out Judaism. Amnon and I were born during that period. They're Bible names."

"I'm a Catholic," Lucas said. "We weren't big on Bibles when I was a kid. Do the names mean something?"

"Jael was maybe a sorceress. Deborah fought Sisera, the Canaanite, and defeated him, and Sisera fled the battlefield and hid in Jael's tent. When he was asleep, she killed him by driving a tent peg through his head."

"Ouch," Lucas said. A tiny flicker of a smile on her sad face? "How about Amnon?"

"Amnon was one of Solomon's sons," Corbeau said.

"What, he was wise?"

"No, no," she said. "He slept with his sister." She scanned the four men, Lucas, Sloan, Swanson, and her own attorney, showed a flicker of a sad smile again, and said, "Were my parents prophets, or what?"

When they were done, they milled in the hallway outside the interview room, and Lucas asked Jael, "Why'd you quit modeling?"

"You think I shouldn't have?"

"I think you could have . . . continued," he said. She made him feel like a provincial clown, and he kind of liked it.

"It's boring," she said. "It's like making movies, except they don't pay you enough."

"Movies are boring?"

"Movies are fuckin' nightmares," she said. She laughed, and grasped his arm, just for a second; she was the kind of woman who liked to touch people, Lucas thought. "Shooting a movie is like watching grass grow."

When Jael and her lawyer left, Lucas and Sloan walked back to homicide. Frank Lester was talking to Rose Marie, and waved Lucas over.

"How'd you guys do?" he asked.

Lucas shrugged. "There's a lot of motive floating around, but not that points at Alie'e or Lansing."

"Who, then?" Rose Marie asked.

"Everybody," Lucas said. "We've got incest, jealousy, drugs, love triangles. You name it, we got it. But nothing that points at anyone."

"That's what I was telling Rose Marie," Lester said. "We've got so many suspects that it's turning into a technical problem. We've got fifty-four people for the party now, and there'll be more. How in the hell do you really interview more than fifty people, and do a good job of it? Who do you push, and how hard? The thing is, if the killer was at the party, and he's our forty-fifth interview . . . there's no *feel* to it anymore."

"You're asking everybody to point at somebody else?" Lucas asked.

"Yeah, but they're all lying through their teeth. Nobody knew that everybody was using drugs. . . . Anyway, we've only been able to *probably* eliminate a half-dozen people who left the party when Alie'e was still circulating. With that open window, we can't eliminate anyone who left after Alie'e went back to the bedroom. Somebody might have unlocked the window for the purpose of leaving, and coming back later."

"If the window was used at all," Sloan said.

"Yeah. If."

"How about the husband of the woman who was with Alie'e and Corbeau on the bed, this Catherine Kinsley. Did he know about the relationship?" Lucas asked.

"They're not in yet," Rose Marie said.

Lester said, "I did just sit in on an interview with Alie'e's boyfriend —"

"I saw him," Lucas said.

"Noxious little penis," Lester said. "His real name used to be Jim Shue. He didn't think he looked like a shoe, so he tried to change it to JX. J for James, X for nothing. The court told him he had to have a vowel, so he winds up Jax. Anyway, he knew all about the relationship with Corbeau. He says it didn't bother him. He called it Alie'e's 'alternate modality.' He said that they were both multisexual. He said pretty soon everybody will be."

"Too late for me," Rose Marie said.

"Yeah. I'm barely unisexual," Lester said. "Anyway, he's a dipshit. He said he had nothing to do with her death, but we're putting him on the shortlist."

"What about the media thing?" Rose Marie asked Lucas. "The human sacrifice?"

"I'll ask Del," Lucas said. "He's setting it up."

6

Del was waiting outside Lucas's office, leaning patiently against the wall. When he saw Lucas coming, he walked down the hall to meet him and said, "I'm clear with IA."

"What about finding somebody we can throw to the media?"

"I can't find a connection. These aren't street people. But the dope guys are set up to raid George Shaw's operation —"

"Shaw is street. He's not Alie'e's dealer," Lucas said.

"I know, but it's what we got," Del said. "We got confirmation last night that he's got a lot of cocaine on hand and maybe some heroin. So they're gonna hit him, and I thought we could ride along. We don't say anything, but we get your picture taken."

"Where?"

"A place down on Thirty-fifth. Shaw has been sleeping there, usually until three o'clock or so. He's there now. We're gonna hit him a little after noon. If we work it right, the TV people are gonna jump to a conclusion. We can deny our ass off and they won't believe us for a minute."

"That's not exactly what we wanted."

"No, but that's as good as we're gonna get it," Del said.

Lucas thought about it for a second. The movie people weren't stupid; if they thought they were being manipulated, there'd be trouble. But if they weren't thrown some kind of meat, they'd be running around like a pack of wolves, and pretty soon the politicians would start to panic, and then the attorney general — you never wanted to stand between the attorney general and a TV camera — would get into it, on some theme like police negligence. In a fairly short time, a world-class pissing match would be going on and . . .

"All right. If that's what we got."

"I've already tipped TV3 to be ready to roll between noon and one o'clock," Del said. "Rose Marie and the mayor already said at the press conference that you'd be monitoring the investigation. So if you're monitoring the raid, and if they want to put two and two together . . . that's their problem."

"But the raid isn't a put-up job, is it? I mean, it's legit?"

"It's fine. Shaw got a ton of shit a week ago, but he's been moving, wholesaling it to all the little assholes. Couldn't find him. Now he's holed up at his sister-in-law's and he's still got some left."

Lucas nodded. "Because if it was a put-up job, and somebody gets hurt, the word would get out and we'd all be in shit city."

Del nodded. "We're okay. The drug guys were talking about it last night, before Alie'e, as soon as they spotted Shaw walking home."

The twelve-man emergency response team met at a south side precinct house and was briefed by a guy named Lapstrake from Intelligence. Lapstrake was a bland, twenty-something guy with a home haircut who wore blue Sears work pants and a blue shirt that said "Cairn's Glass" on the back. He used a flip pad to illustrate the approaches to George Shaw's house. Lucas and Del sat on folding chairs in the back of the room, listening in.

"We're gonna have to move fast," Lapstrake said, pointing with a laser. "George's got relatives all over the neighborhood, and every one of them's got him on speed-dial. Four guys go in the back, coming in from Thirty-fourth. You'll split up and go around this house . . ." He put a red laser-dot on the house behind Shaw's. ". . . and go right over the fence and cover the back door and side windows. It's a hurricane fence, no problem."

"A dog?" somebody asked.

"Used to be, but it died," the Intelligence cop said.

"Aw, shit," somebody said. "They got pit bulls down there."

"He's gone, really," Lapstrake said, grinning. "I promise."

He put another red dot on the front of the house. "We got Group Two coming in from the front, blocking, watching down the sides. Group Three hits the front door. We think George sleeps in what used to be the dining room. When you go in, you'll be in the living room. There'll be a hall straight ahead, and an arch over to the right. The dining room is behind the arch, and that's where George should be, but there's also a connection between the dining room and the kitchen."

Lapstrake sketched it quickly, and made sure the entry group had it. "From the time we hit the sidewalk, we need to be on top of him in one minute, no more. There's a possibility that he'll be upstairs. There's no bathroom upstairs and no way out, and we don't think it's likely he'll be up there. The stairs come down into the front room — you'll see them on your left when you go through the door."

"Who else is in the house?" somebody asked. "And what're we looking for, specifically?"

"We think he's probably got anything from a quarter kilo to a kilo of cocaine on him, and some amount of heroin, but we don't know how much. He usually carries it in plastic squeeze bottles, like the kind you get at camping stores, REI, like that. We heard last week that he'd gotten a delivery the week before, and was putting it on the street, but we couldn't find him, so who knows what he's got left? Maybe he's got a ton, maybe he's sold it all. The coke is definite, one of our guys saw it last night," Lapstrake said. "As for who else in the house, the house is owned by his sister-in-law, Mary Lou Carter. The thing is, you gotta watch Mary Lou. Get her on the floor. She tends to go off."

"She got a gun?" somebody else asked.

"Not her style, but there's probably a few in the house. She basically has a really explosive temper, and she's big and strong. If she comes after you, don't mess around. Take her down. Dick Hardesty ran into her a couple of years ago, and she almost beat his brains out."

"What about Shaw? Is he gonna fight? He's a tough guy."

"Yeah, but he's a pro, and he's getting older and slower. I don't think he'll fight," Lapstrake said. He looked around and asked, "Any more questions? No? Then Chief Davenport wants to say a word. He and Del are gonna ride along."

Lucas stood up and said, "Number one, nobody get hurt. Number two, there's gonna be some media around. The Homicide guys think Shaw's heroin may have been getting to Alie'e Maison, and you've all heard about that situation. Homicide thinks maybe her killing was drug-related. So . . . take it easy, but we want to look sharp."

Lucas looked around, got a few nods. Lapstrake picked up a jacket and said, "So let's go."

Out the door, Del wandered down the sidewalk, pulled out a cell phone, punched in a number, said a few words, and punched off.

"We're set," he said. On the way to the target house, lagging a bit behind the entry team, Del asked, "Do you remember George Shaw?"

"Yeah. I didn't know him real well."

"It's just that Lapstrake said he was getting older and slower and probably wouldn't fight."

"Yeah?"

"Shaw's about our age."

"Fuck Lapstrake," Lucas said.

They turned the corner onto Thirty-fifth just in time to see the armored ERT take down the front door. The entry team flowed inside as Lucas eased the car to the curb; at the same time, doors started opening down the street, and a few kids wandered toward them. Two minutes later, Lapstrake appeared at the front door, looked up and down the street, spotted them, and waved them in. As Lucas and Del walked toward the house, a TV van turned the corner.

"Must of been close," Del muttered. "Lemme get outa sight."

He hurried on ahead, up the steps and into the house, as Lucas idled along the sidewalk. Lapstrake met him at the lot line: "Got him."

"Any coke?"

"Yup. Quite a bit," Lapstrake said, "and some heroin."

"Good. We —"

Another cop appeared at the door. "You guys

gotta come look at this."

"What?"

"Come on."

Whatever it was, was good, Lucas thought. The cop was too cheerful for it to be anything else.

"Got some stuff upstairs, Chief," one of the armored team members said as Lucas ducked inside the house. The house was old, with ceilings that felt an inch too low, floors that creaked underfoot, and rooms that seemed a foot short in both lateral dimensions. The wallpaper on the walls was loose, with warps and water damage near the floor. A couple of rag rugs in once-bright, now dirt-muted, colors made ovals in front of a big-screen television. The place smelled of tacos — hamburger and onions. Most of the cops were crowded into the dining room. Lucas stepped that way, and saw a large black man in olive-green underwear, a dazed expression on his face, handcuffed on an open studio bed. Del was squatting next to him, talking.

"Where's Mary Lou?" Lucas asked.

"She went out a few minutes ago, about the time we were starting over here," Lapstrake said. "She got on a downtown bus, and we let her go."

"Upstairs," said the armored cop, a little impatient.

Upstairs, in the single bedroom, what looked like a full cord of marijuana bricks were stacked on a plastic sheet in the middle of the room.

"All right," said Lapstrake. "Now we're talking."

Lucas picked up one of the bricks, sniffed it, dropped it. A small upstairs window was open, two thin curtains fluttering in a breath of breeze; outside, through the screen, he could see a little boy playing in a tractor-tire sandbox. Ten yards away, a little girl, a few years older than the boy, stood looking diagonally across the yard at what must have been the cops in the street. Her arms and legs were rigid with attention and possibly fear or anger. He was struck by the similarity of the view from the window and a camera shot in a World War II movie he'd seen on television the week before. But then the men in black combat gear, with the helmets and guns, rousting people from their houses, had been Nazis.

Just a movie.

He turned back to Lapstrake. "I'm gonna tell the TV people to hang around. When you get this documented, let them in, let them get some shots of you guys carrying the stuff out," Lucas said. "And flash the cocaine, too."

"Not me," Lapstrake said.

"So get a front guy. Get Jones down here from dope, he's good at this shit," Lucas said.

Downstairs again, Del eased over and said, "I'm outa here — I'll get a ride with one of the squads. We got maybe a kilo and a half of powder cocaine and a bottle of heroin, plus that weed. No crack."

"What do you think about Shaw?"

"George is history," Del said.

"Is there *any* possibility that any of this shit really could have gotten to Alie'e?"

"He's not really in that high end of the trade," Del said. "But who knows? I'll talk to him again downtown."

Del and Lapstrake stayed out of sight while the entry team took George Shaw out to a car and put him inside, and when the cameras started following the head-down figure of Shaw, now dressed in dark slacks and tennis shoes, Del went out the back. Lucas followed the Shaw parade. As soon as the police car was moving, one of the TV reporters shouted his name, and he walked toward them. The reporters were accompanied by three cameramen, who refocused from the car to Lucas.

"Chief Davenport, we understand this raid was a direct reaction to the murder of Alie'e Maison this morning. Is that right?"

Lucas shook his head. "I can't comment on an ongoing investigation. I can tell you that we've found a substantial quantity of illegal drugs."

"What drugs?"

"Both cocaine and heroin and a very large amount of marijuana," Lucas said, looking into the cameras. "The marijuana looks like a stack of firewood."

"We understand that cocaine and heroin may have been involved in Maison's death."

"I have heard that, but my source probably wasn't any better than yours," Lucas said mildly.

"Weren't you at the death scene early this morning?"

"Yes, I was." Reluctantly.

"And now you're here investigating the exact same drugs that were found."

"Look," Lucas said, interrupting, "I don't want to talk about the Maison investigation. Chief Roux is taking direct charge of that investigation, and all comment has to come through her."

"But we understand that you are coordinating —"

"I really can't comment, sorry. Excuse me." Lucas pushed through the group, walking down toward the cars. The interview-on-the-scene was over, and the cameras went down, but the reporters tagged along behind.

"There's gotta be more than that, Lucas," one of the reporters said. She was an intense young woman with short dark hair and small, pretty features.

"I wish I could tell you more, but I can't," Lucas said. "I just can't. But I'll tell you what — if you hang around here, I'll talk to Jim Jones, Lieutenant Jones from Narcotics, and I'll get you inside the house. Marijuana might not be that big a deal, but it is when you've got a mountain of it, and there's a mountain of it in there. And I'll get them to show you the cocaine and heroin."

"Alie'e *was* using heroin, at least in New York she was," another reporter asserted. This one was a honey blonde, with a nose so tidy that it could only be explained as the product of surgery.

"Listen," Lucas said, dropping his voice. "This has honest-to-God gotta be off the record, okay? I'm serious."

The three reporters glanced at each other and nodded. "Alie'e had what's called a short pop of heroin about the time she was murdered. I don't know what they're planning to say downtown, but that's the truth. If you push them on it, they'll confirm it." He looked back at Shaw's house — significantly, he hoped. "That's all I can tell you."

"Wait a minute, wait a minute," the blonde said. "You said, 'short pop,' is that the phrase?"

"Yeah, short pop."

"That's good. That sounds really, you know, ghetto," she said. "And one more question, this can't hurt anyone. When you saw Alie'e this morning . . . was she wearing a green dress?"

"A green dress?"

"Yes, a green dress with a narrow, dropped neck and —"

"This has gotta be off the record." He couldn't see how it could hurt.

"Sure. Of course. We just want to *know*," she said.

"It *was* green. Kind of semitranslucent."

"Excellent." The cameramen had been drifting over to listen in, their cameras pointed away — this was off the record, and they knew the rules. The blonde picked out her cameraman and lifted a hand, palm up, and said, "The dress was green."

They high-fived, and Lucas asked, "What?" The other reporters looked as puzzled as he was.

"Death dress," the reporter said. "We got it on tape yesterday. It's by Gurleon. A twenty-five-thousand-fucking-dollar shroud, and we got it on tape, with Alie'e in it. Are we fuckin' *good,* or what?"

7

"... and became a beautiful filmy-green twenty-five-thousand-dollar shroud for the mysterious women with the jade-green eyes. Back to you, Henry."

The first man hadn't gotten any sleep; he paced his office, watching the TV. The blond reporter was smiling at him. *Filmy green shroud.* She was proud of that. *Filmy green.*

At the tips of his fingers, the man could still feel the soft skin of Alie'e's throat. He hadn't had any choice with her. She'd come along at the precisely wrong time in everybody's life. . . .

Sandy Lansing was panicking, she was going to run. He'd had to *talk* with her, to *discipline* her: You did not run when there was business to be done. He'd reached out, intending to push her against the wall. Somehow the pit of his palm had landed under her chin, and when he pushed, her head snapped back, into a molding around a door. He'd actually felt her skull crack, the vibration through the heel of his hand — like feeling a raw egg crack on the edge of a china cup.

Her eyes had gone up, and she'd slipped down the wall, and he'd glanced back up the hallway toward the party. If the door opened . . . "Get up," he said. "Come on, get the fuck up."

He'd taken her arm and pulled, but her arm was deathly slack. And after a minute, he'd believed. He'd looked for a pulse, tried to find a heartbeat, but could find neither. He'd been seized by fear: Christ, she was dead. He crouched over the body, like a jackal over a baked ham, looking from her face to the still-closed door. He hadn't meant to kill her.

But nobody knew. . . .

The body was next to a door. He pulled the door open: a closet, with a rack of cold-weather jackets and coats. He lifted her, her heels dragging, and shoved her into the closet. She wouldn't fit; she kept slumping, and she had to be upright to fit. He was holding her by the throat with one hand, trying to get the door shut, when a voice said from a few inches behind his ear, "What are you *doing?*"

He'd almost had a heart attack. He turned and saw the green eyes; and the closet door finally clicked shut. Alie'e asked again, "Why did you put her in the closet?"

The second man heard about Alie'e's death from his dashboard radio. At first, he thought he'd misheard; and then it occurred to him that he was crazy — that he wasn't hearing this at all. But the radio kept talking, talking, talking . . . and when he changed stations they were talking, talking . . .

105

Alie'e this, Alie'e that.

Alie'e with lesbians.

Alie'e nude in a photo shoot.

Alie'e dead.

The second man swerved to the side of the road, pulled on the park brake, put his head on the steering wheel, and wept. Couldn't stop: his shoulders shaking, his mouth open, breathing in stuttering gasps.

After a long five minutes, he wiped his eyes on his shirtsleeve, turned, found a clipboard in the back, clipped in a piece of notepaper.

He wrote: *Who did this?* And drew a line under it.

And under that, he wrote the first name.

There would, he thought, be quite a few names before he finished the list.

8

On the way back to police headquarters, Lucas took out his cell phone, thumbed it on, and called Rose Marie Roux on her command line. She picked up and Lucas said, "We got the media fixed. The raid turned up a ton of grass, and a bunch of coke and heroin. I think they all bought it."

"Good. Now we need a second act."

"It's like managing the media has gotten more important than finding the killer."

Roux said, "You know the truth about that, Lucas. We'll either get the killer or we won't, no matter what the media does. But the media can kill *us*. And I don't have anything else I'd rather be doing right now."

For the rest of the day, Lucas hung around the interrogation rooms, listening in. One item came up early — Alie'e didn't have any dope in her possession, or any cooking equipment for the heroin, or a syringe or needles. Somebody else put the dope on her, but nobody at the party was admitting to the use of dope, and nobody knew anybody else who was using.

A question they asked everyone involved the scribble on Sandy Lansing's wrist. They got the answer to that in the early afternoon.

"A woman named Pella," Swanson told Lucas. "She's going to England in December, for three weeks, and Lansing was going to get her a rate at a hotel. She said Lansing wrote her name on her wrist to remember to set it up."

"This holds water?"

Swanson shrugged. "Does with me, I guess. Pella said a decent hotel in London is gonna cost her two hundred a night, but with Lansing's connection, she can get the same room for one and a quarter. That's something like fifteen hundred bucks in savings."

"And this Pella doesn't know anything about the dope?"

"She said she met Alie'e for the first time last night, and said three words to her. But she looks kinda wired. . . . I wouldn't be surprised if she carried a little toot in her purse."

"All we have to do is crack one of them," Lucas said. "Get somebody to rat out her friend."

Lester stopped by: "We grabbed Hanson's computer, but most of what we're getting is bullshit."

"They talked about dope," Lucas said.

"She said it was just rumors."

"She's bullshitting us."

"Of course she is."

Two uniformed cops from St. Paul brought in

a huge man named Clark Buchanan, who, improbably, told them that he was a model and, incidentally, a welder.

"Model what?" one of the interrogating cops asked skeptically. "Lunch buckets?"

"You know, clothes and shit," Clark said. "I was the other guy in the Alie'e shoot. She was doing the clothes up front, I was making some sparks in the back."

Clark didn't know anything about drugs at the party. "I had some drinks, that's all I saw."

"Lotta drinks?"

He shrugged. "Maybe a half-dozen. Maybe ten. Vodka martinis. Goddamn. I'll tell you something, guys — rich people make good fuckin' vodka martinis." He stayed at the party until one o'clock, then caught a cab and went home. He remembered the name of the cab company and that the driver's name was Art. They asked a few more questions and cut him loose.

Early in the afternoon, Alie'e's parents arrived with a group of friends and talked first to the mayor, and then the mayor walked them over to Roux's office. Roux called Lucas, who went down to her office and stood in the back, with Lester, as the chief explained what was happening with the case.

Both Lynn and Lil Olson were dressed from head to toe in black, Lynn in a black-on-black suit that may have come from Manhattan, and Lil in a black lace dress that dropped over a black silken sheath; she also wore a black hat with a net that fell off the front rim over her eyes; her eyebrows matched the hat, severe dark lines, but her hair was a careful, layered honey-over-white blond, like her daughter's. Her eyes, when Lucas could see them, were rimmed with red. Alie'e got her looks from her father, Lucas thought — the cheekbones, the complexion, the green eyes. Lynn Olson was a natural blonde, but his hair was going white. In the black suit, he looked like a famous artist.

The friends were dressed in flannel and jeans and corduroy; they were purely Minnesota.

"She was going to be in the *movies*," Alie'e's mother said, her voice cracking. "We had a project just about set. We were interviewing costars. That was the big step, and now . . ."

Rose Marie was good at dealing with parents: patient, sympathetic. She introduced Lucas and Lester, and outlined how the case would be handled.

Lucas felt a strange disjuncture here: Alie'e's parents, who were probably in their late forties, looked New York, their black-on-black elegant against their blond hair and fair complexions. The words they used were New York, and even their attitude toward Alie'e was New York: all business. Not only was their daughter dead, so was the Alie'e enterprise.

But the sound of the language was small-town Minnesota: round Scandinavian vowels, "oo" instead of "oh," "boot" instead of "boat." And every few sentences, a Minnesota construction would creep out.

Rose Marie was straightforward. She mentioned the relationship with Jael — Lil said, "But that was just a lark, girls . . ." — and the possibility of drugs. The Olsons' eyes drifted away from Rose Marie's . . . and as Rose Marie was finishing, the door opened, and a heavyset man stepped in, looked around.

He wore jeans, black boots, and a heavy tan Carhartt jacket, with oil stains on one sleeve. His hair was cut like a farmer's, shaggy on top but down to the skin over the ears. Lynn Olson stood up and said, "Tom," and Lil stopped sniffling, her head jerking up. The big man scowled at them, nodded at the people from Burnt River, looked at Lucas, Lester, and then at Rose Marie. "I'm Tom Olson," he said, "Alie'e's brother."

"We were just telling your parents what we're doing," Rose Marie said.

"Do you *know* what you're doing?" he asked Rose Marie.

"We handle this kind of —"

"You're dealing with a nest of rattlesnakes," Olson said. "The best thing you could do is beat all of them with a stick. They are sinners, each and every one. They are involved in drugs, illicit sex, theft, and now murder. They're all criminals."

"Tom," Lil said. "Tom, please."

"We're questioning everyone who was with Alie'e in the past day," Rose Marie said. "We're very confident —"

Tom Olson shook his head once and looked away from her, at his parents. "So. After twenty-five years of abuse, she comes to this. Dead in Minneapolis. Full of drugs, the radio says, heroin — a short pop, the radio says — whatever that is. Some kind of evil they have a special name for, huh? We didn't hear about that in Burnt River."

Lester's eyes flicked at Lucas, as Lynn Olson stood up and said "Tom, take it easy, huh?"

Olson squared off to his father and said, "I'm not going to take it easy. I can still remember when we called her Sharon."

"We need to talk to you," Lester said to Tom Olson.

"To question me? That's fine. But I know almost nothing about what she was doing. I had one letter a month."

"Still . . . we'd like to talk."

Olson ignored him, turned to his parents, shook a finger at them. "How many times did I tell you this? How many times did I tell you that you were buying death? You even dress like the devil, in Satan's clothes. Look at you, you spend more money on one shirt than good people spend on a wardrobe. It's a sickness, and it has eaten into you . . ."

He was starting to foam, shaking not just his finger but his entire body. Lucas pushed away from the wall, and Lynn Olson got back on his feet and said, "Tom, Tommy. Tommy . . ."

"*. . . people living in this nightmare, people encour-*

aging this nightmare, willingly doing the business of the devil . . ."

He'd turned to Rose Marie, who was watching him openmouthed, and for a moment he looked as if he was going over the desk at her. Lucas moved quickly, from behind the desk, saying, "Whoa, whoa, whoa, slow down, man, slow down . . ."

Olson stopped talking, but continued to vibrate, then turned away and stepped to the back of the office and leaned on the door. After a moment, in the silence, he turned, with tears running down his cheeks. "Can I see her?" he asked.

Del was working down a line of junkies and dealers, trying to find the source of the drugs going through Silly Hanson's apartment the night before. Lucas's other guy, Lane, was working on Alie'e's genealogy.

"I want all of her family, and I want a chart that shows how they're related," he told Lane. "I want all of her ex-husbands —"

"Aren't any."

"— all of her ex-fiancés, ex-boyfriends, anyone else who might want to do her. Same with this other chick . . ."

"Lansing."

"Yeah. I want the whole chart."

"Listen, I think if we sorted through the people who were at the party last night, ran them —"

Lucas shook his head. "Homicide's halfway through the list. I'll get it tonight or tomorrow, if they don't have a case by then."

"Or working on the cat-burglar angle. I got some sources down there from when I was on patrol."

"Lane — go with the genealogies. Homicide and Property are working the cat-burglar thing. We want stuff that Homicide won't get around to right away. 'Cause if Alie'e getting killed isn't a random thing, if it's not a cat burglar, then it's somebody who knows her well enough to have a motive, and it's gotta be somebody reasonably close."

"But —"

Lucas pointed a finger at him. "The fuckin' genealogies."

He spent an hour in Homicide, listening to returning cops talk about what they'd found, what looked good. Not much looked good. Lester came back from his talk with Tom Olson. "He says his parents trained her like a dog. That's his word. Like a show dog. Used to drag her all over the country for beauty competitions and youth talent contests and modeling gigs."

"But *abuse?*"

"He didn't mean sexual abuse, that wasn't part of the deal," Lester said. "And he doesn't think his parents could have had anything to do with her death. He said they were *living* through her. That they took her life as a kid away from her, and that they were still taking."

"Did Alie'e fight it?" Lucas asked.

Lester shook his head. "He says no. He said she never knew anything else."

"Huh. He seemed a little nuts."

"He's a preacher of some kind," Lester said. "He says he actually loves his parents, but he just doesn't like them very much."

Then Del was on the phone, and said, "Hold on to your shorts."

"What happened?"

"Boo McDonald called me. I'm over at his place." McDonald was a paraplegic who monitored police scanners for a half-dozen TV and radio stations, and sometimes back-fed information to the cops. "He's been cruising the Internet, searching under "Alie'e." There's a story out, from here in the Cities, called 'Muff-Divers' Ball Goes Homicidal.' Guess what it's about."

"Muff-Divers' Ball?" Lucas repeated.

Lester's eyebrows went up. "That doesn't sound good."

Del was still talking. "Yeah. This is an online rock 'n' roll rag called *Spittle*. And they got some detail. It's gotta come out of the department."

"How bad?"

"Well, see, the rag says it's semidocumentary, which means they make up a lot of stuff. You know, to enhance the reality of the moment."

"Enhance?"

"Let me read a part. Move over, Boo." Lucas could hear them clunking around for a moment, then Del read, "Alie'e stretched back toward the

115 >115

115

brass bars at the head of the bed and grasped them in her hands, holding on tight as the waves of pleasure rippled through her lean, taut body. Jael's head bobbed between her thighs, her long pink tongue parting Alie'e's glistening labia, finding at last that little man in the canoe, the center of Alie'e's heat and being. . . ."

"Ah, fuck me," Lucas said. Then he laughed. "You'd sound like a porno flick if you had somebody playing a saxophone behind you."

"Probably will be, sooner or later — a movie, not a saxophone. I called the kid at *Spittle* and asked where he got this shit. He told me he wouldn't talk because of First Amendment considerations. But he said that he had interviews lined up with Channels Three and Four and Eleven."

"An asshole," Lucas suggested.

"Actually, I kinda liked him. Reminded me of myself when I was his age. I tried a little threat, but he told me he was a minor and I could go fuck myself."

"So what'd you say?"

"What could I say? I said, 'The bed wasn't brass, you little prick.' "

"How old is he?"

"Sixteen," Del said.

"So we go fuck ourselves. Anyway, the lesbian thing is out."

"It's out. Another ring in the circus."

Lucas called Rose Marie to warn her, and

when he got off the phone, walked down to his office and a silent space, kicked back in his chair, and stared at the ceiling.

His ceiling was dirtier than it should be.

That's all he got. The case had a bad feel to it: too many suspects, and not enough serious possibilities. Clean murders were the hardest to solve: somebody's killed, everybody denies everything. There were a half-dozen killers walking around the Twin Cities who'd never been touched; the cops knew everything about the murders, without any proof. Husbands killing wives, mostly. Whack the old lady on the head, throw the pipe in the river, go back home and find the body.

What can you do?

He was mulling it over when the phone rang again. More bad news?

No. Catrin.

"Lucas. I've been thinking about you all morning," she said. "God, it was good to see you. I've been thinking about the U — Do you remember Lanny Morton? Do you know what happened to him?"

"Yeah, as a matter of fact," Lucas said, getting comfortable. "He moved to L.A. to get involved in film, and got into real estate instead. He was pretty rich the last time I saw him; he was on his fourth wife."

"Fourth? What happened to Virginia?"

Lucas hunched forward in his chair. "Virginia

died. Didn't you know that? Jeez, it was only maybe five years after we graduated. She had a heart attack one day on the Venice Beach. She was, like, twenty-eight."

"Oh, my God. Do you remember that football game with all the mums, everybody had to buy his girlfriend a mum —"

"The Iowa game."

"Yeah. Virginia was like . . . she was going to live forever."

They talked for twenty minutes, catching up on old times. Catrin remembered all the names from their few months together, and the faces came swimming up from Lucas's memory, along with the sights and the sounds and even the smells of all those old glory days: the field houses all over the Big Ten, smelling of popcorn and dirt; the ice arenas and the odors of cold and blood, wet wool and sweat; diesel fumes from the buses; cheerleaders.

"God, I wish we'd had time to talk," Lucas said. "What do you do now? Do you still paint?"

"No, no, I do some photography, but the painting, I don't know. I just stopped. My husband's a family practice guy. I helped out at the office when we were first getting started. . . ."

"I heard about you marrying a doctor. I remembered on the way over here, after you told me this morning. I think Bill Washington said something about you going out with an older guy."

"Washington. God, I haven't thought about

him in years. The last time I saw him, we were all sitting around on a floor in Dinkytown getting high."

"You're a photographer? Say, you don't know a guy named Amnon Plain, do you? He's hooked up with the Alie'e case."

"Really? Did he do it?"

"He says not, and he probably didn't . . . but he says he's some kind of fashion photographer, and I thought —"

"Jeez, he's more than that. He does fashion photography, got started that way. But he does these most amazing pictures of the prairie. He's like Avedon, he does fashion but he's got this whole other thing."

"Avedon?"

"You were never an intellectual, were you?" She laughed.

"I was majoring in hockey, for Christ's sakes. Criminal justice."

"Yeah, well . . . Plain's a photographer. Big time. Pretty big time. I'm nothing like that — I mostly take care of the kids. Or try to — they're getting to the point where they don't want to hear from me. Oh, my God. . . ."

"What?"

"I just had a terrible thought," she said.

"What?"

"One of them's about to go off to the U. She could run into a Lucas Davenport."

"Hey, how bad could it get?"

But she was laughing. "I read about you in the

newspaper. Sometimes I can't believe that, you know, I *knew* you once. You're kinda famous."

"Yeah. Like they say, world famous in Minneapolis." Pause. "So let me buy you lunch," Lucas said.

A pause on the other end. "Will you tell me all the inside-cop stuff about Alie'e?"

"If you won't tell anybody else."

She laughed again, and said, "When?"

Catrin. As soon as she was off the phone, he wanted to call her again.

And what was he gonna wear tomorrow? Something really cool and expensive, or something tough, coplike? He'd been a hockey jock when they first got together, but she'd confessed then that she wasn't much interested in sports — or jocks, either. He'd talk about taking somebody out on the ice, or he'd come back after the match with a little ding on a cheekbone, a little rub, and she'd be perplexed and disturbed and sometimes even a little amused by his pleasure in the violence. . . .

The adrenaline of Catrin's call got to him. He pushed himself out of the chair, took another turn around the office, and finally launched himself out into the hallway. Frank Lester was sitting in his office, leaning back in his leather chair, the door open, cops coming and going. "Anything new?" Lucas asked.

"Nope. Rose Marie's doing another press conference about the lesbo thing."

"Jesus — don't call them lesbos if you go on TV."

"Hey, am I an idiot?"

Lucas looked at the ceiling, as if thinking about it, and Lester grinned and said, "We're indexing everything we're getting from the interviews, running down every single person at the party, but I'll tell you what: The guys are starting to think it's a cat burglar."

"That'd be tough," Lucas said. "If we haven't got anything yet."

"It'd be damn near impossible, unless somebody turns him in. What's the evidence gonna be? He didn't even get any blood on him, because there wasn't any. We're thinking about putting up a reward."

"You know about George Shaw?" Lucas asked.

Lester nodded. "Nothing there."

"Probably not, but the media seems to have gotten the idea that there is. If you decide to organize a reward, why don't you wait until after the George Shaw angle burns out? A reward would be something new. Keep the goddamn TV off our backs as long as we can."

"All right."

"Besides, I'll tell you what," Lucas said. "The answer is in the party. There wasn't any cat burglar."

"Sez who?"

"Sez me. Rose Marie told me this morning that a man killed Alie'e, that it wasn't a lesbo thing, and by God, she was right. It wasn't a cat burglar, either. God just wouldn't like it, if it was all just a coincidence, a one time thing, and the victim just happened to be Alie'e Maison."

Lester puffed up his cheeks, and then exhaled. Then nodded.

"A cat burglar does *not* crawl though a window and accidentally find a passed-out Alie'e Maison lying there without her underpants," Lucas said. "Not in a million fuckin' years."

Lester grinned again, thinking about it. "Have to be a profoundly lucky cat burglar."

Lucas asked, "Where's Sloan?"

"Still down doing interviews."

Lucas headed for the stairs. Maybe Sloan was pulling a thread.

He wondered what Catrin would be like. What if she'd turned into this small-town mommy housewife? She hadn't looked like that. At the gas station, she'd looked . . . interesting. He tried to gather back the memory of the morning. She was older, obviously, but then, so was he. She had some lines. A couple of extra pounds? Maybe. Maybe ten? Maybe. But still with the good hair, the good moves. The laugh . . .

He flashed back to his college apartment. He'd lived over a dingy auto-parts shop down University Avenue. He had one room with a fold-out couch and fake Oriental carpet from Goodwill, a bathroom permanently frosted over with either mildew or fungus — he was never interested enough to find out which — and a kitchen with a cheap gas stove and a refrigerator that was missing a leg and so listed to the left, and made sloped ice cubes. He also had a tiny bedroom, and in the bedroom was the best piece of furniture in the apartment, a bed he'd brought from home. And a good thing it was that he had the bed, because if he hadn't, Catrin would have broken his back. She liked sex. A lot. She was not promiscuous, just enthusiastic. The two of them had learned a lot together, trying out their chops. There was one cold winter day, but sunny, they'd been in bed late in the morning, the sun coming through the dirty window, splashing across the bed, and Catrin . . .

Flashing back on it, he felt himself . . . stirred.

At the bottom of the stairs he stopped and looked around. What was he doing?

Ah. Sloan.

Sloan was just coming out of the interview room. He carried a piece of paper, and walked a half-step behind a middle-aged man who seemed broken. The man had a hump at the back of his neck, his head pressed forward, his thinning gray hair combed over the top of his balding head. His face was dry, but tear tracks showed down his cheeks.

"Lucas . . . this is Mr. Arthur Lansing. Sandy Lansing was his daughter."

"I'm sorry, Mr. Lansing," Lucas said.

"I can't believe she's gone," he said. "She was so happy. Her career . . ." He trailed off, then said it again: "Her career . . ." He looked at Lucas. "When she was a little girl, her mama and I used to drive over to Como Park and push her though the zoo in a walker. She loved the bears. And the monkeys, she loved the monkeys."

"I'm sure —" Lucas was about to unreel a cliché, but Lansing broke in.

"Do you think you'll catch them?" he asked.

"Yes."

"I'll betcha it was niggers," he said.

"There weren't any black people at the party last night."

Lansing shook a trembling finger at Lucas. "Maybe. But you watch. I betcha it was niggers. You go upstairs, in the courthouse? I go up there all the time. To watch. All you see in them court-rooms is niggers. I mean, some white trash goes through there, but ninety-nine percent of them is niggers. And most of the white trash got nigger blood."

Sloan, standing behind Lansing, rolled his eyes. Lucas said, "Whoever did it, we'll catch him, Mr. Lansing. I'm really sorry about your daughter."

Lansing turned away and spoke to no one. "My daughter. She was an executive." And he wandered away, talking to the air.

"He loved his daughter," Sloan said after him.

"Yeah. That's what all that segregation shit used to be about. All the white people loved their daughters."

"Hate to lose a daughter, though," Sloan said. He had a daughter in college. "Worst thing I could think of. It's not right, dying out of order."

Lucas sighed. "You get anything from anybody?"

"No, but we're working the right people. Whoever killed them was at the party. There was too much going on that sparks off trouble — drugs, former boyfriends and girlfriends, the celebrity thing and the macho shit that goes with it, and just the general craziness of the crowd."

"I just said the same thing to Lester," Lucas said. "So how many people were at the party?"

"We've got sixty-odd, so far, outa maybe a hundred." Sloan held up the piece of paper. "This is the list. Most people don't remember seeing Alie'e after about midnight. I talked to one guy and his girlfriend, who can pin down their arrival at about twelve-fifteen, who say they never saw her. And they heard she was there, so they were looking. Jael and Catherine Kinsley left her in the bedroom sometime before one o'clock. She was alive and drowsy when they left."

"You talked to Kinsley?"

"On the phone. She's on her way back, with her husband. Their cabin is all the way up in Ely — five hours. She didn't hear about it until noon, on public radio."

"And you believe them, that Alie'e was alive?"

"Yes. There's just too much . . . Other people saw Lansing still alive after Jael and Kinsley had left; at least, that's what we're getting now."

"So how many people are eligible to do the killing?"

"Hanson says the party peaked between one and two, which means maybe most of the people were around when Alie'e got it. We've got a few who'd left earlier, that we've been able to confirm. And quite a few more that said they left earlier, but we haven't been able to confirm or are lying," Sloan said.

"What if the killer unlocked that window, left the house, so people could see him leaving — made a deal out of it, kissed a few people, shook a couple of hands, giving himself an alibi — then came back through the window, killed her, and went back out the window?"

"Sounds like too much coming and going," Sloan said.

"But it explains the open window," Lucas said. "And it might even explain why Sandy Lansing was killed. Suppose he came back in the window, does Alie'e, and boom, Lansing is right there in the hall. He's gotta kill her. She knows that he left, and made a big deal out of it, and then came back."

Sloan looked at the paper in his hand. "So we put everybody back on the list."

9

Lane got back. "I got a chart on Alie'e — her folks, her brother."

"I saw her brother," Lucas said.

"Yeah, the preacher. He goes around and ministers to farm people out in the Red River Valley. He fixes farm equipment, sometimes he works part-time at a grain elevator. Won't take any contributions. Gives away everything he earns except what he needs to eat and buy clothes."

"Tell you this: He doesn't spend any money on clothes," Lucas said.

"So the people out there think he's either crazy or a saint, or both. That's what they said in the Fargo newspaper. There was an article."

"On the brother, not Alie'e."

Lane nodded. "Mostly on the brother. The angle was, you know, 'crazy saint related to Alie'e Maison.' "

"Where was he last night?"

Lane had asked that question. "In Fargo. He runs a free kitchen there. He was around the kitchen until eight o'clock or so. He was back in the morning. He could have made a round trip in between."

"And he's got a temper," Lucas said. "What else you got?"

"I got all the shit on Alie'e. That was just a matter of going out on the Net — I got a file of printouts two inches thick. And you know what? There's a cult of Alie'e worshipers out there. And Alie'e haters. They fight on the Net."

"I heard."

"Anyway, I wouldn't be surprised if one of those guys did her."

"Yeah?"

"Yeah. You know, some computer nerd rapist killer nutso builds a fantasy around her, crashes a party where she's supposed to be, she laughs him off, says she'd rather be fuckin' her girl-friends than a pimply little freak —"

Lucas grinned at the runaway description. "Nerd rapist killer nutso?"

"It coulda happened that way," Lane said seriously.

"What else you got?"

"I *got* something else," Lane said, "and it's interesting, but nothing like my previous conjecture about the nerd rapist killer. Nutso."

"And?"

"It's this other chick, Sandy Lansing. I talked to the manager at Brown's Hotel, and it turns out Lansing wasn't exactly a big deal. She was more like a female bellhop. She'd take rich people up to their rooms and show them around."

"Not an executive?" Lucas said.

"No. She was making maybe twenty-five thousand a year. Enough to starve on. But, man, I talked to the guys from Homicide who were down at her apartment. She's got the cool clothes, she's got a decent car — Porsche Boxter? — and she hung out with all these rich people. And held her end up financially. She's gotta have money coming in from somewhere, but I can't find it."

"It ain't coming from her old man," Lucas said. "I just saw him. He looked like he doesn't have two dimes to rub together."

"That's the impression I got," Lane said. "So I was thinking. . . . She works at this hotel, greeting people. Maybe she's on the corner?"

"Any busts?"

"Not a thing. But at that level, it's more by introduction," Lane said. "Some big sports guy comes through town, or big TV guy, and you go hang out. Then you go back to his hotel room and later you get a *gift*. Maybe the hotel knows, maybe not."

"So let's get her friends, and push a little. Find out where the money came from."

"I thought maybe you could do the hotel end," Lane said.

"Me? I'm a deputy chief of police."

"Yeah, but the hotel's assistant manager in charge of keeping things right is an old pal of yours."

"Who's that?" Lucas asked.

"Derrick Deal."

"You gotta be shitting me."

"I shit you not, Deputy Chief of Police."

On the way out of the building, Lucas passed Rose Marie Roux puffing down the hall. " 'Muff-Divers' Ball?' " she asked, hooking his arm.

"That's what the headline said," he answered, mildly flustered.

"How many euphemisms do men have for the female sexual organ?" she asked.

"That's not a place you wanna go," Lucas said.

"How long before we catch the guy?"

"Another place —"

She nodded. " — that I don't want to go."

Derrick Deal had once been an assistant county assessor, more or less. His actual position was bagman for a city council cabal that was selling cut-rate property assessments. The cabal ran into trouble when Deal tried to hit up a machine-shop owner, who happened to be the uncle of a vice cop. The cop did some cop shit and got a tape of Deal soliciting a payoff.

Then the cop made a mistake. He believed that if he simply nailed Deal, that Deal's brother assessors would, in turn, punish his uncle by running up his assessments, even as Deal went off to six weeks in jail. So instead of arresting him, the cop let Deal listen to the tape, and told him to lay off. Deal misinterpreted the threat and ran to his city council protectors. They went to the chief — this was three chiefs ago — who squashed the vice cop like a bug. The vice cop found himself working traffic management on construction sites.

Then *he* rang in his brother cops — notably Lucas. Lucas set up a sting operation and Deal went to jail for nine months. His city council employers managed to slide, and Deal's brother assessors did the expected number on the machine-shop owner, whose taxes went up fifty percent.

When Deal got out of jail, he tried selling cars and then houses, but wasn't good at it. His skills lay in bureaucracy and blackmail, not sales. Lucas heard that he'd gone to California, and until Lane mentioned his name, assumed he was still there.

"Derrick Deal?" he asked himself as he walked across town.

Brown's Hotel was a brick building a block from the IDS tower. From the outside, it barely looked like a hotel; you had to *know* it was there. Lucas nodded at the white-gloved doorman, who held the door for him, and turned right across the plush red carpet, around a circular seat with a spray of out-of-season gladiolas in the center, to the reception desk. A neat young woman stood behind the desk. She was black, with delicate bones in her face; she wore a conservative suit and a silver-and-turquoise necklace with small oval stones. "Yes, sir?"

"I need to see Mr. Deal? Derrick Deal?" Lucas said.

"Can I tell him who's calling?"

"No." Lucas smiled to soften the answer, slipped his ID from his pocket, and showed it to her. "This is sort of a surprise. If you could just show me where he is?"

She reached for a phone. "I'll call the manager on duty."

Lucas stretched across the desk and put his hand on the phone. "Please don't do that. Just show me where Mr. Deal works."

"I'll get in trouble." Her lip trembled.

"No, you won't," Lucas said. "Believe me."

She looked both ways, saw no help, touched her lip with her tongue, and said, "He's in his of-fice . . . down the hall." She looked to her right, a long narrow hallway off the lobby.

"Show me the door."

She looked both ways again, as if the manager might spring out of the red carpet, and finally said, "This way." She came out from behind the desk and started down the hall, walking swiftly. When they were out of sight of the lobby, she slowed. "Is he in trouble?"

"I have a question for him."

"If he's not in trouble, he should be," she said.

"Really?" Lucas asked.

"He's a jerk."

"Wait a minute," Lucas said quietly. They stopped in the hallway. "What's a jerk?"

"He hassles people," she said.

"For money? Sex? Dope?"

"Not dope," she said.

"You've had to fight him off?" Lucas asked.

"Not exactly. I'm a little too dark for him. And I told him that if he hassled me, my brother would cut off his testicles."

"He believed you?"

"Yes. My brother came over and showed him the knife," she said.

"Ah."

"But we have all these little maids, a lot of them are Mexican, and maybe they don't have papers. It's this tight economy is the reason they hire them."

"He puts the bite on them?"

"Yes. Sometimes sex — there are usually a few empty rooms around. Mostly it's money. The guests leave tips for the maids, ten dollars or twenty dollars. He might take out fifty dollars a day, all told. The maids are afraid to turn him down. All he has to do is make an anonymous phone call. He lets them know it."

"Maybe they should bring their brothers up from Mexico," Lucas said.

She shook her head. "Easy to say."

"I know," Lucas said. "All right. I'll go ask him my question, and then maybe later we'll figure out something to slow him down a little."

"The hotel won't fire him," she said. "He's very good at what he does."

"Which is?"

"He fixes things. He gets tickets for shows and basketball games. If somebody gets sick, he gets a doctor."

"Anybody could do that," Lucas said.

"I mean, if a rock star gets sick . . ."

"Because he put something up his nose?"

"Or whatever. Or if there's a little lover's quarrel, and somebody gets beat up or cut up . . ."

"Okay," Lucas said. "We could still have a talk with him about the maids."

Lucas waited until the receptionist was well back toward her desk before he quietly opened Deal's office door. The office was a collection of six shoulder-high fabric cubicles; the clacking sound of a computer keyboard came from the far corner.

Deal was a balding man with a long nose and heavy, petulant lips that he thrust in and out as he peered at his computer screen. He was wearing a dark sport coat, and sprinkles of dandruff decorated the shoulders and lapels. He was intent. He never saw Lucas coming.

Lucas picked up a visitor's chair from a neighboring cubicle and sat it in the aisle just outside Deal's. He sat down heavily, and now Deal, for the first time, realized he wasn't alone. He jerked around, pulled back, startled.

" 'Lo, Derrick," Lucas said, smiling. "Thought you were in California."

Deal pulled himself together. "Goddamnit, Davenport, you scared the shit outa me. What do you want?"

"You heard about the murder? Sandy Lansing?"

"Nothing to do with us," Deal muttered. He picked a piece of paper up from the desktop, squinted at it, and slipped it into a desk drawer, out of sight.

Lucas shrugged. "You know how it is, Derrick. We gotta nail everything down. And this Lansing chick, she sorta puzzles us. She's got no money — she's pulling down twenty-five from this place. But she's driving a Porsche, she's dressing outa those Edina boutiques . . ."

"We give her five grand a year for clothes," Deal said.

"Party dresses?"

"No. Not party dresses," Deal said. He turned casually to his computer screen, which showed a spreadsheet, pushed a couple of keys, and the screen blanked out. "The kind of dresses you see on the other women here. Upper-middle-class conservative matron clothes."

"We thought maybe she was getting the extra money from taking the clothes *off*. You know, the matron dresses."

Deal shook his head. "No."

"Come on, man," Lucas said. He waved his hand, meaning, *Look at this place.* "You got all kinds of jocks and movie stars and singers and theater people and rich guys. . . . I mean, what does a fixer guy like you do when one of them wants a blow job?"

"I tell him to go blow himself," Deal said.

"Derrick —"

Deal put up his hands. "Listen, man. She was

not fucking anybody for money. Not here, anyway. I knew about the car, I even asked her about it. She said something like, 'I got my own money.' I figured it came from Daddy and she was working until she got married."

"She was not a rich kid," Lucas said.

Deal shook his head. "So maybe you should do some real investigation, so you can stop hassling innocent people."

"Derrick, goddamnit, I'm trying to like you, but you make it so hard," Lucas said. He put his hands on the arms of the visitor's chair, ready to stand up. "We know she's getting some extra cash, and sex is the only thing we can think of. I'd hate to think that Brown's is some kind of high-class bordello, but we're gonna have to send some people around to look at the records. Can we use your name as a recommendation?"

"Wait a minute, wait a minute," Deal said. He picked up a telephone, punched in four numbers, listened to it ring once, then again, and then said, "Jean, could you come down here for a second?"

He hung up and said, "You oughta look into dope."

"Why?"

"Because half the time, when Sandy came in, which was usually late in the afternoon, she was hungover. From partying. She was a party girl, and she had a real bad coke habit."

"You think she was selling?" Lucas asked.

Deal opened his mouth, as if with a reflexive response, but his eyes flickered and he changed direction. "I don't know about selling. But she was using. And she wasn't getting any extra cash here, above the board or below it."

He was lying about something, Lucas thought. He'd seen it in Deal's eyes, the momentary flicker. The office door opened, and they both turned toward it. A moment later, a young woman looked down the aisle to Deal's cubicle and saw Lucas. "Mr. Deal?"

Deal stood up and stepped past Lucas. "Yeah, Jean, down here."

The woman walked toward them, and Lucas suddenly realized that she was extraordinarily good-looking. She was a little heavy, round, and had soft brown hair spiked with blond strands, a lush face with placid, pale blue eyes, and a slightly rolled underlip. She wore just a dab of lipstick. Her business suit was as conservative as the receptionist's, but with a difference — hers was cut deeply enough in front to show a soft slice of cleavage. She was, Lucas thought, maternal and sexy at the same time.

"Yes?" she asked.

"Would you take this pencil out to India at the front desk?" He handed her a yellow pencil.

She was puzzled, but compliant. "Yes, sir."

When she was gone, Deal sat down again and said, with just a touch of sarcasm, "*That's* why Sandy Lansing wasn't dating our customers."

Looking after the woman, Lucas thought

about it for a moment and then nodded. "She wasn't enough."

"Not nearly enough, for this place," Deal said, comfortably. "And there are a couple more like Jean. Even better than Jean. Not that I'd know anything about private arrangements between staff members and our guests." He folded his hands across his stomach and leaned back in his office chair. "Anything else, Officer Davenport?"

Lucas leaned into him, smiled, reached out, and tapped him on the kneecap. "Yeah. Lansing and drugs. Where was she getting them?"

"I don't know." He squealed it; he sounded like a startled pig. "I don't know anything about any drugs, I don't do drugs. You know that."

"Yeah, right." Deal was lying about something. "You do assessments."

"Well. I would be, if you hadn't fucked me," he said. "Now I do hotels."

"Like it better?"

"No," Deal said. "I don't. I used to *be* somebody. Now . . ." He looked up between the rows of cubicles. "I'm in a goddamn rat cage."

✥ 10 ✥

Not much more to do: There were cops out everywhere, working on everybody. Writing biographies on the party people; matching their stories, one against the next. Outside, TV trucks were beginning to pile up at the curb. He called Rose Marie, checked out, and went home.

Had a sandwich, got a beer out of the refrigerator — the last one; he'd have to run down to the store. He clicked on the TV: The movie people were going crazy, as expected. The local TV news shows crushed sports and weather into a five-minute segment, everything else into two minutes, and spent the rest of the half hour on Alie'e. Then the networks jumped in, with their talking heads. They'd had all day to explore the topic of fashion and dope, and long lines of solemn middle-aged men deplored the relationship.

Fox and NBC had a stunning Amnon Plain photograph of Alie'e Maison in what looked like men's underwear. The photo was as sexual as could be broadcast on TV without a fuzzy spot over the good parts, Lucas thought — and while Plain was credited as the photographer, all of the commentators gave credit to The Star for the use of the photo.

ABC's news reader said the issue of *The Star* would hit the newsstands by two o'clock the next day, only thirty-six hours after Alie'e was murdered. He seemed to think it was a technological miracle. Lucas got a few seconds of airtime, the interview cut in over movies of a stunned George Shaw, now in jeans and a sweatshirt, being dragged out to a cop car. They'd bitten on George, but not too hard.

"While drugs are acknowledged to be a central point of investigation, rumors have surfaced about a number of sexual escapades involving a former model name Jael Corbeau . . ." And the broadcast cut to a shot of Corbeau in a Chinese-collared black dress that emphasized the planes of her face, the jagged jigsaw quality of the scarring.

After a while, Lucas got tired of it, punched off the TV, and wandered back to the drawing board.

One idea a night, that was all. His idea tonight was that he might need a full-time game master — or better, he thought, a game mistress, somebody cute and blond with gold-rimmed glasses. But game sales wouldn't support a game mistress for long. So there'd have to be a time limit on the game. Say, one year. He pulled out a fresh sheet of paper, sat on his high stool, doodled a bit. Couldn't get going . . .

Catrin. He didn't know what he thought about her, but she was on his mind. . . .

140

Restless, he walked down the hall, picked up the phone, hesitated, then dialed. Calling the nunnery. A nun answered. "This is Chief Davenport with the Minneapolis Police Department," Lucas said. "I need to speak to Sister Mary Joseph."

"I'll find her," the nun said; a young voice with a depressive note.

Sister Mary Joseph was his oldest friend, going back to elementary school. Born Elle Kruger, she was a professor of psychology at St. Anne's College, a few blocks from Lucas's home. Lucas waited two minutes, then heard a phone being fumbled on the other end.

"Lucas."

He smiled when he heard her voice; he almost always did. "Hey, Elle. How's everything?"

"So much for the small talk, Lucas. What's going on with this Alie'e Maison murder?"

"Funny you should ask."

"Is there a lesbian involvement?"

"Ah, man . . ."

"And what's a *muff?*"

Lucas was absolutely befuddled for a moment, though he knew from the first instant that he'd never be able to find an answer to the question. But then Elle laughed merrily and said, "You can restart your heart now."

"Listen, don't do that," he said. "The Alie'e thing . . . it's a mess. There was a lesbian scene, an act, involving three women, some time before she was killed. I don't know what it has to do with the killing. Maybe nothing. That's sorta what I wanted to ask you about."

"What?"

"When gay guys kill each other, it can be pretty rough: a lot of mutilation, a lot of anger. A lot of knives, for some reason. You see guys stabbed twenty or thirty times."

"Passion turns to anger when things go wrong: Passion and anger are linked. What were these women like? Was it all very sexual, or was it less sexual and more something else?"

"That's what I was worrying about. One of the women suggested that while it was sexual, it wasn't aggressively sexual. She said it was more like cuddling. But there was a sexual act — stroking, oral sex. But it didn't seem . . . crazy."

"It might not have been. The cultural prohibition against lesbian sex is not nearly as strong as it is against male homosexuality. If a man becomes involved in gay sex . . . there's a tremendous amount of stress, at least initially," Elle said. "Women sometimes can go from friendship with another woman to occasional touching, to sex, and back to friendship, in a seamless way, without much guilt or stress. That's why you don't see so many violent lesbian murders. The stress isn't so high."

"All of the women involved were also involved with men. The relationships sometimes were simultaneous."

"That's not unusual. There are some women

who are . . . How'll I put this? Reflexively lesbian, that's what they *are*. They are as interested in women as . . . well, as you are. But many women, especially young women . . . they may just drift along, having relationships with women as well as with men. There's even a kind of fashionable element to it."

"All right."

"Have you looked at Alie'e's family?"

"Somebody has. I met her folks. I don't think they'd get the Good Housekeeping seal for parenting. . . . They dragged her all over the country since she was a baby, pushing her into showbiz. Living through her."

"Mmm."

"And she's got a goofy brother."

"That's interesting — it suggests there must've been some serious stresses in the family."

"Yeah. He's a peasant preacher out around Fargo somewhere. Gives away his clothes."

Elle said, "Not . . . Tom Olson?"

Lucas looked at the phone, then put it back to his ear. "Yeah. You know him?"

"He's a saint. Oh, boy."

"Oh boy" was rough language from Elle. "What?"

"He really *is* a saint. He's an evangelical Christian, he believes the rapture is coming next month or next year or whatever, because he can see it coming. Rolling in, like a wave. He might be schizophrenic; he is definitely an ecstatic. We had a novice here, from out that way, the Red

River. She went home to visit her folks. He was preaching at a bowling alley. She went to see him with some of her girlfriends — sort of a lark. She came back and quit the convent and quit the church and began wandering around the Red River preaching Christ's gospel. I try to stay in touch with her: She told me that Olson sometimes gets the stigmata." Her voice hushed with the word "stigmata."

"You gotta be sh . . . kidding me."

"No. I'm not."

As a Catholic, Lucas was severely lapsed, but he nevertheless felt a chill crawl down his spine at the idea of the stigmata. Bleeding from Christ's wounds in the hands, the feet, the side, even from the crown of thorns. "So he thinks he's God?"

"Oh, no. Absolutely not," Elle said. "He sees himself as a messenger, preparing the way."

"John the Baptist, then," Lucas said.

"I don't think he'd put it that way. You're being cop-sarcastic, and he's a very serious man."

"He was in the office today. He was . . . intense."

"Where was he when the murder was committed?" Elle asked.

"In Fargo. Out there somewhere. That's his story. But you think he could have done it?"

"I don't know. Sainthood is generally a mystery, but it involves very deep emotional streams, and often something very dark. He may have very deep feelings about his sister. And because of his emotional condition, he might be very . . . demonstrative."

"He was, with the chief."

They talked for a few more minutes, Lucas filling in the details of the crime. Elle would think about them, and call if anything occurred to her. They said goodbye, and Lucas started back to the study. Halfway there, he turned, went back to the phone, and called the nunnery again. The same young depressive nun answered, and he waited the same two minutes for Elle to pick up.

"Something else?"

"You know what you said to me when you first came to the phone?"

"I don't know. I was teasing you."

"You asked something like, 'What's going on with the Alie'e Maison murder?' "

"Yes?" She was puzzled.

"Nobody ever asks about the other woman. Lansing. She's like a piece of Kleenex that got used."

"Mmm. To be honest, I *haven't* thought of her," Elle confessed.

"You know, when you were hurt . . . you were hurt because somebody was trying to distract *me*. And it worked for a while. With everybody saying Alie'e, Alie'e . . . I hope we're not looking in the wrong direction."

"As long as we keep that in mind," Elle said. After a second of silence, she added, "I'll think about her. Pray for her."

Late that night, as he sat on the bed taking off his socks, Lucas remembered Trick Bentoin — Trick the gambler, the man who wasn't dead, who hadn't been killed by a brand-new lifer out at Stillwater. Lucas had forgotten to call the county attorney, and so, apparently, had Del; they'd talked to each other a dozen times during the day, and neither had mentioned it again.

Lucas muttered a short obscenity to himself. Folks were gonna be pissed about the delay. Even though it *was* kinda funny.

But he wasn't thinking about Trick when he drifted off to sleep. He was thinking about what he should wear to lunch tomorrow.

Lunch with Catrin.

Even later that night, not far from Lucas, but across the Mississippi in Minneapolis, Jael Corbeau heard a scratching 'round her door. Her eyes popped open, and she sat up. She was exhausted, but she hadn't been able to sleep. She'd taken a pill, but her body fought it. Alie'e: Amnon said she was infatuated, that Alie'e was nothing more than a willing reflection of Jael's own need for a special kind of pleasure — for a languid, wicked, fashionable lover. A beautiful lover. And Jael feared it was true, that she was shallow, dissolute. *Trendy.*

The scratching on the door popped her out of the depressive cycle. She recognized the sound as soon as she heard it. Somebody was trying to get in.

Jael lived in a small house on the south side of the loop, not far from the Metrodome. Her bedroom was on the second floor; the first was occupied by her workshop — a throwing room, a glazing room, a kiln room with two big electric Skutts, and a wedging room where she stored clay and did the preliminary workups. The workups that'd built her arms and shoulders: The cops had asked her about that. One had taken her hand, told her to squeeze. She had, and he'd pretended to wince. Fucking with her. Trying to intimidate her. It hadn't worked.

She wasn't intimidated by the cops, and she wasn't intimidated by the scratching at the door. During the worst of the crack years, the scratching would come every week or two. But crack was fading, burning out: She hadn't had an attempt in a year or more.

Still.

She rolled out, knelt as if in prayer, and felt under the edge of the bed. Her fingers picked it up immediately: the cold steel of the barrel. She pulled it out, an old pump Winchester 12-gauge. Moving swiftly through the dark, she went into the bathroom to the barred, frosted-glass window over the tub. The window was double-hung, and the slides were waxed. She unlocked it, slipped it up.

Down below, a heavyset man in black crouched on the stoop, prying amateurishly at the lock. Bushes flanked the stoop, so he would be invisible from the street, unless somebody looked straight up the walk.

She spoke softly but clearly: "Hey, you, down there."

The figure froze, then half-turned. She could see a crescent of his face in the ambient light from the street, like a sliver of the moon seen through a thin cloud, pale, obscure.

"I have a shotgun." She pumped it, the old steel action cycling with the precise *chick-chick* sound effect heard in a thousand movies. "It's a twelve-gauge. I'm pointing it at your head."

The crescent of face disappeared. The man turned, quick as a thought, and bolted from the porch, down through the bushes, around the corner, and down the street, hands and heavy legs pumping frantically.

Watching him go, Jael allowed herself the first smile she'd enjoyed in twenty-four hours. But as she slid the window back down and locked it, a vagrant thought crossed her mind.

He hadn't looked like a crackhead. Not at all.

He looked like some kind of redneck.

⇝ 11 ⇜

Sunday. The second day of the Maison case.

Lucas retrieved the *Pioneer Press* from his front porch, looked at the large dark headline: "Alie'e Maison Murdered." And beneath that, the subhead "Strangled in Minneapolis."

The headline, he thought, was smaller than the moonwalk, and possibly even smaller than reproductions he'd seen of the Pearl Harbor news flash.

But not much.

And he thought: *Trick.*

County Attorney Randall Towson was not exactly a friend, but he was a decent guy. He took the phone call at his breakfast table and said, "Tell me we got everything we need."

"What?"

"On the Alie'e Maison killer — who you're calling to tell me you caught."

"I have something much better. Honest to God." Lucas tried to inject sincerity into his voice. "I've found a chance to serve justice."

The attorney betrayed a cautious curiosity. "You're bullshitting me. Sorry, darlin'."

"No, no, I've found an innocent guy in the prison system. You can get him out. And then you can take the credit, and the grateful taxpayers will undoubtedly return you to office for the — what, fifth time?"

"Sixth," Towson said. "What the fuck . . . sorry darlin' — I'm eating breakfast with my granddaughter. What are you talking about?"

"Del Capslock was at the Alie'e party the other night. He wasn't there at the time of the murder, but he did meet an old friend of ours."

"Who?" Suspicious now.

"Trick Bentoin." Silence. Silence for so long that Lucas added, "Trick had gone to Panama to play gin rummy."

Then, his voice soft and unshaken, Towson said, "This is a problem."

"Yeah." Lucas nodded, though there was nobody to see it.

"I've clearly identified it as a problem. Tomorrow, when I get to work, I'll get my best people working on a solution."

"That would be good," Lucas said.

Another long silence. Then: "Great Jesus fuckin' Christ, Davenport," Towson screamed. And meekly added, "Sorry, darlin'."

Catrin.

What to wear to a Sunday lunch? She was married to a doctor, so she probably had some bucks. She'd be more comfortable with something neat, rather than something out on the edge: Boots and black-leather jackets were out. Lucas dug through his closet, through a stack of dry cleaning, and finally came up with what he hoped would be right — twill pants in a deep khaki, a crisp blue shirt, and a brown suede sport coat. He added dark brown loafers and his dress gun, a P7 in 9mm.

Checked himself in the mirror; smiled a couple of times. Nah. Better to can the little smile, he thought. Go for sincerity and pleasure at seeing her . . .

On Sundays, City Hall was dead quiet. Not today. Lucas went straight for Roux's office; the secretary's desk was empty, but Rose Marie, dressed in slacks and a sweater with fuzzy white sheep on it, was in her office with two visitors. Dick Milton, the department's media specialist, was a former newspaper reporter who'd once written an eight-part investigative series — Sunday through Sunday — on oak wilt. Angela Harris, a departmental contract shrink, was perched on the windowsill.

"What do you think?" Lucas asked as he stuck his head in the door.

"Media-wise?" Roux looked up. "Just about what we expected."

"Been a little rough on George Shaw," Milton said.

"That's not rough," Lucas said. He'd never liked Milton, even when he was reporting. "Rough is sitting in the county jail, waiting to go to Stillwater for ten years, which is what George is gonna do."

"It's not gonna hold, the connection between Shaw and Alie'e," Milton said. He looked at Roux. "This whole lesbian business . . . they stayed pretty delicate about it last night, on the news shows, but I was on the Net and I saw a scan of the first copies of *The Star*, and they got a big sexy picture of this Jael Corbeau. She's hotter than Alie'e, so it ain't gonna stay delicate very long."

"When's *The Star* gonna get here?" Lucas asked.

"This afternoon, I guess. They got stories on the Net about how the *Star* editors tore the ass off a whole issue as it was going out the door, and turned it around to do an Alie'e issue. The *Journal* says all them other rags are suckin' wind."

"So it's gonna pump everything up," Lucas said. He looked at Roux. "You're still working the press pretty hard?"

"We're doing another press conference at ten o'clock, and then the Olson family and friends are supposed to be back around noon. They want the body as soon as they can get it. The funeral's gonna be later in the week, up in Burnt River. Then we'll probably have another press briefing around three o'clock, and if we need another, around seven."

"Nothing came up overnight?"

"Nothing. Except this morning, Randall Towson called about Trick Bentoin."

"I forgot to tell you about it," Lucas said. "The murder washed it away. Del says Trick's in a Days Inn down on 694, so we'll pick him up tomorrow and get a statement. Towson is gonna call Rashid Al-Balah's attorney, I guess, as soon as we get a statement from Trick."

"Maybe nobody will notice?"

"We should announce it the day of the funeral," Milton said. "If we can hold off until then."

"I dunno," Lucas said. "We really ought to get Al-Balah out of Stillwater as soon as we can."

"Al-Balah?" Roux said. "Fuck him. But why don't you get Bentoin today? Just in case."

"Okay." Lucas looked at the shrink. "What do you think about Alie'e? We got a crazy?"

She shook her head. "Too soon to tell. It looks more efficient than crazy, though. Of course, the man is disturbed in some sense."

"He'd be more disturbed if I could get my goddamned hands on him," Rose Marie said.

"Twelve of the people at the party have arrest records, and I'm looking at them for any sign of psychiatric involvement, but I don't see any so far," the shrink continued.

"Twelve?" Lucas asked, looking at Rose Marie.

"Talk to Lester — but it's all small stuff. Shoplifting, petty theft, two misdemeanor domestic assaults, one street fight, a couple of ticket scofflaw cases . . . like that."

Nothing.

A Post-it note was stuck to Lucas's door: *Come get me.* It was signed, *Marcy.* He walked down to Homicide, and found the place full of cops — more homicide cops than he'd ever seen in one spot, at one time, on a Sunday. Lester was perched on a desk at the end of the room, talking to a cop with a notebook. He spotted Lucas and shook his head. Nothing happening.

Lucas stepped back to Marcy Sherrill's desk. She saw him coming, said something into the phone she was holding, and hung up. "I'm really coming over?" She was a pretty woman in her early thirties; she liked to fight. She and Lucas had had a brief, intense affair, which everyone in the office had considered inevitable and overdue. After a couple of months, they'd called the thing off by mutual consent, to their mutual relief.

"Yeah, at least for a while," Lucas said.

"Good. I'm trying to track down more people from the party — I bet we're missing forty people — but I'm not getting anywhere. I'm ready to bag it."

"So you're up? Right now?"

"I could be, if you whispered in Frank's shell-like ear," Marcy said.

"You remember Trick Bentoin?"

Sherrill didn't want to go after Bentoin, but if she could bring him into the state attorney's office, he could keep Del free all day.

"So if I do this, I can work Alie'e for you?"

"We're all working Alie'e after this," Lucas said. "Maybe forever."

Sherrill leaned back in her chair, locked her hands behind her head, and studied him.

"What?" he asked.

"You've got something going on, the way you look. You look sort of . . . snazzy."

"Meeting an old friend for lunch," Lucas said. No point in denying it. During the affair, Sherrill had learned to read his mind.

"Nice-looking, I'd guess." She smiled.

"I don't know. I really haven't talked to her in twenty years."

"Whoa. So what happened? She just came back to town?"

"No, she's been living down south, on the Mississippi, somewhere down there."

And she *could* read his mind. She rocked forward, her face serious. "Lucas, is she married?"

He shrugged. "She's not entirely unmarried, as I understand it. Look, we're just having lunch."

"Oh, God. Don't fuck her up, Lucas."

He was offended, stiffened up. "I won't. And you go get Bentoin, okay? Call me when you've got him."

"Lucas . . ." Even more serious now. "Lucas, man, she's your age, she's married, she's in the danger zone. You could seriously mess her up. I can tell by the way you're acting."

"Find Bentoin." He turned and left. In the hall, under his breath, he said, "Fuck you," and looked at his watch. Plenty of time for an errand.

Carl Knox had taken a fine Sunday morning to look at a stolen Kubota 2900 tractor with a front loader and rear-mounted backhoe; an accessory mower was piled on the front of the trailer that held the tractor. While Carl looked, a freckle-faced, straw-haired, outraged thief was talking about the turf tires, practically unused — the goddamn machine had only 145 hours on it, came straight off the best golf course in southern Minnesota. What was this two-thousand-dollar shit?

Carl couldn't hear him, because he was thinking about a Cree Indian guy named Louis Arnot up in Canada, who'd been calling around looking for just such a machine. Arnot would pay twelve thousand American if Carl could deliver the tractor to Kenora, Ontario, which he could, but his guys would have to change the numbers and he'd have to come up with some Kubota papers, and he hadn't done Kubota in a couple of years.

His daughter had come out to the shop with him. She'd been inside, fooling with the books, but now suddenly broke through the Service Department door and said, "The cops are here."

"Uh-oh," he said. He waved her back inside, and then looked at the tractor. "How hot *is* this thing?"

"Nobody even knows it's stolen yet," Roy said nervously.

Davenport came around the corner of the building, fifty yards away. Knox said, quietly, "Here he comes. Don't look. I know this guy, and he's not here about the tractor."

"I'll take the two thousand," Roy said, his Adam's apple bobbing. Knox stepped away from the trailer to greet Davenport.

"Nice-looking machine," Lucas said as he strolled up. "I use a B20 up north."

"No offense, but that's practically a fucking lawn mower," Knox said. Enough small talk. "What's going on?"

Lucas *was* offended, but tried not to show it. Instead, he looked at the freckle-faced thief: "Why don't you go get a Coke?"

"Sounds good," Roy said. He hopped off the trailer and hotfooted it across the parking lot, toward the Service Department door. Through the glass panel of the door, Lucas could see the pale face of Knox's daughter peering out at them.

"Why's everybody so nervous?" he asked. "What's everybody doing at work on a Sunday?"

"You work every day if you have a small business, and you're not sucking out of the state trough," Knox said.

"That can't be it," Lucas said. He looked at the Kubota. "What, that hick steal this tractor?"

"Jesus, Davenport, he's a goddamn basement excavator who's going broke and has to sell his job. What do you want?"

"A list," Lucas said. "We chase all over town, going after the big dope wholesalers, the gangs,

157

the people pushing shit on the street, and we pretty much know every one of them. The ones we don't know, the ones we can't get at, are the really smart ones who only move a kilo or so a week, to rich people. Nobody ever complains, nobody ever gets caught. Nobody's standing on a street corner. We need some of those names."

"You know I don't mess with dope. Too dangerous."

"But you do loan-sharking, Carl. And you got that layoff business with the sports-book guys. You know a lot of rich people who get their money in strange ways, and put a lot of it up their nose, and who don't buy their shit down in the ghetto."

"You're gonna get my nuts cut off," Knox said.

Lucas shrugged. "So who's ever gonna know that you're talking to me? And it gives us just that much less incentive to figure out what you really *do* for a living. You know, the ugly details."

"Is this part of the Alie'e Maison thing?"

"Yeah, part of it."

"Nobody ought to be killing young girls," Knox said. "I saw the story in the *Star-Tribune* this morning, the interview with her parents." He looked toward the service door, where his daughter's face still floated in the rectangle of black glass in the service door. "I can ask around," he said. "But like the last time, I might come up empty."

"That helped, when you came up empty," Lucas said. "It eliminated some possibilities."

"So I can ask," Knox said. "Now, you wanna take a hike before my kid breaks out in hives?"

Lucas left. Halfway back to the corner of the building, he turned and said, "I'll anxiously await your call."

Knox shook his head and watched until Lucas had turned the corner. The freckle-faced thief eased out of the building and asked, "What'd he want?"

"Just bullshit," Knox said. He turned to the thief. "You said nobody knows the tractor is gone yet?"

"Won't nobody know until tomorrow, when the owner gets back from Vegas."

"Can you get it back there?"

"Get it back? I just stole it," Roy said.

"Yeah, but this guy is gonna look it up, just sure as shit. If it's on a list, he's gonna be back here, and he's gonna want to know where it went. I'd have to tell him I turned you down, and then he'd come looking for you."

"You wouldn't tell him. . . ."

Knox shrugged. "You're not a real big part of my business."

"Well, goddamn, Carl . . ."

"So you take it back," Knox said. "When does your guy go to Vegas again?"

"He goes every couple of months."

"So steal it again, then. I'll give you three thousand," Knox said.

"Three?"

"Take it or leave it."

The thief looked up at the big orange tractor and said, "I'm gonna be out fifty bucks for gas."

"Hey, Roy?"

"Yeah?"

"Tell somebody who gives a shit."

Lucas stopped back at headquarters, left a note for a guy in Property Crimes, asking him to check on stolen Kubota 2900 tractors. He looked at his watch every thirty seconds for ten minutes, then headed for a restaurant called The Bell Jar. No sign of Catrin. He was a few minutes early, but he started to worry. Maybe she'd bailed. . . .

The maître d' put him in a corner, where he could see the room. A waitress came by and dropped off the drinks menu; a couple of minutes later she came back and he ordered a martini. "Will you be dining by yourself today?" she asked.

"No, I . . ." And Catrin came in the door. "I'm meeting that lady right there."

Catrin, he thought, had dressed as carefully as he had, in a light gray-wool skirt, a black cashmere sweater, and low heels. She was wearing small diamond earrings. She looked, he thought, absolutely wonderful. She read his face and might have colored, just a bit, as he stood up to meet her.

"Lucas."

"How are you?" He was fumbling already. "I mean, with your friend . . ."

"Funeral's on Tuesday," she said. "It's over. With what she'd been through, it was time. I don't feel the least bit bad about it."

"Okay. . . ."

She smiled and said, "Did you order?"

"A martini."

"A martini? What happened to the Grain Belt?"

"Only on special occasions," he said. He looked around the restaurant. "If you ordered bratwurst in this place, the chef'd probably faint."

"So I'll have a martini," she said. "An old-time drink with an old-time friend."

And she was fumbling, he thought.

"Last time I saw you — not this morning, but back when — you were really upset."

"I remember," she said. "You were such a punk. You were unbelievable. You were also pretty sure you were God's gift to women, if I remember correctly."

"C'mon. I wasn't God's gift to anyone."

"Easy to say now."

"You weren't exactly a ride in the park yourself."

"Are we gonna fight?" But she said it smiling, almost delighted — like something was still the same.

"The last time I saw you," he said, dropping his voice, "you were absolutely buck naked. The last thing I saw was you standing there with your fists on your hips, looking for your underpants."

"That was something you weren't supposed to bring up," she said, and now she *was* pink. "Though I do remember that we spent quite a bit of time running around naked."

"Yeah. Jesus. Are we old now?"

"No, but we were definitely young then." A waiter came, gave them menus and left water, and promised to come back. Catrin opened the menu and looked over it to say, "You really made me angry, back then. I almost couldn't stand it. I never told Jack about you, and he was a hockey fan, and he used to take me to hockey games the next year, before he graduated. He was one of *your* fans. I remember how pissed off I'd get when you'd be skating around. Cruising around, backward or something, all arrogant macho tough asshole, smiling at the girls . . ."

"Jesus." He was impressed.

"Still pisses me off, thinking about it." Her eyes dropped to the menu.

That was the end of the sex talk. After they ordered, the conversation drifted to their current lives.

"When you said your husband took you to hockey games before he graduated . . . When did he graduate?"

"The next year. We got married June of my sophomore year, and he did his internship with a military hospital in Korea — he was a captain.

162

Then, when we came back, he joined his father's practice in Lake City . . . and that's where we've been."

"What about you? You didn't finish school?"

"No . . . you know. I got pregnant while we were in the army. I mean, I took classes over the years, but I never got back to school full-time. I thought about going this fall, to Macalester, but I just . . . I don't know. I didn't go. Now I'm supposed to go this winter, and I still don't know. . . . I'm kind of fucked up." She heard herself say it, and stopped. "The last time I said that — used those words, 'fucked up' — was when we were dating."

"Yeah, well, the good stuff always comes back," Lucas said wryly.

When they were eating, she said, "Things have really been good. I loved Jack right away, I wouldn't give up any of that for anything. But this is like feminist hell: I keep coming back to *How about me? When do they make my movie?* I always thought I was gonna be the movie star, and the rest of you were gonna be the extras. Instead, I wind up as the one in the background who's changing diapers and doing the books and working for free for United Way.

"I thought you and I were alike, because you always did what you were going to do; you were always the star in your movie. I thought I was like that: I was always going to do what *I* wanted to do, and then the kids came, and I *had* to take care of them. I didn't have any choice, because they were *mine,* and nobody else was going to do it, and it just made sense."

"Now they're moving out," Lucas said. "So do what you want to do."

"But what am I going to do? I have a feeling that if you want to be a movie star, in any movie, you've got to start young and work hard, and the best way to do that is be hungry all the time. But Jack started investing while we were still in the Army, and he always made good money, and you know how much we're worth now? Something like ten million dollars. That's a ridiculous amount. . . . Jack wants to buy a house in Florida, and he's talking about an apartment in London — we both like London, and you can get there in seven hours on Northwest. . . . So what's the point in trying to be a movie star now? To do what?"

"Not to make money, maybe. You were a painter, and you want to do photography. So do photography. Or paint."

"Ahhh . . ." she said. "That all seems too sterile now. Everything is too comfortable."

"So go back to college in criminal justice," Lucas said. "You can be a cop. I can fix it so Minneapolis'll hire you, and you can go around and do murders."

"Really?"

"What do you want to do, Catrin?" Lucas asked.

"Not be a cop," she said.

"So what?"

"I don't know. I'm just so comfortable, everything is so perfect, that I want to scream."

He walked her back to the car. She stood on her tiptoes and kissed him on the cheek, and swiveled into the front seat of the Lincoln. "By the way, the chances of us running into each other up here are just about nil, but if we do — we do get up here every couple of weeks — I didn't tell Jack about meeting you for lunch. There just would have been too many questions. So if we see you . . ."

"Yeah. Don't worry."

He was whistling on the way back to the office, caught himself, and caught himself again. Man, she was married. And it didn't sound like a bad marriage, either. But there was something between the two of them, between himself and a woman he hardly knew anymore, and it had a lot to do with sex. The thought might have brought him down, but it didn't. When he got back to his office, he found another Post-it note on the door: *Find me. Marcy.*

Sherrill was at her desk in Homicide. She didn't ask about the lunch. She said, "No Trick."

"What?"

"The motel manager said he checked out this morning. He's driving a ten-year old lime-green Caddy with a trunk full of golf clubs and one suitcase. We got a license number."

"A real license number?"

"Yeah. Illinois tag. I ran it, and it comes up under a different name, a guy named Robert Petty, but it's a ten-year-old lime-green Caddy. I called Petty, and he said he sold it two weeks ago, and the guy was supposed to change plates. I guess Trick never got around to it."

"Goddamnit," Lucas said. "You put the tag out?"

"Yeah. Pretty much all over the five-state. And I called Del, and he's looking around. The hotel manager said Trick didn't seem to be in a hurry — he checked out about ten minutes before the checkout deadline, and they talked about the Vikings for a while. So . . ."

"He may still be around."

Sloan came in, asked, "Have you seen it?"

He held up a copy of *The Star*, with Alie'e on the front. She was standing in a dark, cavernous space, with fire or sparks flying behind her; she was wearing what looked like men's underpants and a short, torn T-shirt that left her midriff bare. In yellow, inch-high block letters, a headline read, "Alie'e: The Last Shoot."

"Holy shit," Sherrill breathed. She took it from Sloan, and flipped it open to the portfolio in the middle of the issue. Alie'e in a dress the color of froth on the Caribbean Sea, walking down what looked like a line of fire. Another shot of her in the shorts-and-T-shirt ensemble, but this time with one exposed and apparently rouged nipple, and behind her, a giant man in a welder's helmet.

And on the page opposite, a close-up facial shot of a woman Lucas wouldn't have recognized, except for the film he'd seen on television the night before, and the scars. "Is that . . ." Sloan asked.

"Jael Corbeau," Lucas said.

"Looks different," Sloan said.

"Lots better," Lucas said.

She'd been caught full-face, at night. Although the photo had the flash ambience of a news shot, it was obviously done in a studio: Everything was perfect, poised, balanced, designed. Corbeau was looking back over a bare shoulder; a single strand of dark pearls looped around her neck and dropped out of the bottom of the photo. Her hair was cropped and she was not quite snarling at the camera; her lipstick looked dark, maybe purple.

"Hot," Sherrill said. "If I was inclined to do a little muff diving, I'd take either one of them."

"What kind of talk is that?" Sloan asked.

"The kind that turns me on," Lucas said, bumping Sherrill in the arm with his elbow.

"You're not the only one," Sherrill said. She tapped the lap of the giant welder in the photo of Alie'e, the photo with the rouged nipple.

Lucas looked closer. "Is that . . ."

"Unless it's a bigger-than-usual jackknife," Sherrill said. "Like, way bigger than usual."

Nothing was happening. Cops came back shaking their heads, looking for something else to do. Every person that they could find who'd been at the party had been interviewed. Nobody used any dope, nobody knew where it was coming from. Nobody had seen Alie'e after midnight, only a few people could remember Lansing at all.

After an end-of-the-day meeting in Rose Marie Roux's office, Lucas headed home. He changed into a sweatshirt and shorts, ran for forty-five minutes through the quiet Highland Park area of St. Paul. Feeling virtuous. And back home, he picked up the phone to find a message from dispatch: Call Carl Knox.

"Carl," he said. "Lucas Davenport."

"I got two names for you. And I've squeezed as hard as I'm going to — I'm already nervous enough."

"What're the names?"

"Curtis Logan, spelled just like it sounds. He says he's an artist and he used to work in one of the art museums. He started by selling coke and ecstasy and speed to a few of the patrons, and his name got around. In certain groups."

"Okay. Curtis Logan." Lucas noted it on a legal pad.

"And James Bee. That's B–E–E, like in bumble."

"What's he do?"

"Certified financial adviser. Hooks up with rich people through a company called RIO Accounting. Same thing as Logan, mostly handles fashion drugs. Ecstasy, speed."

"What are we talking about in sales? Every once in a while? Or big time?"

"I don't know exactly — I wasn't doing an investigation, I was looking for a connection. But I got the feeling they're semi-big-time. And very careful."

"I owe you," Lucas said.

"Yeah. You do. And for Christ's sakes, don't do anything that'll make them think of me, when you ask about them."

Neither of the two names was on the party list; that would have been too much to expect, anyway. But if they could get the two of them, they might be able to develop a daisy chain of peddlers-to-the-rich, and a name might still be found. . . .

Del was still working. Lucas dialed his cellular number and pulled him out of a bar. "Got two names for you, but you've gotta go gentle."

"Like walking on cotton."

Lucas gave him the names — Del hadn't heard of either of them — and said, "Call me if you get anything."

"Probably won't nothing happen until tomorrow," Del said. "I'll get on some banks, start doing some financials."

"We can't really afford a long-term look," Lucas said.

"I'll do it fast as I can, but I can't just go knock on their doors."

"Hear any more about Trick?"

"No, but people are talking about a big game. Maybe tomorrow night, or the next night. I haven't tracked it down yet, but that'd be a possibility."

"Call me when you get it."

That night he worked on his game, but there were no calls. A call came in the morning, though.

"You awake, sleepyhead?" Rose Marie Roux — and the words, on other days, might have brought up a smile; they didn't this morning, because of her tone of voice.

"What happened?" Lucas asked.

"Amnon Plain's dead."

"Dead?" he said stupidly.

"In St. Paul. Somebody shot him."

❧ 12 ❧

Monday. The third day of the hunt.

There had been no premonition. Lucas was given to premonitions — mostly wrong, and usually involving a variety of plane crash scenarios, beginning as soon as he made a reservation for an airline flight. He also had premonitions involving criminal cases. Some were right. He'd been told by a shrink that his unconscious was probably pushing him to a logical connection that his conscious mind hadn't yet made. He didn't necessarily buy the mumbo-jumbo, but he didn't yet deny it, either. So he paid attention to premonitions, but in this instance, he hadn't had one. And even after he heard about Plain, he felt no foreboding about the rest of the day. . . .

Plain had been murdered in his apartment/studio at the Matrix Building in St. Paul's Lowertown, an out-of-the-loop business district of old converted warehouses occupied by artists and start-up businesses. The Matrix was one of the oldest and least updated: All the elevators were designed for freight, and stank of decades of crushed fruit and rotten onions, paint, beer, and cardboard boxes. The hallways were littered with trash cans, most of them stuffed to overflowing. The Matrix had sold everything at one time or another: produce, hardware, dope, even wholesale leisure suits, sewn in St. Paul's only double-knit sweatshop.

Lately, the big product was art, mostly painting, with some light sculpture. And Plain's photography studio.

A half-dozen St. Paul cop cars were gathered in the street when Lucas rolled up. He dumped the Porsche in a furniture-store parking lot, flashed his badge at a clerk who stood in the window. The clerk nodded, and he headed across the street. A St. Paul cop at the door recognized him, and said, "Nice to see you, chief," when Lucas said "Good morning."

Another cop pointed him at the elevator: "Up to seven, take a right."

A St. Paul police lieutenant named Allport was standing over Amnon Plain's body, making notes on a steno pad with a yellow pencil. Plain, shirtless and shoeless, was facedown in a puddle of drying blood that had spread across a pale hardwood floor. A brown paper grocery bag lay a few feet from his head, its contents spilled out across the floor: bakery, a cereal box, a six-pack of mineral water. Just beyond the grocery bag, a stainless-steel spiral staircase led down to the floor below.

Lucas took it in for a minute, then the St. Paul cop looked up. "Ah, thank God. The Minneapolis cops. We were just about to call for help."

"We heard you had a murder, and thought you probably needed some advice on how to handle it," Lucas said.

"We certainly would. What would you advise?"

"Get your PR guy out of bed and get his ass over here," Lucas said. "In about one hour, you're gonna be up to your knees in CNN, ABC, CBS, NBC, and every goddamn channel that's got initials."

"Yeah." Allport scratched behind his ear with the pencil point. Then he turned and looked at a cop. "Get the chief on the line."

"So what happened?" Lucas asked.

Allport spread his hands over the body. "They just had this big Alie'e spread in *The Star* — have you seen it?"

"Yeah. Sexy."

"You see the boner on that guy?"

"Yeah. So what happened here?"

"I'll tell you what, if I had a dick like that, I sure as shit wouldn't be a welder. . . . Anyway, everybody was screaming for pictures. That's what Plain's assistant says. They were sending them out by phone — I don't know how, exactly."

"So . . ."

"So the assistant was here until four-thirty, and then they decided to break. He said Plain wanted to take a shower, and they needed some food. It was too early for any regular store to be open and they didn't like any of the all-night restaurants, so the assistant drove over to White Bear Avenue. There's an all-night supermarket . . ."

"Where all the cops hang out."

"Used to, when they had the all-night restaurant. Anyway, he bought some rolls and fruit and shredded wheat and a carton of milk and some bottled water." His pencil dipped toward the bag on the floor. "When he came back, he let himself in downstairs, because he thought Plain might still be in the shower, and then he came up the stairs and he found . . . this."

"He dropped the bag?"

"Yup."

"Got a cash-register receipt?" Lucas asked.

"Yup. And the time of the receipt says four-fifty-four. Already worked it out, and it fits."

"You believe him?"

"Yup."

"Why?"

"Because he was freaked out in a way that's hard to fake. Because we had an off-duty cop working at the supermarket who saw the assistant checking the food through, and she said he was mellow enough to bullshit both the cashier *and* the cop."

"Shit."

"I sorta thought the same thing, until it occurred to me that I'll probably get a lot of airtime outa this."

The cop that Allport had sent to the make the phone call came back with a cell phone and handed it to him. "Chief," he said.

Allport took the phone and said, "I got Lucas Davenport here. He says we're gonna need some heavy PR bullshit here, and right away. Yeah. Yeah . . . here he is." He handed the phone to Lucas.

"You working up a new handload?" Lucas asked, when he took the phone.

"Well, uh, not at the moment. Why?"

"All the stray dogs have been disappearing from the neighborhood," Lucas said.

"Yeah, bullshit, Davenport. Listen, how bad's this gonna be?"

"Can't tell. All depends on how you handle it — the movie people are like flies over in Minneapolis right now, and you can bet your ass they'll be over here as soon as the word leaks. I'd be surprised if you got more than an hour. If I were you, I'd get the mayor in and get him briefed, so he doesn't say anything stupid. And I'd talk to Rose Marie. Get her to ship our PR guy here, to brief you on our case. . . . If you sound half bright and on top of all the questions, you'll be okay. For now."

"Until we catch the killer. You guys getting anything over there?"

"No."

"Then spend some time with Allport. If you aren't doing any good over there, maybe something'll catch your eye over here."

When he got off the phone, Lucas went back to the body, squatting as close as he could get without disturbing the puddle of blood. All he could see was the red stain in the middle of Plain's back. An exit wound, he thought; but the cloth was too soaked to show a hole. Lucas looked around the room. "You find a bullet hole anywhere?"

"Yeah. The problem is, the whole place is poured concrete. There's a big goddamn dent in the wall over there." He pointed, and Lucas saw the gray pit. "The slug went somewhere else. I wouldn't be surprised if it more or less evaporated. Hit the wall straight-on."

"When are you gonna roll him over?" he asked.

"*We're* ready." Allport nodded to an assistant medical examiner, who was sitting on a chair in the kitchen, reading a comic book. "But our photo guy is checking what he got on film — we don't want any mistakes on this."

"So how long?"

"He's been out of here for half an hour, so it should be anytime."

"Where's Plain's assistant?" Lucas asked.

"Down in the studio."

"Mind if I chat with him?"

"Go ahead. I'll call you when we roll him."

The studio consisted of five rooms — one big open space with pull-down paper rolls mounted on the walls; a smaller room full of strange-looking tables with curved milky-white plastic tops; a small room with a group of hooded lights and a half-dozen chairs of different kinds, apparently a portrait studio; an office and storage space; and an entry.

Lucas found James Graf in the office. He was dressed in a black turtleneck and black slacks, and had a thin black beard. He looked, Lucas thought, like a picture of one of the old-time beatniks. Graf was lying on a couch, an arm thrown over his eyes. Lucas dragged a director's chair across the floor and sat down next to the couch. Graf lifted his head and looked wordlessly at Lucas. He'd been crying, Lucas thought.

"Did you see or hear anybody outside the studio or the apartment when you left for the grocery store?"

"I already talked."

"I'm from Minneapolis. I'm working on the Alie'e murder," Lucas said. "I just have a couple of questions. Did you see or hear anybody?"

"I didn't see anyone, but we heard people from time to time, when we were working. There's *always* somebody around," Graf said. "People here work all night sometimes. They're always out wandering around in the hallways."

"But you didn't *see* anybody."

"No, but I did recognize one voice. Joyce, I don't know her last name, she's an artist, down the hall. I heard her yelling, and running in the hall. Laughing. This was a few minutes before I went out. I told the St. Paul police."

"How about cars in the parking lot?"

Graf dropped his head back, refocused on the ceiling, thinking, then shook his head. "I'm sorry. I didn't notice anything unusual. We did have a wrong-number phone call about two o'clock, which was pretty unusual, but I told St. Paul and they're checking."

"This artist, Joyce, was wandering around. For what?"

"I don't know." Graf pushed himself up on the couch. "But you know, she was down *here*. He was killed upstairs, and to get upstairs, you have to go all the way to the middle of the building and take the elevator or the public stairs. Unless you take a fire escape. So if he was waiting up there, she probably wouldn't have seen him."

"You don't think he came in through here." Lucas nodded at the studio door.

"No. Ammy was on his way upstairs when I left, and the bolts on all the doors lock automatically. And those doors, they're steel. We've got maybe a hundred thousand dollars' worth of photo equipment and computer stuff in here, and the place is full of thieves — stuff gets stolen all the time — so our doors are *good*. The locks are good. So I think whoever it was, went up and knocked on the door upstairs, and killed Ammy when he answered it."

"Would Plain just open the door if somebody knocked?"

178

"Well . . . maybe. I mean, everybody in the building knows everybody else, so if somebody knocks . . ." He gestured at the door. "The doors upstairs are just like these: solid, no windows. If somebody knocks, you have to open it to see who it is. And maybe . . ."

"What?"

"Maybe he thought it was me, coming back for something," Graf said.

"How often did he send you out?"

"Most nights when we're working. I'd go get some food somewhere and we'd eat it upstairs, in the kitchen. We don't like to have food in here, 'cause you get grease around, and crumbs, and then you get bugs and mice. There's just too much stuff in here."

"So he might have thought it was you, coming back."

"Yes."

"Did he have his shirt on when you last saw him?"

"Yes. And his shoes. He was going to take a shower."

"So whoever attacked him, it probably had to happen within a few minutes of your leaving."

"Probably. I don't think he'd taken his shower yet. His hair didn't look wet. . . . He always washed his hair, because if we were working a long time, it'd get greasy. That's what he always said."

"Do you think —"

Allport shouted down from the apartment

level. "We're gonna roll him."

Lucas went back upstairs. The medical examiner was pulling on yellow rubber gloves; a cop and an ME's assistant were already wearing them. A photographer squatted in the corner, sorting equipment out of a camera bag. An eight-foot-long sheet of plastic had been spread across the floor, just outside the blood puddle.

"Gonna turn him," Allport said.

"Gotta pick him up, straight up, keep him in the air, don't let him dip back into the puddle. Then we're gonna roll onto the plastic," the ME told the other two guys with gloves.

"Did you talk to somebody named Joyce?" Lucas asked Allport.

"Joyce Woo," Allport said, nodding.

The ME interrupted. "You're gonna have to move, we're gonna swing him right past you," he said. Lucas and Allport stepped back. The ME said, "Bill, you gotta hang on to the shoulder at the same time you pick up the hand or we'll lose him. With the blood on there, he could be slippery. . . ."

"She's an Oriental chick," Allport said to Lucas. "She was out in the hallway. She might've seen somebody, she might even have heard the shot, but she was so drunk at the time that she's not sure. I mean, she's sure, but we're not sure. Go talk to her."

"The phone call? The wrong number?"

"Still looking for it."

"Ready?" The medical examiner asked. "Lift . . ."

When they moved the body, Lucas turned away. But he heard it. As it broke free of the partially coagulated blood, it sounded like a boot coming out of a mudhole.

They picked Plain straight up, carried him facedown to the plastic sheet, and then flipped him in midair and dropped him to the plastic. His eyes were open; Lucas winced and turned away for a moment.

"Nothing here," Allport said. "Boom, he falls down."

Lucas squatted, looked Plain in the face. "So strange," he said.

"What?"

"The killings at the party were improvised," Lucas said. "Who'd be crazy enough to go to a big party, *planning* to kill somebody in a hallway, and then strangle a famous model in a bedroom, with a hundred people around? Had to be improvised. It seemed almost accidental."

"This ain't," Allport said. "Maybe this Plain guy knew something and the killer had to shut him up."

Lucas stood up. "That's . . . pretty complicated."

When Joyce Woo answered her door, she was holding a beer mug half full of white wine, and her apartment reeked of the stuff. She was short, stocky, moon-faced, and wore thick-lensed glasses.

She invited him in, and slumped on a couch with paisley cushions. Lucas pulled up a kitchen chair.

"I told the other cops I saw somebody," she said, nipping at the wine, looking at Lucas over the rim of the glass. "Down the hall. But I didn't see him very well, 'cause I was playing catch-me-fuck-me with a friend."

"You were, uh . . ."

"A guy I know from across the street, a computer-art guy. Not what you'd call real good-looking, but, what the hell, I'm not exactly the Queen of the May. And he's big where it counts, if you know what I mean?"

"Yeah, well . . ." Big-where-it-counts was getting a workout, between the computer guy and Clark the welder. But she wasn't finished with the idea.

"It's like that with all the computer guys, you know?" She rolled her head back, staring at the ceiling, as if she were trying to unlock a conundrum. "I don't know why. You'd think the jocks would be the guys with big wieners, but it's never like that. It's always these thin skinny computer guys who got the package."

"You were playing . . . ," Lucas said, trying to wrench her back on track.

She rolled her head forward, focused on him, and said, "Yeah. He gives me a two-minute head start, and then if he can catch me in the building in five minutes, he gets to fuck me."

"Well, that sounds like —"

"Sometimes I cheat and let him catch me," she said. She burped. "Anyway, we run all over the building. I was running down the hall, and I saw this guy in the stairwell. I yelled at him, just, 'Hello,' and kept going."

"Was he going up or down?"

"Don't know. He was just there, in the stairwell," she said.

"He didn't answer?"

"No."

"What time was it?" Lucas asked.

"I don't know, but early. Or late. Whatever. I talked to Jimmy for a minute this morning, after they found the body."

"This is Jimmy, Plain's assistant?"

"Yeah. Anyway, he heard me yelling in the hallway, and the only time I was yelling that they would have heard was about the time I saw the guy. So when I saw him, Plain was still alive."

"You didn't think it was weird that somebody was wandering around the building in the middle of the night?" Lucas asked.

"This building? I'd think it was weird if people weren't wandering around in the middle of the night."

"The St. Paul police said you might have heard a shot."

"Maybe. I heard a loud noise, but it might have been a door banging shut. We've got all these metal doors in here, and they echo off the concrete when you let them bang shut," she said.

"I didn't think about it at the time, except that I heard it."

"This guy in the hallway looked like . . . what?"

"Porky. That's all I can say. Porky. He was sort of turned around from me. . . ." A puzzled look crossed her face. "You know something that crossed my mind? This is stupid. I thought the guy might be the vending machine guy. We got a vending machine guy who looks like this guy."

"Did you tell the other cops that?" Lucas asked.

"No, I just thought of it," she said.

"The vending machine guy wouldn't be here at that time in the morning."

"No."

"But you play catch-me-fuck-me at that time."

"Sure. The way it works is, I drink myself into a stupor in the morning, which I'm doing now. Then I sleep until about three o'clock or maybe four o'clock. Then I get up, and I feel like shit and I eat something, and then I work. I work until midnight, and then . . . you know, whatever. I eat again, and sometimes Neil comes over and we play. And then, when I start getting sleepy, I start drinking."

"Did this Neil guy, your friend, did he see the man in the stairwell?"

"The other cops went and got him up, and he said he didn't see anybody," she said.

"All right." Lucas looked around the apartment, which seemed spartan if not absolutely bare. The only thing hung on the walls was a

Kliban cat calendar. "What kind of art do you do?" he asked.

"Conceptual," she said.

Lucas had just turned the corner at the top of the stairs when he heard the woman scream. The scream came from Plain's apartment, and the cop at the door turned to look inside. A second later, a woman ran out, directly into the green concrete-block wall on the opposite side of the hall. She ran into it full-face, staggered from the blow, ran another step, and then Lucas caught her as she sagged toward the floor. The woman held on and turned her face sideways, and Lucas first registered the scars.

Jael Corbeau. She wrapped her arms around him, blindly, using him for support. Lucas half turned, and Allport came through the door, spotted them.

"Ah, Jesus," he said. "I'm sorry, you shouldn't have . . ." He looked at Lucas. "We told her she'd have to wait until we got him to the medical examiner's to see him. We had the sheet over him and she just stooped down and ripped it off before we could stop her. Jesus, Miz Corbeau, I'm sorry. . . ."

"I gotta go home," she said. "I gotta go home."

"Where's your car?" Lucas asked. He let her go, but she held on to his jacket with one hand. She hadn't looked at his face yet; he was a handy post.

"I don't have a car. A friend brought me."

"Is he still here?"

"No, the police wouldn't let him come up, so I told him I'd catch a cab. I thought, I thought, I thought . . . I thought I'd be here for a long time. But I gotta go home. If I can't have him . . ." She looked back at Plain's door.

"Where do you live?" Lucas asked.

Now she looked up at him. "South Minneapolis."

"I'll give you a lift," Lucas said. He looked at Allport. "Do you need to talk to her?"

Allport shrugged. "Sooner or later, but it doesn't have to be this minute. We can talk to her this afternoon or tomorrow . . . unless you think you might have some information we need, Miz Corbeau."

"I don't know, I don't know, I don't know . . ."

"You better go on home. We'll have somebody call you this afternoon. . . . Get some rest."

Lucas said, "The Woo woman. She said that the guy she saw in the hall looked like the vending machine guy."

Allport's forehead wrinkled. "She didn't say anything about that to us."

"She's a little drunk," Lucas said.

"The vending machine guy?"

Lucas said, "This way," and took Jael toward the door. Halfway down, she stopped suddenly and said, "I have to make the arrangements."

"Not now," Lucas said. "There's nothing you can do here."

"A funeral."

186

"Call somebody from your house. If you don't have a funeral director, I can get you the name of a guy who'll take care of you," Lucas said.

"Oh, God." They started down the hall again.

"Did you call your folks?" Lucas asked.

"My mother's dead. My father . . . I'll have to find him. He's in Australia or someplace right now."

At the first floor, there was a short wide flight of steps down to the door and they could see a cop standing with his back to the glass. Lucas pushed through and the cop half turned, and Lucas heard somebody say, "That's her and that's Davenport."

Jael stopped, and a knot of people in dark coats hurried toward them; down the street were two TV trucks. A still photographer started ratcheting shots with an F5, and a TV cameraman was already shooting, while another ran down the street, towing a reporter on the end of a microphone cord. Lucas recognized the towed reporter as an old friend who'd done a turn as a studio talking-head, and now was back on the street.

Jael squared off against the cameras, looked up at Davenport, waited for the second camera to come up, smiled, and said, "I just want to say, go fuck yourselves." To Lucas: "Where's your car?"

"Across the street." He took her arm and they went left, and the late-arriving reporter followed.

"Lucas, is he dead?"

Lucas turned his head and said, "This is St. Paul. Ask St. Paul."

"Yeah, but . . ."

They hurried across the street into the furniture store parking lot, the reporter trailing behind, the camera on the end of her tether. Lucas stuffed Jael in the driver's side and the reporter, an old friend, followed him around the back of the car and said, in a low tone, "Answer one question."

He leaned toward her and said, "Stick your microphone under your coat." She did, and he whispered, "Plain's dead. He was shot to death. A very bad scene. You didn't get it from me."

In the car, Jael sat silently, hunched, staring straight ahead, as they crossed the interstate, hit a couple of red lights, and then dropped down a ramp onto the roadway heading west toward Minneapolis. After a while, she said, "Honest to God."

"What'd you say? I'm sorry —"

"Nothing. Honest to God, I can't believe he's dead." She looked at him. "You were one of the men who interviewed me. I remember you."

"Yeah."

"You look mean. I kept thinking you were going to say something mean," she said.

"Thanks, I appreciate that. I'll write it in my book of memories."

She said, "I'm sorry if I offended you."

"No. . . ."

"It's the scars," she said. She reached out and touched his neck, a white scar that had resolved itself into a question mark. "How'd that happen?"

"Oh . . . you know."

"No. You'll have to tell me."

"A little girl shot me," Lucas said. "A surgeon had to do a tracheotomy so I could breathe."

"Not a very good surgeon, from the looks of the scar."

"She did it with a jackknife," Lucas said. "She's a pretty good surgeon."

"Why did a little girl shoot you? Like, really a little girl?" Jael asked.

"Yeah. Really. Because she was in love with the guy who was abusing her, and I was chasing him. She was trying to buy him time to get away."

"Did he get away?"

"No."

"What about the girl?"

"Another cop shot her. She was killed."

"Really." She looked at him for another minute, and then asked, "What about the one on your face? The scar?"

"A fishing leader. Snapped it out of a log and it buried itself in my face."

"Bet that hurt."

"No, not really. It stung a little. The real problem was, I didn't do anything about it. Washed it with a can of Coke, pressed it with a shirtsleeve, and kept fishing. It didn't look that bad when I went to bed, but when I woke up the next morning, it was infected."

"I made a lot of money with my scars," Jael said. Her voice had a distant quality, as though she might be sliding into shock. Lucas glanced at her, took in the scars again: three distinct white lines that slashed across her face from the hairline on the left temple. Two of them crossed her nose and ended on her right cheek. The other ran at a steeper angle, missed the left wing of her nose, crossed her lips, and ended on the right side of her chin. They gave her face an odd look of discontinuity, as though she were a piece of paper that had been torn, then Scotch-taped together a little less than perfectly.

"That's because, uh . . ."

"I look terrific. Lots of little boys go home and jerk off when they think about them."

"Yeah? You got them in a car accident?" Lucas asked.

Looking at him again. "How'd you know?"

"I spent a few years in uniform, I've done my share of car accidents. Looks like you hit the glass . . ."

"Yeah."

"Was that when your mother — ?"

"No, no. She took pills. She thought she had Alzheimer's, and sleeping pills were a way out."

"She didn't?" Lucas asked.

"No. She just saw a program about it on TV and did a self-diagnosis. When she told people what she was going to do, nobody believed her. Then she did it. The joke was on them."

Lucas said, "Jesus."

A little later: "How can a cop afford a car like this? Are you on the take?"

"No, no, I'm rich."

"Really? So am I, I guess. That's what they tell me. The bank. I'll be even richer when I inherit from Amny."

"You'll inherit?"

"Yup. Unless he changed his will when he got pissed at me. About Alie'e. I don't think he did."

"A lot?"

"A few million."

"Jeez. If you don't mind me asking . . . where'd you get it?"

"From my mom and dad. When my dad was in college, a long time ago, he invented a new kind of ball for roll-on deodorant." Lucas thought she was joking, but she was solemn as ever. "No, really. The ball has to have some kind of surface thing that I don't know about, to pick up an even coat of deodorant. I mean, they had roll-ons, but they weren't very good. Everybody was looking for a better ball. The problem defeated the best minds of a generation, until Dad came along. Then he got rich, and gave everybody trust funds, and started smoking a lot of dope. When Mom died, Amny and I got her part of the divorce settlement, on top of our trusts."

And later: "How'd you get rich?"

"Computers," Lucas said.

"Ah," she said. "Like everybody."

She was not in a condition to talk much about her brother. Halfway back, she put her head down, the heels of her hands in her eye sockets, and began to sob. Lucas let her go, and drove; she stopped after a while, and wiped her eyes. "God. I can't believe it."

Lucas dropped her at her house. A man was sitting on the steps, fiddling with the wheel on a bicycle. "Don," she said. "A friend. He keeps hoping I'm going to sleep with him, but I'm not going to."

"It's a country song," Lucas said.

She looked at him quickly, and almost smiled. "You'll call me if anything happens. If they catch anybody."

"Yeah."

"Do you think this person . . . I mean, if it's about Alie'e, do you think . . ." Her voice trailed away, then her hand went to her mouth and she said, "Oh." She looked up and down the street.

"What?"

"There used to be a lot of crack around here," she said. "That's why all the houses have bars on the windows, and big doors."

"It's going away now," Lucas said. "Burned itself out."

"I know. But when there was a lot of crack, the crack kids would try to break in all the time. I'd hear them, and I'd go yell at them from a window, and they'd run away. But somebody tried to break in the night before last. I thought it might be crack, but I thought it was weird, too.

The guy didn't look like a crack kid. He was too big, he was . . ." She made a gesture.

"Porky?" Lucas asked.

"Well, I don't know if he was porky. I was gonna say he looked sort of rednecky . . . sort of. Why?"

"White?"

"I think so, but I couldn't really see him. But his clothes looked . . . white."

Lucas peered through the windshield at Don, the friend, who was now standing up, looking at them as they idled by the curb. "Can you trust this guy?"

"Don? He wouldn't hurt a fly."

"Do you have anybody you can trust, who would hurt a fly?" Lucas asked.

"Why? Tell me."

"A woman in your brother's building saw a man last night. She said he was porky. She saw him probably within a few minutes of the time your brother was killed."

"You think?"

"I think we shouldn't take any chances. The guy who killed your brother is a nut. Stick with Don. I'm gonna have a cop drop by and hang out with you."

"How'll I know it's really him? The cop."

"Not a him, it's a her. Ask for her ID. Her name's Marcy Sherrill." He looked at her. "I think you'll probably like each other."

13

Lucas went to Rose Marie's office. The secretary waved him through, and he found her talking to a slender man with a red beard and an expensive black suit. "This is Howard Bennett. He's a curator over at the Walker Art Center," Rose Marie said.

"I've been there a few times," Lucas said.

"Inside?" Rose Marie asked suspiciously, one eyebrow going up.

"Not actually inside," Lucas said. "When I was in uniform, the guards would get us over there to chase people who were trying to, you know . . ."

"Fuck in the spoon," Bennett said.

"The exact words I was looking for," Lucas said. The Walker Center had a Claes Oldenberg sculpture of a spoon with a cherry. Fucking in the spoon was the Twin Cities equivalent of flying a Cessna 185 through the arch in St. Louis.

"Yeah, well, Howard is an expert in photography. He says Amnon Plain's murder is gonna be a bigger deal than Alie'e's."

"I didn't quite say that," Bennett said. "But it'll be bigger with a different crowd." He smiled a thin, marmotlike smile. "You'll get press synergy. A whole new, even more weasel-like element of the press will get on your case, demanding action."

"That's good," Rose Marie said. "We weren't getting enough attention." She looked at Lucas: "How bad was it?"

"Bad. I don't know what you're getting from St. Paul, but I think it's a different killer. Maybe somebody just taking the opportunity, hoping we'll think that whoever did Alie'e and Lansing also did Plain — but I don't think it was the same guy."

"So it might not be directly related."

"Maybe not. On the other hand, it could be. It's possible that a couple of people have seen the killer. They said he was 'porky' and 'big' and 'rednecky.' "

Rose Marie looked at Lucas for a second, then at Bennett. "Howard, I really appreciate your telling me about Plain. Can I call you . . . ?"

Bennett knew when he was being shuffled out. He smiled his marmot smile again and said, "Say hello to your friends in the legislature."

"You can count on it," Rose Marie said. She followed him into the outer office, shook hands, then stepped back inside and closed the door. "You think it was Tom Olson?" she asked Lucas.

"The thought crossed my mind," Lucas said. "He's heavyset. We know he's got a temper. We know he's distraught. We know that he might be a little bit of a nut."

"Or maybe a lot of a nut," she said.

"Maybe the photo spread set him off. I've never seen anything quite like it before."

"Not outside a men's magazine."

"Not even in men's magazines. It was a lot artier than that shit. And decadent. It had this weird end-of-time feel to it, that might have fed straight into his paranoia."

"So what're we going to do?"

"We're doing some research on him. And I'm going to put Sherrill with Jael Corbeau — somebody tried to break into her house the night before last, and the guy was sorta porky."

"Okay. Sherrill for as long as she can stand it, but when she needs a break, I want somebody else with Corbeau. She doesn't get killed in Minneapolis. And we better get somebody with Catherine Kinsley, too."

"The problem is, nobody's looking for Trick," Lucas said.

"Don't worry about Trick."

"We've got to get Al-Balah out. There's gonna be a lawsuit, and we've got to at least keep our heads up on that," Lucas said.

"Sure. If you happen to stumble over Trick, that's fine. But the priority has got to be Alie'e, and keeping people alive. This thing in St. Paul is almost like a good break. We get some time to work without everybody breathing down our necks."

"They'll all be back here tomorrow morning."

"That's twenty-four hours."

Back in his own office, Lucas called Sherrill on her cell phone. She'd heard about Plain, and Lucas told her to get with Jael Corbeau: "A bodyguard job?" she complained. "Why can't you pull somebody in?"

"Look, it's a high-danger point right now. We don't have anybody to chase yet, but somebody killed Plain and somebody may be stalking Jael. I want *you* with her. I *don't* want you looking like a cop. I want you to girl around with Corbeau a little. Her brother's dead, but if you could get her out in the open, making arrangements for the funeral . . ."

"You mean, like *bait?*" Sherrill asked.

"Not a word I'd choose," Lucas said.

"Hmm." She was thinking about it. "That doesn't sound so bad, when you put it that way. Maybe pull this guy right in."

"Yeah. So get over there. She's expecting you."

When he got off, he walked down to Homicide, found Frank Lester, and told him that the chief wanted somebody with Kinsley. "Might as well," Lester said, "since nobody's getting dog shit."

"Nothing at all?"

"Nothing."

Lucas called Del. "I called your office a couple of times," Del said. "I think I'm gonna need a couple of search warrants."

"What happened?"

"The other guy, Curtis Logan, is on vacation somewhere — maybe Vegas. So I hung around James Bee last night, staying out of sight, and at one point he hooked up with Larry Outer. You remember Outer?"

"Vaguely. Wasn't he involved with that Chicago bunch?"

"Yeah. I thought he'd gone away, but I followed Bee down to this pie place on Grand Avenue, and who does he hook up with, but Outer. After a while, they go out to Outer's car, and they talk for a couple of minutes, and then Bee goes back to his own car. Outer's car has Illinois tags, which I got, and I tracked those, and they gave me an apartment in Evanston. I'm willing to bet that Outer is dealing with Bee, and if we stop him on some bullshit, we're gonna find some coke in his car. And if we find some coke in his car, even a little bit, then we can probably get a search warrant for his apartment, and if they find *anything* there, that'd be three felonies in Illinois. And Illinois is a three-strike state."

"You're such a clever fuck."

"Not only that — when I pulled Outer's sheet outa the NCIC, there's a misdemeanor warrant on him for skipping out on child support in Cleveland. He ditched some chick and her kid."

"A vicious criminal. A mad dog."

"No doubt. So we can take down Outer without having to go through any perjury bullshit on a search warrant. When we get him, we've got him in an armlock, unless he's willing to have somebody kick his door in Illinois. So he gives us Bee, and we use that to get a warrant, and we hit Bee's apartment and maybe his office, and get a list. And maybe that gets us back to Alie'e's." He rubbed his eyes. "Convoluted as hell, but it's what we got."

"And for Logan, we have to wait until he gets back from Vegas."

"Unless Outer can give us him along with Bee."

"So it all hangs on Outer," Lucas said.

"Yup."

"You have any idea where he is now?"

"In a motel in Plymouth. I'm standing outside a McDonald's looking at his car, freezing my ass off."

"You been there all night?"

"We've been everywhere all night — we got here about ten minutes ago. Which brings me to the question What are you doing up at this time of day?"

"Amnon Plain," Lucas said.

"Uh-oh. What'd he do?"

"You haven't heard the radio? He was shot to death last night."

"No shit?"

"Over in St. Paul. He's seriously dead."

After a moment of silence, Del said, "Goddamnit."

"Yeah."

"Though it does add a certain frisson to the case."

"A what?"

"Frisson. It's a French word. So get me some guys over here —"

"There's nobody to get," Lucas said. "Everybody over here is already jumping through their ass."

"So what are *you* doing?" Del asked.

Del was sitting in the front window of a McDonald's eating a Big Mac out of a bag and watching the motel across the street. "He's got the blue Olds," he said when Lucas slid into the booth across from him. "You get an okay on the warrant?"

Lucas nodded. "No problem. It's a little old — the Cleveland cops didn't know what I was talking about, and it took about fifteen minutes to find it."

"If it's still good, it's still good," Del said. He was red-eyed, tired.

"You look a little ragged," Lucas said.

"I'm buzzed on caffeine. I'm so buzzed I talked to the counter girl for ten minutes at a hundred miles an hour. Scared the shit out of her."

"Hmm." The counter girl was keeping an eye on both of them. Lucas looked at the Olds parked across the street, nose-in to a motel door. Everything look so quiet, but fifty times a year, somewhere in the country, a cop would kick a door off a nice quiet parking lot and the guy inside the room would shoot him. "So you want to do it?"

200

"Yeah." Del wadded up the bag with half the burger still in it. "Let's go."

They left one at a time, and walked around behind the McDonald's so that if Outer happened to be looking out his window, he wouldn't see them crossing the street. At the hotel office, they showed the day manager the warrant and their badges. He wanted to call the chain headquarters in Rococco, Florida, for instructions, but they got the key to Outer's room and Lucas told the manager to stay out of sight, no matter what they said in Rococco.

"I'll kick it, if you do the key," Del told Lucas on the way down. "I got so much caffeine, I might miss the keyhole."

"All right."

They stopped at the door, listened. A television was on; that was good — it'd cover the noise of the key. Lucas held the key up, and Del stepped into kicking range. When they were ready, Lucas hovered the key a quarter inch outside the lock. The idea was to slip the key quickly into the lock and turn it, and push the door. When the door hit the chain, if it did, Del would kick it. They wouldn't try to sneak the key into the lock for the simple reason that it was almost impossible: The slightest vibration would wake the dead, if the dead was a nervous dope dealer. With the quick open-and-kick, you were usually inside before the target had time to react, whether he heard it or not.

Del nodded. Lucas got right, then jammed the

key and turned the knob, and Del kicked the door and exploded into the room, Lucas two feet behind him, Del screaming, "Police, police. Freeze!"

Outer was sitting on the toilet, a wad of toilet paper in his hands, his slacks down around his ankles. The bathroom door was open — he'd been watching ESPN. When Del landed on the carpet opposite the bed, his pistol pointing, Lucas backing him, Outer sat up, raised his hands, and then, in a deafening silence, said, "Ah, man. Can I wipe?"

Before they had him cuffed, Outer said, "I ain't sayin' shit. I want an attorney."

"Sit on the bed," Del said.

Outer sat, and Lucas started pulling apart Outer's duffle bag. Halfway into it, he ran into a T-shirt built like an I-beam. He shook it out, and found a Smith & Wesson 649. "Gun," he said to Del.

"Jeez, that's too bad," Del said. "Him being a convicted felon and all."

"Attorney," Outer said.

No dope. Lucas looked around the room. He checked the bathroom, but the toilet was the pressure kind, with no tank. He came back into the main room, and Del said, "He wouldn't leave it in the car."

Outer relaxed and leaned back on the bed. "All I have is the gun, which was for self-protection and isn't even mine."

"Get off the bed," Lucas said.

"What?" Outer put on a perplexed look.

"Get off the fuckin' bed."

Del took him by the arm, and Outer said, "Fuckin' cops," and Lucas walked around to the door side of the bed, crouched, grabbed the mattress, and flipped it off the box spring. In the center of the box spring, four Ziploc bags of cocaine nestled in a line.

"That ain't mine. You put it there," Outer said.

"Probably has our fingerprints all over the plastic, then," Lucas said. "And when we get a blood test, we'll probably test for cocaine."

"Attorney," Outer said.

"Sit in the chair," Lucas said.

Del pushed Outer down on an overstuffed chair, and Lucas sat on the box spring.

"I'm gonna make you an offer. I can't make it after you talk to an attorney, I can only make it before. We can fix it so you take a minimum plea on the dope and the gun — three years. That's what we can do."

"Attorney."

"Or we can call the Illinois cops, tell them where your apartment is, tell them we've busted you as a big-time dealer." He looked at the Ziploc bags, and said to Del, "I think we can call that big-time when we talk to Evanston."

"I think so," Del said. "Definitely big-time."

He looked back at Outer. "We can ask them to search your apartment. If there's dope there, if there's a gun there . . ." Lucas spread his arms and shrugged. "Well, that's another felony. And how many felonies you got in Illinois, Larry? Two? Aw, that's terrible. Illinois is a three-strike state, right? What a shame." He leaned forward, the mean smile crossing his face. "You know how long forever is? It's a long fucking time, Larry."

"Jesus . . ."

"We can't offer you this deal after you talk to an attorney, because your attorney might call a friend of yours in Illinois, and the apartment might get cleaned," Del said. "If we don't make a deal right now, we're gonna have to make the call. And get you an attorney, of course."

Outer put his head down. "You're fucks."

"Well, you know, Larry, that comes with our job sometimes," Del said. "That's why we sometimes offer deals to our favorite citizens. To make ourselves feel better."

"What do I gotta do?"

"We've got two names. We know you know the guys, because we've seen you with them. We want a statement."

"Who?"

"James Bee," Del said. "And Curtis Logan."

"Is that it?" Outer said. "I flip on those guys, and I walk?"

"Well, you walk out to Stillwater for a couple," Lucas said. "But you can do a couple standing on your head. And we won't call Evanston. Until later."

Outer seemed to brighten. "Well, shit, if that's

all — I can do that," Outer said.

Lucas and Del looked at each other, then Del looked at Outer and said, "I knew we could be friends."

"Friends — but I want something on paper before I talk," Outer said.

They called a squad, and had Outer transported to the jail with instructions that he didn't get a phone call without Lucas being told. "You call, I call Evanston," Lucas said. "I bet we can get the Evanston cops there before you can get it cleaned out."

Del went over to the county attorney's office to find somebody who could help draw up the deal, and somebody else who could get search warrants for James Bee and Curtis Logan. Lucas walked up the stairs, heading for his office, but got hooked by a secretary: "They're gonna show film from St. Paul. They're bringing somebody in."

"What?"

"It's on TV," she said.

Homicide had a TV, and Lucas stopped there; a half-dozen cops were gathered around the tube. The St. Paul chief was saying, "No, no, no, we just wanted to talk to him. We don't have any indication that he had anything to do with the murder of Mr. Plain . . ."

"Who is it?" Lucas asked.

"Brought in some vending machine guy," one of the cops said. And as he said it, with the chief rambling on in the background, a news clip came up, two St. Paul cops escorting a man in blue coveralls into the front of the police station. He was brown-haired, slat-faced, rawboned.

"Not porky," Lucas said. "He was supposed to be porky."

At his office, he had a *Call me* message from Sherrill, and a note from Lane saying that the Olson family-and-friends genealogy was complete, and he'd put it on a computer disk with Lucas's name on it, in the chief's secretary's out basket.

He dialed Sherrill. "I just kicked open a motel door and arrested a dealer," he said. "What are you doing?"

"We just bought a casket," Sherrill said. "I'm creeped out. You know the last time I was in here —"

"Yeah. Don't think about it." The last time she'd been at the funeral home, she'd been buying a casket for her husband. "How's Corbeau?"

"She's in the can. By herself — I checked. I think you made an impression on her this morning, and it wasn't fatherly," Sherrill said. "My personal feeling is that she's too young for you."

"She can't be any younger than you are."

"*I* was too young for you," Sherrill said.

"I was much younger when we started going together," Lucas said, "than when we called it off."

"Bullshit. You were rejuvenated," Sherrill said. "Anyway, we're shopping. And I'm on the lookout for maniacs."

"St. Paul brought in a guy," Lucas said. He told her about it and said, "I don't think it's anything."

"So what do I do? Stick with Corbeau?"

"Yeah. If anything heats up, I'll call."

He was walking down the hall to the chief's office, to get the computer disk, when Lane returned. He was walking fast, an intent look on his face.

"What?" Lucas asked.

"That genealogy. Excuse me, I meant, that *fuckin'* genealogy. I was getting everything I could on Sandy Lansing's friends, so I went by the hotel to see who she hung out with there. Everybody in the place was looking for Derrick Deal."

"Deal? He's gone?"

"They haven't seen him since he talked to you. Or about then. They been calling his house — nobody home."

"Huh. So I'm not doing anything. I'll go knock on his door."

14

Derrick Deal lived in a town house in Roseville, eight miles northeast of the Minneapolis loop and off Highway 36. The town house, a split-entry end unit with a tuck-under garage, was one of twenty arranged around a pond full of Canada geese.

Lucas knocked on the door, waited, and got the hollow response that an empty house gives. The garage door was locked, so he walked around back. There were windows on the side of the garage and the back door, and he peered inside, but couldn't see much: a corner of the kitchen table from the back door, and on the table, what looked like a stack of bills and a checkbook. The garage was empty. He walked back around to the front, noticed that the mail slot was open just a crack; he pushed it the rest of the way, and could see mail on the floor. More than one day's worth, he thought. No newspapers, though.

He knocked again, then went next door and knocked. No answer from there, either. If you lived in a town house, you worked. Maybe check back in the evening.

208

As he was leaving, Lucas cranked up his cell phone, called Dispatch and asked that they find Deal's license tag, and put it out.

"Lucas, the chief has been trying to get in touch with you," the dispatcher said. "There's a meeting going on . . . well, it's gonna start in ten minutes, in her office. She wants you to come."

"Ten minutes," he said. "I might be a couple minutes late. Tell her."

As he ran the Porsche out onto the interstate, he glanced back toward the town houses. Maybe, he thought, Deal had gone to the same place as Trick Bentoin, wherever that was. But he didn't think so. Deal's disappearance was a shadow across the day.

A huge detective named Franklin was climbing the stairs toward the City Hall's main level when Lucas caught up with him. "What's going on?"

"Just gettin' a Coke and an apple," Franklin said. "Something going on?"

"Meeting," Lucas said. "I was afraid another body had fallen out of a closet somewhere."

"Probably has. But not here, as far as I know," Franklin said.

Lucas went on ahead. The chief's secretary nodded at the closed office door and said, "We've got a crowd. Alie'e's family and some friends. You're supposed to go right in."

Rose Marie was barricaded behind her desk. To her left, Dick Milton, the department PR guy, perched on the edge of a folding chair, his jaws tight. Eight people were arrayed in visitors' chairs in front of the desk: Alie'e's parents; Tom Olson, unshaven, apparently in the same clothes he'd worn at the last visit; and three other men and two women Lucas didn't recognize.

"Lucas, come in, we're just getting started." Rose Marie glanced at one of the men Lucas didn't know and added, "I guess we're trying to get some ground rules going here. Everybody, this is Lucas Davenport, a deputy chief, who often works as a kind of, mmm, key man in these kinds of investigations. Lucas, you know Mr. and Mrs. Olson; and this is Mr. and Mrs. Benton, and Mr. and Mrs. Packard, the Olsons' best friends from Burnt River, who're down to help out; and Lester Moore, the editor of the Burnt River newspaper."

Moore was a gangly man with reddish hair and green watery eyes. He wore wash pants that were an inch too short, and showed a rind of pale skin between the top of his white socks and the cuff of the green pants. "I'm the ground rules problem," he said affably.

"The problem," Rose Marie said, "is that Mr. Moore is also one of the Olsons' good friends." The Olsons both nodded at once, as did the Bentons and the Packards. "They want him here. But if we give him the confidential family briefing that is not available to all the press . . ."

"So will you use what we tell you in confidence?" Lucas asked.

Moore shook his head. "Of course not. I'm here as a friend, not as a reporter. We have our reporter down here right now, and she'll do our coverage."

Milton piped up. "Suppose you think your reporter is reading something wrong, because of privileged information you happen to have."

"We'll go with her story," Moore said. "The people of Burnt River have the right to the information — but not necessarily at this exact minute."

Rose Marie looked at Lucas, who shrugged. "So, you trust him or not. I'd say, go ahead and trust him now, and stop if something comes out."

After thinking about it for a second, Rose Marie nodded. "All right. Mr. Moore stays . . . with the understanding that what is said in this room, stays in this room."

As Rose Marie briefed the group on what had been done in the past twenty-four hours, and filled them in on the murder of Amnon Plain, Lucas watched Tom Olson. Olson sat squarely and solidly in his chair, his chin down almost to his chest, staring fixedly at Rose Marie as she spoke. He really wasn't porky, Lucas thought, although an observer at a distance might think so — especially since pork was almost the default body shape for men in the upper Midwest. But Olson looked hard; he was barrel-shaped and square-faced, but you could see the bones in his cheeks and at his wrists. He *looked* like a farm mechanic: somebody used to pushing around machines, and maybe throwing bales.

The Bentons and Packards, on the other hand, had the pale, round blandness of prosperous Minnesota small-town people. They were not quite blond, but not quite brunette, either. They all spoke softly in rounded Scandinavian vowels, with perfect grammar, and finished each other's sentences. They were, Lucas thought, like two pairs of sugar cookies out of the same nonsexist male-female cookie cutter.

Tom Olson was the one to speak when Rose Marie finished. "So what you just said is, you didn't find out anything. There's no new information."

"That's not at all what I said," Rose Marie snapped. "There was a lot of negative information — we eliminated a lot of possibilities. I will tell you, Mr. Olson, and Chief Davenport will tell you the same thing, that if you don't find the killer standing over the victim and arrest him on the spot, then the elimination of possibilities is one of the most important things we do. We will find the killer. We know it's going to take time —"

"Oh, horseshit," Olson said.

His mother looked at him and said, "Thomas."

The older Olson cleared his throat and said, "The funeral is the day after tomorrow, if you can release Alie'e to us. The ME said he thought that was likely."

"It's done, or will be in the next few minutes," Rose Marie said.

Olson continued, "When the funeral's over, Lil and I are coming back, with Tom, and the Bentons, and the Packards, when Charlie doesn't have to work, and we'd like to stay for a week or two and hope you catch this guy, but we'd like to stay and see what you do."

"That's no problem at all. We can meet every day to keep you up to date."

"Is Amnon Plain's murder related directly to Alie'e?" Lester Moore asked.

"We don't know," Rose Marie said. "We have to treat it as though it is."

Lucas jumped in. "I was at Plain's apartment. Whoever killed him, planned it. There was nothing impulsive about it. The other murder had an ad hoc quality . . . they feel different."

"Two separate killers?" Tom Olson said.

"Possibly. They may be related — they may even have been done by the same person — but I personally think Plain was killed by another person."

"When you say 'person,' are you being politically correct or are you not sure whether the killer was a male or female?" Lester Moore asked.

"I'm being politically correct," Lucas said. "We had a series of very cold, execution-style murders done by a woman, just this past summer. But that's very rare. I think the killer's male. He may even have been seen."

"Well, I hope you find him," the elder Olson

said. He looked at his wife and son and said, "Let's go get Alie'e."

When the door closed, Lucas, Rose Marie, and Milton sat in silence for a few seconds, then Rose Marie asked, "Did you see them on television?"

"No."

"It's like people get media training somewhere," Rose Marie said. "In here, Mrs. Olson sits in her chair like a turtle on a rock, but when you see her on TV, she's the perfect mom. She's as good as most of the professionals you see on the news shows. Every hair in place, except the ones that shouldn't be. She's perfectly distraught. She personifies exactly what a distraught mother *should* be like. And the kid . . ."

"I wouldn't want to meet *him* in a dark alley if he was pissed at me," Milton said. "He's supposed to be some kind of holy guy, but he said, 'horseshit.'"

"Horses shit even around holy people," Lucas said.

"Besides," added Rose Marie, "he was clinically correct. That was a load of horseshit. Lester Moore picked up on it, too. There were no secrets, because we don't have any." She brooded about that for moment, then said, "I think I've heard his name, Lester Moore. Maybe when I was up on the Hill?"

Milton shook his head. "It's a famous name."

"Really?" Rose Marie was curious.

"A guy named Lester Moore was killed in

some place like Tombstone, or Dodge City, and was buried on Boot Hill. His epitapth said something like, " 'Here Lies Lester Moore, Two Shots From a .44, No Les, No More.' "

"Really?"

"Really."

Rose Marie said to Lucas, "We've had some time, now. Now they're gonna start cooking us, the press is. When the funeral's over with, they're all gonna come back here, and we better have something besides horseshit."

Lucas had three messages: one from Catrin that said, "Please call before three," one from Del, and a last one from Sherrill. He called Sherrill first. She answered the cell phone, then said, "I'll call you back in fifteen seconds." In fifteen seconds, his phone rang, and Sherrill said, "I think you better come down here and talk with Jael."

"Why?"

"Some kind of father-figure thing, I think, and all the scars you guys got," she said, and she sounded serious. "She wants to talk — actually, I think she wants to confess something to you."

"She . . ."

"No, no, she didn't kill anyone," Sherrill said.

"Then why doesn't she confess it to you? You got scars."

"Because she's not interested in me. With you, she's thinking it over. Women would much rather confess to a guy they're thinking about sleeping with, because they think *that* way, they might have some control over him."

"Ah."

"So when can you come down?"

"Pretty goddamn quick, but I've got a couple of calls to make. See you in . . . twenty minutes."

Lane stuck his head in as Lucas was hanging up. "I'm heading out to Fargo."

"Why?" Lucas punched in Del's number.

"Because I was looking at Tom Olson's alibi for the night Alie'e was killed. It's loose, and I need to talk to a guy out there. And I've got all the genealogical shit you could ever ask for."

Del's phone started ringing, and Lucas asked, "When will you be back?"

"Tonight, late, or midmorning tomorrow."

Del said, "Hello?" and Lucas lifted a hand to Lane. "Take off." Del asked, "What?" and Lucas said, "I was talking to Lane. . . . So what's happening with the deal, and the warrants?"

"The warrants on Bee and Logan are in the works. Manny Lanscolm is taking Outer's statement right now. We could move in an hour."

"Call me," Lucas said. "Make sure that the warrants specify computer files and disks."

He dialed Catrin's number. The phone rang twice, and Catrin picked it up.

"I'd like to talk again," she said. Her voice was low, tight, anxious. "I know you're busy with the Alie'e thing . . . but could we meet in St. Paul,

216

somewhere, tomorrow?"

"Sure, I guess." He gave her the name of a restaurant near St. Anne's, told her how to find it. "It's got those old-fashioned high plastic booths," he said. "We can talk."

Jael. He was looking forward to seeing her again.

Sherrill met him at the door and said, "She's back in her studio. As long as you're here, I'm gonna run out and get a cheeseburger."

"All right."

Jael Corbeau was sitting on a wooden stool, wearing a clay-spattered apron over jeans and a loose flannel shirt, the sleeves rolled over her elbows. She was turning a cream-colored juglet in her hands. She looked up when Lucas came in. Her eyes were rimmed in red, her nose red and a little swollen; she was still striking. "This thing is three thousand years old," she said. "Look how nice it is."

She handed him the juglet; it was the size of a hand grenade, with a soft, porous surface. "Where'd you get it?"

"My mother gave it to me, because of my name. Amnon got one, too. They come from Israel, the north part of the country, the Galilee."

"I don't know Israel." He handed the juglet back. "You wanted to talk?"

"Where's Marcy?"

"Since I was here, she went to get a bite," Lucas said.

"Okay. So why don't we walk?" Jael said. "I wouldn't mind getting out for a while. Did you bring your gun?"

The last question came with a small hint of humor in her eyes, and Lucas nodded. "Not only that, but it's got a hair trigger."

"Now I feel completely safe," she said. But as they stepped outside, she said, "Do you really think somebody might be trying to hurt me?"

"I don't know, but there's no point in taking a chance."

"I'm not sure I'd be missed that much."

"Maybe not, but if you were killed, the media would trash us. That's what we're trying to avoid."

She smiled now. "*Now* I feel safe. You've got a selfish motive for keeping me alive."

"Damn right."

They walked along for a while in the cold air, and then Jael asked, "What's the thinking on Sandy Lansing?"

"Well, she's kind of a mystery," Lucas said. "She wasn't a hotel executive, and she had no family money, but she had great clothes, a nice apartment, drove a Porsche, and apparently snorted a massive amount of cocaine, which is not free of charge. We're trying to figure out where the money came from. We thought maybe it was sex, that she was taking care of rich people at Brown's, but that seems unlikely now."

Jael stopped and looked up at him, her face

sober. "It's weird, you know, all the people at that party."

"What?"

"Oh, just the way they all made the same excuses: there was no dope, they didn't see any, they didn't know about any. All so worried about their reputations, just like me. And really, in my world, a little dope is no big deal."

"Maybe in the back of their minds, they're worried about something a little more stark, like jail," Lucas said. "Rich people don't like jail. They don't function well in that environment."

"But they didn't tell you about Sandy. And I didn't tell you about Sandy. We were all busy thinking about Alie'e, what a tragedy it was, and just keeping your mouth shut about a little dope. . . ."

"What about Sandy?" But now he knew.

"She was the dealer," Jael said. "Half the people at the party bought dope from her — anything you wanted, she could get. She was discreet, she had to know you before she would sell to you, you had to have a recommendation . . . but she could get it."

"Did you ever buy from her?"

"A little heroin, once or twice. Just little touches of it," she said.

"Jesus Christ, Jael, that stuff is poison."

"But it feels so nice. It smooths you out." Lucas shook his head angrily and stalked off down the sidewalk. She watched him go, then hurried after him. "What?"

"That's so fuckin' stupid, what you just said. It makes my goddamned head hurt." Then he stopped, and faced her. "Will you come in and amend your statement, and say that Sandy Lansing was a dealer?"

"Would I go to jail?"

"No. There's nothing illegal about knowing that somebody deals. Bring your lawyer, so you get all the words right. But it's important that we get it on paper, so we can use the paper to pry information out of other people. I knew something was going on with Lansing, but it was so hard to look in her direction, when everybody was screaming about Alie'e. Did Alie'e get that shit from her?"

"Yeah. Actually, I wasn't there, but I think Sandy had a kit in her purse, and I think she's the one who popped Alie'e. You didn't find a syringe . . ."

"No. Nothing like that. Nothing but the tracks."

"You didn't find Sandy's purse?"

"No."

"Well, she had one. Pretty big — a lot bigger than fashionable. She had some stuff in it."

"Okay," Lucas said.

"I'll come make another statement, but I won't turn in any of my friends. Or anybody else, for that matter."

"Goddamnit."

"I won't."

"Then you just might be covering for a killer," Lucas said impatiently.

"It's more important to me to protect my friends than to catch the killer. Catching the guy won't bring Alie'e or Sandy back. If I turn in my friends . . . well, I won't do that."

"Listen, how about if I put a name on you, and you tell me . . . Look, here's what I want to know. We're ninety-nine percent sure that Sallance Hanson knew that there were drugs all over the place."

"I won't —"

"We're not on the record here. It's just you and me. But I don't want to go off on Hanson if she's really naive. But she can't be that naive, can she?"

Jael kept her mouth shut. Lucas said, "So tell me, can she be that naive? You don't have to accuse her of anything, but tell me that: Is Sallance Hanson naive?"

"You're getting me twisted around."

"Is she naive?"

Jael turned and started back toward her house, her arms wrapped around her body, as if the cold air had suddenly gotten to her. Over her shoulder, she threw one word: "No."

Lucas followed after her, said, "Tell me one more thing — something that won't hurt anyone anymore. Did your brother buy from Sandy Lansing? Did he know her?"

She slowed, and let him catch up. "I don't know if he knew who she was, or what she did. Maybe. Somebody might have told him. But he didn't like dope. He'd get pissed when I used it."

"He said he used it when he was young."

"Yeah. He was precocious. He used *everything* when he was a kid," Jael said. "Then he went to New York and he met Mapplethorpe just before he died, and knowing Mapplethorpe did something to Plain's brain."

"Mapplethorpe. You mean the photographer?

"Yes, completely decadent. Plain used to go on rants, about how Mapplethorpe had this good talent that never came to anything, because he killed himself."

"Suicide?"

"No, he died of AIDS, but he was notorious for putting anything and everything into his body, and into anybody's else's body. Anyway, Plain got to see the end of that whole thing, and he stopped using." She snapped her fingers. "Just like that. He was going to live forever."

"So . . . Lansing. He didn't know her," Lucas said.

"Maybe knew her, didn't buy from her."

"Okay." That's what Plain had told them.

"Does any of this help?" Jael asked.

"Yeah. We couldn't get any traction. We couldn't figure out why anybody would kill either of these women, or your brother, for that matter. Dope was always a possibility, but if Sandy Lansing was dealing, then it becomes a serious possibility."

As they got back to her house, Lucas asked casually, "Are you still using?"

"Oh, you know, sometimes. Just a little pop."

"It'll kill you, Jael." He liked her name; it rolled smoothly off the tongue. "You gotta stop."

"I need to get smoothed out sometimes," Jael said.

"Smoke a little grass. Stay away from the heroin."

"Not the same," she said. But she was amused again. "I should have been recording this: a cop telling me to smoke a little grass."

"Grass'll kill you, too," Lucas said. "But not until you're eighty."

At the house, they sat on the stoop and talked, Lucas trying to tug the conversation back to the party, looking for another name, another hint. "Look, I'm not going to tell you any more names," she said. "If I thought it would really help, I would — but it won't."

A city car pulled to the curb, and Sherrill got out. "Sherrill likes you a lot," Jael said. He could feel her watching his face.

"I like her a lot," Lucas said. He half turned. "Sherrill and I have a little history. That's all over. We weren't good for each other."

"She talks tough," Jael said.

"She *is* tough."

"Tough as you?"

Sherrill was coming up to them. Lucas said, "Maybe."

Sherrill said, "How's it going?"

Her eyes slid from Lucas to Jael, and Jael stood up and said, "Fine. I better go call my lawyer, though."

"What, did he whack you around or something?"

"We're not *that* friendly yet," Jael said.

She went inside, and when she was out of earshot, Sherrill asked, "What happened?"

"She says Sandy Lansing was the dealer. She says Lansing could get anything you want — not like she was a housewife with a neighborhood connection."

"You think somebody killed Lansing for dope?"

"Mmm . . . I don't know about that. But I'll bet it's tied in somehow," Lucas said. "Somebody owed her too much, and was afraid of what was gonna happen. Or blackmail. Maybe she was trying to squeeze one of her clients and he didn't like it. Who knows, maybe she had a competitor in the crowd."

"This is good," Sherrill said. "But you can't stop thinking about Alie'e. If Lansing was killed because she saw something with Alie'e, then there could be a whole 'nother thing going on that we don't see yet."

"I know. That bothers me. But I can't see any connection between Lansing and Amnon Plain, or Lansing and Jael. Plain has to be hooked into Alie'e, or we're completely off the track."

"If it's Olson . . . what, we're talking some kind

of revenge trip for what happened to his sister? Taking out the sinners who led her into the pathways of evil."

"Sounds like a TV show."

"Everything in this case sounds like a TV show," Sherrill said.

"You think we ought to start tracking him? Olson?"

"We oughta think about it," Sherrill said. "We got fifteen guys working on this case, and most of them are standing around bullshitting with each other."

"I'll talk to Lester," Lucas said. He looked back at the house. "You'll take Jael down for the statement?"

"Yeah. I'm gonna take off at five, though. Tom Black is gonna pick up at five."

"Good. Keep her covered."

"Pretty interesting, isn't she?"

Lucas leaned forward, dropped his voice. "You know what I'd like to do? Get about three of them, you know, on a king-size bed. Some really funky blond lesbians stacked up around me, this big Davenport-lesbo sandwich . . ."

She put her hand on his chest and pushed. "So sad, these erotic fantasies in aging men. Three blondes in bed with Lucas, all that relish and one little weenie."

They were laughing together when Jael came out. "He can't do it until three. We're supposed to meet him at his office, and we can walk over to City Hall." She looked at Lucas. "He didn't want me to do it. I told him I wanted to."

Lucas said goodbye and headed back downtown. Del was waiting, ready to go kick doors. "We got a statement from Outer, but his lawyer about had a hernia. He said the deal was a violation of everything sacred in the law."

"What'd Outer say?"

"Not much. But we got him cold on the dope, so we're good. And I've got warrants for Logan's home, and Bee's home and offices."

"Where's the first one?"

"North Oaks. Bee's home." Del read out the address.

"See you there in twenty minutes," Lucas said. He still needed whatever information Bee and Logan had. Lansing may have been Alie'e's dealer, but she had also been the other victim.

James Bee lived in a stone-fronted ranch-style house much like Lucas's own, with frontage on a small, dark lake. Lucas arrived as Del's city car, a Minneapolis squad, and a Ramsey County sheriff's squad were turning up the long blacktopped driveway. Lucas followed them in through a scattering of big oaks, their dead leaves gone a hard stiff brown color.

A narcotics cop named Larry Cohen got out of the passenger side of Del's car, the warrants in hand. The Minneapolis cops got with the sheriff's deputies and headed for the door, while Del dropped back, waiting for Lucas. "This is a long goddamn way around."

"Yeah, but if we can nail him down . . . I'll bet he knows his competitors."

The door was answered by a thin blond woman in black spandex tights and a T-shirt advertising the Twin Cities Marathon. Lucas could hear her screeching at the cops, and then one of the sheriff's deputies broke away and started running around the side of the house, one of the Minneapolis cops six feet behind him.

The other Minneapolis cop was pushing inside, his gun drawn now, while the sheriff's deputy drew his gun and moved up next to a picture window and peeked through. Over his shoulder he yelled, "We got a runner."

Lucas and Del trotted toward the house, drawing their weapons. Inside, the Minneapolis cop had the blonde lying on the floor, facedown. She was screaming, "There's nobody else, for God's sakes, there's nobody else."

They took the house slowly, five minutes to work through it. When Lucas came back up the basement stairs, his pistol reholstered, he found the woman sitting on the couch, her hands cuffed behind her. The second sheriff's deputy was standing over her.

"We got him," the deputy said. "There was no way he was gonna run away from Rick."

"He runs in marathons," the blonde said.

"So does Rick," the deputy said.

Del came out of the back of the house and said, "We're all clear. Office in the back."

Lucas followed him to the office. A paper Rolodex sat on the back of the desk, and Del started going through it while Lucas cranked up the computer. The phone rang, and Lucas picked it up and said hello.

"Hey . . . is this Jim?"

"He's out back," Lucas said. "Can I have him call you?"

"Yeah. Tell him to call Lonnie? Is this Steve?"

"Naw, this is Lucas."

"Okay, whatever. I need to talk to him pretty quick."

"You got a number?"

"He's got it."

"Just in case?"

"Yeah, okay. . . ."

Lucas copied down the phone number and said, "We'll get back to you."

"Thanks."

"Very nice," Del said. He was looking at the Rolodex. "He's gotta have two hundred names in here."

"But nobody from the party list."

"Not so far. But you know what? I'll bet you a buck that we find at least one. If he's dealing high-end. There were a lot of high-end dopers there."

The phone rang again, and a woman's voice said, "Lucas?"

The name startled him; he didn't pick up on it right away. "Yeah?"

"This is Rose Marie," the woman said.

"Jesus, I thought I was talking to a fuckin' psychic or something —"

She broke in. "Listen. I hate this — but Sherrill's been shot."

Lucas didn't understand for a minute. "What? What?"

Del looked at him, straightened.

"Sherrill's been shot. She's on her way to Hennepin."

"Aw, Jesus Christ, is she bad?"

"She's bad. She's bad."

"I'm going."

He threw the phone back at the receiver and started running, and Del shouted, "What?"

Lucas shouted back, "Sherrill's been shot. You stay here, take this."

"Fuck that, Larry can take it." He was right behind Lucas, and together they ran through the front room, and Lucas shouted at Cohen, who was talking to the blonde, "Larry, you gotta take it, Sherrill's been shot, we're going, you know what to do. . . ."

On the sidewalk, the sheriff's deputy, wet up to his hips, was pulling a handcuffed man up the lawn, a short, slender man with a dude's haircut and a small tight mouth; the dude was soaked from head to foot. The deputy said, "Fell in the fuckin' lake."

But Lucas and Del ran past him and piled into Lucas's Porsche and they were gone, streaking through the slow streets of North Oaks past a soccer field and south toward Minneapolis.

15

Lucas focused on driving, blowing past cars as Del gave a running commentary on gaps in the traffic: "Go left behind this red one, move over left, go, go . . ." Down the ramp and around the corner onto I-35W, squeezing between an old Bronco and a generic Chevy pickup.

Halfway back, Lucas said, "We've done this before."

"That fuckin' Sherrill, she's always got her face in it," Del said. "Last time she goddamned near bled to death."

"Rose Marie said it's bad," Lucas groaned. "She said it's bad. . . ."

A pale-faced, blood-spattered Jael Corbeau was standing in the hallway just inside the emergency room door, with two uniformed cops, when Lucas and Del burst in. "Where is she?" Lucas asked.

"They're operating," Jael said, stepping toward him. "They rushed her right in."

Lucas headed for the hall to the operating rooms. Rose Marie was standing there with Lester. Lester grabbed Lucas's arm and said, "Slow down," and Rose Marie said, "You can't see anything down there, Lucas." Lester added, "She's already under, man, they've already got her asleep."

Lucas slowed down, realized Del was right behind him. "How bad?" Del asked, and Lucas asked, "Is she gonna make it?"

"She was hit twice," Lester said. "Once in the left arm, once in the left side of her chest. Busted a lung. She might've died except that she rolled up on her left side . . . they said she might've drowned if she hadn't been on her side."

"Is she gonna make it?" Lucas asked.

"She's bad," Lester said, "but she's still alive. If they get you here alive . . ."

"Aw, Jesus," Lucas said. He slumped against the wall, closed his eyes. Jael. He pushed away from the wall and headed back toward the entrance. Jael was still there.

"What happened?"

The words came out in a spate. "We were coming out of my house, going downtown, and this car came down the street and the window was open and Marcy yelled at me and got her gun out and this man started shooting at us. Marcy shoved me down and then she fell down, and the car kept going, and when I looked at Marcy, she had blood all over her and I ran and called 911 and then I came out and tried to stop the blood and when the ambulance got there I rode down here with her . . ."

"She got off a couple of rounds," one of the uniformed cops said.

Jael nodded, stepped toward Lucas, took his shirt in both hands. "She said to tell you, this is all she said, she said to tell you that she shot the car. She said, 'Tell Lucas I hit the car.' "

"What kind of car? You didn't get a license number —"

"No, no, I barely saw it 'cause she pushed me. I went down."

"You didn't see anything."

She closed her eyes, still holding on to his shirt, and then said, "It was dark. Long and dark."

Lucas pressed. "Long and dark. What do you mean, long and dark? Like a Mercedes-Benz or a Cadillac?"

"No, I don't think so," she said. "It just looked long and dark."

"American?"

"I don't know. Like those big cars from twenty years ago. But I don't know what kind, I don't know, God . . ."

Lucas put an arm around her and gave her a squeeze. "You did good," he said. "I'm amazed that you saw anything."

More cops came rolling in. Everybody was doing right: They were looking at all long dark cars, checking for bullet holes, looping the neighborhood down there. But Jael lived within whistling distance of a half-dozen interstate on-ramps. Everybody was looking, but without much hope.

Another doctor arrived, headed straight back. "Vascular surgeon," a nurse told them.

"What does that mean?" Lucas asked. "Heart?"

"No telling," she said.

One of the on-sterile circulating nurses came out of the operating room on an errand, and they trapped her. "I don't know," she said. "She's alive — they're breathing her."

After an hour, Del said, "We can't do anything here. All we can do is find out that she died, if she dies."

"So what do you suggest?" Lucas was angry and scared, his voice a croak.

"I suggest we go find that fuckin' Olson and look at his car," Del said. Sherrill had been shot once before, and nearly bled to death. Del had ridden with her from the shooting scene to the hospital, in a helicopter, squeezing the artery so hard that for weeks afterward Sherrill had complained about the bruise. "The bullet hole is nothin'," she'd said. "But that goddamn bruise where Del squeezed me . . . that's killing my ass."

"We know what kind of car?" Lucas asked.

"Dark blue 1986 Volvo sedan. And the Olsons said they're staying at the Four Winds. That'd be a place to start."

"I'll drive," Lucas said.

The Four Winds was three blocks from the Mall of America, just south of the I-494 link of the beltway. They spotted the Volvo in the parking lot, stopped behind it, and got out to look. The car was old and dark, with patches of gray primer paint on the left front fender. No bullet holes.

"Goddamnit. That would have been easy," Del said.

Then Tom Olson turned the corner of the motel, carrying a sack of vending machine potato chips and a can of Coke. He saw them, stopped, and then stalked over. "What are you doing?"

"Looking at your car," Lucas said.

"Why?" He set himself squarely, and a half-step too close.

Lucas moved an inch closer yet, and Del moved a foot to the right.

"Because somebody in a long dark car just shot the police officer who was guarding Jael Corbeau."

Olson was amazed, and some of the grimness went out of his face. He shuffled a step back. "You thought it was me? I'd never . . . Is she dead?"

"No. She's in the operating room," Lucas said. "Since whoever is doing the shooting may be taking revenge for the death of your sister, and since you drive an older, dark car . . . we thought we should take a look."

"I didn't do it," Olson said. "If I were you, I'd take a close look at those hellhounds that Alie'e hung out with. They're the crazy ones. Not me. They're the crazies."

"You seem a little loosely wrapped yourself," Del said. He'd edged a few inches closer to Olson, to a spot that would allow him to hook the other man in the solar plexus.

"Only to a sinner," Olson said.

Del tightened up. "Easy, dude," Lucas said.

"Where were you at four-twenty this afternoon?" Del asked.

Olson looked at his watch. "Well, let me see. I must've still been at the mall."

"Mall of America?"

"Yes." They all turned and looked at it. The mall looked like Uncle Scrooge's money bin, without the charm. "I spent a couple of hours walking around the place."

"What'd you buy? Do you have any receipts?" Del was pressing.

"No, I didn't buy anything," Olson said. "Well, a cinnamon roll. I just walked around."

"Talk to anybody?"

"No, not really."

"In other words, you couldn't find anybody to back up your story, if you had to."

Olson shrugged. "I don't think so. I was just walking. I'd never been in the place before. It's astonishing. You know, don't you . . . our whole culture is dying. Something new is being born in places like that. Snake things."

"Yeah, well . . ." Now Del shrugged. "What're you going to do?"

"Pray," Olson said.

There was nothing more to say, and the need

to know what was going on at the hospital was pressing on them. Lucas said, "Let's get back," and Del nodded.

"Sorry about this," Del said to Olson.

Lucas had parked behind Olson's car. Olson watched them get back in, then pushed through a set of glass doors to a stair lobby. Lucas rolled the Porsche out of the parking lot. "I got a bad feeling about Marcy," he said, with a dark hand on his heart.

Del said, "They got her alive, dude. . . ."

"I got a bad feeling, man." At the end of the motel drive, he slowed to let a car go, took a right, idled a hundred feet up the street to a traffic light, and stopped. "This is the second time she's been hit hard."

"You been hit just as hard."

"I never took a shot in —"

Del interrupted, his voice harsh. "What the fuck is this? What the fuck is this?"

He was looking out the passenger-side window, and Lucas leaned forward to look past him. Tom Olson was running toward them, across the motel parking lot, waving his arms. They could see that he was shouting or screaming, but were too far away to hear him. There was a craziness in the way he ran — a violent, high-kick fullback run, as though he were fighting his way through invisible tacklers.

Lucas stopped the car, and both he and Del stepped out as Olson got closer. The traffic light changed to green; the driver of the Lexus that had come up behind them touched his horn. Lucas shook his head at the driver and stepped between the Lexus and the Porsche, heading toward Olson. Olson was fifty yards away when he suddenly stopped, leaned forward, and put his hands on his knees, as though he'd run out of breath. The Lexus guy pushed open his car door and stepped out on the street. The Lexus was trapped behind the Porsche, with more cars behind the Lexus. The driver shouted, "Move the car, asshole" and honked his horn again.

Lucas shouted back, "Police. Go around it." The man *leaned* on the horn, shouting unintelligibly; then another car behind the Lexus started. As suddenly as he'd stopped, Olson heaved himself upright and began running toward them again, crossed out of the blacktopped parking lot onto a grassy verge as Lucas and Del stepped onto the grass from the other side.

Then, with the horns honking behind them, Olson ran to within a few feet of them and stopped, his eyes wide and anguished, grabbed hair on both sides of his head above his ears, opened his mouth, said nothing, his jaw working — and then pitched facedown on the ground.

"Jesus Christ," Del said.

A few of the horns stopped, but one or two continued. They could hear the Lexus driver's voice again: "Hey, asshole, asshole . . ."

They crouched next to Olson, and Lucas turned the unconscious man's face, lifted an eyelid with a thumb. Olson's eyes had rolled up, and Lucas could see nothing but a pearly sliver of white. "He's breathing, but he's out," Lucas said. "Call 911."

Del got his cell phone out and they both stood up, over Olson's crumpled form. A half-dozen horns were going again, and then the sudden *brrrrp* of a cop touching a siren. A squad car rolled around in front of the Porsche, and the honking stopped.

Lucas took his ID out of his pocket and started toward the cop car as a Bloomington cop got out of the near side, another out of the far side of the car. They kept Lucas's Porsche between them. Lucas held his badge case above his head and shouted, "Minneapolis police. We need an ambulance and some help."

The cop behind the Porsche turned to say something to the other cop, and when Lucas closed up he held out the badge case, but the cop on the far side of the squad, the taller of the two, a sergeant, said, "Chief Davenport . . . what's going on?"

"We don't know. We just talked to that guy at the motel and were leaving, and all of a sudden he came running across the lot screaming at us and now he's had some sort of fit. We need a paramedic right now, and we need you guys to hang around. Could you hold on a minute?"

"Sure."

He walked around to the Lexus; the driver had

slid back inside, but Lucas grabbed the handle and jerked the door open. The man was in his fifties, red-faced, wattled. Lucas said, "I'm a police officer. We had a serious problem. My inclination is to jerk your ugly stupid ass out of this car, cuff you, and send you downtown on a charge of interfering with a police officer. A body-cavity search would teach you the real meaning of the word *asshole*."

"I just want to get going." The man was furious, unapologetic. "You had me blocked in. I'm busy, I'm in a goddamned hurry, and you're screwing around with some asshole."

Lucas said, "Put your car in park."

"It *is* in park."

Lucas reached past him, turned the key, killed the engine. "Sit here until I tell you you can go. If you move, you go to jail."

"I'm in a fuckin' hurry," the man screamed.

Lucas went back to the Bloomington cops and explained what had happened with Olson. An ambulance siren started in the distance. The traffic jam intensified as people leaving the mall stopped to gawk at the Porsche and the police car, and the man lying on the grass.

"The thing is, he was fine in the parking lot when we were talking to him," Lucas said. "Then he headed back to his hotel room, and a minute later, here he came running after us. Now he's had whatever this is. A fit."

A car was passing in the outside lane, and a kid

yelled, "Did you shoot him?"

"Maybe a stroke," said the sergeant.

"He's just out," Del said. "He's like somebody knocked him out."

"I think we better go look at the motel," Lucas said. "Could you guys stay here and handle the paramedics and traffic, but send another car over to the motel?"

"Yeah. Have somebody here in a minute." He looked at the Lexus. "What's the story on this guy?"

Lucas told him quickly, and the sergeant nodded. "Fuckhead. We'll keep him around for a while."

"That'd be good," Lucas said. "At least until he's cooled out."

Lucas and Del walked toward the hotel, off the grass, across the parking lot. The desk clerk had come to the front window to watch the commotion at the curb. Lucas showed him the badge case and said, "We need the room number and a key for a guest named Olson."

The clerk stepped behind the desk, punched up a computer. "We've got two Olsons — a Mr. Tom and a Mr. Lynn Olson."

"Give us both keys," Lucas said.

The clerk never hesitated. He looked in a slotted drawer, took out two keys, and pushed them across the desk. "Is there anything else I can do?"

"A Bloomington police car is gonna be here in

a minute," Lucas said. "Send the cops up."

The Olsons' two rooms were adjacent, up an interior stairway and down a long carpeted hall that smelled faintly of disinfectant and something else, like wine or beer. "Would something in his own room freak him out?" Del asked as they counted the room numbers down the hall.

"I was wondering that," Lucas said. "Let's try his folks."

The elder Olsons' door came up first. Lucas knocked. No answer. Knocked louder. They listened, then Del shook his head and Lucas put the key in the lock, turned it, and pushed.

No chain. The door swung open and Lucas stepped inside, smelled the blood and urine.

Lynn Olson lay diagonally across the double bed closest to the door, facedown, fully clothed, his head twisted strangely to the right, away from them. One arm was outstretched; a chromed revolver lay on the floor under his hand. His wife lay on the next bed, rigidly, straight down the middle, shoeless but otherwise clothed. She was faceup, her head on a pillow, a red gunshot wound showing at her temple.

"Oh, fuck," Del said from behind Lucas.

They moved slowly into the room, both of them unconsciously pulling their weapons. The room was actually a small suite, with a sitting area off the main room. The bathroom was in the back. Lucas checked quickly, found it empty,

241

and went back to the main room.

Del, who'd stayed back, said, "Gun by the bed."

Lucas stepped toward Lynn Olson, touched his cheek: cold. He was dead, and had been dead for a while. There was no question about Lil Olson. They could see the spray from the gun-shot wound on the far side of her head where the slug had exited. Lucas knelt next to the gun, got his nose an inch away from it: a nine-millimeter. "I don't think that's the gun that was used on Plain," he said. "That was a pretty big crater in the concrete. I don't think a nine would do that."

"And I can't see the thread. Alie'e goes down, so somebody kills Plain. I can see that: revenge, especially after that photo spread. He's making a buck off Alie'e's death, and maybe some nut takes it the wrong way. Same thing with Corbeau: she's one of the sinners around Alie'e, one of the muff-divers. But the parents. I don't see the parents."

Lucas shook his head. From the hallway, they heard a voice. "Hello?"

Del went to the door, poked his head out. "Down here."

Two new Bloomington cops arrived a moment later, one in his twenties, the other graying, heavier. "Two dead," Lucas said. "We're gonna need the crime lab, big-time, and like right now."

The gray-haired one said, "I saw you on TV. On the Alie'e thing. Is this more of that?"

Lucas nodded. "These are Alie'e's parents."

The cop exhaled, hooked his thumbs over his belt, took another long look as though memorizing the scene. "Gotta hand it to you," he said, as though it were Lucas's doing. "This is some weird shit." He looked at his younger partner. "Call it in."

Lucas said, "I just thought of something. I'm gonna have to . . . I need Lynn Olson's billfold."

"Aw, man, I don't know," the older cop said. Crime scenes were not to be messed with.

"Yeah, I know, but I need it." Lucas stepped back inside the room, looked around, saw a plastic bag stuffed into an ice bucket, got it, and walked over to Olson's body. He could see the lump of the wallet in Olson's back pocket, carefully lifted the pocket flap, gripped the wallet through the plastic bag, and slipped it out. With the wallet inside the bag, he opened it, found the driver's license in a credit-card slot, and maneuvered it out.

"Could you call this in?" he asked the older cop. "Ask them to run Lynn Olson, DOB 2-23-44. He lives in Burnt River, Minnesota. We need cars registered to him."

Bloomington came back in thirty seconds. Olson had three cars: a new dark-blue Volvo, a two-year-old Ford Explorer, and a green 1968 Pontiac GTO.

"You guys got it," Lucas told the Bloomington cops. "We need to look for this car in the parking lot." And to Del: "Come on."

On the way down the stairs, Del said, "Marcy's gonna make it."

Lucas looked at him. "You didn't talk to anyone?"

"No, man. You bummed me out with that bad vibe. But *this* was the vibe. Not Marcy. You were getting a vibe from this."

"Del, you can't be smokin' that shit while you're working."

"Yeah, well, watch. She's good." He seemed marginally more cheerful.

They found the Olsons' car in a minute, the blue Volvo, much like Tom Olson's car but a decade newer. Lucas walked around to the passenger side, squeezing between the Volvo and a red Chevy Camaro. He saw the bullet hole before he got to the door, reached down and touched it. Hard to mistake, either by sight or feel.

"That's Olympic-quality shooting," Del said. He knelt in the narrow space to look at the hole, while Lucas turned to look back up the parking lot. Three Bloomington squad cars rounded the corner of the hotel, one after another, lights flashing, like a Shriners parade.

"I better call Rose Marie," he said. "I left my phone in the car."

Del handed him the cell phone, and he punched in Rose Marie's number. "This is Lucas," he said. "How is she?"

Lucas listened, Del peering at him. Lucas took the phone away from his ear and told him, "She's still on the table."

"She's okay," Del said, but now he sounded uncertain.

Lucas said to Rose Marie, "Okay. We've had a development down here."

🙠 16 🙢

While Del waited at the car, Lucas led the arriving Bloomington cops up the stairs to the Olsons' room, then violated the crime scene again. This time, over the Bloomington cops' protests, he took the Olsons' car keys off a dresser.

"The keys are completely out of the scene," he told them. "You won't get anything off the car keys. . . . But we need to look in their trunk."

"Yeah, but . . . ," the sergeant said uneasily. It was all against his training.

"Look, it's okay. I'll take the responsibility," Lucas said. "But I'd appreciate it if you could come down and watch while we open the car."

The sergeant agreed to walk along. Lucas opened the car trunk, found nothing but odd bits of traveling luggage — a camera bag, a half-full laundry bag, two golf clubs and a couple of loose balls, an open box of plastic garbage bags, an empty cooler, and, under a purple Minnesota Vikings jacket, a gray-metal toolbox.

"Looking for a big gun?" Del asked.

"If this is what it looks like, if this is murder-suicide . . . man, it'd make life easier," Lucas said.

He dipped into the box of garbage bags, pulled one out, ripped a couple of chunks out of it, made mittens out of the chunks and opened the toolbox. The top of the box was a lift-out tray with a socketwrench and sockets. He lifted the tray out. Tools. "Nothing," he said.

Del had taken the keys out of the truck to open the passenger-side door. "I don't see anything."

Del stood up. "But the hole in the door . . . This could clean up Marcy and probably Plain. Revenge shootings. Either that or . . ."

"What?"

"What if Lynn Olson was trying to fuck his daughter, and something happened? He was drunk at the party . . . and maybe Lansing . . . I don't know."

"Where'd Plain come into it?" Lucas asked, thinking it over.

"Maybe he saw something?"

"Why wouldn't he tell us? He said he didn't like them much, the whole crowd around Alie'e."

"I don't know," Del said.

They stayed at the motel for an hour, watched the preliminary crime-scene work, and made arrangements for a statement for the Bloomington cops.

"You gotta do the gun right now," Lucas said as a crime-scene tech crawled over the room. "It may be the gun used to shoot Marcy Sherrill."

"We'll have it in a couple of hours, no more," the tech said. "Have they taken a bullet out of her?"

"I don't know." Lucas called to ask, and was told that both bullets that hit Sherrill had done clean pass-throughs. Another crime-scene team was at Jael Corbeau's studio, trying to recover a slug from what looked like a bullet hole in a wooden railing. Jael was still at the hospital.

A cluster of television camera trucks had appeared at a diner across the street. Bloomington was keeping them away from the motel, and a Bloomington cop had moved Lucas's Porsche back into the lot. As they left the motel, Lucas could see sudden movement among the cameramen, the cameras going up on their shoulders.

"We're about to go on TV," he said. Del dipped his head and stepped behind Lucas. At the car, he kept his head down, one hand over his face. As they pulled out of the parking lot, a TV truck pulled out behind them in pursuit. Lucas lost it on the interstate, cutting through evening traffic like a shark.

They'd made the phone checks: Sherrill was still on the table. She'd taken a lot of blood, but the prognosis had improved. Tom Olson was asleep. He'd been disoriented at the hospital, his body overcome with shock. He'd been sedated.

North of town, at James Bee's house, the cops had cleaned out the computers and the Rolodex. There'd been one cross-match between the Rolodex and the names on the party list from Silly Hanson's, and a competent Minneapolis cop named Loring was running down the cross. The cops at Bee's house also found three ounces of cocaine in a bedroom. Bee claimed it belonged to his wife, the blonde, who denied it. They were both being transported to the county jail.

They still had the outstanding warrant for the second house, but Del shook his head: "Everything's too heavy right how," he said. "If we need it, let's do it tomorrow. Let's go talk to Bee — maybe he'll give us what we need."

"Let's stop at the hospital first."

"Yeah, well — I assumed that," Del said.

They weren't allowed to look into the operating room, and Sherrill was still on the table.

"Jesus, how long's it been?" Lucas asked Rose Marie.

Rose Marie had taken an empty hospital room, and was working two separate patient telephones. She looked at her watch. "Four hours."

"How much more can they have to do?"

"I don't know what they've done, Lucas. Look . . . go away. Go do something."

"Like what?" he asked.

"I don't care, but this isn't good for you." She looked at Del. "You either."

Del said, "So let's go talk to Bee."

Bee was with his lawyer. Lucas knocked on the door, poked his head in. "Wanted you to know . . . we're looking for some information and we might be able to talk."

"I don't think so," the lawyer said. "Your search warrant is a piece of toilet paper."

"Au contraire," Del said. "That thing is a piece of gold. Your client here is going straight to jail, and he won't be passing Go."

Bee looked troubled. He said, "I don't think I've exactly got a problem. For one thing, it wasn't my cocaine, it was Connie's. But say I wanted to help Connie . . . what would you need to know?"

"We're trying to find out who was running Sandy Lansing, the woman killed with Alie'e Maison. She was dealing, but she was retail. We're looking for the guy behind her."

Bee shrugged. "Let me talk to Ralph here. I don't know if I could help you even if I wanted to. But let me talk to Ralph."

"Talk to Ralph," Lucas said. And to Ralph: "I understand you've been shootin' beaver again."

Ralph grinned and said, "Shhh," and Bee said, "What?"

Ralph said, "I got a little beaver problem up at my cabin."

"Larry Connell said about once an hour he'd hear a high-powered rifle," Lucas said.

"Deer season's coming up," the lawyer said. "I need the practice. And those fuckin' beaver, if they block up that creek, it's gonna flood my whole property. Goddamn rodents. I hate them almost as much as I hate the DNR."

"What beaver?" Bee asked.

"Talk to you later," Lucas said.

"You know what you dumb shits did?" Bee said. "You took the one guy who'd know about this for sure — you took and put him in prison. He hates your ass, and he ain't never gonna talk to you."

Del said, "What?" and he and Lucas looked at each other, then simultaneously said, "Rashid Al-Balah."

Outside, Lucas said, "We gotta nail down that poker game. If Trick's gonna be anywhere, that'd be it."

"Gimme two hours," Del said. "You going back to the hospital?"

"Yeah."

"Turn on your cell phone."

"Okay."

"No. I wanna see you do it," Del said.

Lucas took out the cell phone and turned it on. Del took out his, punched a speed-dial code, and Lucas's phone buzzed. "Satisfied?"

"Keep it on," Del said. "I don't want to be kicking down the door of a high-stakes game by myself."

Lucas walked through the tunnel to the government center and took an elevator up to the county attorney's office. Randall Towson was in conference. Lucas got him out, into a hallway.

"What's going on?" Towson asked. He was

holding a printout of what looked like a financial spreadsheet.

"Have you talked to Al-Balah's attorney about Del bumping into Trick Bentoin?"

"Not yet, but I can't put it off much longer," Towson said.

"Could you call him now?" Lucas asked. "And tell him that we've lost Trick, and can't do anything yet, but we're looking. And that we might want to talk to Al-Balah tomorrow."

"Makes us look retarded," Towson said. "He'll be calling the papers two minutes after he hangs up."

"We really need to talk to Al-Balah," Lucas said. "It's the Maison case."

He gave Towson a quick explanation, and Towson said finally, "All right. I gotta call him anyway. I'll do it right now. You sure you'll find Bentoin?"

"No. But Del's heard that it's a big game, and that normally would be a magnet for the guy. Even if he's not there, somebody else at the game might know where he is."

"How's Marcy?"

"I'm going over there now. She was still on the table, the last I heard."

"Listen, she's gonna make it," Towson said. He knew that Lucas and Marcy had had a relationship. "She's in good shape, and once they get her on the table . . ."

"Yeah, well. I hope."

"She's gonna make it, man."

At the hospital, Lucas nodded at a couple of loitering cops and headed straight for the desk. A nurse saw him coming, shook her head, and said, "She's still not out, but Dr. Gunderson came out for a Coke and said they've got almost everything hooked up again. It shouldn't be much longer."

"She's doing okay?"

The nurse equivocated. "She's doing as good as she could. I understand . . ." She looked both ways, as though worried she might be caught giving out unauthorized information.

"Yeah, yeah?"

"I understand that the bullet hit her just below her breast and a couple of inches off the center-line, so there's a lung problem and they've got a problem with bone splinters from her ribs, but there's no spinal involvement. I think if they've got the bleeding under control and if she's strong enough, she should make it. That's what *I* think, but I'm not in there."

"Bless you," Lucas said. "She's pretty strong."

He headed down to the room that Rose Marie had commandeered, and found her talking with Frank Lester.

"Anything new?" Lester asked.

"Maybe the edge of something," Lucas said. "How about you? And where's Jael?"

"You talk first."

Lucas gave them a quick account of the raid on Bee's house, Bee's suggestion that Al-Balah might come up with the name, and Del's search for Trick Bentoin. Rose Marie took it all in and said, finally, "You're still about three levels away from the killer."

"Or maybe four or five," Lucas said. "Where's Jael?"

"We had Franklin take her back to her place to get some clothes. We're gonna ditch her someplace safe, maybe over in Hudson, keep her covered. She wants to talk to you again. I think she blames herself for what happened to Marcy."

"Good — keep her out of the way," Lucas said. "What'd you get?"

The police shrink, Angela Harris, had come in to talk with Lester an hour earlier, after she'd heard about the death of Alie'e's parents. "She doesn't think it's a murder-suicide," Lester said.

"She knows about the bullet hole in the car door?"

"Yeah, but she's predicting that we'll find the killings weren't murder-suicide. She thinks that they were killed in revenge for the murder of Alie'e. Along with Plain, and along with the attempt on Corbeau, if that's what it was. She thinks we need to take another very close look at Tom Olson. She's talked to some guys who know him, and he's apparently had some odd psychological episodes in the past that suggest he may have multiple personalities. Harris thinks one of the personalities is a psycho."

"Aw, man. That's too weird," Lucas said.

"Yeah, but she says it explains what happened

with the parents. Olson gets in psycho mode, and starts eliminating people who he blames for killing Alie'e — people who led her into her life-style with dope and lesbians and all that. The tabloid pictures set him off: the rouged nipples and all of that, some kind of psychosexual trip with his sister.

"So he goes after Plain, then he goes for Corbeau because of this lesbian stuff that's been coming out — he hits Marcy instead, but he was going for Corbeau. Then he kills his parents, the people who are really responsible for putting her in this life . . . and we *know* he blames them for that. Then, having killed them, he wanders off in psychological exhaustion to the mall, changes personalities. This personality has no idea what the other personality did . . . and then in that same personality comes back to the motel, runs into you, then goes up to his parents' room and finds the bodies. He comes running after you, but in the shock, he begins to disassociate."

"Disassociate?"

"Fuck me, I don't know," Lester said. "That's what she said."

"He falls apart," Rose Marie said. "Some-where, his main personality knows what he did but can't handle it. So his whole jury-rigged per-sona starts falling to pieces. He has what you saw — some kind of fit."

Lucas thought about it, then said, "He'd have access to his father's car. If it's not murder-suicide . . ."

"We thought about that. What we're doing right now is waiting for the crime-scene guys and the ME to finish down there. If they say it's a murder-suicide, then we slow down a little; if they say it's not, then we look at Olson. He's not going anyplace; he's asleep, in the hospital. The paramedics said the shock really got on top of him."

"All right," Lucas said. "Things are looking a little better for Marcy."

Rose Marie nodded. "She's gonna make it, Lucas."

They all thought about that for a minute, and Lucas felt a finger of darkness — the first premonition of the day. But he didn't say anything. He said, "There's a science thing that I picked up from the computer jocks I used to work with."

"Yeah?" Lester asked.

"Yeah. If you have enough information to make a good prediction, then you're probably getting a grip on the situation. If Harris is predicting that the Olsons aren't a murder-suicide, despite appearances, then maybe she's onto something."

"You oughta talk to your girlfriend the nun," Rose Marie said.

"I'll call her," Lucas said.

He hung around awhile, watching Rose Marie work the telephones. Lester went out and got a Diet Coke and brought one back for Lucas. They were talking about nothing, waiting, when

Lucas's cell phone rang.

"It's Del," Lucas said, fumbling the phone out of his pocket.

But it wasn't Del. A surprised dispatcher said, "Is this Lucas?"

"It's me. I mean, it's my phone, anyway."

"How come you're answering the phone?"

"I'm running around. . . . What's going on?"

"I'm relaying a message from the Maplewood cops. They found that car you were looking for."

"Car?"

"Yeah, that, uh, I wrote the name. . . . Derrick Deal?"

"Oh, yeah." From about ten years ago. He looked at his watch: six hours, two more dead bodies, one shot cop. "Where was it?"

"In some executive's reserved spot out in a 3M parking lot."

"At 3M?" And he thought, *Uh-oh.*

"Yes. That's what they say. They want to know what you want to do with it."

"Can you patch me through? To the cop?"

"Uh, just a minute . . ." A few seconds later, she came back. "I talked to them, and the executive whose space it is has a cell phone in his pocket, so you can call them directly. He's standing right there with them."

The executive's name was Marx; he sounded interested. "The car's been here since yesterday. I finally called the cops, the police, to get it towed, because I was getting angry about it. They say it's on some kind of hit list."

"Yeah . . . lemme talk to the cop."

The cop came up, and when Lucas identified himself, said, "Hey, Chief, what's happening with the car?"

Lucas gave him a quick story and asked, "Is there anything unusual about it?"

"Yeah, one thing — you can see the keys on the floor of the driver's side. A key ring. They might've fallen out when he got out, and he locked it behind him."

"Nothing else?"

"Nope. The car's clean. Nothing else inside that we can see, except some maps and a *Wall Street Journal* on the floor of the backseat."

"Listen, this has to do with the Maison case . . . and that car could be pretty important. I wonder if I could get you to open the door and use the keys to pop the trunk."

"Jeez, I don't know. We don't carry the door openers anymore," the cop said.

"How about if you break the window? It's pretty important."

"Aw, man . . . I'd have to call in. Can I get back to you?"

"Can I hold?"

"Sure, just take a second."

While the cop was calling in, Lucas said to Lester, "I'm gonna start using this phone, and then people are gonna start calling me on it, and pretty soon I'll be as crazy as the rest of you fuckers."

"It feels kind of good after a while," Lester said. "People call you up, you feel important. Pretty soon, you start thinking about a beeper."

"Yeah, in a pig's eye," Lucas said.

"You just haven't experienced it yet," Lester said. "The connectivity rush."

Franklin leaned into the doorway, and Lucas and Lester both looked up at him. Lucas said, "I thought you were with Jael Corbeau."

"She's right there," Franklin said, pointing to his left. "Talking to a nurse. I can shoot the nurse, if you want."

"That's okay," Rose Marie said. Franklin asked about Marcy, and Rose Marie began filling him in.

Then the Maplewood cop called back and said, "Listen, Chief, my chief wants to talk with you. You got a number he can call?"

"Hang on," Lucas said. He handed the phone to Lester and said, "Give him your cell-phone number."

Lester read his number off, then handed the phone back to Lucas. Lucas could hear the Maplewood cop repeating the number to somebody else, and a second later, Lester's phone rang. He handed it to Lucas, who said, "Hello?"

The Maplewood chief asked, "If we bust this car, are we gonna get sued?"

"There's a suspicion of foul play, so we really don't want to move it, just in case," Lucas said, rolling his eyes at Lester. "We'll take responsibility. If the city won't, I'll pay for the window myself."

"On your head," the Maplewood chief said, and Lucas could hear him talking in the background. He put his own phone to his ear, and the Maplewood cop at 3M said, "Okay, we're gonna bust it."

Lucas said, "If you gotta pick up the keys, use gloves. Just in case." In his other ear, the Maplewood chief said, "Take it easy," and Lucas said, "Yeah, thanks," and handed the phone back to Lester, while the cop was saying, "We can leave the keys. I can see a trunk latch."

From 3M, Lucas heard a crunch, then a door, and the Maplewood cop said, "We're popping the trunk." And a moment later, "Ah, shit."

Lester, who'd been looking at Lucas's face, asked, "What?" and Franklin and Rose Marie, hearing the tone, stopped talking and looked at Lucas. Then the Maplewood cop came back and said, "I hope this guy ain't a friend of yours."

"Aw, man." Lucas stood up. "What does it look like?"

"Looks like somebody busted him in the head with a shovel. He's way dead."

"Little guy? Maybe sixty? Long haircut for his age?"

"Yeah. You got him. What's the deal?"

Lucas looked at Rose Marie and said, "We got another one. I don't think it's about Alie'e. I think it's about Sandy Lansing."

"Is this about Maison?" the cop asked in his ear.

"So where does Alie'e's family fit in?" Rose Marie asked.

"Maybe Tom Olson is on a revenge trip — but the first killings, that started it off, that's about Lansing."

"Who're you talking to?" the Maplewood cop asked.

To Rose Marie, Lucas said, "Just a minute," and into the phone, "I'll be out there in a few minutes. Exactly where're you at?" He made a mental note of the address, and hung up.

"Can we avoid talking about Deal?" Lester asked. "To the media?"

"I don't think so. The Maplewood cops know we're talking about Alie'e, and you know — word's gonna get out."

"We've had a cop shot and four killings in one day." Rose Marie looked at Lester and then Franklin and back to Lucas. "What're we gonna do?"

Lucas left them, found Jael huddled next to the nurses' station, Franklin standing by the outer door. Jael saw him and stood up, and Lucas said, "How are . . ." Jael reached around his neck with both arms and put her head against his chest and hung on.

"I'm coming apart," she said after a while. "I can't do this."

17

Derrick Deal was distinctly deceased; the Maplewood cop hadn't been lying when he said he looked like he'd been hit with a shovel. The cop played a flashlight over Deal's face. The left side of his forehead and left eye socket had been crushed, and another indentation followed the line of his eyebrows across the right side of his face. Deal's right eyebrow looked like a stepped-on millipede, while his left one was gone entirely.

"Wasn't a shovel, though," Lucas said, looking at the body. "Looks like he was hit with a chair."

"You think so?"

"Yeah. I once went to a killing where this guy hit his old lady with a kitchen chair. He said he thought it was gonna break, like they do in the movies. He might as well of hit her with a pipe. Her face looked just like this." He pointed at the dent leading out the right side of Deal's face. "I'll bet you it was an old wooden chair. The other guy swung it by the back, just like in the movies, and hit him in the face with the edge of the seat. One of the legs busted his brow ridge. You might find a mark from the other leg on his neck, or his chest."

"I'll tell the ME," the cop said. "I never seen a chair job."

Lucas stood around the melancholy scene until the ME got there, and convinced a crime-scene guy to check Deal's pockets. They found a wallet with eight dollars, two dollars and eleven cents in change, a withdrawal slip for twenty-five dollars from an ATM, and a small black-leather card case. The case had a dozen cards from Brown's Hotel.

"No address book?" Lucas asked.

"I don't find one," the crime-scene cop said.

Lucas took a last, pensive look at the dead man's crushed face, got in his car, and started toward Deal's town house.

Deal had known something. Lucas had seen it in his face when he went to talk with him, but hadn't known what Deal was lying about. After Lucas left him in the hotel, Deal probably had gone out looking for a little schmear. A few bucks to meet the rent, or whatever needed meeting. But it wasn't nice to blackmail a killer, who had nothing to lose. . . . But now they had a connection. Deal had known the killer, or had known how to make a connection to get to him. They weren't three steps away anymore. One step, and they'd have him.

The Maplewood cops had already opened Deal's town house. The place was a melancholy collection of small cubicles, an efficient, uninflected space for sleeping, eating, and watching television. He had no computer; nor could they find an address book or Rolodex. There had to be one, unless the killer had taken it.

Lucas lingered at the house until he was sure there was no more to find, then headed for Brown's Hotel. On the way, he called the hospital. They'd finished with Marcy, Rose Marie told him, but she wasn't out of the operating room yet. They were rigging her up for intensive care.

"The doc thinks she's gonna make it," Rose Marie said. "They're gonna keep her under for a while, though. They don't want her popping anything loose."

A knot in Lucas's neck loosened a notch. "Good. As long as there's no heart involvement."

"It was lower than that, lower than what we heard. The slug went in below her breast at an outward angle, so it came out almost on her side. She must've been turning sideways when it hit her."

"What about the slug in the railing? Have they ID'd it yet?"

"They got it, but it's wrecked. We won't be able to ID the gun. They can say it's a .44 Magnum jacketed hollowpoint."

"Then it's a different gun than the Bloomington gun," Lucas said. "And if it was a murder-suicide, why'd they bother to hide the big one?"

At Brown's, the good-looking black woman was working behind the reception desk. When she saw Lucas come in, she said a word to the woman working with her and slipped out. Lucas glanced at her name tag and remembered: India. She said, "We heard about Derrick. Is it because you talked with him?"

"I don't know," Lucas said. "But I need to look at his desk. I can get a search warrant, or we can just go look."

"Can I ask the manager this time?"

"If you have to. But I want to go down and stand by Derrick's cubicle while you ask," Lucas said.

"I'll go ask," she said. And "I'm sorry, but my job . . ."

"Sure."

Lucas went down to Deal's office space. Another man was sitting in a cubicle, three down from Deal's, working with an old mechanical adding machine. He glanced at Lucas and said, "Can I help you?"

"Waiting for the manager."

"You the police?"

"Yup."

The man leaned back from his chair. He was Deal's age, and like Deal, a little heavy, balding, with wiry black hair on his arms. He locked his hands behind his head and said, "I don't know exactly what he was up to, but he seemed a little shady. He always had get-rich-quick deals."

"You know anybody who bit?" Lucas asked.

"No, not around here. He did not exactly inspire confidence."

"He was not that bad a guy, though."

"Hey, some of the best guys I know sell used cars. They've all got big deals cooking somewhere. I like them, but I'd never put my money with them."

The outer door opened, and a tall man in a dark blue suit came through, trailed by India. The man had a beaked nose, close-set water-green eyes, and a black — too black — widow's peak. He resembled Prince Philip just a little, and must've known it, because he had a red silk handkerchief peeking from his breast pocket. He looked Lucas up and down, and before the manager had a chance to open his mouth, Lucas didn't like him.

"You're the police?" As if he doubted it. "Do you have identification?" He had a perfect, round, baritone English voice.

"Yeah, but you usually don't want to flash the old buzzer in a high-class joint like this," Lucas said, looking around the room, as if the ceiling tiles might turn hostile. India's eyes cut sideways at him, and the corners of her mouth twitched. Lucas flipped open his ID, held it in front of the manager's eyes, and said, "We can lay some paper on you if you want. Otherwise, I'll just take a quick gander at Derrick's desk."

"Well, I don't think you need a search warrant. We're all anxious to help find out what happened with Derrick," the manager said. He tilted his head back, the better to peer down his nose. "He'd reformed, you know. He was doing so well."

Lucas shrugged. "So maybe it was an accident."

The manager lifted an eyebrow, just one. "We heard he was found locked in a car trunk, with his face smashed in."

Lucas nodded judiciously. "Maybe you're right. Probably wasn't an accident. I never thought so, myself." He was getting tired of it. "So I can look around?"

"I'd like to leave a staff member with you." Prince Philip tipped his head at India.

"Sure . . . no problem."

When he was gone, India giggled and asked, "Where'd you get that accent?"

"Where'd he get his?" Lucas asked as they walked down to Deal's desk.

"Same place as Cary Grant."

"Really? Cary Grant?"

"They were both born in Bristol. England."

"Yeah?" He'd spotted an old-fashioned plastic Rolodex on Deal's desk. "And this" — he touched the Rolodex — "is what I've been looking for."

He found a name, two-thirds of the way through the Rolodex. He checked it twice: Terrance Bloom. He checked the printed party list to confirm it, then called Lester at Homicide.

"I'm looking at Derrick Deal's Rolodex and I find the name Terrance Bloom, and Bloom is on the party list."

"Give me the address and phone number," Lester said.

Lucas read them off the Rolodex, and Lester, rattling on some computer keys, said, "Hang on a sec. I'm just bringing the screen up. . . ." Then: "Yup, that's him."

"We gotta get on him," Lucas said. "This could be something."

"Hang on, hang on. . . ." Lucas hung on for another moment, listening to the computer keys at the other end of the line, then Lester again: "He's not on Lansing's phone list."

"Shit."

"Well — that could be deliberate, if he's her guy. She probably wouldn't need it, and he wouldn't want her carrying it."

"Yeah, but . . . listen, put somebody good on it. This is the first hint we've had."

"Absolutely. Did you hear about Marcy? I mean, going into intensive care?"

"Yeah, that's the last I heard."

"Same with me. . . . She's gonna make it."

"If there's any goddamn justice in the world. Talk to you later."

Lucas spent fifteen minutes with India, going through Deal's computer, but Deal apparently didn't use e-mail, and Lucas couldn't find any data files. There had to be some, but they could be on a removable disk. He closed the computer down, stuck a handwritten note that said, "Don't use — Minneapolis police" on the monitor screen, and said, "I'm sending a computer guy over here to take a look at this thing. Don't let anybody touch it, okay?"

"I'll tell Philip," she said.

"Who's he?"

"The manager?"

"Honest to God? Philip?"

Del called when Lucas was on the way back to the hospital. "I got the game. Started last night, continues until five a.m. tomorrow. Twenty-five grand to get in." That was good. They had Bloom's name now, but there was no guarantee that Bloom was their guy. They still needed Trick — and Al-Balah.

"Where at?"

"Pat Kelly. Remember him?"

"Yeah. . . . Where's he at now?"

"Bought a place down on the south end, right on Minnehaha Creek. He's got a brand-new two-story fully-heated triple garage in his back-yard. The word is, it's upstairs in the garage."

"Going on now?" Lucas asked.

"Yup. Want to meet me?"

"Absolutely. Let's get . . . uh, what's Franklin doing?"

"He's still with Corbeau," Del said.

"How about Loring?"

"I saw him early today, so he's probably off — but he's always up for overtime."

"Give him a ring. I'll meet you at Pasties in an hour."

Rose Marie had gone home, but a night nurse at the hospital let Lucas look in on Marcy. She was half propped up in a bed, a breathing tube in her nose, more tube in her arms, wires scrambled around the top of the bed, running to monitors. She smelled of disinfectant and something else: corruption, or cut flesh. Lucas knew the odor, but had never been able to put a name to it.

He sat down on a chair next to the bed, watched her breathe for five minutes, then said, "We got a couple of things going, couple of leads." You're gonna make it. We talked to the docs. But you gotta keep sleeping for now." Maybe she could understand it, somewhere down in her brain. He backed out of the room, turned, and nearly ran over a woman who'd been standing by the door.

"Lucas," she said, and showed a tiny smile.

"Weather." His heart thumped. That hardly ever happened anymore; now, three times in three days, with Catrin, with Jael Corbeau. "I was just . . . Marcy . . . you know."

"I heard. I was coming down to take a look," Weather said. She was a small woman, with wide athletic shoulders and a slightly crooked nose that might have been just a shade too large. Her eyes were dark blue, her short hair just touched with white. She'd be thirty-eight, Lucas thought. And, God, she looked good. "I talked to Hirschfeld — he did the surgery — and he said she's got a good chance. She was pretty torn up when she first came in, and he was worried, but they got it together."

"She was hit hard."

"Another nutcase, Lucas. They keep coming."
She was a surgeon. She saw the victims, especially the children.

"Four times a year, about," Lucas said. "Crime's down. Burglary's down, rape's down, robbery's down, even murder's down, except for nutcases."

"Everybody's getting too old for crime," she said.

"Everybody's got a job," Lucas said. "Jobs cure everything. And crack's going away. . . ."

She looked up at him — she was a small woman, with shoulders that were slightly too broad, like an acrobat's — and asked, "What're we talking about?"

"I don't know."

"Want a cup of coffee?"

"I've gotta go. I'm running down south, I've got a door to kick down," Lucas said.

Now she did smile. "Lucas. So see you around, huh?"

He didn't say anything for a few seconds, then: "Really?"

"If you've got the time . . . sometime."

"Anytime," he said. "Anytime but now. I just gotta, I just gotta . . . go." He backed away from her as he'd backed out of the room, backed up almost to the outer door, then turned and pushed through.

Behind him, Weather's smile softened; she'd heard him talking to Marcy. In that few seconds, she thought, something had changed. Maybe . . .

Lucas drove south through town, replaying the talk with Weather. Played it once, played it again. What she looked like, what she sounded like. She'd once owned a dress that she planned to wear for her wedding to Lucas; that hadn't happened. The relationship had dissolved in blood, in the very hospital where they'd talked, where Marcy had gone under the knife; another nutcase who'd died for his efforts. Weather Karkinnen. She'd wanted kids, two or three. . . .

Pasties was an all-night greasy spoon off Lyndale Avenue. When it first opened, it sold indigestible meat pies, but now it was all fried bacon, fried sausage, and fried hamburger, with home fries or french fries and catsup, and suspicious-looking pecan pie. Lettuce was not in demand; the coffee was mediocre. On the other hand, it was open all night, had racks of free papers inside the front door, and nobody cared if a customer spent an hour drinking a cup of coffee.

Del was deep in conversation with the counterman when Lucas showed up. He broke off the conversation and they took a booth, and the counterman followed him over with a plastic carafe of coffee and two cups. The counterman was tubercularly thin, with round John Lennon glasses and shaggy hair; he was rolling an unlit, unfiltered cigarette between his dry lips. "Anyway, that's what happened," he told Del. He shook his head. "Shoulda known better. He said

272

he only wanted to stay a couple of days."

"I'll tell you what — those accordion guys are sneakier than they look," Del said. "Some of that music is pretty damn romantic. The *Blue Skirt Waltz*? You know that one? And you *know* women like to dance."

"I wouldn't have no more suspected him than I would've suspected a . . . a . . . banjo player or something."

"Coulda been worse," Del said.

"Yeah? How?"

"She could've run off with one of the Eagles."

The bartender didn't laugh. He shook his head and shuffled back to the counter. Del looked at Lucas and said, "Love problems."

Lucas didn't want to hear that. He said, "Did you find Loring?"

"Yeah, he'll be here anytime. Did you stop at the hospital?"

"She looks like shit, Del. Her skin's the color of a piece of paper."

"She's gonna make it," Del said.

"She had about a million units of blood. It was running out of her as fast as they could put it in."

"Look, they stopped the bleeding, right? That's most of it with that kind of wound. Stop the bleeding."

"Yeah." Suddenly Lucas felt tired. He hadn't gotten much sleep since he'd left his cabin three days before, and now it jumped him. And he felt greasy, he thought. Literally greasy, like he needed to shower, right now. He took a sip of the coffee. It lived up to its billing: mediocre. "This isn't fun anymore."

"Was it ever?"

"Of course it was," Lucas said. "When all we had was Alie'e and Lansing — all the goddamn media pouring in, all the attention, everybody running around — that was kind of fun."

"I'd pick a different word."

"Fuck it — it was *fun*. You were enjoying yourself, Del. So was I. So were the mayor and Rose Marie. Right up to when Marcy was shot."

"Yeah, well . . ."

They were talking aimlessly, pointlessly, when Loring came in. Loring was a very large man; nature had given him square teeth and a naturally mean expression. He was wearing a black raincoat over jeans and brown penny loafers. He got a coffee cup from the counterman, slid in next to Del, poured a cup of coffee, and stirred in a couple of ounces of sugar.

"Pat Kelly," Lucas said.

"Yeah. He's got that three-stall garage. He's been doing a game or two every month. Supposed to be a nice layout," Loring said.

"You been inside?" Lucas asked.

"No, but I heard about it. There's a back door, then some stairs, and a door at the top of the stairs. There's a toilet up there, and a refrigerator and a Coke machine full of cold drinks and beer. Big table. Kelly deals."

"Security?"

"Depends. I asked, but the guy I asked said he didn't see any," Loring said. "That was small stakes, two or three grand. If Del's right about this one, and they got seven guys playing, then there's a hundred and seventy-five thousand in cash on the table. So — probably security."

"Don't want to go walking into some asshole with an AK," Del said. He yawned, and poured out the last of the coffee.

"Kelly's too smart for that," Loring said. "His security would be good."

"Hate bad security," Del said. "Some god-damned workout fag with a baseball hat and a gun."

"That's why I wanted Loring," Lucas said. "We can stand behind him."

"I thought it was my brains, and it was my body all the time," Loring said.

Pat Kelly's house was on a narrow tree-lined street where the cheapest hovel went for a half-million dollars. His house was shingled with cedar; the cedar had turned old and dark over the years. One yellow light was visible through the front-room curtains, a lamp with a white shade and fringe. A double driveway led toward the back, where a hulking garage peeked out from behind the house. The garage had been built in the same style as the house, but the shingles were paler, redder. New. The only light near the garage was on the house's back porch — a yellow light, the kind that's supposed to discourage insects.

They parked their cars down the street, hooked up, and walked toward the drive. "No light in the garage," Lucas said.

"Made that way," Loring said. "No windows. You drive by, it looks like anything but a casino."

"Looks like a rich dude's house," Del said.

They turned up the drive, shoulder to shoulder, and unconsciously began spreading out, and each of them touched his own hip as they walked, feeling for the tender comfort of a gun. They were passing the house when a voice in the dark called, "Can we help you gentlemen?"

"Police officers," Lucas said toward the voice. How many was "we"? No way to tell. "We're looking for a particular player."

"Do you have some ID?"

Lucas still couldn't spot the voice. He could feel Del edging farther away from him on one side, Loring idling away on the other, an inch at a time, so they wouldn't all get taken down with a single burst. A little stress. He grinned and held up his card case. "Lucas Davenport," he said. "And friends."

The voice spoke softly — into a cell phone, Lucas thought — and two minutes later, a side door opened on the garage. Pat Kelly stepped out, a thin, white-haired man wearing a white dress shirt open at the throat. He looked tentatively down the driveway and said, "Davenport?"

"Yeah. Me and Loring and Del."

"Jesus, like old home week. What's going on?"

"You got Trick Bentoin up there?"

"What's he done?"

"You got him?" Lucas asked.

"Well . . ."

"So we'll just run up and get him," Lucas said.

"You're gonna scare the shit out of my guests," Kelly said. "We're just a bunch of friends."

"Yeah, yeah, yeah," Lucas said impatiently. "Look, you heard this lady cop got shot this afternoon?"

"Yeah? What's that got to do with Trick?"

"Something," Lucas said. "So we're gonna go up."

"Why don't I just ask him to step down?"

"Nah. If people knew exactly what was going on, they might start running. We're gonna have to go up, Pat. I guess it's up to you how we do it."

Kelly shook his head. "Hey, if you wanna go up, you're the cops."

They found seven guys sitting around an empty green-baize table on a beige carpet. There was no money in sight, no chips, no cards — an air of innocence smudged with cigar smoke. A television in the corner was tuned to ESPN; Trick Bentoin's chair was turned toward the TV. With the exception of Trick, the guys were all beefy, and every one of them wore a dress shirt. Suit jackets and sport coats hung off the back of plain wooden chairs. Trick was thin, and looked a little like a cowboy in a cigarette ad.

"Trick," Lucas said. "You gotta cash out. We need you downtown."

"Me?" He was surprised. The other six players looked at him.

"Yeah, it's that Rashid Al-Balah thing," Lucas said.

"Man, we're right in the middle of *Sports* . . ."

"*Sports* what?" Del asked.

"*Sports Talk?*"

"Sorry, that's the radio," Del said. "And the only goddamn place you ever watched sports was a book in Las Vegas. Come on along."

"What if I told you I was on a roll?" Trick asked.

"You could just ask the guys to wait until you get back," Loring said.

One of the guys grunted, "Huh," and a couple of them grinned.

"Sorry. We need you," Lucas said. He looked at the other men — other than the single grunt, none of them had said a single word, or had met his eyes — and said, "We'll wait at the bottom of the stairs."

Pat Kelly followed them down. "That was relatively civilized," he said.

"This is a nice place," Lucas said. "But . . . don't push it."

"I never push," Kelly said genially. "Never, ever."

Trick Bentoin appeared a minute later, pulling on a rumpled jacket, shook his head, and said, "Down four."

"I thought you were on a roll," Lucas said.

"I was. I'd been down nine. Another two hours, I'd of owned their asses, each and every one." He looked at the three cops and said, "Well, I'm not gonna run. What're we doing?"

"We need to haul your ass out to Stillwater tomorrow, for a little discussion with Rashid Al-Balah."

"You could've called," Trick said. "I would've come in."

"Couldn't find you. Didn't even know you were at the game for sure. And if we'd called, and you'd found it inconvenient . . ." Lucas let his voice trail away.

"So you're gonna put me in the fuckin' jail?" Trick asked.

"Well," Lucas said, "we don't want to take a chance."

"That's such a pain in the ass. I'll get some psycho up all night screaming. I need some sleep."

"I got a spare bedroom," Loring said. "If you really won't run."

"I won't run," Trick said. "You guys know me better than that."

Lucas thought about it for a minute, then said, "All right. Let's do that. Then we won't have any bullshit, either, checking him in."

"You want me to bring him over to your place?" Loring asked. "I'm up early tomorrow."

"I'll be down at the office about eight. Let's meet there," Lucas said. "I'll make some calls tonight and get the interview set up."

Del said, "I'll be there, too. I'll come out to Stillwater with you."

"Marcy's gonna be okay," Loring said.

"Yeah. I just don't want any early calls tomorrow," Lucas said. "No goddamn early calls."

❧ 18 ❧

Tuesday. Fourth day of the case.

As beaten up as he was, he hadn't been able to sleep. Hadn't been able to drive Marcy out of his head, or Weather. Or Catrin. And Jael Corbeau was there in a corner, watching. He even thought about standing in the barnyard with Mrs. Clay, the night he delivered the fishing boat, and what might've happened with their lives in other circumstances.

And he thought about the Olsons, dead together in the hotel, and their son, running toward the highway, pulling his hair out to the sides of his head, as though trying to pull a devil out of his skull.

He hadn't been able to sleep, but somehow must have, for a while. He might have been asleep, he thought, when the alarm went off, and shook him out of bed — it was one of those nights when he couldn't tell whether he was awake or only dreaming that he was awake, the dreams punctuated by the liquid green light from the clock as he touched it at two, three, four, and five o'clock. He didn't remember touching it at six, and now at seven the alarm went. . . .

Marcy. He called the hospital and identified himself. She was still listed as critical, in intensive care. Still alive, still asleep. He stood in the shower for ten minutes, slowly waking up. Drove out to a SuperAmerica store for a shot of coffee. Rolled into the parking ramp a few minutes after eight.

Loring was waiting in homicide with Trick Bentoin. "Del called. He's on the way," Loring said. "He says to turn on your cell phone."

"Yeah, yeah."

Del looked as beat up as Lucas felt, grinned when he arrived, said, "Well, you look like shit," and Lucas said, "So that's two of us." Del asked, "Have you been to the hospital?"

"No. I called. She's still asleep."

"Let's go over for a minute," Del said. "You can get more face-to-face."

They walked over in the cold morning, breathing steam into the air. The streets were crowded with cheerful going-to-work people. Not long, Lucas thought, before Thanksgiving and then Christmas.

"Christmas coming," Del said, picking up the thought.

At the hospital, they got almost nothing from the nurses, because the nurses knew almost nothing.

"Let's go see if Weather's in," Lucas suggested.

"Yeah?" Dell looked at him curiously. Weather couldn't look at Lucas; not last year, anyway.

Had something changed?

"Yeah. Come on."

Weather was in the women's locker room. A nurse went in and got her, and she came out in her scrubs and booties. She said, " 'Lo, Del. You're looking like . . . you look a little tired."

"Thanks," Del said dryly.

Lucas asked, "You talk to any of your pals about Marcy? We can't get anything downstairs."

"Her blood pressure's a little funky," Weather said. "It could be shock, but Hirschfeld's afraid she might've sprung a leak. They're watching her."

Lucas panicked. "Sprung a leak? What does that mean? Sprung a leak?"

Weather touched his hand. "Lucas, it can happen. As messed up as she was, it'd be a miracle if they did everything perfectly. If it's a leak, it's not huge. She's just a little funky."

"Jesus Christ, Weather. . . ."

Weather said to Del, "You're gonna have to watch our boy, here. There's nothing he can do about this, but he's going into full Lucas mode."

Lucas was still shaken when they left, and Del was more curious than ever. "You've been talking to Weather?"

"Bumped into her last night. First time we'd talked . . . forever."

"She seems different," Del ventured. The unfinished part of the thought was *like she didn't hate you anymore.*

"Time passes," Lucas said.

On the way out to the prison, they talked tactics with Trick.

"According to your brilliant plan," Trick said, "I sit on my ass until you tell me to walk. Then I come in."

"Yeah, but when you come in, you come in shining like the fuckin' *sun*," Del said.

"Shining like the fuckin' sun for Al-Balah," Trick said in disgust. "If that cocksucker died this afternoon, we'd have to go over to the cathedral and light candles in thanksgiving."

"You a Catholic?" Lucas asked.

"Fuck no," Bentoin said. "Fuckin' bead-rattlin', genuflectin', ring-kissin' assholes."

"Me'n Lucas are Catholic," Del observed. "Since you got a Frenchy name —"

"You figured wrong," Bentoin said.

"So what are you?"

Bentoin looked out the car window at the cornfield going by and said, sourly, "An ex-Catholic."

Lucas started laughing, and then Del, for the first time since Marcy was shot.

The interview room was painted an indefinite pastel color, as though the painters had a bunch of pastels but not enough of anything, so they poured them altogether and came up with a lime–cream–rose–baby blue, which resolved itself into a pastel sludge. Al-Balah's lawyer, a pretty good three-cushion-billiards player named Laziard, was sitting on a bench with his briefcase by his left foot, reading a pamphlet about items forbidden as gifts to inmates. He looked up when Lucas came in with Del.

"My, my, a deputy chief," Laziard said. "You must be a little worried. Hey, Del."

"We figure you're gonna sue us for a billion dollars," Lucas said.

"You got the number right," Laziard said genially as Lucas and Del chose spots on the benches.

"So we thought we should show a little concern, just in case we find Trick again," Lucas said.

"Just in case?" A wrinkle appeared on Laziard's forehead. "I thought Del had him."

Del shrugged. "I talked to him, but I didn't *arrest* him. I didn't have anything to arrest him *on*. He told me he was checked into the Days Inn down on the strip, and when I snuck out and checked, he *was*. But the next day, when we went down to pick him up, he'd checked out. We just missed him."

Lucas said, "The problem is, he might've gone back to Panama. The guys in the county attorney's office don't want to hear any of this 'Del saw him' shit. They want to see *Trick*."

"What are you telling me?" Laziard demanded. "What . . ."

The door opened in the back wall, and they all turned. Rashid Al-Balah stepped into the room, a guard a step behind him. Al-Balah was a shaved-head black man with a heavy face and two-day beard. He glowered at Lucas, gave a few seconds of hate to Del. The guard pointed him at a bench. Al-Balah sat down and asked Laziard, "How much longer?"

"We're trying to figure that out," Laziard said.

"What? What're you trying to figure out?" Al-Balah's voice was rising. *"Get me the fuck outa here."*

"There's a problem," Lucas said. "Trick went away, and the county attorney's office is being a stick-in-the-mud about it. They want to actually see his ass before they do anything. I'm sure we'll find him, sooner or later."

"Sooner or fuckin' later?" Al-Balah shouted. "I packed my shit this morning. I'm ready to go. Right now, motherfucker."

"This is not going well," Del muttered to Lucas.

"What? What'd you say?" Al-Balah was getting angrier.

The guard snapped, "Cool down." Al-Balah looked at him, and the guard took a half-step forward and set his feet. "Just cool down. Keep your place."

Al-Balah sagged on the bench. "I packed my shit," he said to Lucas. "You're supposed to get me the fuck out of here. I packed my shit up, man."

"We're doing what we can," Del said. "I'm the guy who brought the whole thing up, you know?"

Lucas jumped in. "I didn't actually come out

here myself to talk about cutting you loose. I actually came out with a question." He looked at Laziard. "A question for your client."

"A question?"

"You know about the Alie'e Maison case," Lucas said to Al-Balah. "There was another woman killed the same night, the same place."

"Yeah, yeah, I been seeing it on my TV," Al-Balah said.

"This woman, Sandy Lansing, she was dealing. But she was just the street hookup, we don't know who was running her. We'd like to find out, and we thought you might know. You know all that shit."

Al-Balah shook his head. "Fuck you."

"All right." Lucas stood up. "I figured there wasn't much chance."

"When you gonna get me out of here?" Al-Balah asked.

"Soon as we find Trick. We've got some staffing problems with this Alie'e thing, but we can probably spring a guy on it. You know, half-time, anyway. As soon as the Alie'e thing is done with. If Trick hasn't gone back to Panama or something. I mean, I'll bet you're out by spring. Summer at the latest."

Al-Balah almost got up this time, and the guard stepped away from the wall: *"Spring? Fuckin' spring?"*

Lucas shrugged. "It's this goddamn Alie'e thing. We can't catch a break. We're working on it."

"Richie Rodriguez," Al-Balah said. His lawyer said, "Stop!" but Al-Balah continued. "The bitch was run by Richie Rodriguez, who gots a place in Woodbury. He gotta a whole bunch of apartment buildings or some shit."

Del looked at Lucas and said, "There's a Richard Rodriguez on the party list."

"That's him. *Richard*," Al-Balah said. "You call him 'Dick' if you want to piss him off."

"Goddamn it," Laziard said.

Lucas looked at Al-Balah and said, "Thanks. We'll push the Trick Bentoin thing. We owe you."

"You owe me, and you gotta get me outa here. I'm fuckin' *innocent*." Al-Balah was pleading now.

"Yeah, well . . . more or less," Lucas said. He took a step toward the outer door, following Del.

Laziard asked, "Will I hear from you this afternoon?"

Before Lucas could answer, Del, who'd opened the door, said, "Whoa!" He reached out and, a second later, pulled Trick Bentoin into the room by his shirtsleeve.

"Hi, guys," Bentoin said, shining like the fuckin' sun.

"You pricks," Laziard said.

Al-Balah was stunned, but after gaping at Bentoin for a second, he started to laugh, and a minute later, was laughing so hard that he had to lean on his attorney for support. So hard that Lucas, Del, Laziard, and Bentoin started to laugh, and finally, even the guard.

On the way back to town, Del's phone rang. He answered, listened for a second, and said, "Yeah, he's right here. He just hasn't turned his fuckin' phone on." He handed the phone to Lucas. "It's Frank."

Lester was calling with three pieces of news. "We're rolling on this multiple-personality idea. The Olsons were murdered, dude. The shrink called it. Mrs. Olson's head was on *top* of some blood spray from her old man, and from the way the spray hit her face, she was looking toward him when she was shot. When her body was recovered, she was looking straight up toward the ceiling."

"So he was killed first," Lucas said.

"Absolutely. But the gun was next to him."

"All right," Lucas said. "What happened to that Bloom guy we were checking out?"

"Black checked him, and isn't getting any-place. The guy seems really straight."

"We got a better name," Lucas said. "A Richard Rodriguez. He's on the list."

"How good?"

"Very good. Have you seen Lane around there? He should be back from Fargo."

"Yeah. He's here," Lester said.

"Get him on the Rodriguez guy. Full bio. We'll be back in half an hour."

"See you then."

"How's Marcy?" Lucas asked.

"Same, I guess. I checked this morning when I

came in, and nobody's said anything else."

"Half hour," Lucas said.

Things were beginning to move, like watching the ice go off the river in spring. Nothing happening, nothing happening, and then boom: breakup.

When they got back, they walked Trick over to the county attorney's office, left him, and headed back to City Hall. Lane was waiting outside Lucas's office with a wad of paper in his hand. He saw them coming, and walked down the hall waving the paper.

"He's our guy. He's a dealer, anyway. Moved here from Detroit eleven years ago, got busted a couple of times for vagrancy. Now he owns a bunch of small apartment buildings here and in St. Paul and out in Washington County, through a real-estate investment company in Miami." Lane was talking at a hundred miles and hour, and they were swirling around each other in the hall, looking at pieces of paper. "He lists himself as an apartment manager on his state tax returns. I looked at the returns going all the way back, and he showed up nine years ago at twenty-two thousand, and now he's up to ninety, but he never lists his ownership anywhere. He doesn't have to."

"Goddamnit, this looks good," Lucas said.

Del nodded. "Hiding the money. But I wonder why he's still selling dope if he's got the apartments?"

"He pyramided them, I think," Lane said. "He can't stop yet. Maybe he's got a pal at the bank who knows he has another income, 'cause it looks like he bought the first apartment with a cash down-payment — and nobody asked any questions — then used the equity in that one to finance the next one, paid on that a while, then used the equity in the two of them to buy the third, and then the equity in the three to buy another one, and kept doing that until he got where he is now. The total assessed value in twelve buildings is nine point five million, and they're really worth twelve or thirteen. But his own money, he's got maybe a million into them."

"The rents don't cover the payments?"

"Oh, they cover them, barely, as long as he never has a vacancy," Lane said. "But you're never a hundred percent in apartments — not for long, anyway. What he's doing is, if somebody moves out, he keeps paying the rent out of the dope money until he gets another tenant. I bet he's getting a lot of his maintenance done on the underground economy, paying in cash. So the dope money is invisible. It just goes away."

"And he gets paid out of Miami, and nobody looks at that up here," Del said.

"That's right," said Lane. "He files all of his taxes, he's clean. A few more years of this, and he can sell the whole thing out. Pay some capital gains, and he's a multimillionaire."

"What happens if the dope stops?" Lucas asked.

"Can't stop," said Lane. "He needs a hundred percent occupancy to pay his financing costs, and the only way he can get a hundred percent is to pay the rents on the vacant apartments himself."

"Strange nobody noticed," Lucas said.

"How they gonna notice?" Lane asked.

Lucas and Del looked at each other, thought about it for a moment, then Lucas shrugged. "I don't know."

"I talked to some guys up at the assessor's office, and they don't know a way," Lane said.

And Del said, "You know what it reminds me of? The Namiami Entertainment porno houses."

Namiami Entertainment was a mob-related company out of Naples, Florida, that bought three porno theaters around the Twin Cities. The Cities liked them because they'd agreed to business conditions that were more restrictive than the previous owners would agree to. Namiami had done away with the jerk-off-booth peep shows, ended the sale of adult novelties, had taken down outside advertising signs, and though they still ran porno films in the theaters, had generally blended into their neighborhoods. They'd operated for years before the tax people got curious about how they managed to get seventy or eighty percent of theater capacity for their film showings; a little investigation suggested that actual capacity was more like ten percent. The theaters, it turned out, were the most excellent device for laundering large numbers of small bills.

"So what we got," Lucas said, "is a dead woman who dealt dope to rich people. She's killed at a party where her dope-dealer boss happens to be, and who claims he didn't know her. Nobody else seems to have a motive — most people barely know her. But one guy who does know her, Derrick Deal, all he has to do is think about it, and he figures out who killed her. He must've known Rodriguez."

"And he did it without even knowing that Rodriguez was at the party," Del said. "He didn't have our list."

"Right. And Derrick's not above a little blackmail. He tries it, and gets himself killed for his trouble," Lucas said.

"Gotta be this guy," Lane said. "Nothing else fits."

"What'd he say when we talked to him?"

"Says he got to the party late, never saw Alie'e, didn't know Lansing. Got bored, and left around two o'clock," Lane said.

"So he admits he was there pretty late."

"Yeah."

"Let's talk to Sallance Hanson about this," Lucas said. To Del: "Let's go see Marcy, and then go see Hanson. See what she knows about Rodriguez."

"Okay."

And to Lane: "Find this Rodriguez. Don't approach him, just spot him for us. Stay with him. Start tracking him."

When Lucas and Del walked into the hospital, a nurse saw them coming and cut them off. "There's been a problem. They've had to take Officer Sherrill back into the operating room."

"What?"

She looked at her watch. "About fifteen minutes ago, they decided they had to go back in."

"Ah, Jesus," Lucas said. "How bad?"

The nurse shook her head. "I don't know. I know they were watching her blood pressure, and they were worried about it. Dr. Hirschfeld made the call about a half hour ago. She was pretty strong when she went in, though."

"Was she awake?"

"No."

"How long will they be in there?" He looked down the hall toward the emergency operating theater.

"There's no way to tell. Until she's fixed."

Lucas looked at Del. "I told you man, I got a bad feeling."

Del asked the nurse, "Have you seen Dr. Weather Karkinnen around?"

"Yes. She was down asking about Officer Sherrill just a few minutes ago. I think she's doing her morning rounds."

"Let's go," Lucas said.

They tracked her down in the surgery wards, talking to the parents of a child who'd had some reconstruction work after a car accident. Lucas stuck his head in the room, and Weather saw him and said, "I'll be just a minute."

They waited in the hall, listening to the murmur of voices, Lucas pacing, until Weather came out. "I don't think it's too bad," she said. "I think it's that one leak."

"They said she was pretty strong," Del said.

"Well . . ." Weather's eyes slid away from Lucas. "She was in a lot better physical condition than most people who come in."

"Aw, man, you're saying she wasn't that strong."

"Lucas, this had to be done. If they'd waited, she would have gotten weaker, and that would have been worse. Hirschfeld thought he had to go in now."

"Is she gonna make it?"

Weather nodded once, quickly. "Yes." This time her eyes held on to his.

Sallance Hanson knew Rodriguez only slightly. "He's quite a respected real estate investor, but he's not part of the usual . . . group. The group that comes to my parties. Do you think he's the one? Who killed Alie'e?"

"We're just doing a second round on everybody," Lucas lied. He went back to Rodriguez. "I'm curious about the investor part. Our preliminary workup showed him as an employee . . . an apartment manager, not an investor."

"Well, like I said, I don't know him that well, but that's not the way he talks. That's not the way he dresses, either. He's a coarse man, but he has a nice taste in clothes. So do you, by the way." She reached out, folded back the lapel on Lucas's jacket, read the label, and asked, "Where'd you get this?"

"Barneys."

"Really. Nice material. You went to New York?"

"I have a friend there. I visit sometimes," Lucas said. He pushed the topic back to Rodriguez. "Why is he coarse? What makes you think that?"

"He's just . . . Every once in a while, something slips out. He'll say, 'twat,' or something. A lot of guys say 'twat,' you know, when they're looking for an effect, or they're trying to shock you or piss you off. I even know one guy who tried to tell me it was a variation of twit."

Lucas grinned. "He had to be a moron."

"Yes, well . . . yes. But with Richie . . . I've heard — overheard — Richard say it sort of casually. Like that was the word he'd normally use in that place, and if he said 'woman,' it was because he was trying to be polite. He's a coarse man, with a layer of politeness that he learned somewhere. Maybe a book or something."

"Do you know anything about his financial dealings?"

"No, no. Nothing. Although every time I talked to him, that's what he wanted to talk about. He was always complaining about his tenants — late with the rent, or skipping out, or whatever."

Del chipped in. "You never saw him with Sandy Lansing?"

"I just don't remember."

"You know Lansing was dealing drugs."

She looked at Del for a moment, then at Lucas, then back to Del. "Look, I know . . . I've talked to my lawyer, and he says telling you this is no crime. . . . I know some people at the party were using drugs. And I'd heard that you could sometimes get something from Sandy. But I didn't want to slander a dead woman."

Del leaned back on the couch. He was wearing a black leather jacket, jeans, and a ragged thirty-year-old political T-shirt on which the words "Lick Dick in '72" were barely legible. He grinned, showing his yellow teeth. "You oughta tell that to Derrick Deal."

"Derrick . . . ?" She was puzzled.

"A guy we know," Del said. "He's in the icebox down at the morgue."

"Right up to that point, I was trying to make nice with her," Lucas said when they were out on the sidewalk.

"Fuck the bitch. She's one of those people who'll drive you to communism," Del said. He scratched the side of his face; he hadn't shaved in a couple of days. "After we see about Marcy, maybe you oughta talk to your friend Bone."

"Not a bad idea," Lucas said. "But first . . ." He took out his cell phone, turned it on, and punched in a number.

Lane answered. "Yo."

"This is Lucas. You find him?"

"I've *seen* him. I took Hendrix along, Hendrix interviewed him after the party. He's got an office in St. Paul, on the street level down from a Skyway, and we can see him in his office."

"You can see him now?"

"No, but I can see the door he's gotta come out. I'm with him."

"Let's get some pictures of him — we might want to take them around."

"Okay."

"And if he gets closer to Minneapolis, call me. I'll leave the phone on. I'm probably gonna want to look at him this afternoon, wherever he is."

Marcy was out of the operating room and back in the recovery room. Tom Black was standing in the corridor outside the operating suite with a nurse; when Lucas and Del walked in, Black stepped toward them. "She came through it okay. They had a pretty good leak, but they stopped it, and everything else seems to be holding."

"But she's not awake."

"They're keeping her asleep. They want everything tying together before she wakes up and starts moving around."

They talked about that for a minute: the way Lucas had been tied down once when he got shot in the throat, and hadn't been able to move his head for three days; and about the pinkingshears incident, when Del's hips had been immobilized for two days. Then Del said, "I'm gonna go see this gal over at the BCA. See if the state's got anything on Rodriguez. What're you gonna do?"

Lucas looked at his watch. "I've got a date, God help me."

Catrin was sitting in a back booth, facing the door, when Lucas arrived. He smiled when he saw her, and she nodded and then paid a lot of attention to picking up a cup of coffee and taking a sip.

"Hey." He slid into the booth on the opposite side and waved at a waitress.

"I hope I'm not tearing your day apart," she said. She'd dressed down this time, in jeans and a cornflower blue shirt that didn't seem to have a button — a subtle, outdoorsy peek-a-boo blouse. "I was watching the Alie'e thing on television, and it seems like people are going crazy."

Lucas nodded and tried to keep his eyes on her face. "It's worse than I've ever seen it. We've had some bad ones before, but this is nuts."

"Are you making any progress? Or can't you tell me?"

"If we were making progress, I might not be able to tell you, but since we aren't, I can tell you. We aren't."

The waitress came by, and they both ordered salads and coffee. Then they spent a couple of minutes in dragging chitchat until Catrin said, "I called you up because you're the only person I can call up and talk to. I'm in pretty bad shape."

"You look . . . terrific. You even look happy."

"More like anesthetized," she said. Then she shook her head. "I shouldn't be here."

"Why not?"

"I can't even tell you that. I mean, I would tell you if I knew."

"Have a little trouble sleeping? Can't stop your head going around, big dark dreams keeping you up?"

She tilted her head to one side and looked at him curiously. "I'm not suffering from depression, if that's what you're asking. But you did, huh? I recognize the description."

"Yeah."

"I had a friend with the problem. We were worried about her. She eventually got straightened out."

"Chemicals."

"Of course. What'd you do?"

"I had this superstition about chemicals, so I just . . . waited until it went away. I knew what was going on, and I read about it, and in most cases, it'll go away. So I waited. I hope to Jesus it doesn't happen again, but if it does, I'll do the chemicals. I'm not going through it again."

"Good call," she said. "But my problem . . . it's the good old midlife crisis, Lucas."

"Haven't really had mine yet," he said.

"Knowing you, you probably won't. Not until you're about sixty-five, and realize that you're not married and you don't have any grandchildren, and then you'll wonder what happened."

"I could have grandchildren," Lucas said, a little truculently. "I've got a kid."

"Who you don't see much."

"What are we talking about here?" he asked, suddenly irritated.

"Maybe I'm dragging you into your midlife crisis with mine," she said. The waitress came with the salads and nobody said anything until she was gone, and then Catrin said, "Way back when, after I left you, and you didn't call —"

"I called."

"Yeah. Twice. If you'd have called four times, I would've come back. The next time I saw you, you were walking around with some skinny blonde with a terrific ass and these little bell-bottoms, and you stopped on a street corner and she tried to stick her tongue down to your tonsils."

Now Lucas blushed. "I don't even remember," he said.

She maneuvered a lettuce leaf into her mouth and crunched on it, watching him. He pushed his salad bowl away and waited. "Anyway," she said, "About two days after I saw you with the blonde, I met Jack and we started dating and I liked him a lot and I liked his parents and they liked me, and my parents were delighted, he was one year away from his M.D. So we . . . just got married and he did his hitch in the Army and then we went down to Lake City and bought a house and had kids and dogs and sailboats and goddamnit" — testing the word, *goddamnit* — "here I am, twenty-five years later. What happened to *me?* I thought I was gonna have a movie, but all I've ever been is the woman in the background of somebody else's movie."

She thought about that, and poked her salad fork at Lucas and said, "That's what we're talking about. Metaphors. The other day when we met, I used that movie metaphor. It just jumped up and I said it. I've been thinking about it ever since. When's *my* movie?"

Lucas sat looking at her for a long moment, and Catrin said, "Say something," and Lucas sighed and said, "If I could only figure out a way to run for the door without freakin' out the restaurant."

She sat back and didn't quite snarl at him, "You'd run for the door?"

"Catrin . . . I know women who run businesses and make a zillion dollars a year and drive around in Mercedes-Benzes and every night they go home and wonder what the hell happened, how they could've forgotten to have kids. They're forty-five years old and have everything but kids, and that's all they think about: no kids. Then I meet people like you who have these great kids and they're all messed up because they're not running General Mills."

She'd wiped her mouth with a napkin, and now tossed the napkin into the middle of her unfinished salad. Her eyes were bright and a little too wide, and he started to remember her temper. He thought, *Uh-oh,* and she said, her voice rising a notch, "So all I'm going through is some kind of routine female bullshit that I'll get over."

He shook his head. "No. You see women thinking along these lines, and about half the time it ends in disaster. They walk on their old man and their kids and they get their freedom and they wind up living in a crummy apartment and selling cupcakes in the local foo-foo dessert bar. If you ask them if they'd go back, they think a long time and most of them say, 'There's no way to go back,' but if they could, on some kind of negotiated terms, they would."

"What about the other half, the ones who don't walk?"

"Then, they come to some kind of accommodation, but . . . I'm not sure how happy they ever are, not having tried it."

"So you're saying I'm fucked," she said.

"Well, you've got a problem. You've got to think about it a long time."

She looked away and said, "I'm thinking about moving out. I didn't tell you that the other day. I wanted to impress you with how wonderful I was, after all these years."

"Does your husband know?" Lucas asked.

"At some level, maybe — but he wouldn't want to think about it. I mean, he seems happy enough. He's got all the prestige and his patients like him and he's delivered half the kids in town and we've got a sailing club and he's got a hunting shack across the river in Wisconsin, and all his buddies."

"*You've* got friends, too, don't you?"

"Housewives. Waiting for death. Three or four of them have actually taken off."

"What happened to them?"

"They're selling cupcakes in foo-foo dessert bars," she said, and grinned at him.

"Not really."

"One sells real estate and not very well. One works in a decorating business and doesn't make much. One went back to school and became a social worker and got a job in St. Paul, and she's okay. One's a waitress who's trying to paint."

"And you'd take pictures. Photographs."

"Maybe. You think I couldn't?"

"I don't even know how you'd go about it."

"It's not like I'd be broke. Like I said the other day, we've *got* money."

"So why don't you just go ahead and do what you want, without walking? Just tell him, 'Look, I'm gonna be busy for the next couple of years. Remind me to stop by once in a while.' "

" 'Cause he's in the way," she said. "Anything I'd do, it'd be a hobby. We'd have to go to London for shows and someplace for family medical conventions, and I'd have to cook at Thanksgiving and Christmas for the kids and we'd have to keep up with our friends. . . . I couldn't *think*. I just need to *think*."

"And what happens to Jack?"

"You know what I think?" She looked at him steadily. "I think if we got divorced in January, he'd be married again by December."

"You've got somebody in mind for the job?" Lucas asked.

"No. He doesn't fool around. But he needs a wife to hold him up, and if I moved out, there are plenty of women around town who'd sign up as candidates."

Lucas shook his head. "You know what? I bet he'd be devastated. I bet he wouldn't be married in five years. You'd be a little hard to . . . get over."

She smiled at him, a sad smile. "Thanks."

"You gotta think about it," Lucas said. "Probably the most important thing you've thought about since you got married, or got pregnant."

"I didn't think about those things. I just did them," she said.

"So think about this."

She nodded. "Let's get out of here."

Outside, on the sidewalk, she said, "This whole conversation took a kind of unexpected turn. It was more like therapy than anything. . . . You've thought about this more than I expected you would have."

"I had a woman I wanted to marry, and didn't. She wouldn't. I'm still not over it," Lucas said. "When I look around City Hall, or the County Courthouse, the place is full of wounded people. I don't know what happened. I don't remember this happening to our parents' generation."

"It probably did, but they just never told us," Catrin said.

"Yeah." Lucas took a step back. "So think about it."

"One of the things I'm thinking about," she said, "is sleeping with you. But I've got to decide whether to do it before I walk, just to try it out, to see if I've got anything left . . . or just go ahead and walk out, and sleep with you later."

Lucas was offended. "Like I don't have a say in it."

She regarded him for a minute, then shook her head. "Not much. You already want to sleep with me. If I really wanted to force it, I could press up against you and you'd get all kinds of Catholic guilt and everything, and you'd go raving up and down the house waving your arms, and then you'd do it."

"Jesus, I'm a piece of meat."

"Not that," she said. She reached out with an index finger and pushed against his chest. "You're just one of those guys who likes to sleep with women. You need the comfort. And you're not seeing anyone now. So I could do it, if I wanted to. . . . I just have to think."

He took another step back. "Well . . . let me know."

Now she laughed, and for a moment she looked like she was nineteen again. "I will."

From his car, Lucas used his cell phone to call

his friend Bone; fifteen minutes later, Bone's secretary pushed him past a panel of waiting middle managers in the banker's outer office.

Bone was looking at two computer monitors at the same time. He turned away from them when Lucas came in and said, "Sometimes I feel like I've got so much radiation going through my skull, you could put a roll of film behind my head and get an X ray."

"How's your ankle?"

"Hurts. Should be okay by next week." They played pickup basketball twice a week. Bone had once been a suspect in a case Lucas had worked. Now he was not only a friend, but his banker connections could get Lucas useful financial information. "I got that stuff on your guy."

"Confidentially."

"Of course. But there wasn't much."

"Would you loan him money?"

Bone leaned back. "There are two things you look at before you loan a guy money: history and security. He never had much security, but, boy, his history is good."

"Too good?"

"No such thing as too *good*," Bone said. "It just can't be too *bad*."

"What if you depend on a hundred percent tenancy in your apartment buildings to meet your financing? And then make it? Is that too good?"

"He can't be doing that," Bone said. He rocked forward and shuffled through the papers, looked from one to another, punched a few numbers into one of his computers, and pushed a key. Then he said, "Jeez, that's a little tight, isn't it?"

"He's greasing it with dope money," Lucas said.

"Ah."

"What I need to know — this'll never get to a second person, past me — would the guy who's making his loan know about this? About the dope?"

Bone spun his chair around until his back was to Lucas. He was looking at a walnut bookcase full of financial manuals, a few computer guides, the complete works of Joseph Conrad, and a tattered multivolume set of Proust's *Remembrance of Things Past.* A copy of the Oxford Study Bible was jammed sideways on top of the Proust. After a minute, without turning back, Bone said, "He'd have to know *something.*"

"But maybe not the dope?" Lucas asked of the chair.

Bone spun the chair around. He had a lean, wolflike face. He grinned, showing his teeth. "Maybe not, because there's another good possibility that bankers don't like to talk about — the other possibility is, he found a guy at the bank and either bribed him to okay the loan, or kicked back part of the loan itself."

"But whatever happened, the bank guy would have to know."

"I don't see how he could avoid it, if his IQ's

over eighty," Bone said. Then: "I hope I haven't screwed anybody here."

"You might be reading about it," Lucas said. "This Rodriguez . . ."

Bone was a smart guy. He knew Lucas wouldn't be on a routine errand. "Alie'e?"

"You might be reading about it," Lucas said again.

Del called to suggest they meet in St. Paul. Lucas checked on Marcy by phone, then got his car and headed across the river. Rodriguez's office was in the Windshuttle Building, hooked by Skyway to Galtier Plaza. Lucas dumped the Porsche in the Galtier parking garage and found Lane and Del loitering in the Skyway.

"He's down there now, talking to his secretary. See the Temps office? Look one window to the left, the guy in the pink shirt. That's him." Lane handed Lucas a pair of miniature Pentax binoculars, and Lucas looked down through the Skyway windows at the man in the pink shirt.

Rodriguez was ordinary. At six-two or six-three, he had thinning brown hair and a gut. He didn't look Latino; he looked like an everyday Minnesota white guy. He was intent on the secretary's computer screen. He said something to her, looked at a printer, looked back at the computer, tapped the screen, then turned back to the printer as a piece of paper rolled out.

As he turned back and forth, Lucas got a good

view of his face. "You're sure this is the guy?"

"This is the guy," Lane said.

"He looks like a city councilman." Lucas turned to Del, "What'd the BCA say?"

"He had a fairly heavy juvenile record in Detroit, burglary mostly. They think he was running dope early on, just deliveries on his bike, then got his nose into it. He didn't do much in the way of sales. . . . Then he just disappeared. They never tried to find out where he went, they were just happy he was gone. They did some assessments on him when he was in juvenile care. They say he's smart, but as far as they can tell, he never went to school after the fifth grade."

"All right," Lucas said. He handed the glasses back to Lane and said, "You go home, relax, have a couple beers, visit your girlfriend, whatever. But I want you back on this guy tomorrow morning at nine o'clock, wherever he is, and you can plan to stay on him every day, all day, until we take him down."

"Good." Lane nodded. "Where're you guys going?"

Lucas looked at Del. "We better go talk to Rose Marie."

Rose Marie had just broken free of a press conference when Lucas and Del arrived. They could see her through the glass door of her outer office, waving her arms around, as the receptionist shook her head in sympathy. Lucas pushed through the door. Rose Marie nodded at them, turned back toward the receptionist to finish what she was saying, saw Del's "Lick Dick" T-shirt, did a worried double-take, lost her thought, and asked, "What?"

"We gotta talk."

Inside her office, with the door closed, Lucas said, "I think we got the Alie'e killer. I'd say maybe eighty-five percent."

Rose Marie looked from Lucas to Del and back to Lucas and asked, "Who?"

"A guy named Rodriguez." They laid it out for her. At the end, she said, "So we know who it is, but we can't convict him."

"That's pretty much it," Lucas admitted. "When you make the leaps, you can convince yourself that he's the guy . . . but a jury, I don't think so. One thing, he doesn't look like a dope dealer. He looks like a washing-machine salesman."

"What if he isn't the guy?"

"We put together a case. If we can put together a solid enough case to convince ourselves . . . maybe we'll have a chance. Or maybe we'll stumble over something," Lucas said. "I mean, we convicted Rashid Al-Balah and he didn't even do it."

"So . . . we brace the loan officer from the bank."

"As soon as we do it, he's gonna go out the back door, make a phone call, and Rodriguez will know we're on his ass," Del said.

"Good thought. We ought to have Rodriguez

tapped," Lucas said. "If we can get him talking about it . . ."

"Do we have enough for a tap?" Rose Marie asked.

"Probably," Lucas said. "We can get that going this afternoon. The best thing that could happen to the county attorney's office is to have something to distract from the Al-Balah story, when it breaks. If we can hang Rodriguez for Alie'e, Al-Balah moves to page nine."

"Al-Balah has already broken," Rose Marie said. "The county attorney's guys decided it'd be better to get out there first with the news, put some of their own spin on it."

"Still . . ."

Rose Marie nodded. "I'll get them started on a tap."

Then Rose Marie laid out the situation with Tom Olson. He was out of the hospital, but was being tailed by relays of Homicide and Intelligence cops, who would stay with him twenty-four hours a day. Alie'e's funeral had been delayed until the elder Olsons' bodies were released, so they could all be buried together — and that might be a while yet, because the situation in the Bloomington motel room was so complicated.

"If Olson's the guy — the one who's going after everybody *else*, in revenge for his sister — we think he might go after Jael Corbeau again, or the other woman, Catherine Kinsley."

"Or that Jax guy."

"Jax checked out," Rose Marie said. "He's gone to New York, but says he'll be back for the funeral. He's probably shopping for the right outfit to wear when he throws himself in her grave."

"So we're just watching?" Lucas asked.

"No. We've had these family briefings every day, and we're going to continue them. In fact, Olson's coming here in" — she looked at her watch — "about twenty-five minutes. We're going to try to point him at Kinsley. We'll talk a little about Alie'e's relationship with her. Kinsley and her husband are going up north to their cabin, which is way the hell out in the woods. You can't even find them with a map. We'll have a team at her house, waiting, if Olson goes that way."

"How about Jael?" Lucas asked.

"We think he's less likely to try her, because he tried once, and she ran him off," Rose Marie said. "But we'll have a team there, too. I'd appreciate it if you'd stop by and talk to her. She's scared, and she'd like to have you around."

"All right," Lucas said. "And listen, I know Angela Harris is a smart shrink, but I saw Olson's face when he came running across the grass to tell us about his folks. And man, I don't know about this multiple-personality stuff, but that was . . . real. That was so strong that if his personalities were gonna dissolve, or whatever they do, that would have happened right then. I mean . . . I've never seen anything like it. Ever."

"We're keeping that in mind, of course," Rose Marie said. "But it's what we've got, right now."

"So we're set?" Del asked, stepping toward the door.

"If everything went exactly right — exactly right — we could have both these guys in twenty-four hours," Rose Marie said. "If the bank guy calls Rodriguez, if Olson goes for Kinsley . . ."

"There's gotta be at least one time in life when everything works," Del said. "One time."

"Bullshit," Lucas said. Out in the hall, when they were away from Rose Marie, he added, "She says they're keeping in mind that it might be somebody else, but they're not. They just put all their chips on Olson."

"And we put all of ours on Rodriguez," Del said.

"Yeah, but there's a major difference," Lucas said.

"What's that?"

"We're right. They might not be."

19

Del went off to coordinate with the county attorney's office on the wiretaps and the subpoena for Rodriguez's bank records. Lucas went down to the Homicide office and spent an hour looking over the typescript of the Rodriguez interview, and talked to Frank Lester and Sloan about the multiple-personality idea.

"Everything I know about it I learned from TV," Sloan said. "But you gotta admit, the guy looks good. He's got motive, he had access to the shooting car, he could get close enough to take his parents out . . ."

"When he came running after us, after he found the bodies . . . he looked like his head was trying to explode," Lucas said. "He was trying to pull the hair out of the sides of his head; I've never seen anything like it. Then he dropped in his tracks."

"Could be psychological pressure from the other personality," Lester said. "Or maybe he's just goofy."

"What we saw was real. He wasn't faking anything. If his other personality killed his parents, the personality we saw didn't know it," Lucas said.

Lucas left the City Hall as the streetlights were coming on. Fifteen minutes later, he slid to the curb at Jael Corbeau's house and headed up the walk. Every room inside the house was lit; everything outside was dark, including the front porch. When Lucas reached for the doorbell, a voice from the corner of the porch said, "Go on in, Chief."

"Who is that?" he asked. He didn't turn his head.

"Jimmy Smith. From dope."

"You cold?" Lucas asked, still speaking at the door panel.

"Nah. I'm wearing my deer-hunting camies."

"Excellent." Lucas pushed through the door into the living room, where he met another dope cop, Alex Hutton, who stood to one side with a hammerless .357 in his right hand. He slipped it away when he saw Lucas's face, and said, "Franklin and Jael are upstairs. Cooking."

"Franklin cooks?" It seemed unlikely.

"He's teaching her how to make one-minute meals, you know, for during football commercials."

"The guy has talent," Lucas said.

Hutton took a step closer, dropped his voice, and said, "I don't know where this chick has been for the first part of my life, but she is *hot.*"

"I thought you were married with about nine kids," Lucas said, dropping his voice. He added, "Besides, she sorta likes other girls."

"I only got three kids . . . and I think Jael likes a little of everything," Hutton said, glancing at the door that led into the back of the house and the kitchen. "If she wanted to bring another chick along, I could handle that — conceptually, anyway."

"Except that your wife would stab you to death."

"Fuck my wife. She's history. I'm abandoning her. I figure if I abandon a wife and three kids, the papers will pass on the story. You only get in trouble for five or more."

"I forgot all about stakeouts," Lucas said. "The sexual fantasies, and all that, when you've got nothing to do."

As he walked up the stairs, Lucas could hear Franklin's gravelly voice. He was saying, "All right, hands clear of the counter. Hands clear . . ." Jael: "I'm arranging the cheese sacks."

"Nope. No good. Gotta be like you just threw them in the 'fridge. . . ."

Lucas leaned in the kitchen door, and a second later, Hutton came to stand behind him. Franklin and Jael had their backs to them, and Jael was closing the refrigerator door. Franklin looked at his watch and asked, "Ready?"

"Ready."

"Five seconds . . . four, three, two, one, GO!"

Jael jerked the refrigerator open, pulled out two sacks of grated cheese, threw them at the kitchen counter, snatched a plate out of the cupboard, opened a bag of blue-corn nacho chips, and spilled them on the plate.

"Too many chips, too many chips," Franklin warned. She grabbed a handful of them off the plate, threw them back in the bag, quickly arranged the others on the plate, and Franklin said, "Fifteen seconds." Jael opened the two bags of cheese, working frantically, spread a small handful from one bag over the plate of chips, opened the other, spread another small handful, and asked, "Is that good?"

"You're looking good, but you're a few seconds behind," Franklin said. "Gotta keep rolling."

She picked up the plate and pushed it into the microwave, said, "One minute," pressed a series of buttons, and the microwave started to hum. Then she went back to the refrigerator, grabbed a jar of salsa, popped the top, got a spoon and dumped three large spoonfuls into a small glass dessert bowl, glanced at the microwave timer, put the top back on the salsa jar, stuck it in the refrigerator, and wrapped up the top of one of the cheese bags, while watching the timer. Then she reached out. . . .

"Not too soon, not too soon," Franklin said. Jael jabbed a button, popped open the microwave door, thrust the salsa bowl inside, slammed the door, and pushed the Resume button.

"Might be too much time," Franklin said.

"No, I think we're okay," Jael said. Working quickly, she wrapped up the top of the second cheese bag, put both cheese bags back into the refrigerator, took out two beers, stepped back to the microwave, said, "Three seconds."

There was a popping sound, then another. Franklin said, "Shit. I told you. There goes the salsa."

The microwave beeped and Jael opened the door and looked inside. The interior was spattered with little gobbets of salsa. "I'll get it later," she said.

"Classic line," Franklin said with approval.

She pulled out the dish full of chips and the bowl of salsa, turned to the cooking island, saw Lucas for the first time, put the chips on the butcher-block top, and said, "Time."

Franklin looked at his watch. "One minute, twenty-nine seconds. If you add ten seconds going and coming, you could've missed a pass play."

"I don't think I can cut much time," she said.

"You just don't have the moves worked out yet," Franklin said. "You lost time with the chips, arranging them, you lost time getting the salsa out. And now you gotta go back and clean the microwave."

Jael looked at Lucas and asked, "Did you know that if you heat up salsa too fast, the onions pop like popcorn?"

"Everybody knows that," he said as Franklin turned around. Franklin seemed mildly embarrassed.

"I've been cooking seriously for half of my life,

and I didn't know that," she said. "Even the idea of heating it up seemed pretty brutal."

"Gotta have it about medium-warm, a little better than room temperature."

Hutton chipped in. "You want boiling-hot cheese on the chips, medium-warm salsa, very cold beer. You want that range."

"Do all men know this?" she asked.

All three of them nodded, and said at once, "Of course."

The house originally had four bedrooms and a full bathroom upstairs. Jael had wiped out the bottom floor as a studio; had rebuilt a kitchen upstairs, in what had been the master bedroom; the other three she'd turned into a snug little living room/dining room, a small library/office, and her own bedroom. The space was carefully assembled and connected, and Lucas felt comfortable.

They'd chatted with Franklin and Hutton for a few minutes, eating the nachos with melted cheese — "I can feel my heart clogging up. This stuff is absolute shit," Jael said — and then Jael said to Lucas, "Let's go talk."

As she stepped past him, she caught his wrist in her hand and led him out of the room; Hutton raised an eyebrow. In the living room, Lucas sprawled on a couch while Jael settled back in an oversized chair. Lucas said, "Great chair," and Jael said, "All guys don't really know about that nacho-cheese thing."

"You're right. There's probably some raggedy-ass cowboy out on a ranch in North Dakota somewhere who doesn't have either a TV or a microwave."

She said, "It really . . . wasn't bad."

"If you eat that stuff three days in a row, you'll be as big as Franklin." Franklin completely filled an average doorway. "In fact, Franklin used to be about your size."

She nodded, getting rid of the topic. "I went to see Marcy a couple of hours ago. I just missed you."

"She's hanging on," Lucas said, his face going grim. "But she's harder than goddamn nails. If anybody can make it back, she's the one."

"I feel . . . you know. Guilt, I guess."

"Don't," he said. "This has nothing to do with you, really. It has something to do with a nut, and some asshole who killed Alie'e and Sandy Lansing."

"I can't get Plain's body," she said. "But I finally found Dad. He's on St. Paul Island, which is about as far from here as you can get and still be on Earth. It'll take him a few days to get here."

"How is he?" Lucas asked.

"Devastated. I'd like to get the thing . . . done with."

"I'll see about it," Lucas promised. "This thing with Plain . . . when did that end?"

"A year ago."

"A year? I thought it might be more recent . . . the way he acted."

"Time was not a big deal with Plain. Everything was right now. He could read a history book about Rome and get angry about the Roman empire."

"Tell me about Alie'e," Lucas said. "Was there anybody that she talked about? Anybody who might be a little over the edge?"

"Are you questioning me?" But she smiled, and when she did, her torn-paper face was beautiful, tough and vulnerable at once.

"No, no. Of course not. And if you want to talk about something else, that's fine. But I start brooding about this kind of stuff. You know, *why?* Most people are freaked out by the idea of shoplifting. If you get somebody killing several people, he's either completely psychotic, delusional, nuts, living in a different world, listening to God . . . or he thinks he's got a reason. This guy we're looking for, he thinks he's got a reason. So there should be some connection to Alie'e. Somewhere, a connection."

"Her dad . . . was weird. He came on to me a couple of times. I often thought he was a little . . . wrong. Not a killer, but he, I think . . . I don't know." She lifted her hands to her temples. "His relationship to Alie'e and the other girls, he tried to act paternal, but he was always looking at them. . . . If you know what I mean."

"Yeah. He was turned on."

"Yeah. And Alie'e's mom wasn't much of a prize, either. My mom didn't care what I did for a living; she thought the earth owed me one, and

let it go at that. But Lil was living through Alie'e
. . . and I think she knew about Lynn's interest in
sex."

"You think Lynn might have abused Alie'e?"

"No. Nope. I think Alie'e would have told
me, and I think I would have seen it in her, the
way she acted around her father. No, maybe it
was just my expectations. Somebody's a dad —
you don't think of his standing around trying
to get a shot at the asses of his daughter's
friends."

"Happens all the time," Lucas said. "I'll do it.
For sure."

"But he was creepy about it."

"So . . . no ideas."

"I told you before, I really think you've got to
look at the people on the Internet. Those
people . . ."

"We've got somebody checking that, a computer guy named Anderson. If you can think of
anything specific along those lines, call him. But
the thing is, when he ran Alie'e's name through
Alta Vista, he got 122,000 matches. We're trying
to narrow them down."

"What's Alta Vista?"

"A search engine on the Net. You can look for
names and so on."

"Okay. Well, I'll think about it. You know all
about her brother, Tom."

"We're looking into him," Lucas said.

"He's an amazing guy. From what she said."

"Is he nuts?"

"She didn't think so. She thought he was holy," Jael said.

"How bright was she?" Lucas asked.

"Mmm, you've got to be smarter than average to make it as a model, but not a lot smarter. She wasn't intensely bright."

"So why were you hanging out with her?"

She smiled. "I thought everybody knew that."

"They know you were sleeping with her, but I thought there had to be a better reason."

"There wasn't," Jael said. "She was deep into herself, into feeling good. Into . . . *feeling.* That's what she did best, and she spread it around. She could make you discard everything else and feel good. The sex was wonderful. Very intimate and very playful and very sexual. I mean, I can't really explain it to you, because you don't know what I'm talking about and you're not in a position to find out."

"Did her appearance have anything to do with it? And her being famous?"

"Probably. There was a whole package. When you were with her, you felt sexy and important and wicked and fun. And she'd make you forget everything else and just *feel.* That's why she did those short pops: It was another aspect of feeling for her."

"So what about her boyfriend, Jax? What'd he think about all this? Sleeping with other women."

She shrugged. "Jax carried her bags. And slept with her every once in a while. He's basically a remora. He's probably back in New York right now, looking for somebody else."

"He is. You didn't like him?"

"It's not that. I just didn't *care* about him. Didn't even think about him when he was standing in front of me. He made himself into what he is. Not my fault. He wants to carry bags and hang out with pretty women, and that's what he does."

"Sounds bad," Lucas said.

"He doesn't think so." They sat in silence for a moment, then Jael said, "You and Marcy had a relationship."

"For six weeks or so. It was a little too intense."

She cocked her head. "Why would you walk away from intensity? Other people go their whole lives without intensity. They dream about it."

"Like I said, this was a little too much. We were headed for a disaster."

"You mean, like, you'd strangle her or something?"

"No. But something was going to happen, and we'd wind up hating each other," Lucas said. "We didn't want to do that. Risk it."

"She's still sort of hung up on you," Jael said. "You know what would've been fun? For the three of us to go away. You and me and Marcy."

She said it so conversationally that Lucas was neither embarrassed nor surprised. He said, "I'm a little too Catholic for that. Marcy would be, too, if she was a Catholic."

"Oh, I don't think so," Jael said. "Not Marcy,

anyway. I think she might be interested in the idea."

"Really?" She'd said it with some certainty, and now he *was* surprised. He looked a question at her.

"No, no, we weren't playing. We hardly had a chance to talk," Jael said. "But you can sort of pick out people who like to *feel*. Marcy's one of us."

"You mean, a little gay?" Lucas asked.

"No. That's not what I mean. You're one of us. I could tell from talking to you, and the way you look at women."

"I gotta stop talking about this," Lucas said.

"Sure," she said.

"It really makes me nervous."

"That's the Catholic part," she said. "You've probably been fighting it all of your life."

"Maybe," he said.

"You know," she said later, "I'm a little scared."

"I know. You should be."

"The way Plain was killed. He probably never had a chance even to say anything."

"The guy is nuts. But he's not some great force. We just haven't been able to find him. We will."

"Soon, I hope. I don't like being cooped up. I'm thinking of heading out to New York, as soon as I can get Plain taken care of."

"You could leave that to your father."

She shook her head. "Dad . . . couldn't handle it."

"So New York's an idea," Lucas said. "But you wouldn't have any protection."

"I could stay in a hotel. How could he find me?"

"Something to think about," Lucas said.

Downstairs, as Lucas was leaving, Hutton asked, "Learn anything new?"

It wasn't meant as a double entrendre, but Lucas turned it into one. "A little more than I wanted," he said.

On the way home, he called St. Anne's, and got Elle on the line. "I know it's cold, but I could take you for an ice cream."

"Never too cold for an ice cream," she said. "I'll walk over, meet you there."

The ice cream shop was across the street from St. Anne's, and was recognized as the local nun hangout. Elle was sitting with three other nuns in a booth near the front of the shop when he walked in, and she laughed and said something to one of the other women and then stood up, and led the way toward the back — a scene, Lucas thought, virtually identical to millions that had taken place in bars that night, if you took away the odor of spilled milk, and, of course, the nuns.

"Get a break?" she asked, and added, "I told Jim to make you a chocolate malt."

"That's fine. We've got a couple of things

working. I think we've got an eye on the guy who killed Alie'e, and we've booby-trapped everybody the second guy might be going after."

"You're sure there's a second guy."

"I think so. And he's the guy who's bothering me. The homicide people have a candidate. Tom Olson."

"Ohhh . . . no."

"The thing is, they have a theory," Lucas said. "The theory is, the same kind of mental pressures that made him an ecstatic also made him a multiple personality, and one of those personalities is a psychotic who made a run at Jael Corbeau but got chased off, killed Plain, came back after Jael Corbeau but shot Marcy instead, and then killed his parents."

"You say theory . . ."

The malt came. He took it, shucked the straw, and told her what they had: the police shrink, the prediction on the apparent double suicide. At the end, she was shaking her head. "I would love to talk to this man. If you convict him and send him to the state hospital, I will go see him. Multiple personalities are so rare. They're rarer than . . . than supernovas."

He smiled at the comparison. "Now, if I knew how rare supernovas are . . ."

"On the basis of pure chance, you'd say that the chances of Tom Olson being a multiple personality are nil," Elle said. "Just like your chances of winning the lottery. But somebody will win the lottery."

"So he could be."

"I would really like to talk to him," Elle said.

"If he is . . . disassociating, whatever that means, what's going to happen?"

"He'll break down. He could go so far down that he essentially becomes vegetative . . . and might not ever recover. Probably wouldn't. He'd probably die in a bed."

"That bad."

"That bad."

They made desultory small talk for a few minutes: about her fall classes at the school, about students developing a new interest in the Old Testament. "Amnon and Jael. They knew who they were," she said.

"Terrific," he said. Then: "I've talked to Weather a couple of times at the hospital."

Her eyes shifted away, quickly, furtively, and then back. She knew about guile, but she wasn't instinctively good at it. She had to plan. "What?" he asked.

"Nothing."

"Elle, God . . . bless me . . . what?"

"God bless me?"

"*What?*"

"I can't. I don't really want to talk about Weather."

"She called you," Lucas said. "She called and asked about me."

Elle wouldn't look at him. "I can't talk to you. Everything that's been said by . . . everybody . . . is in confidence."

"Aw, man, this could be a problem," Lucas said.

Now she sat up. "Why? You don't have another relationship."

"Some things have come up lately."

"Lucas . . . if you have any chance of recovering with Weather, you'd be a moron not to take it."

"Oh . . . boy," he said. "Mmman-oh-man."

After he left Elle, he went home, turned out the lights, and sat in the dark in the living room. Tried to make sense of the Alie'e case. Tried to make sense of his relationship with Weather.

Weather had become entangled in one of Lucas's cases, and had been taken hostage by a crazy peckerwood killer on a revenge trip. She'd talked him into surrendering, but Lucas hadn't known that. He'd set up an ambush involving a police sniper, who'd fired a high-powered varmint bullet down a hospital corridor, exploding the peckerwood's head like a pumpkin. The idea had been to get him out in the open, to get his weapon pointed in some direction other than Weather's head, and then take him out. The plan had worked to perfection.

Except for one small item: Weather had been looking at Lucas, straining toward him, full of a kind of strange goodwill toward her captor, who'd seemed to be not an entirely bad man — that in one minute, and in the next, the man's brains were literally blown across her face, with fragments of bone.

She was a surgeon, and no stranger either to blood or death; nor was she a sentimentalist. But this was something else, and when it was done, she'd been unable to talk to Lucas. She'd known the trouble was a kind of psychological reflex, a kind of phobia, a mental tic, but knowing it didn't help. She drifted away . . . went faster than that, actually. Walked away. Hurried away. Didn't hate him, nothing like that — just couldn't deal with his nearness, and the constantly played sound/sight/feel of the slug going through a man's brain three inches from her own.

But, Lucas thought, time passes.

Time passes. He closed his eyes in the dark. And saw the scarred face and teasing eyes of Jael Corbeau; the slightly plump, intense face of Catrin; the shoulders, the too-big nose, the *feel* of Weather.

Time passes, but sometimes it beats the shit out of you as it goes.

⋘ 20 ⋙

Wednesday. The fifth day of Alie'e Maison.

Lucas checked on Marcy. Black was slumped in a visitor's chair, and when he saw Lucas, got up. He was a little shaky, unshaven. "Nothing happening, but she started to wake up. She went back down, but they say she was close to the surface. She should wake up today."

Lucas looked in. Marcy had always been the most active person in the office, always had something rolling, something moving. She didn't look right, propped in the bed. She looked thinner, gaunt, wasted. He patted Black on the shoulder and said, "Take it easy."

The main offices of the Atheneum State Bank were off University Avenue three blocks from the state capitol building in St. Paul, in a redbrick building with four white wooden pillars out front. The neighborhood started trending up when the porno movies moved out and the hookers had been pushed farther west, away from the state legislators. The upward trend had stalled, and now the whole strip had a shabby, going-nowhere ambiance, like a squashed paper cup outside a convenience store.

The taps on four of Rodriguez's phones — one home, two business, and a cell — were in place, along with taps on the home and cell phones used by Bill Spooner, an assistant vice president in the commercial loans department.

Lucas and Del drove to the bank in a beat-up city car, trailed by an assistant county attorney named Tim Long. From the parking lot, Lucas called Rose Marie. Rose Marie, who had been waiting for the call, phoned the bank president and asked him to make time for a quick talk with Lucas. She got back to Lucas and said, "He's waiting. Be a little careful: He's one of those hail-fellow types who's always ready to help a member of the legislature, and never forgets when he has."

Lucas said to Del, "See if you can find Spooner's car."

Del nodded. "Crunch him," he said.

Lucas and Long went inside, spoke to the bank president's secretary. She went back into his office and popped out a minute later, followed by the president himself. "Already? I just talked to Rose Marie a couple of minutes ago."

"Traffic was light," Lucas said.

The bank president's name was Reed. He was a genial man, overweight, a patriotic panoply: red face, white hair, blue eyes; red tie, white shirt, blue suit; an American flag in the corner, with a plastic eagle atop the staff, in gold.

When Lucas outlined the general nature of their questions, Reed leaned back in his leather executive chair and said, "I've known Bill since we were kids. He was six years behind me at Cretin. His parents, God bless 'em — they're both dead now — used to play canasta with my parents. There's never been anything wrong with any of his accounts; he's one of our best loan officers. I was godfather for his oldest son."

"I'm sure there's nothing wrong now," Lucas said. "We just want to talk with him about Mr. Rodriguez. Their personal relationship. Anything he might be able to tell us that could help us in our investigation."

"I don't know that we could help much. Our financial records are confidential —"

Long interrupted. "Mr. Reed, we know about your confidentiality requirements, and we're just trying to handle this whole matter as discreetly as possible. If you wish, we can get a subpoena for your loan records, and we can call a squad car and transport Mr. Spooner to Minneapolis for questioning. We thought this would be better. *Chief Roux* thought it would be better."

"I appreciate that. Senator Roux was a good friend," Reed said. After a moment of silence and a thoughtful inspection of Lucas, he said, "Let's go talk to Billy and see what he has to say."

Billy was a Minnesota WASP, fair-haired, once slight, but now carrying a few too many pounds. He was wearing a gray off-the-rack suit and black lace-up shoes. And he was guilty of something, Lucas thought: His eyes went flat at the introductions, and when they settled into their chairs and Lucas explained what they wanted, he said, "As far as I know, Richard Rodriguez is entirely legitimate. He has a perfect payment record."

"That's our *problem*," Lucas said. "It's a little too perfect. From our review, it appears that he needs a one-hundred-percent residency rate to make his payments. We're wondering why you would give somebody a loan under those conditions."

"A lot of small reasons, and one big one," Spooner said. "The big one was, he helped our minority loan level. In our neighborhood, we have to be sensitive to redlining issues, and as a responsible, hardworking, intelligent minority person, we decided we could go with him as long as the risk wasn't too great. The first building he was interested in was for sale at such a good price that we could have loaned him almost all of the money even if he hadn't had a down payment. But he did have a down payment. Not much, but it was all of his savings, and guaranteed that he'd stay right on top of the business. And he had the minority status, of course. That swung it. After that, with a lot of hard work, he kept his record perfect, and we were always ready to help when he wanted to expand his horizons."

"So he got a great price on the original building," Long said. "What are the chances that he delivered part of the original purchase price to the seller, under the table, to drive down the apparent price?"

"I wouldn't know about that," Spooner said stiffly.

"What are the chances that he uses dope-dealing money to make up shortfalls in tenant rents?" Lucas asked.

"Dope? Richard Rodriguez? I don't think so."

Lucas leaned into Spooner's desk. "If we got a subpoena for your loan records and asked a state examiner to look them over, you think he'd say they met state loan standards?"

"Absolutely. The minority status alone would bring applause from the state banking department." Spooner leaned back and relaxed a hair, the way a fence relaxes when he realizes that a cop doesn't really have anything on him.

Lucas looked at Long and shrugged. Long dipped into his briefcase, found a paper, and handed it to Reed. "It's a subpoena for your loan records."

Reed's face turned a little redder. "I thought we were handling this on a friendly basis."

"We wanted to," Lucas said. "But Bill here is bullshitting us, so we're gonna have to see all the records."

"I'm *not* bullshitting you," Spooner said.

"You're bullshitting us, Billy, yes, you are," Lucas said. "And I'll tell you what. This case is part of the Alie'e Maison murder investigation. If Rodriguez turns out to be involved, because of his drug dealing, and you're helping him cover up . . . well, then, you're involved. That's called murder one on the TV shows. Murder one in Minnesota is a minimum of thirty years in a cell the size of your desk. You look like you might be young enough to do the whole thirty."

"Wait, wait, wait," Spooner said. "I have absolutely nothing to do with any of this. I want a lawyer. Right now."

"Those are the magic words," Long said to Lucas. "No more questions, and read him his rights."

When they were done with the reading of the rights, Reed agreed to print out the loan records and Long walked out to the parking lot with Lucas. "It's the reading of the rights that scares the shit out of them," he said.

Lucas nodded. "The question is, will Spooner make a call?"

He made the call.

Long went back into the bank and Lucas climbed in the passenger side of the city car. "He's driving the Lexus in the corner," Del said.

Lucas looked down at a silver-toned car nosed in next to a power transformer. "So he's spending some money."

"He's a banker," Del said. "He's gotta have some kind of car to impress the neighbors."

Del took the car to the end of the block and found a spot where they could see Spooner's car.

Del's phone rang twenty minutes later, and Long came on. "I'm not going to make lunch. I've got a thing I've got to do with a subpoena," he said.

"He's moving?"

"Absolutely, sweetheart," Long said.

Del said, "He's moving," and a minute later they spotted Spooner pushing through the front door, carrying his briefcase, pulling on a thigh-length black trench coat. He went to the Lexus, tossed the briefcase across the front seat onto the passenger side, and rolled out of the lot. They followed, a block behind, a half-dozen cars between them, past the capitol, down the hill toward downtown St. Paul, where Del closed up and Lucas eased down in the seat.

Halfway through downtown, Spooner took the Lexus into a parking ramp. Del pulled to the side, shoved the gearshift into park, said, "I'll catch him at the Skyway exit. Turn on your phone," and jumped out. When Spooner was out of sight, up the ramp, Lucas walked around the car and went looking for a parking meter.

Del called ten minutes later. "Got him. He's at an attorney's office."

"Goddamnit."

"So what do we do?"

"I'll call you back in two minutes," Lucas said. He punched the Off button, redialed Lane's cell phone number. Lane answered, and Lucas said, "Where's Rodriguez?"

"In his office. I can see his sleeve."

"Nothing going on?"

"A few things. My feet hurt like hell; I've got Homicide's interview notebook on the case, and I'm reading all the interviews; a nine-year-old kid tried to sell me what I believe are counterfeit baseball cards; and the St. Paul cops rousted me. That's about it."

"No trouble with St. Paul?"

"Nah. Just checking on why I'd been standing in the Skyway for two hours, reading a note-book," Lane said.

"Okay. Our guy's at an attorney's office. He's about two blocks from you."

"Let me know if anything happens."

"A Mickey Mantle rookie card's gotta be worth more than twenty, doesn't it?"

"Chump." Lucas redialed Del. "Rodriguez is at his office."

"So . . ."

"So let's hang for a while. Give it an hour, anyway."

Twenty-five minutes into the hour, Del called. "He's moving."

"Where?"

"Looks like the parking garage."

"Goddamnit. Stay with him. If he heads to the car, I'll pick you up where you jumped out."

Five minutes later, Del was back in the car. Lucas drove around to the parking garage exit, and as they picked up Spooner, Del's phone rang. He took it out, listened for a second, said, "Lucas's phone is on now," and then handed it to

Lucas. "I'm a fuckin' secretary," he said.

"Your boy made the call," Lester said.

"Yeah? When?"

"Six or seven minutes ago. He was calling from a lawyer's office."

"Yeah, we took him there. He's out, and we're on him again. What'd he say?"

"Sounded like he was reading out of a script. He said, 'Mr. Rodriguez, allegations have been made against you by the Minneapolis police. I will no longer be allowed to have any direct dealings with you on the mortgages on your buildings, and I wanted to inform you that in the future your account will be handled by Mrs. Ellen Feldman.' Then Rodriguez said, 'What are you talking about? The police?' And then Spooner said, 'I'm not at liberty to discuss it, but you can get more information from Minneapolis Deputy Chief of Police Lucas Davenport or Mr. Tim Long, assistant Hennepin County Attorney.' Then Rodriguez said, 'Is this about the party?' And Spooner says, 'I'm really not at liberty to discuss it. I suggest you call Chief Davenport or Mr. Long. I'm sorry this had to happen. I felt we had an excellent working relationship. I have to go now. I hope this works out for the best.' Then Rodriguez says, 'Okay. Well, thanks for everything, you know.' And that's it."

"Thanks for everything," Lucas said. "He means the phone call."

"Pretty goddamn neat phone call, too," Lester said. "He warns him, but there's nothing in it to hang him with. Either one of them."

After Lucas hung up, they tracked Spooner back to the bank. He drove back slowly, well within the speed limit. When he was inside, Lucas said, "Fuck him. Let's go see Marcy."

Weather was outside the intensive care ward talking to Tom Black. They saw Lucas and Del coming, and Weather smiled and Del said, "Something good happened."

"What?" Lucas asked as they came up.

"She's somewhat awake. Everything's pretty much stabilized. She's still critical, but it's looking pretty good. For the first time."

Lucas went to the ward window and looked in. "Can we go in?"

"Let me get a nurse. They just took a guy in."

The nurse came, said, severely, "One minute. Say hello, and out." She gave them masks to hold over their faces, and led the way in.

Marcy's eyelids were at half-mast. When Lucas, Del, and Black loomed beside her, her eyes opened fractionally, and after a moment, the corners of her lips twitched.

"Sleeping on the job," Black said.

"I ain't signing off on the overtime — you're still on the Homicide payroll," Lucas said.

"If you die, can I have your gun?" Del asked.

She tried to say something, but Lucas couldn't hear and he leaned forward. Her lips looked parched, almost burnt. "What?"

"Fuck all of you," she whispered, and she

turned her head another fraction of an inch.

"She's better," Lucas said, delighted. "She says go fuck ourselves."

Weather said, "I can't believe cops. I never could. The bullshit gets *so* deep." She was smiling when she said it.

Lucas squatted next to the bed, speaking through the blue mask. "You're hurting," he said, "but you're gonna make it. We're tracking the guy who shot you."

Her head rolled away, and her eyelids drooped again.

"Everybody out," the nurse said.

In the hall, Lucas said, "She looked pretty good, huh? She looked pretty good."

"Pretty good," Black said.

"I was amazed," Del said. "She took a fuckin' .44, man. Man, she looked a *lot* better." He hitched up his jeans, and they all nodded at each other.

"She's not out of the woods," Weather said. "Keep that in mind. It's a long trip back."

On the way out the door with Del, Lucas stopped, said, "Hang on a minute," and went back inside. Weather was walking away, back to the interior of the hospital. "Hey, Weather."

She stopped, waited. He came up, took a card out of his ID case, scribbled his cell phone number on the back of it, and said, "Keep an eye on her while you're here, okay? You know the docs better than any of us. If anything changes . . ."

"I'll call," she said. She took the card, and Lucas headed back out.

On the sidewalk, Del said, "What?"

"Gave her my number in case anything happens with Marcy," Lucas lied. She could have gotten to him through the police switchboard, and she *had* that number. He'd actually gone back because of a little subconscious twitch: He went back to look at her ears. She was wearing inky blue sapphire earrings, one-carat stones. He recognized them, because he'd given them to her.

He smiled on the way back to the office, and Del said, "Our girl's gonna be all right."

"Maybe," he said.

Back at the office, Lucas put in a call to Louis Mallard at the FBI in Washington. Mallard had enough clout to extract anything from any government computer anywhere. He agreed to find and send along everything available on Rodriguez's Miami company. When he got off the phone with Mallard, Lucas walked down to Rose Marie's office.

"Need a meeting," he said.

"Marcy's awake."

"I know. She's gonna make it."

Rose Marie put a finger to her lips. "Shhh. Don't hex her."

While they were waiting for the meeting to get together, Lane called. "I got bored and walked by Rodriguez's office window. He was working on the computer in his office."

"How many people saw you? The secretary?"

"Maybe. But I was disguised as a cool guy, which, for me, takes no effort, and I put a little shine on her, through the window."

"Lane, you fucking —"

"Anyway, Rodriguez was signed on to E-Trade."

"E-Trade."

"Yeah. I bet he's scared and dumping stock."

"Like I was saying, you're a fucking genius." Lucas called Mallard back. "Can you get into E-Trade records?"

"If I wanted to," Mallard said.

Del came to the meeting, along with Frank Lester; Towson, the county attorney; and Long, the assistant county attorney, just back from the Atheneum bank with a pile of paper. No public relations people.

"I wanted to make sure everybody knows what we're doing," Lucas said. "We're looking at this guy Rodriguez, and I will tell you this, just based on feel and experience and a few things we know about him: He killed Alie'e and Sandy Lansing."

"You're pretty sure," Towson said.

"Pretty sure. Lansing was dealing several kinds of dope to rich people and wanna-bes, working for Rodriguez. Rodriguez is at the party. They have some kind of conflict, and Rodriguez kills her right there in the hallway. Maybe it's even an accident — the ME's saying it looks like her head was smashed against a doorjamb. So

Rodriguez tried to stuff her in the closet and is surprised by Alie'e, who was in the bedroom. Maybe Alie'e heard the noise of Lansing's head hitting the doorjamb — or maybe she just woke up at the wrong time. Anyway, she sees something, and Rodriguez takes her out. At this point, he walks away, maybe down the hall to the next room, and goes out the window. Or maybe he just walks through the crowd and drifts away."

"What do we have for sure?" Towson asked.

"We have the fact that Rodriguez was a punk in Detroit, came here with no money, and got rich fast. We have a guy who'll tell us that he's a dope wholesaler, and that Sandy Lansing worked for him, selling dope. I don't doubt that once we start working on that angle, now that we've got his name, we'll be able to find a few other ties between them. We've got Rodriguez at the party. We've got a guy — Derrick Deal — who knew Lansing pretty well, and thought she might be selling a little dope; and he was a guy who would do a little blackmail if it looked profitable. He almost certainly knew who her boss was, because a day after I talked to him, he was murdered in a way that was at least reminiscent of the way Alie'e and Lansing were killed: no passion, just brutal efficiency."

"I don't see how you tie Deal to Rodriguez," Rose Marie said.

"I don't, directly. What I'm saying is, Deal didn't know Alie'e. So if he was going to blackmail somebody for murder, it had to be somebody tied to Lansing. The only person at that party tied to Lansing, as far as we know, was Rodriguez."

Long looked at Towson. "We'd need some kind of color chart, or maybe a PowerPoint presentation, to sell that to a jury."

Towson shook his head. "We're not at a jury yet. We need more."

"We're just starting on the guy," Del said.

Long leaned into the discussion. "I got all the paper from Atheneum. Spooner's boss was looking over my shoulder, and you know what? If we push the guy, he'll tell us the loans shouldn't have been made. The goddamn things are dirty. Rodriguez was paying him off."

"Can we crack him?" Towson asked.

"I don't know. He's sort of a nebbish, but he's scared, and if he keeps his mouth shut . . . I mean, he's got a lawyer, and if he claims that the loans were on the up-and-up and keeps going back to this minority business, and if Rodriguez doesn't talk, there's not much we can get him on."

"We'll get some paper going on him," Lucas said. "If he's been paid off by Rodriguez, he might have an income-tax problem."

Towson said to Long, "Talk to the IRS."

Lester summarized the case against Tom Olson. "He had motive, he had opportunity, he had access to a car that we now know for sure was used in the Marcy Sherrill shooting —"

"How do you know that?" Long asked.

"We took the slug out of the car door. It didn't penetrate the passenger compartment, it wound up inside a plastic handle inside the door. It came from Marcy's revolver."

Long nodded. "Okay."

"But you haven't found the .44 that was used on Marcy," Lucas said.

"No."

"That's a problem," Del said.

"Yup. Especially since he's been here, and not back in Fargo, ever since the shooting. We went through his motel room, and his car, after his parents were killed. No gun. The gun that was used to kill his parents belonged to his father: It was his father's car gun."

"Where'd you get that?" Lucas asked.

"Olson told us. His father kept it under the front-seat cushion. We ran the serial numbers, traced it to a gun store up in Burnt River. Lynn Olson bought it six years ago."

"You think he did his parents?" Towson asked.

"We've got this whole theory. . . ." Lester explained the multiple-personality concept, and explained the trap they'd set for Olson.

"The trap better work," Towson said, "Because the multiple-personality theory sounds like bullshit."

A secretary stuck her head in and said, "Lucas, you've got a call from the White House."

The group all looked at him, and Lucas said, "What?"

"The guy said he's with the White House. He didn't sound like he was joking."

"You better take it," Rose Marie said.

Lucas took it on the secretary's desk. Mallard said, "I bet that impressed everybody. The switchboard lady told me you were in a meeting in the chief's office."

"It certainly impressed the shit out me," Lucas said. "What's happening?"

"Your boy Rodriguez started selling out his accounts Monday morning. It'll be a couple of days before he gets the checks, but he's got a quarter million in the mail."

"Goddamn," Lucas said.

"I've only got one thing from Miami. Rodriguez set up the Miami company nine years ago. The attorney's name is Haynes, and as far as the guys in the Miami office know, he's straight — small time, private office, business-oriented guy. Does real estate, that kind of stuff."

"Mallard, you're a good egg," Lucas said.

"Ho ho, very funny," Mallard said. "By the way, you remember Malone?"

"Of course. How is she?"

"She's fox-trotting with somebody else," Mallard said.

"Uh-oh. Gonna be number five?"

"Could happen. Anyway, we'll grind some more on Rodriguez, but I thought you'd want to know he was collecting cash."

"That's one more thing," Towson said when Lucas told them about Mallard's call. "And it's a good one. We've got to slow him down, though."

"So what do we do?" Rose Marie asked.

"Some lawyer shit," Del said, looking at Towson.

"The IRS," Towson said. "Tell them about the dope — maybe they can do something about the money he's got coming."

Rose Marie said, "So we push on Rodriguez, and we keep baiting Olson. Everybody agree?"

Everybody nodded.

"Best we got," Lester said.

🐝 21 🐝

Del took a call from Narcotics and headed that way. Lucas borrowed a uniformed cop from the patrol division, put him in plainclothes, and sent him to relieve Lane.

On the phone to Lane, he said, "When he gets there, I want you to brief him, then go on over to the county attorney's office, talk to Tim Long, and look at all that loan paperwork on Spooner. Spooner's critical: If he knows anything at all about Rodriguez, then he probably knows about everything. If we crack him, we may have enough."

"How much paper?" Lane asked.

"About a ton," Lucas said.

"Goddamnit, Lucas, how come I'm always the one stuck with paper?"

" 'Cause you can read; I'm not so sure about the other guys. So get your ass over here. Also, an FBI computer file just came in on Rodriguez and his money. I'll print it out and leave it with Lester. Take it with you, see if there's anything that, you know . . ."

"What?"

"Shit, I don't know. Correlates, or something."

When he was done with Lane, he got out the phone book, got the number for Brown's, dialed, and asked for India. She came on the phone a minute later. Lucas identified himself and asked, "Are you gonna be around for a few minutes?"

"Until six."

"I want to stop by," he said.

When he got off the phone, Lucas walked down to Homicide with the printed-out FBI file, left it with Lester. "Did you guys print those pictures of Rodriguez?"

"Uh, yeah. . . . I think they're down in ID. They handled it."

Lucas went down to the Identification division. The photo guy's name was Harold McNeil, a former uniform cop who got tired of cold squad cars and got the photo job by lying. Photography, he said, was a longtime hobby, although he didn't know a small-format camera from a yak. He read a book called *Learn Photography in a Weekend*, fooled around with the department's cameras, and after a week or so, was better than the last guy, and kept the job.

He had two good shots of Rodriguez: a full-frontal head shot, and one side view.

"Got some heads I can use in a spread?" Lucas asked.

"Yup." McNeil turned around, opened the bottom drawer of his filing cabinet, and took out a handful of photos. They found sets, front and back, of a half-dozen guys. Lucas stuck them in his pocket.

"I'll bring them back," he promised.

"That's what everybody says. Nobody ever does," McNeil said.

Lucas got his coat and walked across town to Brown's; the cold air felt good; the walking felt good. India was behind the desk and smiled when she saw him coming.

"Did you ever see any of these guys with Sandy Lansing?" Lucas pushed the stack of photos at her. "There are two photos of each guy."

India took her time looking at them. Another woman came along and asked, "What's going on?"

Lucas said, "Police. We're trying to see if we can find somebody Sandy Lansing might have gone out with."

"I've seen her with a guy a few times," the other woman said.

She stood at India's elbow, and they went through the photos together, India slowly shaking her head. "I don't think so," she said finally. "This guy . . . but I don't think it was him."

The other woman said, "I don't think so, either. Sorta like that, though. If you put him in a suit."

"It's not him. This guy looks a little rough," India said.

"You're right," the other woman said. She looked at Lucas. "I don't think I've ever seen any of them."

Lucas looked at the one photo they'd talked about. A honey-haired white guy, round-faced, but without Rodriguez's heft. He and Rodriguez looked nothing alike.

"Thanks," he said.

Strikeout.

Back at the office, Lucas had a note to call Tim Long at the county attorney's office. He did. "You can't count on getting anything from the IRS," Long said. "I talked to a guy over there, and they said if we get anything that looks like hidden income, to send them a copy of what we get. But they've had too much trouble with citizen complaints to go after a guy who they've never had a problem with. He was audited a couple of years ago, in a random audit, and everything worked out to the penny."

"Which it would, if he's faking his cash flow with drug money."

"Yeah, well, the IRS guy said, 'You catch 'em, we fry 'em.' But they ain't gonna hang up his investment money and have a congressman screaming at them. Not when they've got a whole file that says the guy is clean."

Another strikeout.

Rose Marie said, "Olson isn't moving. He's not doing anything."

"You're talking to him, aren't you? In the family briefing?"

"Yeah." She looked up at the office clock.

"We're gonna do it again in about fifteen minutes."

"Why don't you tell him, in utter confidence, that we've got a candidate for the guy who actually killed his sister. If he's nuts, and anything is going to get him stirred up, that should do it."

"Lucas —"

"Don't give him the name," Lucas said. "Tell him you can't do that, but there's a possibility that we'll know something in a couple of days. The idea is to get him cranked, get him back in the mood, if he's the one doing the killings."

"I don't know . . ."

"Another benefit is, it'd keep him from pissing on us in the press."

After leaving Rose Marie, Lucas walked over to see Marcy. Tom Black was sitting next to her bed, and her head was turned toward him. When Lucas walked in, Black said, "She comes and she goes. She's asleep right now."

Lucas got another chair and carried it over to Marcy's bed. Two beds down, an old man with a shock of white hair, a desiccated face, and a thin, hawk nose, tried to breathe; worked at it.

"What do you think of this Olson guy?" Black asked.

"He's maybe crazy," Lucas said.

"You think, uh, he'll be doing a trip down to the state hospital?"

"Hard call. A guy executes his parents, it's pretty easy to say he's nuts."

"Yeah, well . . ." Black exhaled, and looked down at the tile floor.

"What?" Lucas asked.

"I'd hate to see the fucker get away with what he did to Marcy," Black said. "No goddamn justice in the world if you can blow her up and get away with it."

Lucas looked at him for a moment. Black was Marcy's best friend on the force. And he was gay, so they didn't have the sex problem that tended to come up around her — that had come up with Lucas. "Listen, Thomas my friend, if you're thinking what I think you're thinking, stop thinking it."

"You haven't thought about it?"

"No, I haven't. You get some guy you can't stop, a pederast or a serial rapist and you just can't get at him . . . then I might do some thinking, but I sure as hell wouldn't mention it to *anyone*. To anyone. And I wouldn't pop somebody for shooting a cop. You know? Cops get shot; that's part of the job. Marcy knew it could happen — hell, it already happened to her, once. It's not like she's an innocent little lamb."

"But if he gets away . . ."

"Jesus, Tom, give it some time. We'll get him. I'll tell you what, I think maybe it's fifty percent Olson, maybe fifty percent somebody else. You can't go popping a guy on fifty-fifty chance."

"It's got me fucked up, dude," Black said.

"I know."

Marcy woke up a couple of minutes later, recognized both of them, croaked, "I could use a beer."

"I got one, but I already used it once," Black said. "If we could find a bottle someplace . . ."

She smiled. She looked almost okay, Lucas thought. "How're you feeling?"

"Like I got hit pretty hard."

"You did, you dumb shit. You ain't the goddamn Secret Service, and Jael ain't the President," Lucas said.

She closed her eyes for a minute, seemed to drift off, then snapped back. "How's Jael?"

"We've got her covered twenty-four hours a day," Lucas said. "Franklin taught her how to cook nachos."

"I feel hollow," she said. She licked her dry lips. "I don't hurt."

Black stood up. "You want me to get the nurse?"

"No, no . . . I just feel . . . hollow."

Del shuffled in, said hello, squatted next to the bed, and looked at Marcy. After a minute, he grunted and said, "You're doing okay. I'm gonna stop coming over here every five minutes. You want some magazines?"

"Not for a few days yet," she said, her voice going weak. She turned her head back straight, closed her eyes, and took a couple of breaths. Lucas thought she'd gone back to sleep again. Then she turned back and looked for Lucas, her eyes going in and out of focus. "Did you meet . . . that old friend?"

He nodded. "Yes."

"You're careful?"

"We can talk about it next week."

"You're teasing me. . . ."

"She's going through her midlife," Lucas said. "I don't know if anybody can help her."

Marcy said, "Mmmm."

"Great. Office gossip in intensive care," Black said.

Marcy asked, "What else is there?" and closed her eyes again. This time she did sleep. After two minutes, Del stood up, looked at Lucas, put a finger to his lips, and tipped his head toward the door.

Lucas whispered, "We're going. . . . You take it easy," to Black, and followed Del to the door. Outside, Del said, "You remember that Logan guy? The other dealer that Outer gave us, along with Bee?"

"Yeah, we never had time —"

"Dope hit him three hours ago — that's the call I got. They got almost a kilo of coke and a couple of sacks of meth. We're doing a little dance with him. Gave him a stack of photos and told him if he could put two of them together, he might have something to deal with. He chose Rodriguez and Lansing."

"Did you talk to Tim Long about it?" Lucas asked.

"Not yet."

"Get with him, figure out a plea, and run it past Logan's attorney. We'll want a statement as quick as we can get it. Today," Lucas said.

"That's pretty quick, with a lawyer involved."

"I know. You gotta tell his attorney that there's a short-term expiration date on the offer. Right now, Logan can give us something new. If we find another connection, we don't need his client. If that happens, Logan goes to Stillwater and does the whole enchilada."

"I'm outa here," Del said.

Lucas looked at his watch and headed back to the office, stopped again to talk to Rose Marie.

"What happened with Olson? You tell him?"

She nodded. "That we've got a candidate."

"And I'm going to push Rodriguez, see if we can get him to panic," Lucas said.

"Why?"

" 'Cause the only case we're going to get against him will be circumstantial. The stuff is starting to pile up, but if we can get him to do something irrational, like dump a bunch of money and run for it, if we can bust him with a plane ticket to Venezuela or something . . . that'd look good to a jury."

"All right. We need some public action for the movie people anyway. Ever since Alie'e's funeral was put off, they've been pissed. What are you gonna do?"

"That depends on Rodriguez. He knows that we're onto him. We'll watch him the rest of today. Tomorrow — I don't know. Maybe I'll go over and talk to him. Maybe bust him for the cameras, haul his ass over here, then turn him loose again. Shake him."

"Let me know."

Lucas went back to his office, sat in his chair, put his feet up on a desk drawer and thought about it, and, ten minutes later, walked down to Homicide and found Lester.

"When you guys cleaned out Sandy Lansing's house, did you get any photos? Albums, anything like that?"

"A few dozen photos — nothing real recent. Family stuff," Lester said. "We didn't find a camera in the place. Well — there was an old Polaroid in the bedroom closet, but it was so old I don't think you could get film for it anymore."

"How about video?"

"She had a VCR and a few tapes, but the tapes were all movies, and some low-rent commercial porn. No video camera."

"What she do in her life? Everybody's got a camera."

"She went to parties," Lester said. "And bars. As close as we can tell, that's it. She went out every night of her life. She worked out at a fitness place three times a week. She had about six CDs and a compact stereo that probably cost her two hundred dollars, a medium-sized Sony TV, and the basic cable package. That was about it."

"We need to tie her tighter to Rodriguez."

"Gonna have to do it from the other end," Lester said. "This girl was a little strange. As far as I can tell, she didn't have any interests except going out. A million dresses, fifty pairs of shoes, a big collection of costume jewelry. Larry Martin checked the workout club and found out that they use these magnetic cards to check you in. She went Monday, Wednesday, and Friday, and all she did was a forty-five minute class designed to keep your butt looking good. So she wasn't even interested in working out. Wasn't interested in music, not interested in TV, had about six books."

"And no pictures."

"Not many," Lester said.

"Did you look at the porn?"

"No, but Larry did. She wasn't in it. Other than that, it was just standard jerk-off stuff out of California. Hot tubs and swimming pools and blow jobs."

"Huh. Ever wonder why we live in Minnesota?"

"So we don't have to put up with that scum," Lester said.

"What a poop," Lucas said. He stood up and stretched.

"Scratching for anything, huh?"

"At this point . . ."

Just after dark, with rush-hour building outside the door, Lucas started thinking about dinner; then took a call from the cop sent to watch Rodriguez.

"This is really exciting stuff," the cop said.

"Wish I was plainclothes and got to stand in Sky-ways all the time."

"You calling to thank me, or what?"

"Some dude pulled into Rodriguez's office, he's got a briefcase bigger than my dick, and they sat down and started looking at paper. This dude is pushing all kinds of paper across the desk. I can't tell you anything about it, because all I can see is their shirtsleeves. So, after about an hour, the guy puts all the paper back in the briefcase and comes out, and Rodriguez pulls up his computer and I figure he isn't going anyplace, and maybe I ought to check this other dude . . ."

"And you went after the second guy and Rodriguez skipped on you," Lucas finished.

"Fuck no. I'm looking at him right now. Rodriguez, I mean. Anyway, I followed the other guy into the parking ramp and he gets into a car that's got magnetic signs on the doors. Coffey Realty. I got the phone number off the door and the tag number off the car, and then I ran back to make sure Rodriguez wasn't going away. . . . Anyway, Rodriguez is still here, and he was dealing heavy with a guy from a real estate company."

"All right. You done good. I owe you a donut or something."

"*Two* donuts. With them little sprinkles. You want these numbers?"

Lucas looked up the tag number for the dealer's car, and got a name and an address. When he called Coffey Realty and asked for Kirk

Smalley, Smalley was in, and working. "I need to talk to you," Lucas said after identifying himself. "I can be there before five o'clock."

Coffey Realty was located on University Avenue just down from the state capitol, a block from the Atheneum bank. As he parked his car in the gathering darkness, Lucas made a mental note to check on connections between the real estate company and the bank, then walked up and pulled on the real estate company's door. Locked. There was a light inside, and he knocked. A moment later, a balding man with rolled-up shirtsleeves came to the door, peered at Lucas, then opened it.

"Officer Davenport?"

"Yeah."

"Come on in. I'm Kirk Smalley." Smalley locked the door behind them and led Lucas back to an interior office.

"Big place," Lucas said as they walked back.

"We're a pretty good-sized company," Smalley said. "We specialize in commercial real estate, so we don't do a lot of mass advertising. But we do pretty well." He dropped into a swivel chair behind his desk, waved Lucas at a visitor's chair, and asked, "What can I do for you?"

"Are you handling a real estate deal for Richard Rodriguez?"

Smalley swung back and forth in his chair, thinking about the question, and then said, "Can you tell me why you want to know?"

"I can tell you some things . . . if you're handling a real estate deal."

"Is this confidential?"

"If we need your official testimony, we'll sub-poena you — you'd have no choice about talking, if you see what I mean."

"What, Richard Rodriguez is in the Mafia?" Smalley grinned at Lucas.

"It's serious," Lucas said.

Now Smalley sat forward. "You've got to keep it confidential, unless you subpoena me."

"Sure." That didn't sound like enough. "We will," Lucas added.

Smalley shrugged. "He called me today, Richard did, and asked me how hard it would be to sell off his real estate holdings. He wanted to know how long, and how much. I told him how much depends a little on how long, but if he was in a hurry, we could lay them off on a real estate investment trust in a couple of weeks. But unless we were lucky, he'd take a hit."

"How big a hit?" Lucas asked.

"Can't tell. Could be two hundred thousand dollars. Right now, after his mortgages are paid off, Richard could take out a couple of million. If you take two hundred off the top of that, he's down to a million eight. Then you've got to take capital gains and state taxes out, plus our commission. He'd wind up with something like a million three, walk-away."

"Lot of money," Lucas said.

"Sure. But that two hundred thousand is purely thrown away — a little bit would go to taxes and commission and so on, but he's basically taking a fifteen percent hit by trying to sell it quick. Two hundred thousand, in the context of a million three, is a big chunk."

"What'd he say?" Lucas asked.

Smalley came back with his own question. "Why're you investigating him?"

"There's a possibility that he's using large amounts of drug money to make up the difference between actual rents, on one side, and his mortgage and maintenance payments on the other," Lucas said.

Smalley considered that for a moment, then said, "You mean he cooked the books? But he cooked them *up?* I never heard of that."

"That's what we think. It's a form of money laundering," Lucas said. "The investigation is in the context of the overall investigation of the Alie'e Maison murder."

"Holy shit." Smalley was impressed. And he was a smart guy. "You think he did it? Strangled Alie'e?"

"I can't tell you that — we're conducting an investigation," Lucas said. "So answer my question. What'd he say when you told him about the hit?"

"He said, 'Sell it.' I said, 'Listen, Richard' — he doesn't like to be called Dick — I said 'Listen, Richard, if you could give us two months,' and he just cut me off and said, 'Dump 'em.'"

Then it was Lucas's turn to think. After a moment, he asked, "If you'd heard about this investigation unofficially, what would you do?"

"Do? I'd drop the deal like a hot rock," Smalley said. "We don't need to mess around with Alie'e Maison and all of that. We sure as hell don't need to peddle a couple million bucks' worth of real estate to a REIT" — he said "reet" — "and then have them come back and tell us that we sold them a bunch of cooked books. That's not the kind of reputation you want to build."

"So do what you want," Lucas said.

"Drop him? You want us to drop him?"

"I don't care what you do," Lucas said. "Drop him, if that's best for your company. This is an official call — you'll be subpoenaed in the next day or two. But if you were to call him and drop him, we wouldn't object, certainly."

Smalley scratched his chin, looked at the telephone, then back at Lucas. "You're using me to fuck with him."

"I'm just trying to uphold the law, Mr. Smalley."

"Right. I almost forgot." They sat together for a few seconds, contemplating the law, and then Smalley said, "I'll call him tomorrow morning."

Lucas took Dale Street down to I-94 and got on the interstate heading west. He was inching toward his own exit at Cretin, then, at the last second, moved back left and continued across the Mississippi River bridge, into Minneapolis, and down south to Jael Corbeau's studio. Lucas rang the bell and a voice fifteen feet away said, "Go on in, Chief."

Lucas jumped. "Jesus, I thought you were a bush."

"I feel like a fuckin' bush." Then, sotto voce, on a radio: "It's Davenport." As Lucas pushed through the door, he said, "Tell dickweed it's his turn out here."

Two more bored cops were sitting in the studio, watching a portable TV that was set up on the floor, plugged into a DVD. When Lucas walked in, one of the cops paused the picture; they were watching *The Mummy*.

"Whichever one of you is the dickweed, I'm supposed to tell you it's your turn out there."

One of the cops looked at his watch. "Bullshit. I got fifteen minutes yet. You looking for Jael?"

"Yeah."

"She's upstairs, reading."

"Is she decent?"

"Aw, man, don't ask me that. It gives me a hard-on."

"Let me put you down for sensitivity training. We have it every Saturday morning at six."

"I'll be there. Count on it." The cop re-started The Mummy halfway through a street riot; it resembled the media scrum outside City Hall.

Lucas went halfway up the stairs, called, "Jael?"

She came to the top of the stairs and said, "Hey — Davenport. What's going on?"

"What're you doing?" Lucas asked.

"I'm down to reading a book called *Natural Ash Glazes*. What'd you have in mind?"

"I don't know. I thought I'd check you out, we could roll around town for a while," he said.

Her face brightened. "That's the best offer I've had in weeks. If I have to sit around here anymore, I'll scream."

Lucas told the other cops that they'd be gone for a while. One of them said, "Hang on," and pulled on a pair of camo coveralls. "I'm going to sneak out through the garage. Give me two minutes. Give us a chance to see if anything moves after you leave."

So they sat watching *The Mummy* for a couple of minutes, and then Lucas said, "Let's go." Outside the door, Jael took his arm, and the bush said, "Wish I could go." Jael jumped. Lucas laughed and said, "Got me coming in."

Down the sidewalk, she asked, "See anybody?"

"No. Don't look around."

"What if the guy follows us?" she asked.

"Then *we* follow *him*."

"But what if he's watching from further away, and we don't see him, but he follows us anyway."

Lucas loaded her into the Porsche. "Not possible," he said.

They pulled away from the curb, Lucas watching ahead and in the rearview mirror, Jael craning left and right, looking for headlights.

"Lots of cars, but I didn't see any headlights come on," she said.

"So he's probably not around."

"But what if —"

"Reach behind your seat there, there's like a black plastic bag. . . ."

She got the bag, opened it, took out the little bubble light, and looked at it.

"Gimme it," Lucas said. He look the light, licked the suction cup, and stuck it on the dash; the cord plugged into the cigarette lighter. A minute later, they rolled down the ramp on I-35W and Lucas dropped the hammer.

The Porsche took off, running through moderate traffic, and a half-mile down, he flipped the switch on the flasher and Jael laughed and the speed went up and Jael braced herself against the dashboard and said, "Now you're showing off," as they went past the 100 mark. They flew along along the interstate, cars ahead of them scattering like chickens. At an open spot, Lucas killed the flasher and said, "No point in advertising," and backed off the speed a notch, bringing it down to ninety-five.

A minute later, they burned past a highway patrol car that had been hidden behind a Ryder truck.

"Aw, shit," Lucas said.

"Highway patrol," she said.

"Yeah, I know. Stop or go?"

"Go," she said.

He went, and the needle pushed past 100 to

108, and Jael said, "He turned his flashing lights on. . . . I think he's coming. . . . He's coming, but you're still gaining."

Exit coming up. Diamond Lake Road. One car at the top of the ramp. Lucas pushed it until the last second, then cut right, took the ramp. The car at the top was turning left, so Lucas went right, around the corner, down a long block, and turned left: He accelerated to the end of the block, turned left again, and rolled down the window. They could hear the siren from the Highway Patrol car, but it was north and then west of them — going the wrong way.

"They usually turn right if they lose a guy," Lucas grunted. "We gotta get south."

They zigzagged south and west, past Oak Hill cemetery, under another limited-access road, Jael teasing Lucas as he lurked through residential neighborhoods, avoiding headlights. "Shut up, shut up," he said, and she laughed and said, "Mr. Speed-o."

They finally made I-694, and Lucas took the car onto the highway, two exits, off, into a bookstore parking lot, part of a shopping complex. "Now what?" Jael asked.

"We go to the bookstore for an hour, then walk over and get something to eat, and maybe go shopping for a while. Gotta stay off the road for a couple of hours. There aren't that many black Porsches around."

"What if they stop us anyway?" she asked.

"Then I lie like a motherfucker," Lucas said.

"I thought cops got free passes."

"Not if they're showing off for a girl," Lucas said. "I hope you like books."

She did like books, and disappeared into the Art section. Lucas browsed through Literature, slowed down at Poetry, found a collection of Philip Larkin's stuff, and was reading through it when she snuck up behind him. "*Guns 'n' Ammo*," she predicted, reaching for the book. He let her have it, and she turned it over in her hands and then looked up at him. "Showing off for a girl, eh?"

He shrugged. "Not really. I don't read much fiction, but I read poetry."

She closed one eye and examined him. "You're lying like a motherfucker."

"Nope."

"One of the other cops told me you once owned a computer company."

"Yeah, but it was really somebody else who did the computer stuff," Lucas said. "I just had some good ideas at the right time."

"That's what it's all about, isn't it? Having the right ideas at the right time." She turned the book over. "You think I'd like him?"

He thought for a minute, then said, "Nope. He's a little too *guy* for you."

"Who, then?"

"Emily Dickinson? She's my favorite — probably the best American poet ever."

"All right, I'll try her," she said. "Otherwise,

all I got was this." She held up a book with a pot on the cover that said, *Japanese Ash Glazes.*

"I got a deep interest in ash myself," Lucas said.

After the bookstore, they went to a bagel place and got healthy bagels. As they were eating, Jael paging through her collection of Dickinson, she suggested that they go back to the bookstore so she could buy some mysteries. "I always go into the bookstores and wind up buying books for work, or something serious, but if I've got to keep sitting in that house, I gotta have something else. I can't stand TV anymore."

"If you want to buy mysteries, there's a place on the way back that we could stop. Nothing but mysteries."

"Sounds good." She licked a drip of sun-dried tomato hummus off her thumb. "We need to kill some more time." But in the car, she said, "At your house, do you have both a bathtub and a shower? Or are you just a shower guy?"

"No, I have both."

"Since we've gotta kill time, why don't we go back to your place and jump in the tub? It's been a while since I had a really great back-washing."

They were sitting at an uphill stop sign, and Lucas had one foot on the clutch and let the car roll back a few feet, then accelerated forward, and rolled back, thinking. "Maybe I need a little more romancing," he said finally. "Besides . . ."

"Another commitment?"

"Not exactly. But . . . I'm sort of between everything," he said.

"I know you're not gay, the way you look at me."

"That's not the problem." But it had been a long time: He remembered standing outside the cabin and looking up at the great smear of the Milky Way stars and feeling not insignificant, but lonely. And alone.

"It's just casual sex, Lucas. Therapy," she said.

"Maybe I'm still too Catholic. Besides, what about the guys at the bookstore? They need the sales. What're their children gonna eat if we don't buy books?"

"You remember what it feels like? Sitting in a tub, with a woman between your legs, all slippery and slidey, and you've got the soap in your hands . . ." She was laughing at him again.

Lucas let the car roll back, and accelerated, and let it roll back, and accelerated, and said, "All right."

"Good choice," she said. "Fuck the guys at the bookstore."

She was laughing, but later that evening she said, "For three hours, I almost forgot about Plain."

❧ 22 ❧

Thursday. Day six of Alie'e Maison.

Frank Lester was carrying a brown sandwich bag up the City Hall steps when Lucas caught up with him the next morning, half jogging through the cold twilight, trailing a long streamer of steam. "Baloney sandwiches?"

"Peanut butter and jelly," Lester said. He held up the bag; he was wearing ski gloves. "I understand you were out late with Jael Corbeau."

"Yeah, a little late, rolling around town," Lucas said evasively. "She didn't want to go back home."

"Not a goddamn thing happening. Not with Corbeau, not with Kinsley. Maybe we're fucked up. Maybe Olson's not the guy. He's been preaching every night, he goes around to all these churches. The guys who're tracking him say he's completely loony, but the people at these churches, they love him. Last night, he started to bleed —"

"Aw, man, I don't want to hear that," Lucas said.

"Can't figure out how he did it. Thought maybe he has a little razor blade stuck on his belt, or something, but they say he got all cranked up and he spread his arms above his head, screaming, and all of a sudden, the blood started seeping out of his palms, and then he gets a red spot on his shirt, right . . . you know. Right where the spear went in."

"Jesus."

"Exactly. . . . What's happening with Rodriguez?"

"Pushed a button last night," Lucas said. "Maybe today we'll see something."

"Hope so." He looked past Lucas, and Lucas turned. A TV remote van squatted down on the street, its engine running. "Wonder if they've got a microphone on us?"

"Better not," Lucas said. "I'd slam their butts in jail for that. Talk to the judge, we could probably get them three years."

"Yeah."

They both watched the van for a few more seconds — no signs of life, just the exhaust; and they went inside.

Lane came by ten minutes after Lucas got to his office. "We need an accountant to look at some of that paper from the bank," he said. "I've got it narrowed down to a few questions, but I can't answer the questions without an expert."

"What are the questions?"

"How could Spooner give him the loans? That's the basic question. If I could have gotten a home loan on the same terms, I'd be living on

374

one of the lakes. The loans stink."

Lucas leaned back in his chair. "See? That's why I had you reading the paper."

"I'd rather be bustin' somebody's balls. So get me the accountant, and I'll go over and bust Spooner's."

"Let's talk to Rose Marie."

Rose Marie had a better idea. She knew the banking commissioner from the old days, made a call, and got Lane lined up with a bank examiner. She'd just gotten off the phone when the secretary buzzed her. Rose Marie picked up, listened for a minute, then said, "It's Rodriguez," and pushed another button.

"Rose Marie Roux. . . . Yes, this is . . ." She listened for a long minute, then said, "I'm not aware of any of this. Chief Davenport is leading that aspect of the investigation, and we haven't met yet this morning. . . . No, I can't tell you anything. If he did that, as part of the investigation, I assume he had good reason. I appreciate that, Mr. Rodriguez, but there's really no more that I can tell you. I can have Chief Davenport call you when he comes in. . . . Yes, I'm sure he would. Yes, I'm sure he would. . . ."

After another minute of back-and-forth, she politely said goodbye, hung up, and said to Lucas, "Not a happy man. Some real estate deal was canceled. . . .You *did* have good reason?"

"Sure. We're trying to panic him. We've got him tapped." He stopped, scratched his head, said, "How come a cop called me and told me about his appointment with a real estate dealer, but we didn't get it on the wiretaps? He had to have called the guy."

Lane said, "He's a dope dealer, dummy. He's got a blind phone."

Lucas stood up and said, "Shit! How'd we miss that? All of his good calls have been going out somewhere else."

Rose Marie asked, "But how would you find a blind phone if —"

Lucas shook a finger at her. "We need to talk to the phone company, and get incoming phone numbers yesterday afternoon. Wait a minute — who's watching the lines?"

"Somebody from Narcotics, I guess," Rose Marie said.

"Call down and get a number."

Two minutes later, Lucas was talking with the Narcotics cop who was monitoring Rodriguez's lines. "Did he just take a call from a real estate dealer?"

"Nope. He's gotten a couple of calls from one of his apartment managers. They had an electric panel fire last night. He's been making calls to some of his other managers, and a maintenance company. He just talked to the chief, I assume you know that."

"What line was that?"

The cop gave Lucas a number. "But no real estate dealer?"

"Nope."

Lucas rang off, got Rose Marie to dig a St. Paul phone book out of her desk, looked up Coffey Realty, dialed, and asked for Smalley. Smalley came up, and Lucas asked, "We just got a call from Mr. Rodriguez. He sounded a little upset. I assume you called him?"

"Yeah, just a little while ago. He was not a happy camper."

"Can you give me the number you called?"

"Well, sure. I guess," Coffey said.

"I don't have it here. I want to call him back," Lucas said.

"Just a sec, I've got it on a piece of paper. Where . . . Here it is."

Lucas copied the number and said, "Thanks. I would stay away from Mr. Rodriguez for a while. Until he cools off, anyway."

"I plan to stay away from him forever," Smalley said.

Lucas hung up, and Rose Marie said, "Different number?"

"Yeah." He punched in the number for the monitoring cop, got him, and said, "We think Rodriguez is using a blind phone that we're not monitoring. I want you to call him, make like you dialed a wrong number . . . see if it's him. If the voice is right."

The cop said, "Gimme the number."

"He might have caller ID," Lucas said.

"He won't get it from this phone."

"Get back to me," Lucas said.

"Goddamnit, we should have known this,"

Rose Marie said when Lucas had hung up. "A blind phone's pretty basic for a dealer."

"Water under the rug," Lucas said. He looked at Lane. "You get over to the bank guy. If it's like you think, call me. We'll go bust Spooner's balls."

"All right. I should be back to you before noon," Lane said.

"Are you going to call Rodriguez?" Rose Marie asked.

"I'm gonna get Sloan to go over and see him," Lucas said. "I want to see how he handles himself."

Rose Marie's phone burped. She picked it up, listened, pushed a button, said, "This is Rose Marie . . ." then looked at Lucas. "That's Rodriguez's number. It's his voice on the other end."

"Excellent," Lucas said. "Now maybe we make some progress. But we've got to get him talking."

Sloan was on his cell phone. Lucas got him, told him to bring a car around to the hospital. "We're gonna go talk to Rodriguez."

Marcy was sitting up, still paper-pale, five years older than she'd been the week before, the corners of her eyes creased with pain lines. But her eyes were clear, and Black, perched on a chair next to her bed, said, "They're gonna put her in a regular room."

"That's progress," Lucas said. He bent over the bed and kissed her on the forehead. "Man,

I'm glad to see you up. I had all these premonitions."

She looked at him for a moment, then asked, "What've you been up to?"

"What?" He shrugged.

"You've got that innocent look, and that really close shave you get when you're really satisfied with yourself. What have you been doing?"

Lucas grinned. "I don't have the guy who shot you, but I think we've got the guy who did Alie'e. Sloan and I are gonna go bust his chops."

"Yeah?" She still looked suspicious. "Who is it?"

As he filled her in on Rodriguez, he caught her attention wavering once or twice. She really wasn't back yet, he realized. Almost, not quite. When he finished with Rodriguez, he asked, "What are they telling you about recovery time? Think you could be back by Wednesday?"

"Maybe not," she said. "They said, if everything goes well, I'm gonna have to do some rehab. . . . Maybe May?"

"May? Jesus . . . You were hit hard."

"They might have to go back in," Black said. "There're a couple pieces of bone floating around inside that oughta come out. But that's gonna be a while yet."

"You hurt?" Lucas asked her.

She nodded. "Yeah. Started this morning. I don't think it's gonna stop for a while."

"Drugs," Lucas said.

Sloan showed up and chatted for a while, then

he and Lucas left, headed for St. Paul and Rodriguez. Outside the door, on the way to the car, Lucas said, "Before, I was scared about her. Now I'm pissed. She's hurting, and there's not a goddamn thing we can do about it."

"Get the guy who did it," Sloan suggested.

"The guy who did it thinks he's the Messiah," Lucas said.

"There's a difference between *thinks he is* and *is*," Sloan said. "To me, he's just another fat asshole on his way to a cell at Stillwater."

On the way to St. Paul, Lucas said, "Let's stop and see if Spooner is at his office. Bust his balls a little bit."

"Want me to be the nice guy?" Sloan asked.

"We don't need one. We just need to scare this guy."

But Spooner wasn't in. Reed, the bank president, came out to see them and said, "I suspended him. With pay. I think he's innocent, but we don't want a question. I pray to God that he and Alicia understand that."

"Who's Alicia?"

"His wife," Reed said.

"We really need to see him. . . . You think he'd be at home?"

"He was earlier today."

"Do you have his address?" Lucas asked.

Reed frowned, looked at the secretary, and then said, "Give him Billy's address." Then, with just a hint of defiance: "And call Billy and tell him that these gentlemen are on their way."

Spooner lived a block from Highland Park, an affluent residential area ten minutes from the bank. The house was an upright, two-story, white-clapboard place set well back from the street, with oak trees in the front yard. Sloan pulled into the driveway and they got out; as they did, Spooner came to stand in the picture window, and for a second Lucas had the strange feeling that Spooner was somebody else — but who, he didn't know. When Spooner saw them, he headed to the door. A dishwater blonde replaced him in the window. She was wearing a pink blouse and a gold watch.

Spooner met them on the front steps, pulling on a coat as he stepped outside. He shut the door behind him.

"I've talked to my attorney, and he said that I shouldn't talk to you unless he's present," he said.

"Well . . . shoot," Lucas said. To Sloan: "A wasted trip."

Sloan said to Spooner, "What does your attorney think about us talking to you — you not talking back?"

"I'm just not supposed to talk to you."

"So tell your attorney we're here, and want to set up a meeting. The loan papers we subpoenaed are being reviewed by a bank examiner and an accountant right now, and we need to talk about it," Sloan said.

"And tell your attorney that we're making the case against Rodriguez — for dope dealing and murder — and the more we look at him, the more we find," Lucas said. "That the case on Rodriguez is a hell of a lot more serious than a little fudging around with loans, and that you're going to buy a piece of his prison sentence if we don't start seeing some cooperation."

Spooner had his hands in his pockets, and he flapped his coat panels like wings. "Jeez, jeez, you guys, I don't want this. But you come on like I'm going to jail, what can I do but call my lawyer? So why don't you call him and talk to him? I'll come in. I'll tell you everything I know about Richard, but I've got to have some legal protection."

"When?" Lucas asked. "When will you come in?"

"Anytime. Jeez . . . When do you want me to come? This afternoon? When? But I want my lawyer there."

The blond woman was standing in the window with her arms crossed, peering out at them. "Is this your wife?" Sloan asked.

Spooner looked, then said, "Yes, she's really freaking out. My God, my job . . ."

Lucas was thinking: Lane had just gone to see the examiner, and they would want that opinion before they talked to Spooner. "So come in tomorrow. Tomorrow morning. Call your attorney, make an appointment with the chief's secretary. I'll be available anytime you are."

"Okay." Spooner shuffled uncertainly, opened the screen door as if to go back in the house, then said, just as Lucas and Sloan were turning away, "You know, I wasn't lying the other day. I still don't think Richard is involved with any of this."

"You're wrong."

"You're watching him. You know he's done this?"

"We're all over him," Lucas said, "and there's not a lot of doubt. The question is, how much do you know? If you know enough . . ."

"I'll tell you everything, but there's just not much that I know. I mean, his loans, they were a little risky, but his record . . . Thinking that he's a dope dealer, I . . ." His mouth opened and closed a few times, as though he were flabbergasted. "I mean, I don't believe it. He's a *nice* guy."

"Tell me something nice that he's done," Lucas said.

"Well . . ." Spooner seemed to grope for something, then said, "I can't think of anything specific, but he's been to our *house,* and he's nice to my wife, and he's nice to other people. . . . I mean, he's just a nice guy to sit around and have a drink with."

"Well," Lucas said. "It's something to think about."

In the car, Sloan said, "A nice guy."

"Man, he's dealing dope. People who deal dope know about him — they pick him out of blind photo spreads," Lucas said. "And if you look at those loans . . . the guy's a goddamn hustler."

"Even if he is nice," Sloan said.

"You remember Dan Marks?" Lucas said.

"Now, there was a *nice* guy," Sloan said.

"Everybody agreed, until the trouble started and they took apart his garbage disposal," Lucas said.

"I didn't know fingernails would do that," Sloan said. They thought about fingernails, and headed back into St. Paul.

Rodriguez was at his office. Another patrol cop had been stuffed into a sport coat and left to keep an eye on him. They found him shifting from foot to foot in the Skyway, eating popcorn out of an oversized box. "Hey, guys," he said when Lucas and Sloan stepped into the Skyway. He looked at the popcorn box in his hand and said, "Gift from the St. Paul guys. Their precinct is right inside."

"What's he doing?" Lucas asked.

"Working on his computer. He went away for a while, and I lost him, but he came back."

"In his car?"

"No, he walked back into the building somewhere. You see the building entrance . . . his office opens off that hallway. When he put on his coat, I ran down, but he was already out the door into the hallway. He was out of sight when I got there, so I went back to the parking garage and waited to see if he was coming out. . . . He never came out, and when I checked again, he was back in the office."

"So he went someplace inside."

"Yeah, but it's all hooked into the Skyway through there, so he could have gone anywhere. He was gone for maybe twenty minutes."

"Put on his coat."

"Yeah."

They thought about that for a minute, but nothing occurred to them except that he probably hadn't been on his way to the can.

"Maybe we need a couple more guys," Lucas said.

"If we're serious about him," the cop agreed. "As it is, I've got my car parked down on the street, but if he comes out the ramp and turns the wrong way, I'm gonna be pretty obvious doing a U-turn fifteen feet behind him."

Lucas looked at Sloan and said, "More guys."

"And soon — my feet are killing me," the cop said.

Rodriguez was not what Lucas expected. He was not Latino: He didn't look Latino, or sound Latino. He didn't sound like a drug dealer, either. Most drug dealers had a streak of macho in them, or if not that, then a bit of backslapper bullshit.

Rodriguez looked and sounded like a white middle-class businessman who'd crawled up out of the working class, sweating the details of whatever kind of business he was in. He was a large guy, thick-necked, thick-waisted, round-shouldered. Maybe he drank too much, and if so, it'd be beer, or if not beer, something serious — vodka martinis with a pearl onion. Lucas had seen the same guy in car salesmen, machine-shop owners, bartenders, union officials. He saw it sometimes in lawyers who came from a working-class background.

And Rodriguez was mad: "What the fuck are you doing, what the fuck do you think you're doing, bustin' my reputation and my bidness dealings? I'll tell you what: I'm getting my lawyer down here right now" — he snatched up a telephone — "and we're gonna add this little patch of harassment to the lawsuit. I don't need no goddamn apartment buildings, because I'm gonna get rich suing the city of Minneapolis for about a billion bucks, and this ain't the first time you Minneapolis cops got nailed doing this kind of harassment bullshit and —"

"You're dealing drugs, Richard," Lucas said. "We can prove that. We can prove you ran Sandy Lansing: We've got people who will stand up in court and say so. We can prove you got a bunch of bullshit loans that you supported with dope money, and the IRS is gonna come after your ass. We've got all that. The question is, can we get you for killing Alie'e? We know you did it, we just gotta fit the suit to you."

"Bullshit. I never touched that bitch." He'd been punching numbers into his phone set, and now he spoke into the phone. "Let me talk to

Sam. The cops are here, hassling me. Davenport and some other guy." He listened for a moment, then thrust the phone at Lucas. "Talk to him."

"No. We're leaving," Lucas said. "I just wanted to get a look at your ass. We're coming for you, Richard."

"Fuck you," Rodriguez said, and into the phone, "He won't talk to you. They're leaving. . . . Yeah, yeah."

As Lucas and Sloan went through the office door into the hallway, they heard the phone clattering on the desk, and a minute later Rodriguez was in the hall behind them. "Let me tell you assholes something," he said. "Let me tell you something. You and me. My goddamn mother was no better'n a whore in Detroit. I don't even know who my daddy is. Even my name is some kind of joke. My old man was probably a Polack or a Litvak or some other fuckin' Eastern European." He was building steam as the words rattled out of his face. "I got outa Detroit by my fingernails, and I busted my ass every day of my life to get where I am. Now some two-bit fuckin' cops are saying I killed somebody. . . . I'll tell you what, I never killed anybody. I never killed *anybody*. I never even slapped anybody in the face. I just wanted to get out of that fuckin' Detroit and be somebody, and now I am, and you assholes —"

"Enough on the assholes," Lucas snapped.

"You're an asshole," Rodriguez said. "Both of you are. So why don't you slap me around a little, or something, huh?" He inched closer to Lucas.

"C'mon, hit me, I won't hit you back. It'll just give me a little more to sue you with, you motherfuckers. You're ruining my bidness. . . ."

And suddenly, his face crinkled up and he said, "My bidness. You're ruinin' my bidness." And he turned around and went back through the door into his office.

"Jesus," Sloan said, impressed. "The guy was . . . I mean, those were tears."

"Yeah." Lucas scratched his head, then shrugged. "Let's go."

"We're sure he's dealing drugs?" Sloan asked.

"Unless he's got an evil twin."

The Rodriguez interview put a blight on the day, and they drove, mostly in silence, back toward Minneapolis. "Drop you at the hospital?" Sloan asked.

"Nah. . . . I'm gonna . . . I don't know what I'm gonna do."

"What if we're wrong about Rodriguez?"

"I've been sitting here thinking about that," Lucas said. "But we're not. You know what we're doing? We've gotten to the place where we think dope dealers are automatically subhumans . . . but both of us could think of guys who push a little dope and aren't all that bad as guys. Love their wives."

"Not a lot of them," Sloan said. "Most of them are dirt."

"Not a lot, but some. Some of them are human beings. You know what it reminds me of? Remember when you were interviewing Sandy Lansing's father, and he started off on 'niggers' and all that?"

"Yeah."

"He's the flip side of Rodriguez. Here was a guy who coulda played the nice old candy-shop owner on a TV show, but then he opens his mouth, and this bullshit comes out. Rodriguez is a dope dealer, and *his* story is this pathetic struggle to get out of the slums. Fuck, I don't know." He thought about it for a minute, then said, "What I do know is, Rodriguez is a drug dealer, he was running Sandy Lansing, he was at the party where Sandy Lansing was killed, he denies all of it, and that's the only tie we've got."

Del called. Sloan handed Lucas his cell phone and asked, irritably, "Why don't you turn on your fuckin' phone?"

"What's going on?" Lucas asked.

"I'm at Boo McDonald's, and I got some seriously bad fuckin' news," Del said. McDonald was the paraplegic radio and computer monitor.

"All right."

"You know that little rat who publishes *Spittle*? He's got a new story out, and it names Rodriguez."

"*What?*"

"Yeah, the little jerk. I'm going over to scream at him, scream at his parents. But Rodriguez's name is out."

Rose Marie was livid. "You gotta tell me the

truth, Lucas — this isn't the little push you were talking about?"

"No. Nobody got the name from me or any of my people."

"Not from me, or anybody I know," Lester said. "There's gotta be fifty or sixty people in the department who know the names."

"I've had about nine calls in the last half hour, and what do I say?" Rose Marie asked. "I can't say no, it's not Rodriguez, because it *is*. So I say, I can't comment on an ongoing investigation. And you know what that means? That means, *yes*. And everybody knows it."

"The *Spittle* kid's got a leak," Lucas said. "We know this goddamn place leaks."

"If I find the fuckin' leak, that guy will find himself out on his ass, and I'll spend the rest of my term trying to fuck his pension," Rose Marie snarled. "I want you to put that word out — that I'm looking for the guy, and his job and his pension are on the line."

"That's a little strong," Lester said. "I'm not sure they'll believe it."

"It'll give them something to think about," she said. "By God, I'm gonna have IA look into this. Brace a few people. I'm not gonna have this shit. I'm not going to have it!"

Lucas said, "I can tell you one thing. This morning I asked you guys to send a couple more people over to watch Rodriguez. We better put a serious net around the guy now. I mean, forget about Jael Corbeau and Catherine Kinsley —

he's gotta be number one on this other fruit-cake's hit list."

Lucas went back to his office, found two notes. One said, "Call Jael." The other, "Call Catrin."

He called Jael, who said, "The dozen long-stemmed roses you sent to my house haven't arrived yet."

"I'm sorry, I thought . . . uh . . . well, I mean, I thought *you* were supposed to send them to *me*. I've been waiting," Lucas said.

"God, he's such a wit," Jael said. "I need a man with wit . . . maybe. So . . . anything going on? Can I get out of here?"

"Not yet." He told her quickly about the leak in the department. "It'll be on the news."

"What're you doing tonight?" she asked. "I mean, this isn't another proposition. I'd like to rejoice in the blood of the lamb."

"What?" He was confused.

"This guy who's trying to kill me — he's preaching at some church tonight," Jael said. "I'd like to see him. One of your guys here did, and it's supposed to be something else."

"Man, I don't know," Lucas said. "That might not be such a good idea."

"C'mon, don't be a stick-in-the-mud," she said. "Besides, you can bring a gun. And I'm going nuts. Let's get the sports car, let's go see him."

"I'll call you. Things are going on over here. If I can get away . . . maybe."

He called Catrin; she was on a cell phone, and answered in her car. "Let me pull over to the side," she said. Her voice was showing stress; he thought she might have been crying.

"What happened?" But she'd put the phone down.

A moment later, she came back. "Well I told him that I thought we had some problems, and that I was thinking of going away, that I thought I might want to be by myself for a while. You know what he said?"

"I don't —"

"He said, 'Well, whatever you think you have to do. Let me know.' It was like I wasn't sure I could make it to lunch."

"Catrin, I really can't advise you, I just don't know —"

"He just walked away from me," Catrin said. "Now I wonder if he isn't having an affair or something. It was like he was waiting for me to say something."

"If the guy has any sensitivity at all, if he knows you at all, then he knew something was coming," Lucas said. "It's like waiting for the ax to fall. When it does, there isn't much to say. You know about everything that anybody might say. . . ."

"Lucas, what are you talking about? We were married for more than twenty years."

"When we were talking at lunch . . . when you asked if you were just screwed . . . I mean, look at your old man. If he argues with you, he's being domineering and he's not letting you lead your own life. If he doesn't argue with you, but is absolutely supportive, tells you to do whatever you want, then he's being patronizing and you feel like your life is a hobby, because he's got all the money and you're going to London for plays, and all that. And if he lets you go, he doesn't care. So — I mean, when you talk about being screwed, he's about as screwed as you can get. Whatever he does is wrong."

"It sounds like you're on his side," she said. There was an undertone of disbelief.

"Absolutely not. Look, half of my friends have been divorced, and most of the other half are fucked up. I'm fucked up. I've been through this . . . Jesus. I'm on your side, Catrin, because we're old friends. If I was your husband's friend, I'd be on his side, because nobody's right or wrong. And in that case, you've just got to go with your friends."

"Well, I talked to one of my girlfriends down here — actually, I had lunch with three of them, my best friend and a couple that I've always been friends with — and I knew by the way one of them was acting she's on Jack's side."

"That's gonna happen," Lucas said. "And some old friends of Jack's will be on your side. That'll surprise you, too. You said you belong to a golf club?"

"Yes."

"What's gonna amaze you is, a couple of his

male friends are going to put the moves on you."

"The loose woman . . ."

"Not just trying to get laid — I mean, some of them will — but some of them will have been looking at you for a long time, and liking you."

"Lucas —"

"Hey, it's gonna happen. If you walk —"

"I don't think I've got any choice now," she said.

"Listen, what you're telling me . . . have you thought about telling Jack? Scream at him a little bit? Throw a little crockery? I mean, do you still love him?"

After a long silence, she said, "I don't think so."

"Aw, jeez."

"What happened was, his reaction made me angry," she said. "So angry. But I feel like . . . I don't know. I'm a little excited in a dirty way. Like I just broke out of jail."

"Aw, man."

"You keep saying 'aw, jeez.' What's that supposed to mean?"

"You're hurting a lot worse than you know, but you're going to find out," he said. "So's Jack. I can't hardly stand to think about it."

"Well. Maybe. But I'm getting out."

He couldn't think of anything to say. Thinking about her, sitting on the side of a road, talking about the end of her marriage on a cell phone to somebody she hadn't seen in twenty-five years.

"So congratulate me," she said. Now she did start crying.

"Awww . . . jeez."

Rose Marie came down. "The media's got Rodriguez surrounded. His lawyer just called the county. . . . What happened to you?"

"I was talking to an old friend. Her marriage is breaking up," Lucas said.

"Did you have anything to do with it?"

"No. Not directly. I mean, I'm not fooling around with her. Maybe I could have said something that would have changed things . . . I don't know. She's just an old friend."

"Huh." Rose Marie might have been skeptical. "You can't take care of everybody, Lucas. They don't even want you to."

"She needs a little help," Lucas said.

"I've got no advice," Rose Marie said. "Now: Rodriguez is gonna sue us, of course. And Tom Olson has called twice in the past half hour, asking about Rodriguez, but I'm not in. I've got to come up with a story."

"When's he coming in? You've got a briefing?"

"Yes. In a half hour. I'd like you to be there," she said.

"Sure. I don't know what I can say."

"If he tries to throttle me, you could hit him over the head."

They were still talking when the phone-tap monitor called: "We got some stuff on Rodriguez's blind phone. Three calls in a hurry."

"Where?"

"The first one, to Miami, to an unlisted number. I mean, we've got the number, but when we tried to check on it, the directory supervisor said she needed to see some paper before she can give us a name."

"Another blind phone, I bet."

"I think so. Anyway, he told whoever answered not to send Jerry up, that he had a problem. We think it might have been a delivery. Hell, I know it was a delivery. I've heard the same thing two hundred times, in almost the same words," the cop said. "Nothing specific mentioned, like it would be if it was legitimate. Just 'You know that delivery we talked about, with Jerry? Better hold off, I've got some problems up here.' "

"Good. Give me the Miami phone number," Lucas said. He scribbled the number on a pad. "I've got a guy with the FBI who might be able to help."

"Great. Then there was another call, this one to a real estate guy. He asked the guy to look into selling the apartments, and suggest that a Reet might want to buy them. I don't know the name."

"It's R–E–I–T, real estate investment trust," Lucas said. "It could be a way to get out in a hurry."

"Well, the guy he talked to . . . he was hot to handle it. You want the name?"

"Yeah." Lucas wrote down the name.

"And the third thing is he called another dope

guy. He said, 'I've got to shut down my business for a while. Tell everybody I'm sorry.'

"The other guy said, 'What's the problem?'

"Rodriguez said, 'Just a problem. The cops think I had something to do with that Alie'e thing. They're messing with me.'

"And the guy said, 'Where're you calling from?'

"And Rodriguez said, 'I got a good phone.'

"And the other guy said, 'I'd throw it in the river, if I was you. If they think you were involved with Alie'e, they're gonna tap you three ways from Sunday.'

"And Rodriguez said, 'Well, tell everybody. I'll call you back when it's over.'

"And that was it."

"We need that number, and times and transcripts," Lucas said. He jotted down the number, and when he got off, he looked at Rose Marie and said, "It's piling up."

When Rose Marie was gone, he called Mallard and gave him the Miami number, and called Del and gave him the local number. Del called back fifteen minutes later and said, "That number is out to another blind phone, but Narcotics knows it. They picked it up on a pen register a couple of months ago, a guy named Herb Scott. That's all they know, a number and a name in the computer. Want them to look a little closer?"

"Absolutely. Put him on the list. If nothing happens by tomorrow night, we're gonna sweep them all, and see if we can shake anything loose."

Mallard called back a few minutes after Del. "That number goes with a guy who lists his address in a place called Gables-By-The-Sea. I guess it's a ritzy neighborhood. I've got a guy checking with the locals."

"Thanks."

Piling it up.

For a moment, he thought about running down the new real estate dealer, but decided against it: That might make the phone tap obvious, and the phone might still be valuable.

Sloan called. "Come on down to Homicide. There's something you got to see."

Lucas walked down, and found a half-dozen cops laughing around a small-screen TV. "What?"

"That's Rodriguez's apartment," Sloan said.

"Penthouse," somebody said.

A wavering picture was focused on a window surrounded by reddish concrete. Then, moving in slow motion, Rodriguez appeared in the window and pulled the curtain across it. When he was out of sight, the loop started again: the window, Rodriguez, the curtain.

"Guilty, guilty, guilty," a cop said.

And somebody else, with a little edge of sarcasm: "If he wasn't guilty, why would he pull the curtain?"

And a third guy: "If it was me, I'd be pointing a

rifle out the window."

"They'd love that."

"Yeah, until a little bullet hole appeared on the forehead of one of them blonde c—"

A woman with a gun said, "Watch it."

"— cameramen."

Olson came by, trailing the Bentons, the Packards, and Lester Moore, the newspaper editor. "Who is this Rodriguez?" Olson demanded. "Everybody's saying he did it."

Rose Marie said, "He's a suspect. Lucas . . ."

Lucas said, "We think he's a drug dealer — actually, we're sure he is. And we have at least two sources who say that he was running Sandy Lansing. That is, Sandy Lansing was the street dealer for drugs brought in by Rodriguez."

"Rodriguez was the wholesaler?"

"More like the local franchise owner, and Lansing was one of his employees."

"Amazing," Olson said. "Franchises and employees. Did he pay her Social Security?"

Moore broke in: "Can you get him?"

"Not yet," Lucas said. "Maybe on drugs. We have no direct connection to the murder, but we can put him at the party, we can connect him with Lansing, we have him denying that he knew her, we can probably show that they dealt drugs together. We can project it as a drug argument that went bad. He killed Lansing, maybe even accidentally, by cracking her head against a doorjamb. Alie'e comes out of the bedroom just at that point, and he kills her, to get rid of a witness."

Olson stood up slowly, peered at the Bentons and then at Moore. "You mean . . . she was killed as a bystander? That all this happened because she was at the wrong place?"

"That's a possibility," Lucas said.

Olson said, "I don't believe it. This is not a casual killing. All these people dead. It can't just be chance. It can't be."

"We don't really know that it is," Rose Marie interjected. "Lucas is just outlining one possible theory."

"My good God," Olson said. He put his hands on the side of his head, as he had the day he found his parents, and pulled the hair straight out, as he had that day, just before his collapse.

Lucas stood up, stepped toward him, took his arm. "Easy."

"I can't, I can't . . ."

"Sit down."

Olson stumbled, and Lucas guided him around to the chair. Olson looked around the room, at the faces all pointed toward him, and said, "This cannot stand. This cannot."

When he was gone, Frank Lester said, "If that doesn't get him cranked, I don't know what will."

Lane came back. "Took all goddamn day, but the bank examiner comes in on our side. She says the loans are funky."

"That's the technical expression: funky."

"Exactly. But there's a problem," Lane said. "I created it. I made the fundamental investigatory error: I asked one too many questions. No — I asked two too many."

"I've told you about that," Lucas said.

"Yeah. So I've got this bank examiner — who's got nice legs, by the way, even if she wasn't a big rock 'n' roller — and I say, 'What would you do if you'd caught him doing this? During a bank examination.' And she says, 'We'd tell him that the loan was weak, and depending on the status of their other loans, we might require action.' And I say, 'That's it?' And she says, 'What'd you think we were gonna do? Shoot him?'"

"So then I make the next mistake. I ask another question."

"You already had two questions."

"Naw, that was like question one and one-a. Now I'm at question two. I ask, 'How many commercial loans are there in Minnesota? Gotta be hundreds of thousands, huh?' And she says, 'Well, many tens of thousands, anyway.' And I ask — this is question two-b — 'How many are this bad?' I figured she'd say something like, we get one or two a year. You know what she said?"

"I'm afraid to know," Lucas said.

"Be very afraid," Lane said. "She said, 'There might be a few thousand.'"

Lucas said, "Goddamnit."

"Yeah. Our hold on Spooner just got slipperier. On the other hand — I thought of this on the way over here. . . ."

"What?"

"Spooner doesn't know it," Lane said.

"You're a sneaky fuck," Lucas said. "It's a quality I admire in a cop."

As the earlier darkness settled in and the lights came up, Del came by with an ice cream cone and said, "I'm gonna go see Marcy. Wanna come?"

"Yeah, let me get my coat."

On the way over, Lucas told Del about Catrin. Del listened, finished the cone in the cold night, and then said, "She's probably gonna want to jump in bed with you. To prove to herself that she's still desirable and that she's as good as she was in the old days."

"What am I gonna do?"

"Well, I don't think jumping her is gonna be the answer." He looked at Lucas. "Or is it?"

"No. I mean . . . man, she's really nice, but she's really fucked up."

"So give her a really understanding talk about how she *is* fucked up — you might want to find a different phrase — and that she shouldn't do anything until she's gotten herself straight again."

"That doesn't sound like something Catrin would go for," Lucas said.

"How do you meet these women, anyway? They're all so fuckin' tangled up."

"I don't know. It's a special talent."

"What you need is some chick that comes up and says, 'Wanna see my Harley?' And you say, 'Is it a Sportster?' And she says, 'It's whatever you want it to be.' "

"I've often wondered if you had a fantasy life," Lucas said. "I guess that question's answered."

"Yeah, well, if I were you, I'd go home and think about this Catrin chick for a long time. Especially if she's still a friend." They walked along for half a block, and then Del added, "There is one bright side to the problem."

"Yeah?"

"Yeah. It's your problem, and not mine."

Marcy was sitting up, awake, but she looked distant, her eyes a little too bright. "The docs are worried that she might have a touch of pneumonia," Black said. "They say it shouldn't be serious . . . but they've got to deal with it."

Lucas squatted to look straight into her face. "How're you feeling?"

"A little warm."

"Still hurt?"

"Always hurt."

"Goddamnit." He stood up. "There's got to be better drugs."

"Yeah, but they fuck up my head. I'd rather have a little pain," Marcy said. "How's the case? I understand this Rodriguez guy is out in the open."

They talked about Rodriguez, and she stayed

awake, but she didn't look as good as she had, Lucas thought. She looked like she had the flu. After chatting for a while, he told the others he was going to get a Coke, and wandered out of the room. As soon as he was out, he headed for the desk and asked, "Is Weather Karkinnen . . . ?"

The nurse looked past him: Weather was headed down the hall toward them. He walked toward her and said, "You've heard about Marcy? This pneumonia thing?"

"Yeah, I've been keeping up," she said. "It's not too serious yet. They're managing it."

"C'mon, Weather. Is this gonna turn into something?"

She shook her head. "I can't tell you that, Lucas. She's young enough and healthy enough that it shouldn't, and we're right on top of it . . . but she was hit hard, and her lung took some of it. So . . . we gotta stay on top of it."

"That's all."

"Lucas, I don't know any more," she said in exasperation. "I just don't know."

"All right."

They stood, awkwardly, then she touched his arm and said, "I've been seeing this Rodriguez guy on television. That's you, isn't it? Your part of the case?"

"Yeah. He's the guy. the problem is, how do we get at him? There's almost nothing at the scene that would help. We're building a circumstantial case. . . ."

They walked along, Lucas talking about the

case. They'd done this when they were living together, Lucas talking out problem cases. The
talking seemed to help, seemed to straighten out
his thinking, even when Weather didn't say
much. They fell back into the pattern, Weather
prodding him with an occasional Why do you
think that? or, Where did you get that? or, How
does that connect?

They turned at the end of the long hall, and
Del stepped out of Marcy's room, looked down
at them, and went back inside. On the way back,
Weather said, "What're you doing tonight? Want
to go out for pasta?"

"I can't," he said, shaking his head. "You know
what it gets like. . . . I'm going nuts. But could I
call you?"

"Yeah. I think you can," she said. She grabbed
his ear, pulled his head down, and kissed him on
the cheek. "See ya," she said.

⋙ 23 ⋘

Lucas ate alone, a quick sliced-beef-and-cucumber sandwich in the kitchen, stood in the shower for a few minutes, soaking, then changed into jeans, a sweatshirt over a golf shirt, a leather jacket, and boots. He thought about taking the Tahoe; it would fit better with the crowd. But Jael really liked the Porsche.

He took the Porsche, across the Ford Bridge and up the Mississippi, then west to Jael's studio. She'd picked out an outfit like his: leather jacket and jeans, cowboy boots, and a turquoise-and-silver necklace. "We look like we're going to a square dance," she said.

"C'mon." Downstairs, in the studio, she said, "I left my house keys in the back, just a minute . . ." and when she went to get them, one of the ambush cops, sitting on the floor with a PlayStation, looked up and said, "You're breaking my fuckin' heart, Davenport."

"Hey, we're going to church."

"Yeah," the cop said, and, "Aw, shit, now I missed the yellow block."

Jael came back with her keys and said, "We're rolling."

The cop looked up at Lucas, one eye closed, and Lucas shrugged and followed her out the door.

Olson was preaching at the Christ Triumphant Evangelical Church, a good part of an hour west of Minneapolis in the town of Young America. The church was a long, narrow-faced white clapboard building with a bell tower, in the New England style, with a nearly full gravel parking lot to one side. Lucas parked between a tricked-out Ford F-150 and a Chevy S-10 with a snow blade, in a slot where the Tahoe would have fit perfectly. The Porsche, crouched between them, looked like a cockroach between two refrigerators. And down about ten slots, Lucas noticed, a nondescript city car huddled behind a van.

Outside the church, a thin pink-faced man in a long black trench coat stood next to a Salvation Army–style kettle, with a sign that said, "Please Donate," and under that, in small letters, "Suggested donation: $2 per person."

Jael said, "I thought Reverend Olson didn't accept compensation," and the man standing with the kettle said, "This is for the church, ma'am. Reverend Olson doesn't even take gas money out."

Lucas put a five-dollar bill in the kettle, and the man said, "Thanks very much, folks — you better get inside if you want to get a seat."

The church was severely plain inside: white

walls, natural-wood floors, a center aisle between two ranks of pews, and a rough wooden cross at the far end. The pews were two-thirds full, with a couple of dozen people still milling around; Lucas and Jael sat near the back. The place was warm, and they took off their coats. In the far left corner of the church, two women from Narcotics chatted quietly with each other. In five minutes, the pews were full, and people began sitting in the aisle.

"The fire marshal would have a heart attack if he saw this," Lucas muttered as people continued to jam into the church.

Jael leaned toward him and said, "See the women?"

"What women?"

"In the dark blue vests." She pointed with her chin.

Lucas took a minute to pick them out: A half-dozen women were working around the front of the room, passing out sheets of paper, stopping to talk to people, laughing, chatting. Then Lucas picked out a couple of blue-vested men, also working the crowd. "Couple of guys, too. See the guy in the parka? He's got one on underneath."

"Oh, yeah. I didn't see him. . . . I wonder . . ."

They were whispering, and Lucas whispered, "What?"

"Is this a cult?"

The lights began to dim, and Lucas shrugged. Then one of the women in blue vests gave them a stack of paper to pass down their pew, and they each took one and passed the rest. Lucas peered at the writing in the dimming light: the words to a half-dozen songs, and on the back, some kind of drawing. He put the paper in his lap and looked up as Olson appeared at the front of the church, stepped up on the dais, and started with, "How're y'all tonight?"

Some people said, "Fine," or "Good." Olson said, "I'm not very good. How many of you knew that Alie'e Maison was my sister? Hold up your hands."

Two thirds of the audience lifted their hands.

"So you know my sister was murdered, and my parents were murdered, and that a man named Amnon Plain was murdered. I want to talk to you about that." He talked about his sister and his parents for twenty minutes; how he and Sharon Olson and their parents lived their lives in Burnt River, a quiet, family-oriented small-town existence for the most part, with the one difference that Alie'e's looks and talents made.

"I didn't know any difference. I didn't know that even there, in Burnt River, running along the water, fishing with Dad, getting in apple fights with my friends, and BB gun fights — I'm sure more than a few of you have been in BB gun fights, even a few of you women, huh?" A ripple of laughter and acknowledgment ran through the audience. "I didn't know in all of that young, childish fun, even there, the evil was reaching out to us. Long tentacles, reaching out of New York, out of Los Angeles, long wispy fingers of evil settling over the minds of us all. . . ."

Lucas felt a creepy tingle. Olson had a deep, resonant voice, and knew how to play it: Although it seemed to drop to a whisper, and though it seemed to be aimed at each individual, it was loud enough to be heard perfectly. And he had the deep, stocky build, and the square, powerful head, that gave him a quality of suppressed violence.

He talked about the evil, and about its expression on television, in the movies, in fast-food businesses and on the Internet. "I have been around a little bit. I was in the Marine Corps, I worked as a shore patrolman at Subic Bay on payday. I know all the trouble that people can get into with sex, and with dope, and with greed and with the need of possession. I knows that there's some of it in all of us — but I also know that an adult can fight it. Maybe not win, but can choose to fight. But have you personally looked into this newest evil, this Internet, that all the schools and libraries now are trying to sell us? Have you looked on the Internet? I have — I looked at a library, with a librarian, one of our people, showing me — and the evil on the Internet is beyond belief, beyond anything you might encounter at Subic, beyond anything you veterans of the world have seen, beyond all of that. And it is flowing straight to our children."

With that as a base, Olson began to preach: on the evil of the world, and the light to come; on Jesus, who was with us all the time, and who would be visible in the next few years. The end of times was upon us. . . .

The preaching lasted for twenty minutes, a rising and ebbing of emotion, the emotional appeals coming in waves that would crest, each higher than the last, with Olson wandering halfway down the aisle, talking, calling on the children of God, reaching into the pews to touch people, both men and women. The audience rocked with him in a shoulder-pushing rhythm. The noise of the audience, the heat inside the church, and Olson's voice together finally climaxed in a long, desperate wail. . . .

And when the wail died, Olson was smiling.

"But we're gonna be okay, because we're the children of the Lord."

And that, Lucas thought, was it for the night. Olson, in an almost businesslike way, began talking about Amnon Plain. "A biblical name, Amnon. And Plain, that's important. As soon as I heard the name, I thought this was a message; as soon as I heard of his murder, I was sure of it. I've spoken in this church about my admiration for the Plain people, our brothers the Amish and the Mennonites, and although our beliefs may be different, in that thing, in the belief in the Plain, we agree. The Plain will save you. You have seen some people here in blue vests; those are handmade blue vests, they all made them themselves. If you accept the Plain, make yourself a vest. Put it on. Then kill your TV. Kill your Internet connection. Turn away from the magazines that overflow with the Evil."

Suddenly they were back in it, but this time it was different, humping along in an almost orgasmic frenzy built around the word *Plain,* and the evocation of the death of Amnon Plain, and the clear message to God's children.

As the frenzy built, Jael's fingers dug into Lucas's leg, dug in and held, and as Olson talked, the lights in the church continued to dim until it was nearly dark inside, with the only light around Olson at the front as he preached. He was tying himself in a knot, Lucas thought; his body was shaking with the violence of his words. People began to stand up and cry out — then the entire congregation was on its feet, and the wailing began again. . . .

And Olson, in the light, reached a new climax, dropped to his knees in an agony and threw up his hands, palms to the audience. Blood ran from wounds in his palms down his forearms, and the wailing became so intense that Lucas could hardly bear it.

Then Olson collapsed, and the wailing stopped as though a switch had been thrown, and the people of the audience looked at each other in stunned appreciation. A man from one of the front rows went to kneel beside Olson, and then another, and between them they got him back on his feet and led him to the side of the room, and then out of sight.

The thin man who'd been collecting money outside stepped into the light at the front of the church and said into the now-hushed room, "Reverend Olson will be back in a moment. For those of you who are new to the church, or our community, and are interested in Reverend Olson's concept of Plain, I would like to say a few words.

"There is no church of Plain. No money is collected, there is no organization. If you feel that you can be Plain, and you wish to be Plain, then make a vest. Or don't make a vest, if you don't wish to. Some of us find it easier to make the vest, as a reminder of what we are about. But I don't want any of you women making vests for your men. They should make their own, and if it doesn't come out just right . . . then show them how, but let them do the work. The vest won't save you, it's just a piece of cloth. But you'll find that it keeps you very, very warm. . . . On the back of your song sheet, we've included a little sketch, a little pattern, for making your vest."

There was a rustle of paper as people looked, and the man said, "If you'd like to sing, you're welcome to. If anyone is a bit too warm, you're welcome to step outside for a bit. So why don't we start with, 'You Are My Sunshine,' and all of you singers make room for those who need to get out for a breath."

A number of people started moving toward the back, and Lucas grabbed Jael's arm and they stepped over the last couple at the end of the pew, into the aisle, and out into the churchyard. "I'd say we got our money's worth," Jael said,

413

looking back at the church. The first chorus of "You Are My Sunshine" broke through the doors.

Lucas was looking at the paper in his hand. "None of these songs are religious songs," he said. "They're all, like, old-timey sing-along songs."

"You want to go back and sing?" Jael asked.

"No. I've had about enough," Lucas said.

"So have I. When he started talking about Plain, that was like being electrocuted." They walked back to the car, climbed in. And she said, "I know this is going to sound like the Hollywood bullshit Olson's trying to get away from, but . . . he's good. He's really good at it. Something about the way he looks, like a big tough hillbilly, and his voice . . ."

"You gonna make a vest?" Lucas asked.

"There's something in what he says," Jael said. "Especially if you don't have to sign up for the great Christian march to the Pearly Gates. The way he was talking, anyone could be Plain. There's a lot of that Plain feeling with potters."

"Except that it's too late," Lucas said. "At this point, being Plain is purely a luxury that most of us can't afford. Like big expensive artist pots."

In the car, she asked, "Do you think that the blood was faked? That he cut himself?"

"Not unless he's the biggest hypocritical phony on the face of the earth, and he sure doesn't give off that vibration."

"But if he was the biggest hypocritical phony, he *wouldn't* give off that vibration."

"I don't know, but I'll tell you what: I saw him go down — faint, or have some kind of a fit — after his parents were killed, and he wasn't faking that. This thing tonight was over in that direction: It looked real to me."

"So he's nuts?"

"Depends on your definition of nuts," Lucas said. "There are some genuine ecstatics running around out there, and he apparently is one of them. Maybe they're nuts, I don't know."

"You don't think he did it. You don't think he killed Plain," Jael said.

"There's some evidence that he did."

"I wasn't asking you a question," Jael said. "I know there's some evidence, but I can tell: You don't think he did it."

"You're wrong. I think it's possible that he did it. But the . . . being . . . who did it is not the one we see. Tonight we saw a saint; maybe there's a devil in there, too. We just haven't seen it yet."

They were halfway back when Lucas's phone buzzed. "You turned your phone on?" Jael asked. "I thought the joke was you never turned it on."

"Things are coming together," Lucas said as he fumbled it out. "If somebody makes a move, I want to know it." He thumbed the answer button. "Yeah."

"This is Frank, Lucas. Where're you at?"

"Down on 494 by France. Somebody moving?"

"Your boy Rodriguez is dead," Lester said.

"What?"

"He might've killed himself," Lester said. "That's what they're saying."

"C'mon, man, how'd he —"

"Jumped. Down that open space thing inside a building, what do you call it — an atrium. He jumped down the atrium in his building. He's pretty busted up."

"Who's there?"

"Couple of our guys, and now St. Paul's coming in. I'm heading over. I've got to call Rose Marie, and then I'm going."

"See you there."

24

Jael bitched and moaned, but Lucas dropped her at her studio before he went on to St. Paul. The St. Paul scene was a business-district replay of the murder scene at Silly Hanson's, with cop cars piled up along the curb and four big TV vans parked illegally down the street, reporters and cameramen milling around them.

A woman from one of the stations pointed at him, at the Porsche, and lights came up, putting a nearly opaque glare on the windshield. As he threaded his way past them, he could hear a woman shouting, "Lucas, *Lucas* . . ." and somebody slapped the car.

He pulled in beside a Jeep that he recognized as Lester's, got out, showed his badge to a St. Paul cop, and asked, "Where?"

The cop pointed at the building's main doors, and Lucas walked in, down a hallway toward a cluster of cops, then out into the open atrium space. Rodriguez was still on the floor, uncovered. His face had been crushed like a milk carton. Lester nodded as Lucas walked up.

"Ah, for Christ sakes," Lucas said in disgust. "Who was on him?"

"Pat Stone and Nancy Winter," he said. "Over there."

Stone and Winter were both patrol cops, borrowed for the loose net they'd had on Rodriguez. Lucas walked over and asked, "What happened?"

Winter said, "He left here, went out to his apartment, went inside. We saw the light come on in his living room, and we were just getting snug when he walked back out and got in his car. So then he drove over to a CompUSA and went inside and bought some stuff, we didn't get close enough to really see what he was getting, and then he came back out and drove back down here."

"You couldn't see what he bought?"

"No, I'd already gone back outside, but I could see him through the window at the cash register. Nothing big, whatever it was. Still got to have it on him, unless somebody took it. In his briefcase."

"All right. Then what happened?"

"I watched the ramp exit while Pat ran back to the Skyway and watched his office," Winter said.

"When he showed up in his office, then I was gonna call Nancy back," Stone said, picking up the story. "But he never showed up in the office. I was in the Skyway, so we know he didn't go out that way."

"Aren't there other Skyway exits?"

"Not open this late," Stone said. "Only open my way. You can only get out of the building three ways: the Skyway past me, the parking ramp, and the front door — that has a push bar. The other ground-floor doors are locked."

"We thought maybe he'd stopped in the can," Winter said. "I showed my badge to the lady in the ramp's pay booth, and then I got my keys out and started jingling them like I was looking for my car, and walked up the ramp until I saw his car, to make sure he'd parked. Then I walked back out and Pat still hadn't seen him. So I sorta strolled over to the door and looked in — I didn't have a key, so I couldn't *get* in at that point — and I saw this lump way down on the floor. I wasn't sure what it was, but I got the lady in the pay booth to let me inside, and . . . You saw him."

"How long from the time he drove in the garage until you saw the lump?" Lucas asked.

"We've been trying to figure that out. We were talking on cell phones, so you can probably get the exact time from the calls, but I figure it was about ten minutes," Winter said.

"I think it might have been a little longer," Stone said. "I think it might have been ten minutes before you walked up the ramp, then another few before you came back out, then walked down and looked in the door. . . . Maybe twelve or thirteen minutes."

"You can tell from the phone calls," Winter repeated. The two cops were anxious to get out from under, Lucas realized. And he couldn't see what else they might've done.

"All right," Lucas said. "You done good, guys."

Stone glanced at Winter, relieved. Lucas went back to the circle of cops around Rodriguez's body.

"Where's his briefcase?"

"Up there." He pointed up, at the railing around the second floor of the atrium. "He set it down before he took the dive — if he took a dive."

"He's a big guy to have somebody throw him over without a fight," one of the St. Paul cops said.

"Goddamn TV was all over him. He was about to lose his ass," another one said.

Lucas said, "I want to look in his briefcase."

"Crime-scene guys working it," one of the St. Paul cops said. "Take the elevator."

Lucas went up, found a crime-scene cop probing the briefcase. "Papers," he said. "This thing." He held up a plastic box in his latex-covered hand.

"What is it?" Lucas asked.

The crime-scene guy turned it in his hand. "Zip disk, two-pack."

"How about a receipt? You see a receipt in there?"

The cop dug back into the briefcase and came up with a slip of paper. He held it away from himself, in better light: "CompUSA. Zip disk. Two-pack."

Lucas walked back downstairs. The St. Paul chief of police was coming down the hall, two steps behind Del. Del lifted a hand, and the St.

Paul chief said, "He jump?"

Lucas said, "I don't know, but I'd send a guy down to get his computer. I think he came down to clean out his disk drive. Maybe changed his mind when he walked up to the railing."

They all looked up at the railing. The St. Paul chief said, "Woodbury is out at his apartment. They say there's no note."

"Didn't have time to write one." Lucas looked at Del. "You wanna ride out to Woodbury?"

Del looked down at Rodriguez's body, then up at the railing, and said, "Might as well. Elvis has left the building."

As they stepped away, the St. Paul chief said, "If he jumped . . . he took a lot of problems with him."

On the way out to Woodbury, Del called the Woodbury cops and got directions. Rodriguez's apartment was in one of his own buildings. "The Penthouse suite," the cop said, deploying a capital *P*. "That's what I'm told."

"Find out who was watching his phones tonight," Lucas said. "Find out if there was a call."

Del checked. "Not a single call at his apartment today," he said.

"Goddamnit."

Rodriguez's building was a routine-looking apartment with a pea-gravel finish over concrete block, double-glass doors, and a line of mailboxes and buzzers between the two doors. A Woodbury patrolman sent them to four, the top floor. His apartment door was open, and Lucas stepped in, with Del just behind. "Dope money," Del said as soon as he was inside.

All the walls had flocked wallpaper; the furniture all came from the same store, and that was Swedish modern; high-style graphics on the walls. A plainclothes cop stepped toward them. "Chief Davenport. I'm Dave Thompson."

"How are ya? This is Del . . . what'd you get?"

"Not much. Yet. He's got a lot of paper in his office, taxes mostly. . . . No suicide note, nothing like that. We checked the answering machine, nothing there. No computer in the house."

"Talk to his neighbors?"

"He's only got one on this floor," the cop said. "We haven't been able to find them yet. It's a married couple, they left here about six. People downstairs said they looked like they were going out. A little dressed up."

"All right. . . . Mind if I walk through?"

"No, like I said. There just isn't much to see. Mirrors in the bedroom. . . . Big TV, he's got a home theater."

Lucas and Del did a quick walk-through, all the way to the back. The master bedroom was at the end of a central hall: mirrors on the bedroom wall beside the bed, and two more on the ceiling. Heavy pine chests and chest of drawers, with black metal fixtures. The next room up was a small office, with a built-in desk, a Rolodex, a two-drawer filing cabinet, and a telephone. A cop was on his knees, going through the cabinet.

"Grab the Rolodex," Lucas said.

"We will."

The theater had a projection TV and a wall of video and stereo equipment, with a big black-leather circular couch facing it; a leather-covered refrigerator sat next to the couch. The room originally had been two bedrooms, Lucas thought: The join was imperfect, a ridge running around the ceiling and walls. "Dope money," Del said. "A goddamn dealer's wet dream."

The Woodbury plainclothesman wandered toward them, and Lucas asked, "Find anything like a wall safe?"

"No, no, nothing like that."

"You might want to tear the place up a little," Lucas said. "It's about five-to-one that he has a little hideout someplace in here."

"Check the power outlets, see if any of them don't work," Del said. "That's a longtime crowd favorite."

Lucas had stopped in the kitchen. A book of matches lay open on the counter next to the sink.

"You think he smoked?" Lucas asked Del.

Del looked at the ceiling, then at the curtains, sniffed, and said, "I don't think so. Why?"

"Had these matches sitting here. . . ." Lucas picked them up, then looked at the sink. Grains of black stuff in the strainer. He put his finger in it, rubbed lightly, and took it out.

"What?" Del asked. The Woodbury cop strained to see.

"Looks like ash," Lucas said.

"He burnt something?"

"Maybe," Lucas said.

And that was it: a group of cops standing around on a carpet with too-deep burgundy pile, looking at the Leroy Neiman print.

"What're we gonna do now?" Del asked.

"You think it's a suicide?"

"Yeah, I could buy it — it *would* solve a lot of problems. I'd like to know a little bit about his medical history, though," Del said.

"Doctors?"

"Yeah. See if he was depressed, if he'd ever been treated. But maybe he just saw the walls coming down, walked up to that atrium and just . . . an impulse."

"From the second floor? Christ . . ." Lucas shook his head.

"That's a high second floor. You look down from there, you know you ain't gonna bounce. I'm seeing a guy who's freaked out, he's got TV all over his ass, he knows he's in trouble on the dope, he's built up this fortune and he sees it drifting away . . . maybe he's even guilty about Alie'e. Who knows? Anyway, he puts down his bag and dives over the rail."

Sounded good. "Maybe."

"I'd give it a strong maybe," Del said. "Reserving the right to change my mind."

"So let's see what the ME says."

Lucas dropped Del back downtown, thought

about going over to see Jael, decided against. Thought about calling Weather — but she wasn't the one to talk to about death and destruction, not when they might be limping back to some kind of reconciliation.

And was that what they were talking about? Is that what she meant when she said he could call her? What the fuck did she mean? And why was he screwing around with Jael? And Jesus, he didn't even want to *think* about Catrin.

So he went home, thought about the game for a few minutes, then took a shower and crawled onto his bed. Ran it all around his head, and drifted off to sleep.

He woke twice during the night, lay awake for an hour each time, running it through. In the morning, he shaved, showered, and, still tired, headed into downtown St. Paul. On the way, he took out his cell phone and called the department photo guy.

"I got a picture I want you to take," he said.

25

Friday. The seventh day of Alie'e.

Rodriguez's building had been cleaned up and was open for business; except for the cops working on his computer, nobody would have known. Lucas stopped at Rodriguez's office and was introduced to Rodriguez's secretary, a young woman who was dealing with her loss with equanimity. "I'll be working tomorrow night," she told Lucas. "In this economy, a dead guy could get a job. Whoops — maybe I oughta rephrase that."

"Do you think that Richard would have committed suicide?" Lucas asked.

"He wasn't the moody type," she said. But she pressed a finger to her lips, thinking. "On the other hand, when he decided to do something, he'd do it, impulsive-like. Real quick. So, I mean, with all this publicity . . . But I don't know. Maybe you really don't know a person until he does something like this. And then, of course, you don't know him at all, because he's dead. So, like you never really get a chance to know anybody, you know? When you think about it."

In the hall, Lucas told the St. Paul cop, "She

426

seems to be dealing with it."

"Yeah. A little too well, if you ask me. I wouldn't be surprised if she was holding a little cash for the boss, or a little product."

"Cash, maybe. Not dope. She's too ditzy to be trusted with dope," Lucas said.

"We'll probably find out that she's the brains behind the operation." They both looked at her through the window slit beside the office door. She was talking to another cop, unconsciously twirling a ringlet of hair with an index finger. Lucas and the St. Paul cop looked back at each other and simultaneously said, "Maybe not."

"You know what I really need," Lucas said. "I need to find the maintenance guy."

The maintenance man looked worried. "I'll do anything I can to help."

"What I need to know is, how would you get out of this building if you couldn't go out the ramp and you couldn't go out the front door and you couldn't go out the Skyway?"

"You mean, like, if there was a mystery man here last night?"

"Exactly."

The maintenance man thought about it. "Couldn't do it," he said finally. "He'd need a key. But all the keys are on two rings, and you have to know what you're looking for before you can use one. Otherwise, it's just a bunch of numbers on the keys. So if you wanted to get just one, you'd have to steal the whole ring — which nobody did. Even then, you still wouldn't know which key opened what until you tried them all. That'd take a couple of days if that's all you did."

"So let's say the guy didn't have a key."

"Well, there are some windows on the second floor that open, so he could lower himself down — but that'd be pretty obvious. I mean, there *are* cars on the street at that time of night."

"And it's a long way down," Lucas said. "He'd need a big rope."

"Yeah." The maintenance man thought for another minute, puzzled. "You say he can't go out through the garage."

"Nope."

"Well, if it were me, I'd hide in the building until the cops were gone, and then I'd just jump out and walk away with the crowd. Lots of places to hide."

"St. Paul went through here pretty thoroughly, last night and this morning."

"No kidding — had me running around like a madman."

"How about access to the alley?"

"Nope. Them overhead doors lock with padlocks and . . . Ohh. Wait a minute."

"What?"

"The regular door there. There's a great big dead bolt on it, but . . ."

"It opens from the inside," Lucas said.

"Yeah. I never use it. If we got a big delivery, they ring and we open the overheads. . . ."

"Let's go look," Lucas suggested.

The maintenance man started toward the far end of the building. "It locks with a key from the outside."

"You can't just pull it shut?"

"No. Nope. Gotta lock it with a key from the outside, or with the knob from inside," the maintenance man said.

They walked down the basement stairs, then along a dark corridor to a loading dock. Lucas stepped over to the access door. The door was metal, with a small window with inset wire mesh. He said, "Don't touch the lock. . . . You got any lights?"

"Yeah."

The maintenance man found a wall switch and turned the lights on. They both looked at the lock, and Lucas said, "The bolt's open."

"Aw, man."

Lucas looked around the dock and asked, "Did Rodriguez ever get anything here?"

"His furniture, probably."

"You ever see him here otherwise?"

"No. Nobody comes down here, except for deliveries. Unless there's something wrong with the plant."

"Hmph. Better go talk to St. Paul," Lucas said.

"What'd St. Paul say?" Del asked.

"First they said it was all bullshit, it didn't make any difference. There was no indication that there was anyone else in the building. Then they started pissing on each other," Lucas said.

"Over here, we'd be shooting at each other."

"That's a kinder, gentler city," Lucas said. They were walking across town, Lucas with a large-sized manila envelope in one gloved hand. The day was even colder than it had been early in the week, and though the sky had turned blue, a gusty wind was cutting along the streets. Shoppers were bundled in long coats, and businessmen snarled into the wind.

"If you don't tell me what's in the envelope, I'm gonna be pretty embarrassed when we get there," Del said.

"Pretend like you knew all along."

"You're just bustin' my balls because you got up crabby."

"Nope. I'm actually pretty cheerful," Lucas said.

"And that surprises me," Del said. "I figure you've either solved the case or you're fuckin' Jael Corbeau."

"Why couldn't it be both?" Lucas asked cheerfully.

"Nobody's that's lucky," Del said. "So what's in the envelope?"

"Let India tell you," Lucas said. "When we get to Brown's."

India, Philip the manager, and the other woman who'd looked at Rodriguez's picture were waiting at the desk when Lucas and Del arrived at Brown's Hotel. Lucas slipped a photograph out of the envelope and passed it across;

the photograph had been taken that morning with a digital camera, and had been printed out only a half hour earlier. "Do you know this guy?"

Del tried to edge sideways to get a look, but Lucas cheerfully blocked him off.

"That's him," India said. The other woman nodded, and Philip, looking down his nose at the photo, said, "Yes, I've seen him."

"Did he know Derrick Deal?"

"He may have," Philip said. "He probably did. I think I saw the three of them talking once. At least once. So maybe . . ."

"He was definitely around here," India said.

Del reached out, took the picture, glanced at it, and said, "It's like I been telling you since the start, Lucas. It's that fuckin' Spooner."

"You've got to be kidding," Rose Marie Roux said. She was leaning back as far as she could in her office chair, hands covering her eyes as if to block out the horror of it all. "We've already started taking credit on Rodriguez."

"He was murdered," Lucas said. "It kept me up half the night, thinking about it. And remember how we decided that if Angela Harris could make an accurate prediction about the murders of the Olsons, then we'd have to pay close attention?"

"I remember."

"So I was awake half the night, working this out. And when I got done, I made *two* predictions. First, that I'd find a way the killer could

431

have gotten out of Rodriguez's building. And second, that the people at Brown's would recognize Spooner. I'm also making a third prediction. We know we only got about half the people at the party — Frank's got his people running pictures of Spooner around to the party people we interviewed. I'm predicting that somebody will put him at the party."

"Ah, mother. Run it down for me," Rose Marie said.

Lucas ticked the points off:

- "We had a guy who came out of the slums of Detroit with no education — and two years later, is setting up a Miami corporation to buy legitimate apartments which he uses to wash his drug money. That's a little too sophisticated.
- "If it's too sophisticated, where did he figure out how to do it? How about a banker?
- "What does the banker get out of it? How about dope, money, and women?
- "What does Rodriguez get? How about financing, a way to wash his dope money, and legitimacy. He was a *smart* guy, even if he didn't have much education.
- "What happens at the party? Who knows? But Spooner winds up killing Sandy Lansing, maybe accidentally. Alie'e witnesses the killing, so he has to kill her. He then evaporates — maybe goes out the window,

I don't know. In any case, he doesn't come up on our party list. He's not part of that crowd, he's just Lansing's boyfriend, and lot of people don't even know *her*."

"Wait a minute," Rose Marie said. "There's a fairly big jump in there. All the other stuff is linked, but that's a pure jump —"
"Let me finish," Lucas said.

- "We identify Rodriguez as being at that party, because, unlike Spooner, he's known to be rich and single, and so he gets some attention from the other partygoers.
- "When Al-Balah links Rodriguez and Lansing, we *assume* that since they were dealer-employee, that there'd been a falling-out. We then *assume* that Derek Deal knew about them, because we knew Rodriguez was Lansing's boss. We assume that Deal went to Rodriguez, tried to black-mail him, and got killed for his trouble. But when I took a photo of Rodriguez over to Brown's, nobody recognized him. And I remembered that, back when I first talked to Deal, he wasn't absolutely sure that Sandy Lansing was a dealer. He *thought* she might be, but he didn't know. And that suggests to me that he didn't know who her boss was. He definitely knew who her boyfriend was — we confirmed that today, with the photo of Spooner. He went to

Spooner, not Rodriguez, and he got killed.

- "Of all the people who were at the party, the ones most likely to finger Spooner as being there were Lansing, who was dead, and Rodriguez, who couldn't, because that would drag the whole drug-apartment deal out into the open.
- So then I talk to Spooner. I try to intimidate him by suggesting that we're about to bust Rodriguez, and let him know that we're watching Rodriguez, that we're all over him.
- "Spooner realizes that if we *really* come down on Rodriguez, his goose is cooked — Rodriguez will try to stay clean as long as he can, but he's not gonna suck it up for first-degree murder. He'll talk to us, and one thing that will come out is that Spooner was at the party. And Spooner had some kind of relationship with Lansing. Sex, dope, something. He'd be as good a suspect as Rodriguez. But if Rodriguez commits suicide . . ."
- "Spooner knows we're watching Rodriguez, and probably suspects that includes tapping the phone. So he goes to Rodriguez's apartment and slips a note under the door. Probably something unsigned, maybe even typed. It says something like, 'They're coming for you — you gotta get anything incriminating off your computer. Burn this note.' "

"And we find ashes in the sink at Rodriguez's apartment," Del said. "Though he could of flushed it."

"Nothing gets rid of paper like burning," Lucas said. He continued:

- "So Spooner watches Rodriguez until he sees him leave for home, then hides out in the building where he can watch the entrance from the ramp. Rodriguez goes home, gets the note, thinks, 'Oh, man, if they get the computer, my goose is cooked.' He stops at CompUSA to get a Zip disk, because he plans to dump his files to the Zip disk, then either write over the hard drive or just take it out and throw it in the river. They're cheap enough.

- "Spooner knows we're watching, so he can't just whack Rodriguez and walk out the Skyway or the ramp or the front door, which would be the logical way to get out, especially if you're in a little bit of a hurry. He has to sneak out. The basement door."

"How'd he know about that?" Del asked.

"Who knows? Maybe from hanging around with Rodriguez. Maybe he actually scouted the building the day before. Whatever the reason, if Rodriguez was murdered, the killer *snuck* out, as though he knew the place were being watched."

"How'd he kill him?" Rose Marie asked.

"Hit him with something flat and hard. Not a

baseball bat, because the wound would be wrong. Maybe a two-by-four."

"Oooh. Sting the hands," Del said.

"He then hauls Rodriguez over to the railing, hangs him over, head down, and lets go. Rodriguez hits headfirst and he's gone," Lucas said.

"I'll tell you something," Rose Marie said. "Remember when those people were doing their swan dives over in the county government building? I saw a couple of those. They didn't go headfirst — they just let themselves fall, and generally landed flat. Rodriguez would have had to made a conscious decision to *dive* — to land headfirst. That doesn't feel right. Even people who want to die don't want their identities erased. Their faces broken up."

"I hadn't thought about that, but you're right," Lucas said. Del nodded.

They all sat and thought about it, Rose Marie swinging back and forth in her chair, and finally she asked, "Have you guys figured out the rest of it?"

"We've figured out that we'll never get him, if that's what you mean," Del said.

Lucas nodded. "We've publicly said, or let it be known, that we think there are two killers working: one who killed Lansing and Alie'e, and somebody who's killing in revenge for those murders. Therefore, the most likely candidate as the Rodriguez killer is that second man, especially since Rodriguez's name was leaked. But we know it can't be, because we were watching the guy who's probably the second man, and he was clear over on the other side of town. And the second man, even if it isn't Olson, also wouldn't have known how to lure Rodriguez back to his office, wouldn't have known that Rodriguez had a twenty-four-hour police escort, wouldn't have known about the phone taps. All of which would count about zilch with a jury."

"And we'd already pretty much pinned the Alie'e and Lansing killings on Rodriguez, and the details were leaking. Even the suicide fits. . . . It's too late to change our minds," Del said.

"If we did change our minds, and we bust Spooner, the defense would put Rodriguez on trial and they'd win," Rose Marie said. "You've got me two-thirds convinced it's Spooner, but if you were talking to a jury, it'd still be eighty-twenty for Rodriguez. All we've got as evidence on Spooner is this long chain of Lucas Davenport suppositions."

"Suppositories," Del amended.

"That's not totally true," Lucas said. "We can put him with both Lansing and Deal. Nobody could put Deal with Rodriguez. If we can put him at the party . . ."

"It'd be weak but usable, if Rodriguez wasn't there as an alternative candidate," Rose Marie said. "You haven't even suggested why he'd kill Lansing. With Rodriguez, we could suppose it was some kind of criminal falling-out between wholesaler and retailer."

437

Another ten seconds passed in silence, then Rose Marie said, "So what do I tell Olson? He's coming in here in fifteen minutes, so I can give him the official word on Rodriguez and say that we're satisfied that Alie'e's killer is dead. What do I say now?"

"Bullshit him," Lucas said. "Tell him that there's some evidence that Rodriguez was the one, but we're continuing to examine other possibilities."

"He's gonna want some kind of closure," Rose Marie said.

"Fuck closure," Lucas said. "Nobody gets closure."

"With this bunch, nobody deserves it," Del muttered.

Lucas asked Del to check with the Homicide cops who were circulating Spooner's picture among the known partygoers. "I've got to do some paper," he said. "Maybe when you're up-to-date with Homicide, you could check with Marcy. Tell her I'll be over as soon as I can."

When Del was gone, Lucas went back to his office, locked the door, looked at his watch, leaned back in his chair, and closed his eyes. Ten minutes later, his eyes popped open. Time to move. He got up, walked back down to Rose Marie's office, and peeked: door closed. He stepped inside and asked the secretary, "The Olson bunch in there?"

"Yup. A pretty sad-looking bunch, too."

Lucas backed out of the office, got his coat, put it over his arm, and went to the end of the hall, where he could see the chief's office door but where somebody also might think he was waiting for somebody to come in the front door. Out on the street, the media wagons were piled up; a square-jawed trench-coated reporter was doing a stand-up, with City Hall as background. More airtime for Alie'e.

A cop named Hampstad wandered by, leered at Lucas, and said, "You hear the one about the guy with the headache?"

"Aw, Jesus," Lucas said.

"Guy goes to the doc, and he says, 'Doc, you gotta help me. I got this terrible headache. It feels like somebody is pounding a nail through my forehead. Like I got a big pair of pliers squeezing behind my ears. It's tension from my job. I can't stop working right now, but the head-ache's killing me. You gotta help.' So the doc says, 'You know, I *do* have a cure. Exactly the same thing happened to me — I was working too much, and I got exactly the same headache. Then one night I was performing oral sex on my wife, and her legs were squeezing my head really tight, really hard, and the pressure must have done something, because the headache was a lot better. So I did this every night for two weeks, and at the end of two weeks, the headache was gone.' And the guy says, 'I'm desperate, Doc, I'll try anything.' The doc said, 'Well, then, I'll see you in two weeks.' So the guy goes away, and two weeks later he comes back for his appointment and he's the most *cheerful* guy in the world. And he says, 'Doc, you're a miracle worker. I did just what you told me, and the headache's gone. Vanished. I feel great. I think it's got to be the pressure, and — by the way, you've got a beautiful home.' "

"Saw it coming," Lucas said without cracking a smile.

"Bullshit, saw it coming. You're cracking up inside," Hampstad said.

"Have I mentioned our sensitivity sessions? We have them —"

"Fuck a bunch of sensitivity," Hampstad grumbled. "Nobody has a sense of humor around this place anymore."

At the end of the hall, Olson stepped through the chief's door. Lucas pushed away from the wall. "Gotta go," he said. He walked down to the front doors, looked at the media wagons for a count of twenty, then started back toward the chief's office. He heard them as he was coming to the corner, and nearly ran headlong into Olson. They milled for a second, Lucas said, "Sorry, sorry, excuse me," and then Olson said, "Chief Davenport . . . we just talked to the chief."

"Yes, I knew you were coming."

"Not very satisfying," Olson said. "She was much more — I don't want to save evasive, but she was much less positive than I had expected. About this Rodriguez man."

Lucas looked at him for a long beat, then at the rest of the group from Burnt River. "Could I speak to you privately for just a minute?" Lucas said.

Olson nodded, looked at the Burnt River people, said, "Excuse me for a minute," and he and Lucas walked down the hall toward the front door.

"The chief is, uh . . . Did you know I came to see you preach last night?"

"I thought that might be you in the back. I wasn't sure," Olson said.

"I was impressed. I'm not from the same stream of . . . Christianity . . . as you, I'm a Roman Catholic, but I was . . . affected." Lucas said, letting himself grope for the words. "What I'm trying to say is, I know you're a good man, I could see it last night. I hate lying to you. The chief wasn't lying, but, to tell you the truth, most of us think that Rodriguez was innocent. That he may have been murdered himself."

"*What?*" Olson was stunned, but his voice was hushed. "Then who . . ."

"A banker named William Spooner. He essentially set Rodriguez up in the drug business, showed him how to launder his money. . . . He was carrying on an affair with Sandy Lansing."

"Then why don't you . . ."

"We're investigating him every way we can, but to be honest — please don't tell anyone I told you this — it's going to be very difficult to get him on this. The two chief witnesses against him would be Sandy Lansing and Rodriguez himself. They're both dead. And even if we arrested him, a defense attorney could simply prosecute Rodriguez during Spooner's trial, and frankly, Rodriguez is a much more inviting suspect. Even if he didn't do it."

"Are you saying that Spooner'll never be punished?" Olson asked.

"I don't know what's going to happen, I really don't," Lucas said.

"I don't know what to say," Olson said. "I should talk to Chief Roux again."

"Don't do that, it'll just cause problems for her. She's trying as hard as she can with all this media attention. . . . She wants the media to concentrate on Rodriguez for a few days, since it can't hurt him anymore, while we go after Spooner."

"This is . . . I don't know."

"I'll tell you what you can do," Lucas said, trying to *feel* the sincerity. "You can pray for us. After what I saw last night, I believe it will do some good."

Olson looked at him for a moment, a speculative examination of several seconds, then said, "I will."

Lucas said goodbye, shaking Olson's hand, then walked through the group of Burnt River people, down the hall, and to his office. Felt the dark finger of hypocrisy stroking his soul. All for justice, he thought. Or for something. *Winning,* maybe.

Lucas waited in his office until he figured Olson would be gone, then walked down to Homicide to talk to Lester. "We need to put a couple of people on William Spooner," he said. "More to cover him than to watch him."

"What's going on?" Lester asked.

"I just gave Spooner's name to Olson. I didn't tell Rose Marie, so she'll have a little insulation. But if Olson starts wandering around in his car, and we're too far back . . . he could walk right up to Spooner's front door and nail him before we could catch up."

"Man, I don't know about this," Lester said, shaking his head.

"We were willing to do it with Jael and Catherine Kinsley — use them as decoys — and they weren't even guilty of anything."

"Yeah, but they sorta volunteered," Lester said.

"They had no choice, Frank. Their names got leaked and played in the papers and on television, and somebody in this department leaked them. They wouldn't have volunteered if their names hadn't already been out there."

"All right, all right. . . . I get a little puckered up sometimes."

"Will you put some guys with him?"

"Yup. I'll do it now."

"One more thing, if you don't mind," Lucas said. "I talked to Spooner about coming in today with his attorney — I don't want to do that now.

Tell him that after Rodriguez's death, we're re-assessing the case and it may not be necessary for him to come in at all."

"I can do that."

"I'd do it, but I don't want to talk to him," Lucas said. "We don't want to lie to him at this point."

After leaving Homicide, Lucas walked over to the hospital. Del was just leaving. "Took her back into intensive care," he said; he looked a little frightened. "Pneumonia's getting on top of her."

"Can she talk?" Lucas asked.

"She's asleep. They say it's controllable, but she looks worse to me than she did yesterday."

"Ah, man. Let me see . . ." Del went back inside with him. A nurse led them in, but Marcy was asleep, as Del said. Back outside, Lucas led the way to Weather's office. Nobody home. "What do you do around here to find out what's going on?"

"Black left ten minutes ago, to get something to eat — he said they're still optimistic."

"What does *he* think?"

"He's not a doctor," Del said.

"I know, but what does he think?"

"He thinks she's getting into trouble," Del said.

They went back down to intensive care and stood outside and looked at her. After a while, they walked back to City Hall.

Lucas's door had a "See me ASAP" note on it from Loring. Lucas and Del walked down to Homicide and found Loring taking a statement from a pale blond man dressed all in black. In a different age, he might have been an undertaker.

"What's going on?" Lucas asked.

"There you are," Loring said. "This is John Dukeljin, he was at the party at Sallance Hanson's. He picked William Spooner out of a photo spread, says he was at the party."

"Oooh," Lucas said. "That's excellent."

"*Almost sure*," Dukeljin said. "He was leaving, we were coming back. I saw him coming down the front walk — Silly has that low-voltage lighting all along there, we could see him quite clearly — and I pointed him out to my friend. But he got to the end of the walk before we did, and he went the other way."

"Why did you point him out to your friend? Was there something about him?" Lucas asked.

"I thought he might be gay," Dukeljin said.

"Mr. Dukeljin and his friend are gay," Loring said.

"Why . . . ?"

"He was carrying a bag. Carrying a bag is way over with, for men. But usually, if you see a man carrying one, you know, unselfconsciously . . . it's something to think about."

Lucas looked at Loring. "Sometimes you show a tiny flicker of intelligence."

"You're just jealous," Loring said.

"What?" Del asked.

"We never found Sandy Lansing's purse," Loring said. "If we had, we probably would have made her as a dealer."

Lucas looked at Dukeljin. "Do you think your friend would recognize Spooner?"

"I haven't been able to get in touch. He's out on a project — he's an engineer — but I pointed this fellow out. I'm sure he'll remember *that*. And the bag, you know, because it's so over with. I don't know if he'll exactly remember the face."

"Where's this project?" Lucas asked.

"In Rochester, something to do with the Mayo Clinic. . . . He'll be back tonight," Dukeljin said.

Lester came in while they were talking, and said, "Loring told you."

"Yup."

"Pain in the ass, Lucas. It'd be better for everyone if it was Rodriguez. Close the books and walk away."

"Can't do that."

"Yeah, I know," Lester said. "I just talked to Rose Marie, and she said the Spooner ID was your third prediction; she's a believer. So I've got four guys all night with Spooner. And we're tracking Olson."

"Something's got to pop soon: there's just too much pressure building. If anything happens, have them call me."

Weather called. "I understand you were checking on Marcy Sherrill and stopped up."

"Yeah. We're pretty worried," Lucas said.

"I talked to the people in Medicine, and they still think she'll be okay. They got on it right away. She's in intensive care so they can keep a closer eye on her."

"Tom Black is probably hanging around there. Could you tell him that? He's really sweating it," Lucas said.

"Sure. I'll walk down there now."

"And I want to get together. I need to talk with you," Lucas said. "But you know what it's like. . . ."

"I heard about the Rodriguez fellow. Doesn't that solve a lot of problems?"

"No. Not really. I'll tell you about it. Could we get lunch tomorrow?"

"Sure. It might be a little late. I've got two jobs tomorrow, and the second one's scheduled for ten o'clock."

"That's okay. I'll try to get over there. . . . Listen, just call me anytime. I'll keep my cell phone on, and I'll run over whenever you're ready."

At the end the day, Lucas stopped back to look in on Marcy; no change. He walked back to the parking ramp, got his car, and headed south to Jael Corbeau's studio. She'd been making pots; a couple of new cops were sitting around in her studio, watching. When Lucas walked, in she looked up and said, "Dinnertime?"

"Talked me into it," he said.

One of the cops said, "That's the god-damnedest thing I've ever seen. You oughta see her make pots. It's, like, weird."

"Interesting," Jael said.

"If I got interested in that," the cop asked, "is there someplace I can take lessons?"

"Yeah, about a hundred," she said. "This is one of the big ceramics places in the country."

"It's so goddamned neat," he said.

The other cop raised his eyebrows and shook his head. "Playing with mud."

Jael looked at him and said, "Playing with mud can be fun." And she dragged the tip of her tongue over her upper lip.

"Oh, God, take me now, I'm ready to go," the cop said, and Jael laughed and said to Lucas, "Ten minutes to clean up."

They ate at a fast-food place on Ford Parkway, a few blocks from Lucas's house. "We could go see a movie," Lucas suggested.

"Why don't we go for a hike? Walk up the river path."

"Pretty cold."

"It'd feel good. I'm stuck in that house. I'm not staying in much longer," Jael said. "Another couple of days, and then I'm leaving for New York. Let him find me if he can."

They dropped the Porsche at Lucas's house and walked a mile up River Road, talking about the day. Lucas told her his doubts about Rodriguez, and the possibility that somebody else was involved. She told him about talking with the cops as she shifted through her day, and the one cop who might actually be interested in ceramics.

"Or interested in your ass," Lucas said.

"I can tell the difference. You can tell the way a person's face lights up when he sees a pot being thrown," she said. "He really thought it was neat. He was amazed."

"Well . . . maybe he'll get into it."

"You're not the potter type," she said.

"No, but I like the potter types."

"You certainly demonstrated —"

"That's not what I meant," he said with a little impatience. "I like people who can do things. Craftsmen. Good carpenters. Good bricklayers. Good reporters. Good cops. It's all sort of the same."

They walked out to Cretin, turned south, back toward Lucas's house. "Weird name for a street," she said.

"Named after a bishop," he said. "I've got a friend who went to school in Normal, Illinois, and another guy who went to Cretin, the high school in St. Paul. They've always had this idea that they ought to get 'Cretin' and 'Normal' T-shirts, and hang out."

"That would be funny for about one second," she said. "After that it would get annoying."

Back at the house, Lucas shut the door behind them and Jael said, "Now I feel hot, after all that cold air."

"Want a beer? I got a movie the other day, *Streets of Fire*, looks neat in a cheesy way."

"All right."

Lucas went and got two beers, and when he came out she had the DVD case and was dropping the disk in the DVD player. Lucas punched up the TV with the remote, handed her one of the beer bottles, and dropped onto the couch. The movie came up and Jael took a hit on the beer, then set it on the coffee table and peeled off her sweatshirt. She was wearing a plaid shirt under that, and under that, a bra. She dropped them all on the floor, then peeled off her jeans and underpants, and picked up the beer.

"Maybe we could have some sex while we're watching the movie," she said.

"If you play your cards right," Lucas said, manipulating the remote. "Move over to the left, you're blocking the screen."

"I'll block the screen," she said. She straddled one of his legs and started tugging at his belt buckle. "I'll block the damn screen."

26

Saturday. Day eight.

He took Jael back home at two o'clock. Then, restless and awake, a little moody from the sex, he took I-394 west to the 494–694 beltline, decided at the last minute to go north, and drove the 694 north, then east across the north side of the Metro area, then south again, and back into St. Paul on I-94. The trip took most of an hour, and he used the time to think about Jael, and Weather, and Catrin.

He felt a strong tie to Weather; he couldn't help it. If she called in the morning and said, "To hell with it, let's get married next week," he'd probably say yes. On the other hand, she was making some preliminary moves toward what might be a reconciliation, and he was sleeping — well, not sleeping — with Jael. He was risking the Weather tie with a woman who wouldn't be around long. He knew Jael would be moving on, and Jael knew he knew it; and when he wasn't looking at her, he hardly thought about her, at least on a conscious level.

But his car kept steering itself to her doorstep, and he kept winding up in a bed or on a couch or on the floor with her. And he *liked* it. Most of that was Jael herself: She was not self-conscious about sex, and not particularly concerned that Lucas enjoy himself. She was getting her own, and letting Lucas take care of himself, which he did. And he liked *that*. This was *serious* casual sex.

So now he was going to lunch with Weather; the lunch had the feel of a crisis meeting. If nothing happened tomorrow, it was likely nothing would happen at all. A *moment* was occurring. He could pick it up or let it go, and he really wanted to pick it up, but maybe if he could just get another week of rolling around with Jael . . . Maybe two weeks?

He thought of the legendary quote from St. Augustine that so beguiled his high school classmates who were headed for a seminary: "Please, Lord, make me pure . . . but not yet."

Then there was Catrin, a problem that might be more serious than Jael. She pulled on him. And he couldn't help thinking that if it didn't work with Weather, it might yet work with Catrin. He was curious about her; liked her a lot twenty years before, might have gotten serious about her twenty years ago. And, as he thought about it, he wondered if one reason that he'd never married was the relationship he'd had with her so long ago: She had somehow immunized him against marriage. That *that* had been a moment, and on that moment, he'd passed.

He pushed the Porsche down the ramp onto I-

94, let it wind, kicked it out of the chute and past a Firebird like the Pontiac was *parked,* and decided that his brain was getting tired of italics. Had to make a decision.

But if he could just get another week . . . or two . . . out of Jael, could he be happy? Did he even want to be?

"Fuck it," he said aloud. But he didn't mean it. He was hanging a little over 125 on a nearly empty interstate when he passed Snelling Avenue. Thirty seconds later, he flashed past a highway patrolman going the other way, on the other side of the highway. He saw the flashers come up and grinned, took the Porsche up the ramp at Cretin-Vandalia, and turned left toward home.

The guy had no chance.

At ten o'clock the next morning, a cop called to say that Olson was moving. "We don't know what he's doing. He got out on the interstate and he's done a couple of laps around the St. Paul side. He stopped once at White Bear Avenue to get gas."

"How close has he gotten to Highland Park?"

"He took 35E from 94 to 494, so he went right past Spooner's exit at Randolph or at Seventh. If he'd gotten off at either one, we would have been screaming our heads off — but he's just driving."

"Keep calling me," Lucas said.

Weather called while he was in the shower. "I've got a problem," she said.

"No lunch?" he asked, dripping water on the hallway floor.

She could hear the disappointment. "I'm sorry, but this . . . thing . . . just came up and I've got to deal with it."

"Doesn't sound medical," Lucas said.

"It's not. Lucas, I'm being . . . damnit, we need to sit down and talk this out. I have not had a sexual relationship since we split up."

"Why face a disappointment any sooner —"

"Will you shut up? Will you just shut the fuck up for a minute?" she said.

"All right," he said.

"I have not had a sexual relationship, but there was this doctor . . ."

"The Frenchman?"

"You know about this?" she asked.

"I know you were going out with some Frenchman."

"Not going out with. I went out with him three times. Or four times. Or maybe, I don't know, five or six times. We never really stopped or anything. I was busy or he was busy and it sort of drifted, and then he had to go back to Paris for a while."

"He came back."

"Yeah. He called last night and he wanted to have lunch today," she said. "He was pretty insistent, even when I said I was pretty busy. . . . I think I've got to go talk to him."

"And . . . ?"

"I'm ultimately not interested in Frenchmen," she said.

"Well, Jesus, Weather, why don't you just tell him to blow it out his froggy ass?"

"I don't think that would exactly be a diplomatic way to handle it . . ."

"You aren't the fuckin' State Department." He let himself get a little angry about it.

". . . and I've got to work with him. He's an important guy around here."

They talked for another minute or two, and he let himself get a little angrier — and at the bottom of it, was satisfied that she was impressed by the anger. Then he went back to the shower, finished cleaning up, and got dressed. *All right.* He picked up the phone and dialed Jael.

She answered on the third ring, and he said, "Your problem is, you're too Victorian."

"That's my problem, all right," she said lazily. "Hang on. . . ." He could hear her yell, "It's okay, it's for me," and then she was back.

"Have you had breakfast?"

"I'm barely awake. It's not even ten-thirty," she said.

"I'll come get you if you want."

"Can't. I've got a half-dozen people coming at noon. We're working out a joint show, and we've got way too many people. We're trying to figure out how to screw some of them. You're welcome to come over, but you wouldn't like the people, and I don't want any of them thrown out any windows."

"Goddamnit. I can't find anyone to talk to this morning," he said.

"And tonight, my dad's getting in. We're all going over to the airport to pick him up. So . . ."

"No dinner. No midnight snack."

"You ever tried phone sex?" she asked.

"Tried once, but it doesn't work. I feel like a silly jerk-off."

"That's sort of inevitable," she said.

"On the other hand, I'm good at giving it. I wouldn't want to use the word *brilliant*, but then, I'm a modest kind of guy."

"Really? That's interesting," she said. "I mean, how would you start it?"

"Are you still in bed?"

"Yeah."

"What are you wearing?" he asked.

"A flannel nightshirt and underpants and socks," she said.

"Socks? Jesus. That makes it a little harder," Lucas said.

"Come on, Davenport."

"All right. You know that fake Indian dreamcatcher you've got hanging over your sink?"

"Yeah . . . ?"

"Go get it," he said.

"Go get it? What for?"

"Listen, are you going to do this, or not?"

"Well . . . I just wanted to know . . ."

"You're gonna need that hawk feather," he said.

After a moment, she said, "Hang on."

"Wait a minute! You still there?"

She came back. "Yes?"

"Didn't I see one of those Lady Remington leg shavers in the bathroom?"

"Yes?"

"Bring that too," Lucas said.

"I'll tell you right now, I'm not shaving anything," she said.

"You don't use those things to *shave*," Lucas said. "You use them to *shave*? You naive little waif, you."

"I'll be right back," she said.

The City Hall was quiet; there were fewer TV trucks at the curb, and the Homicide office was mostly empty. Del called on the cell phone and said, "Hot damn, you've turned it on."

"Yeah. What's going on?"

"Nothing. I was just calling to ask."

"All right. I'm turning this fucking thing off."

"No — don't do that. Listen, I'm gonna take off with the old lady this afternoon. Go see an aunt of hers, and then maybe go look at some carpet."

"You're doing carpet?"

"Yeah, maybe for the family room."

"All right. Well. See you later."

He wound up in his office with all the paper on the case; he found nothing new, but strengthened his sense that Spooner was at the bottom of it. Then Lester called, and said that the gay friend of John Dukeljin, who had identified

Spooner as being at the party, and carrying a shoulder bag, remembered seeing a man with a bag but couldn't pick Spooner out of a photo spread.

"Par for the course," Lucas said. "You find anybody else?"

"Two other people think they saw him. But the guy is sort of a nebbish, and the light was bad, they had those strobe things you dance to. . . . So that's what we got."

Rose Marie called and said, "Here's a mystery for you. Why would the head of the state highway patrol call me up at home and say, 'Tell that fuckin' Davenport to knock it the fuck off'?"

Lucas thought for a moment. "Must be political," he said. "He's a Republican."

"I thought it might be something like that," she said.

"Is Olson coming in this afternoon?" Lucas asked.

"No. I told him we'd call if there were any serious developments."

"All right. I'm outa here."

"See you Monday. . . . And Lucas, knock it the fuck off, whatever it is."

He called Catrin at her home, ready to hang up at a man's voice. "What are you doing?"

She didn't need to ask who it was — a good sign. "Well. I'm moving out."

"When?"

"I'm staying with a friend tonight. Jack seems to be mostly amused," she said. "Maybe he thinks I'm going through some kind of phase. It's making me really angry."

"If you'd like to get a bite and talk, I'll meet you halfway."

"God, Lucas, could we tomorrow?" she asked. "I'm just really jammed today. I mean, I packed away my daughter's First Communion pictures."

"Okay, okay. Don't tell me. You've got my cell phone?"

"You never answer."

"It's now permanently on — at least for the duration of the Alie'e thing."

"I'll call you."

He had wicked designs on three women, was worried sick about how he could possibly juggle them . . . and he couldn't get a date. "They'll always take you at Saks," he said to his office walls.

They took him at Saks. For a lot. "Lucas, how are you . . ." the custom-shop salesman said. "We have *got* something for you. I've been saving it. Two new fabrics from Italy, you won't believe that they're wool."

He killed two hours at Saks and wrote a check for three thousand dollars. He took a call halfway through the fitting from the cops who were tailing Olson.

"We got a concept," the cop said.

"I'm interested."

"We just took Olson back to his motel. He's

preaching tonight down in West St. Paul . . . you know where the Southview Country Club is?"

"Yeah."

"He'll be at a church right around there. He actually got off this tour he was doing, and drove into the church parking lot, like he was just figuring out where it was. Then he went back to driving, and finally wound up here at the motel. And what we got to thinking was, what if he's timing something?"

"Huh."

"Yeah. When you think about it, West St. Paul and Spooner's place in Highland Park, you don't connect them, but if you look at a map, it ain't far — about six miles, and most of that is Interstate. He could do a round-trip in less than fifteen minutes. What if he does his weird preaching thing, then tells the pastor or whoever that he needs to be alone for a bit, to recover — or thinks of some shit like that — goes out to his car, runs over to Highland Park, wastes Spooner, runs back, and there he is: all those witnesses who say he was at the church."

"Sounds Hollywood."

"Yeah, well . . . that's our concept."

"Could be his concept, too. How many guys we got on Spooner tonight?"

"Two or four."

"I'll make sure it's four. You need any more help on Olson?" Lucas asked.

"If he goes to the church, we could use one more car, for a while, anyway."

"All right, get me a radio, and I'll come out and sit with you. I'm not doing anything."

He spent the rest of the afternoon walking around town — got his hair cut, visited a game store, three bars, and a gun shop, where a dealer tried to sell him a $2,600 Scout rifle by Steyr.

"I'd have to shoot a deer that dressed out at thirteen hundred pounds to get my money back," Lucas said, looking at the rifle. "On the hoof, that's a two-thousand-pound whitetail. That's a whitetail the size of a Chevy pickup."

"It's not the deer, it's the aesthetics of the machinery," the dealer said. The dealer had quit his job as an English teacher to take up gun sales. "Look at this piece. . . ."

"The bolt handle's weird," Lucas said.

"It's German."

"It's weird."

"Forget the bolt for a minute, look —"

"Why's the scope way out there on the end?"

"I'll tell you why." The dealer pointed out the window. "Swing it at something across the street. Keep both eyes open and then let your right eye just look through the scope."

Lucas swung. "Whoa . . . that's nice. You shoot where you're looking."

"They didn't mean it to be, but this is the perfect North Woods deer rifle. There's never been anything better."

"Caliber's too small."

"A .308's too small? Have you been smokin' something strange? A .308 is absolutely —"

"Not for a two-thousand-pound deer. And the bolt handle's weird."

"You aren't the artist I thought you were, Davenport," the dealer said. "I can barely contain my disappointment."

At six o'clock, he drifted down toward West St. Paul, located the church, then got dinner at a steak house and made it back to the church a little before seven-thirty. He hooked up with one of the surveillance cops, a guy from Intelligence, and got a radio and a pair of binoculars. "I'm getting pretty tired of this," the cop said.

"Maybe something will pop," Lucas said. "Where do you want me?"

"See that hill? If you go up there, there are a row of houses where the backyards look right down on the parking lot. If you could go up there, find somebody at home and hustle them a little —"

"How will I know which car is Olson's?"

"Call us when you're set, and when Olson rolls in, and he's inside, I'll walk over to his car and point a flashlight up at you. We'll have somebody inside the church watching Olson. We're most concerned that he might find a way to sneak out and get rolling before we know it. Or maybe have another car ditched here by one of his Burnt River pals."

"All right. I'll set up."

Lucas found a house with lights, showed his ID, and got permission to sit out on the patio. The owner dug a webbed folding chair out of a lawn shed and gave it to him.

Olson was already moving, a little early. He arrived twenty minutes before he was to preach; the Intelligence cop spotted the car for him, and Lucas settled down to wait. The radio burped every few minutes: when Olson started preaching; when other cars came or went; and an occasional observation on life.

Four people in two cars were at Spooner's, watching front and back, and they weighed in from time to time. Spooner was at home, but the front drapes were drawn. Then Spooner's garage lights came on, and a minute later Spooner backed out in his car. The people watching him scrambled. Spooner drove five blocks to a SuperAmerica, bought something, walked half a block to a Blockbuster Video, rented a movie, and drove back home. The garage door went down. The watchers settled in.

The guy on the radio said, "Olson's getting cranked. The crowd's rolling with him."

A minute later: "There's a guy coming from the north side, he's walking a pooch. . . ."

"Got him."

Then one of the cops watching Spooner said, "Spooner just came out in his shirt. He's looking up at his roof. What the fuck is he . . . SPOONER'S DOWN, SPOONER'S DOWN.

463

HOLY SHIT, DAVE, DAVE. Do you see . . ."

And they lost them; and then they were back. "WEST WEST WEST. JESUS GO BACK. NO, GO BACK. JESUS GET EMS DOWN HERE. GET EMS . . ."

Lucas was running — around the house, into his car.

Every step of the way, he could hear people screaming on the radio. In one minute he was on Mendota Road, in two minutes on Robert Street, then on 110, and he was moving as fast as he could without killing anyone, flashing past cars, weaving through traffic, praying that he wouldn't run into a highway patrolman, running, and all the time the traffic on the radio became more shrill: "GODDAMNIT, WE'RE LOSING HIM. WE'RE LOSING HIM. WE NEED SOME GODDAMN HELP, SOME-BODY . . ."

Lucas made I-35 and headed north, and called, "I'm coming up. If you've got a runner, tell me which way."

Then a cop, coming back: "We don't know. We don't know."

"I thought you said you were losing him."

"Spooner, Spooner, we're losing Spooner."

"Where's the shooter, where's the shooter?"

"I don't know, man, I don't know, we never saw him. Dave, where are you? Dave, did you get west?" Then Dave: "I got west, man, but I don't see anything, nothing moving. Lucas, if you're coming in, get up on the Seventh Street ramp and put on your flashers and see if anybody shies away."

Lucas thought: He's gone. If they were down to blocking ramps, the shooter was gone.

And he was.

Spooner died on his front lawn with his wife screaming over him, and two cops trying to stop the blood with their hands. He took a .44 Magnum slug four inches to the left of his sternum; he took a couple of minutes to die, but he didn't know it. Except for technical purposes, he was dead when the slug hit.

27

Lester drove over from Minneapolis in time to see the body hauled away. He and Lucas stood on the Spooners' lawn and watched the Ramsey County ME working, and Lester said, "We may be fucked. Personally, I mean. We gotta go talk to Rose Marie so she won't be blindsided by the press."

"I know," Lucas said. "Before we do that, we ought to wring out Olson. And we have to fill in St. Paul on what we were doing, and get them to grab Spooner's paper and his computers and close off his safe-deposit boxes — get some people in early tomorrow and notify every bank inside a couple hours' driving time about the boxes, and maybe get a warrant for the house and grab any keys he's got."

"Jesus, Lucas, it's gonna look like we got him killed, and then we're persecuting his wife," Lester said.

"Persecuting his wife won't make a hell of a lot of difference if they hang us for killing her husband," Lucas said. "But if Spooner's dirty, then we might kick loose of the whole thing. We've got to go after him hard."

"Aw, man . . ." Lester was shaken up. He kept coming back to the body, still on the ground, now under a tarp.

"Listen, this ain't you," Lucas said. "This is me. I'm the one who tipped Olson. There are only two possibilities: Olson tipped the killer — he's managing the killer — or somebody else put the killer on Spooner. I don't think anybody else leaked Spooner's name — it's gotta be Olson."

"So what do we do?"

"I'll go talk to Rose Marie. You stay out of it. I won't mention your name. I'll just tell her that I asked you to put a couple people on Spooner. And that's really what happened."

"Except that I went along with it," Lester said.

"Bullshit. I didn't ask you before I did it. Afterwards, what were you gonna do? Tell Olson to forget the name? And you were just helping protect Rose Marie."

"Aw, man . . ."

"Just sit tight," Lucas said. He got on the phone and called Del, filled him in. "I'm gonna go shake Olson, if you want to come along."

"I'll meet you," Del said. "Do you know where he is?"

"I'll have the guys at the church call us when he heads back to his motel. We want to get him alone."

A St. Paul cop across the street, in the backyard of the house opposite Spooner's, was yelling something, and two St. Paul plainclothesmen trotted toward him. "Something going on," Lester said.

Lucas hung up his phone and got on the radio, called the cops watching Olson. "Tell me when he's heading back to the motel. The minute he heads that way."

"You got it, Chief."

Back on the phone, calling the cops who were watching Jael: "Somebody may be coming. Keep her away from the windows, keep her away from the doors. If anything moves, shoot it."

He and Lester walked across the street. One of the St. Paul plainclothesmen said, "We got a shell."

"What kind?"

One of the patrol cops who'd found it said, "Forty-four Mag."

"He's shooting a rifle," Lucas said. "One of those Ruger carbines, I bet. The shell ejected, and this one he couldn't find."

"What does that tell us?" Lester asked.

"Damned if I know," Lucas said.

Lucas called Rose Marie. "I've got a problem. I've got to come see you."

"What happened?"

"I'll come see you," Lucas said.

Rose Marie lived in a comfortable neighborhood on the south side of Minneapolis, a fifteen-minute drive from Spooner's. Lucas didn't think about what he was going to say, except that whatever it was, he had to cover Lester and the other cops. Rose Marie's husband was just walking out the door with the family cocker spaniel when Lucas arrived. "As long as it's not another killing," he said genially.

"I hate to wreck your mood," Lucas told him grimly.

"Oh, boy. Here in town?"

"Over in St. Paul."

"That's a little break."

Rose Marie was reading. She dropped the book on the floor when Lucas pushed through the front door and called, "Hello?"

"Lucas . . . what's going on?"

"William Spooner was shot to death. A half hour ago, over in St. Paul."

"My God." She was appalled.

"It's worse than that," he said. He told her the story, made it as flat as he could. She listened without much change of expression, and when he finished, said, "Let me think for a minute." She took the full minute, then said, "We're gonna have to talk to the mayor. I can put it off until early afternoon."

"Then what?"

"I don't know. You've saved several people's butts over the years, but this could be tough. Especially if we can't make Spooner as the guy who killed Rodriguez and the others."

"You don't sound nearly as pissed off as I thought you'd be," Lucas said.

"Well . . ." She shrugged. "I'm not. I know

what you were doing. The fact is, Spooner's name would have leaked sooner or later, just like Rodriguez's, and just like the muff-diving thing. This way, we controlled it."

"I controlled it," Lucas said. "I think, for damage-control purposes, we ought to keep the emphasis on me. I'd especially hate to see anyone else get hurt."

She shook her head. "I think it's just you and me — if they hang you, they'll get me for not controlling the department."

"Which is bullshit."

"It's politics," she said. "Anyway, I can put it off until after lunch. You say you want to shake Olson. Go do it. I'll get the St. Paul chief moving, and serve some warrants on Mrs. Spooner, God help her. If we can get something going by noon, or one o'clock, the mayor'll think twice before he throws us to the dogs."

"If we actually get somebody, if we start a hunt, with an actual name . . ."

"Then we've solved the crimes. Especially if we can make the case against Spooner. Then we've solved the crimes, and the whole thing becomes moot."

Lucas looked at his watch. "Fifteen hours."

He left Rose Marie's house in a better mood than when he arrived, but the leaking of Spooner's name seemed, in retrospect, unforgivably stupid. On the other hand, if it had worked, it would have seemed brilliant: like Napoleon at

Waterloo — beaten by a hairsbreadth, but beaten.

The cops at the church called. Olson was moving west on 494, headed back toward his motel. Lucas scrambled to get to Del's, picked him up, and filled him in on the Spooner ploy. "So you're now one of four people who know what happened," he said.

"Should have worked," Del said.

"We had a wrong concept in our heads," Lucas said. "We figured the killer walked up, close range, like he had to with Plain, and bang! A pistol. But he was only close with Plain because he had to be. He was inside a building. A fuckin' rifle, man — if we'd found a shell from a .30-06, I would have had a two-block-wide net around Spooner. But a .44? I assumed it was a pistol."

"So'd we all," Del said. "I wonder why that chick in the Matrix building —"

"Yeah, the Oriental chick."

"— why she didn't see the rifle. If that was him?"

"It's a small gun, man. You could put it down your pants leg, if you wanted to walk with a limp."

Del thought it over, looking out the window at the dark. Then: "How'd he get Spooner to come outside?"

"Huh. I didn't ask that," Lucas said. "The surveillance guys said he came out and looked at his chimney. You got your phone?"

"Yeah."

"Call St. Paul. See if Spooner took a call."

St. Paul was already working it. Spooner took a call, the St. Paul cops said, supposedly from a neighbor down the block, who said Spooner might have a chimney fire. Spooner had run outside to look, his wife said. St. Paul was in the process of tracking the calling number.

"That could be interesting," Lucas said.

"Got a buck that says it's from a pay phone," Del said.

Olson beat them to the motel by ten minutes. Lucas and Del checked in with the surveillance cops, then headed up to Olson's room. "I want you down the hallway, out of sight," Lucas said. "I'm going in hard. If I need you to interrupt, I'll call you on the cell phone and I'll ask for an update, as though I were calling downtown. Give me a minute, then come knock on the door."

"How do I come in?"

"Soft. He might need somebody to give him a little sympathy."

Del stayed out of sight. Lucas knocked on the door, heard a man's voice call, "Just a minute," and a minute later, Olson came to the door, buckling his belt. He looked out past the privacy chain, frowned, and said, "Chief Davenport?"

"We got to talk," Lucas said.

"Sure." Olson slipped the chain out, and Lucas banged in hard, put a hand on Olson's chest before he had a chance to react, and shoved him back against the bed. Olson fell back on it, and Lucas kicked the door shut and screamed, "How the fuck did you do it? Who are you working with?"

Olson, eyes wide, tried to sit up, but Lucas crowded against his legs, slipped his .45 out of its holster, and held it by his side. "What . . . what're . . ."

"Don't give me that shit," Lucas said. "You set him up, you know you set him up. You got your own parents killed, and I don't want to hear any bullshit."

"What . . . what . . ."

Lucas took a breath. "I told one guy about Bill Spooner. One guy. You. So tonight Bill Spooner is shot to death on his own lawn, in front of his wife's eyes. Cold-blooded murder. Shot with a rifle."

"I don't , I . . . Oh, no. No, no," Olson stuttered. "I told, I told, I told, oh no. I told four people. I told four people, my God, I told four people."

"Who?"

But the question died with a knock on the door. Del should have stopped any visitors. Lucas stepped back, opened the door, looked. Del was standing in the corridor. "Something came up," he said. He looked past Lucas at Olson, who was now sitting up on the bed. Lucas stepped back, and Del asked, "You already tell him about Spooner?"

"Yes."

Del looked at Olson. "Spooner was lured out on his front lawn by somebody who told him he had a chimney fire. The St. Paul police traced the phone call. It came from a cell phone registered to your mother."

"What?"

"To your mother," Del repeated.

Olson looked from Lucas to Del. "My God, I'm sorry," he said. "I didn't know she had her own phone."

"You didn't have anything to do with it," Lucas said skeptically.

"I told four people," Olson said. "At dinner Friday night. I told the Bentons and the Packards."

"Where are they now?"

"They went back home for the weekend," Olson said.

"How far is Burnt River?" Lucas asked.

"Five hours. By car."

"Do you have their phone numbers?" Lucas asked.

"Yes. Of course."

"I want you to call them," Lucas said. "If somebody answers, like Mrs. Benton, I want you to ask for her husband. If Mr. Benton answers, I want you to come up with a reason to talk with his wife. Just thank them for helping you out."

"I'd feel like I'd be betraying them," Olson said.

"But you won't be, if they're home," Lucas said.

"I'll know —"

"People are dying," Del said.

Olson made the calls from the motel phone, with Lucas listening on an extension. Both couples were at home. "Couldn't be them," Olson said.

"You only told four people," Lucas said.

"Only those four. We walked across the street to Perkins and had dinner together before they left. Right after dark, on Friday."

Lucas thought for a moment. Burnt River, Burnt River. What if they'd been going about this all wrong? Or half wrong? A deep, old connection, but not family. Someone who'd known her from the old days, someone who'd — He picked up the phone and called Lane. "You know that genealogy you made up? Who was the guy who nailed Alie'e on the baseball diamond?"

"Gimme a minute, I'm watching the game," Lane said. A moment later, he was back. "Louis Friar," he said. "The people up there call him the Reverend, but he doesn't know why."

"Thanks. I'm running. Talk to you tomorrow," Lucas said. He turned back to Olson. "Who is Louis Friar?"

"He's a guy up in Burnt River."

"Would either the Bentons or Packards know him?" Lucas asked.

"Yes. His parents, especially. Louie's parents and my parents and the Bentons and the Packards and a few other families, we're all in the same social circle. Play cards and stuff."

"He once had a sexual relationship with Alie'e."

"That's just a rumor."

"Everybody in Burnt River believes it. They all seem to think it happened."

"Yes. I know," Olson said.

"Do you think he might have felt protective toward her? You think he might have —"

"No, no . . . he's just a guy. He's got a lawn service. He goes around to resorts and stuff, and does landscape maintenance."

"Single guy?" Del asked.

"Yes."

"Deer hunter?"

"Probably. I don't know him that well. He was a couple years behind me in school."

Lucas got back on the phone, called Rose Marie. "Call the airport, authorize the big chopper. We need to go to Burnt River, right now, tonight. Three of us."

"You think you might make the fifteen hours?" she asked.

"Got my fingers crossed," Lucas said.

"Get over to the airport. I'll call."

⤜⤞ 28 ⤜⤞

To Lucas it felt like three in the morning — like he'd been up forever — but the chopper lifted off a few minutes before ten o'clock, with Lucas, Del, and Olson in the back. Before they left the metro area, Lucas called the Howell County sheriff's department, got switched to the sheriff, and gave him a quick summary. He asked if a sheriff's department car could meet them at the Sheridan airport, the nearest to Burnt River. The sheriff said he'd send a couple of cars, and would ride along himself. "Kind of interesting," he said.

The flight took a little over an hour. Lucas was unaffected. Fixed-wing planes scared him; when they came down unexpectedly, the people inside wound up as postage stamp–sized pieces of meat. With a helicopter, you always had a chance.

The sky had been mostly cloudy in the Cities, but they put down at Sheridan under crystalline skies, with stars as brilliant as those that Lucas had watched from his cabin the week before. They were met by two Ford Explorers with light racks. The sheriff and two deputies climbed out to shake hands, and the sheriff said, "Who do we want to find first? This Friar guy?"

"Yeah," Lucas said. "If he's not around, we'll want to talk with his parents, and take a look at his house — see if there's any sign that he might be involved with Alie'e."

"You might have trouble getting a warrant if you've got nothing more than an urge to look around," the sheriff said. He was a square-shouldered, square-faced man with a brush mustache. He wore jeans and cowboy boots, even with the snow. "Our judges aren't all that cooperative."

"We've narrowed down the number of people outside the police department who knew about the man who was shot tonight," Lucas said. "There were exactly five. That includes Mr. Olson here — and we know where he was tonight — and two Burnt River couples, who are here, at home. But if Friar isn't here — and he couldn't be, if he's involved in the shooting tonight, not unless he's got his own chopper — then we think he's worth looking at. He once had a sexual involvement with Alie'e."

"Okay, I know the guy now," one of the deputies said. "If he's the guy who nailed Alie'e. They call him the Reverend."

"What do you think?" the sheriff asked the deputy. "You think he could do it?"

"Far as I know, he's just a good ol' boy," the deputy said. "He might've had a couple of DWIs over the years. Nothing serious."

"How about if his parents tell us they told him about Spooner?" Lucas asked.

"Might get you a warrant on that," the sheriff said. "Especially since it's Alie'e."

"So let's go," Lucas said.

Del and Lucas got in the back of the sheriff's truck, while Olson got in with the other two deputies. Once inside, Del told the sheriff, "I told your guys to kinda keep an eye on Olson," he said. "He's not entirely out of the woods yet."

"They can do that," the sheriff said. He pulled a cell phone from his pocket, turned it on, ran through a call list, and pushed a button. A minute later, he said, "Hey, Carl, this is me, you get anything on Friar? Yeah? When? At McLeod's? Uh-huh. Uh-huh. Okay, we're going out that way, then."

He rang off and looked at Lucas. "You may have wasted a trip. The Burnt River town cop says a guy he ran into at the Yer-In-And-Out Store saw Friar shooting pool with some friends at McLeod's Tavern out on the lake. They were there a half hour ago."

"Goddamnit," Lucas said.

"So what do you want to do?" the sheriff asked.

"We're here, let's talk to him," Lucas said. "Then we can go wake up the Bentons and Packards and find out what they have to say. It had to come out of here — someplace along the line, it had to come from Olson, the Bentons, or the Packards." But he was no longer sure of it; what if it was a departmental leak? Or what if Olson was lying, and he was running another guy, one of his disciples? Maybe somebody who thought Olson was Jesus?

"Whatever you say," the sheriff said. He called the other car, and they swung toward McLeod's.

McLeod's looked exactly like five hundred other lakeside taverns: snow-covered parking lot with mounds of plowed snow on the side; fake dark-brown log-cabin styling; small windows under the eaves at the front; a Christmas wreath on the door; snowmobile parking at the lakeside. "We don't have any snow in the Cities yet," Lucas said as they pulled in.

"That's because you're practically living in Miami," the sheriff said.

"I guess that accounts for the palm trees outside the office," Del said to Lucas.

Talk in the bar stopped when they all walked in; Lucas could feel the heads turning. They clumped down toward the game room, through a haze of barbecue smoke. The deputy who knew the Reverend said, "That's him in the red shirt."

Louis Friar was focusing on the five-ball when he saw them all coming. He stood up and grounded his cue and said, "Evening, Sheriff." He looked puzzled, then saw Olson and said, "Hi, Tom. Sorry about Alie'e, jeez —"

The sheriff said, "Could you come back over here and talk with us for a bit?"

"Sure . . . what'd I do?" Friar handed his cue to a friend.

"Nothing, apparently. But we need to talk," the sheriff said.

They got in a corner, away from the bar, and Lucas quickly told Friar the problem. "Well, yeah, my folks told me," he said. "I mean, I couldn't have told you the guy's name tonight, but I could've told you Friday night and all day yesterday. Spooner, right? Banker."

"Did you tell anybody?" Lucas asked.

"Well, sure . . . those guys over there."

They all turned and looked at the three men Friar had been shooting pool with. "When did you tell them?"

"Friday night, I guess. My folks got home about ten o'clock, and we just had that snow come through. I was over there blowing out their drive, and they told me. I came down here afterwards for a couple brewskies, you know. . . . I told a couple people."

"Do you think . . . they might have told anybody?" Lucas asked.

"Look," Friar said. "I doubt there's anybody in Burnt River who hasn't heard this guy's name by now. The Bentons told my folks, and my folks probably told a couple more friends, and I imagine the Bentons told more. Everybody's interested in what happened to Alie'e, she's the most famous person ever come from here — or ever will. She's the only person in the whole county or maybe all the counties around whoever had her face on a magazine."

"Goddamnit," Lucas said.

The sheriff waved at the three guys around the pool table. "You guys, could you step over here for a minute?" When they did, clustering around, he said, "We want to know, did any of you hear about this banker fellow, the suspect in the Alie'e case, from anybody besides Louie? Nobody's gonna get in trouble, we just need to know how much the name's gotten around."

Two of them admitted passing the name along; two of the three had heard the name in conversation on Saturday or Sunday.

"So everybody knows," Lucas said.

"Everybody," said a guy in a green shirt. "What happened, anyway? Somebody shoot that asshole?"

Lucas looked at him. "Exactly. Somebody shot that asshole."

"Really?" They wanted details. Lucas shook his head and said, "Man, the question is, is there anybody in town who might pull something like this?"

A guy in a gold flannel shirt said, "What was he shot with?"

"A rifle, we think. The shooter was fifty yards out or so and hit him in the chest."

"That ain't much of a shot with a rifle," a blue flannel shirt said. "I woulda gone for a neck shot."

"You always go for a fuckin' neck shot, and the next time you come back with a deer, I expect to be a grandpa," Friar said.

"Wasn't a .44 Mag, was it?" gold shirt asked. Lucas and Del both focused on him. "What?"

"A .44 Mag?"

"Yeah. It was," Lucas said. They all looked at gold shirt. "Who's got a .44 Mag?"

Gold shirt swallowed, looked at his friends. "You know who it is? It's that jack-off Martin Scott."

Friar slapped his forehead. "Goddamn, Steve." He looked at Lucas. "It was Martin Scott."

"Who's that?"

"He's the jack-off Coca-Cola truck driver for Howell County," gold shirt said. "He shoots a .44 Mag, a Ruger, and he's always had this thing about Alie'e. I mean, bad. He works free for her parents, mowing their yard and shoveling snow and shit, because he thinks that when she comes back, they'll let him hang out with her."

"He says he saw her tits once, when she was out in their pool," green shirt said. "I called him a lyin' SOB, I said nobody in Howell County ever saw her tits but the Reverend here, and he never saw them but once. But Martin said he's seen them."

"Only about sixty-six billion people seen them by now," gold shirt said, then he remembered Olson and swallowed and said, "Jeez, sorry, Tom."

"He's nuts. He thinks he's in the Coca-Cola army, walks around twenty-four hours a day in his Coke uniform," said blue shirt.

"Yeah, but you know what?" green shirt said. "Couldn't be him."

"You're full a shit. Gotta be him," Friar said.

"Nope. Because, guess what?" Green shirt crossed his arms.

Lucas bit. "What?"

"Because a whole bunch of those people got shot on Monday. Wasn't it a Monday?"

Lucas had to think: it seemed like a thousand years ago. But Marcy was shot on Monday afternoon, and all the others. "Yeah," he said. "Monday."

Green shirt looked at his friends. "Martin works on Mondays."

"Oh, yeah," Friar said.

"And the chances of that carp-sucker Rand Waters letting him off are slim and none. He's a slave driver," green shirt said.

"I wouldn't work for him," said blue shirt. "He's a mean son of a bitch. I saw him pick up the back end of a Chevy Camaro one day, right down on River Street."

"Light car," gold shirt said.

"Let's see you pick one up," green shirt said. "Your balls would pop like birthday balloons."

Lucas jumped in. "So could somebody call this Waters guy, and find out if Scott *was* here last Monday? That'd settle a lot."

"I can call him," the sheriff said.

"If he ain't home, he and his old lady'll probably be up at the Port," Friar said.

Gold shirt bought a round as they clustered

around the bar. The sheriff got the bartender's phone book and made a series of calls from the kitchen. When he came out, he said to Lucas and Del, "We better run out to Martin's house."

"Yeah?"

"Yeah. He had last Monday off. He told Waters he had to go to the Cities to help the Olsons with Alie'e. He told him if he didn't get the day off, he'd quit. That's how serious he was."

Lucas looked at Friar. "So where's this guy live?" Lucas asked.

"Hard to explain, but we can show you," Friar said.

They left the bar in a convoy of two pickups and the two sheriff's department Explorers. They went into Burnt River, then out the other side, then off on a side road for a hundred yards. Martin Scott lived in a small log cabin, with a stick-built garage across a wide, snow-covered drive. The snow had been driven on, but there was no sign of truck at the house, and only a single lighted window. A pizza pan–sized satellite dish perched on the corner of the house, aimed at the satellite over Reno. A propane tank sat off on one side of the driveway, and next to the garage, a lean-to covered four or five cords of split wood. All of it was illuminated by a blue yard light.

"He ain't home," Friar said, looking at the dark house. They'd all gotten out of the truck and gathered next to one of the Explorers.

"How do you know?" Del asked. "Maybe he's asleep."

"He burns wood, and the wood-stove ain't going," Friar said. "That smoke there" — he pointed at a thin stream of smoke burbling out of a four-inch-wide stack — "that's from the propane burner. You only turn that on when you ain't home, to keep the wood stove going."

"Why don't you guys wait," Lucas said to the sheriff. "Del . . ."

Lucas and Del took out their pistols and walked up toward the house. Lucas knocked, then pounded on the door; no sign of life. He opened the storm door and tried the door knob. Locked. The sheriff came up and said, "Let's look around back."

The house had a back porch, but the door apparently wasn't used much: It hadn't been shoveled since the last snow fall, and there were no tracks crossing it. Lucas stood up on the back porch and tried to peer through the window. "Want a flash?" the sheriff asked. He handed Lucas a flashlight. Lucas shined it in the window and saw a kitchen.

Gold shirt had wandered over to the garage and pulled the center-opening doors far enough apart to see inside. "Truck's gone," he said.

Lucas started down the far side of the house, Del and the sheriff trailing behind. One window showed a five-inch slit in the curtains. Lucas looked at Del and said, "If I boosted you up, could you look in there?"

"I guess."

Lucas made a stirrup out of his hands, Del

stood in it, and Lucas boosted him up the side of the house. The sheriff handed him a flashlight, and Del looked through the window. A minute later he said, "All right," and Lucas let him down.

Del handed the flashlight to the sheriff and said to Lucas, "This is the guy."

"What'd you see?" The four shirts and two deputies and the sheriff pressed around.

"I'll let you look," Del said. "Could you pull one of those pickups up here?"

Gold shirt ran back to his pickup, gunned it out of the driveway and up to the house. Lucas took the flashlight from Del, and they all scrambled into the truck bed. Lucas shined the light though the window.

They were looking into what might have been a bedroom at one time; now it was a shrine. The walls were covered with the thousand faces of Alie'e Maison, all carefully cut out, all pasted flat to the wall, thousands of green eyes looking out at them from the wall opposite. In the center of the room sat a single lonely wooden chair, where a man might sit to look into the eyes.

The sheriff took it in, muttered something under his breath, then turned to a deputy. "Go yank Swede out of bed and get a warrant. Tell him I need it right now. Tell him I need it ten minutes ago, because I'm already in the house."

And Lucas added, "Get this guy's tag number and the make on his truck and call me. Quick as you can."

"Nineteen ninety-seven Dodge ram, metallic black in color, black-pipe running boards, impact bars on the front, and red script on the door that says, 'Martin Scott,' " gold shirt said.

As they walked around the front of the house, Lucas called Rose Marie. "We ain't got him, but we know who he is," he said. "A deputy up here's gonna call Dispatch, and we need to get a truck description and tag out on the streets."

The sheriff opened the house by the simple expedient of punching out the window on the front door, reaching inside, and unlocking it. He told the four shirts to hang around, but wouldn't let them inside.

The sheriff, Lucas, Del, and one other deputy went into the house. The house smelled bad from the first step, "like he's been skinning some mink in here," the sheriff said. They went back to the shrine and looked in. From the outside, they could see only the wall opposite; from the inside, they could see that all four walls, plus the ceiling, had been done in Alie'e's face.

The sheriff shook his head. "This gives me the creeps," he said. "If he'd showed me this on a nice summer day with Alie'e running around alive, it'd give me the creeps."

"It's a little too much," Lucas agreed.

Green shirt was up on the porch. "Us guys just want to come in and take a quick look, or go back to McLeod's. It's too goddamn cold out here to be hanging around."

The sheriff looked at Lucas, who shrugged. "I don't care . . . maybe they'll see something we don't."

So the sheriff let them come in as Del and Lucas probed Scott's bedroom and kitchen; they found a box of twelve-gauge shotgun shells — skeet shot — in a bedroom closet, but no shotgun; a scoped .300 Winchester Magnum; and a Ruger .22 semiauto carbine.

"So maybe he's got a shotgun with him, too," Lucas said.

"I'll call it in," Del said.

A small living room had black velvet curtains to block the light; a love seat was pushed against one wall; opposite the couch was a projection TV, a Sony, with a screen five feet wide; and next to the TV, a rack of tuning and sound equipment. A Nintendo console sat on the floor next to the couch, with a dozen game boxes — and next to that, a Dreamcast console with even more games. Five small speakers were spotted around the room, with a subwoofer the size of a trash can next to the TV.

"Nine hundred and ninety-nine channels of shit on the TV to choose from," Del said, sounding like he might be quoting someone.

In the kitchen, they found nothing at all. The last of the shirts had taken a look at the shrine, and gold shirt came out in the kitchen, opened the refrigerator, took out a beer, and screwed off the top.

"What the hell are you doing?" the sheriff asked.

"He ain't gonna need it," gold shirt said. "Gonna go to waste."

"Gimme one of those," Friar said. Gold shirt opened the refrigerator, handed him a beer. As he unscrewed the cap, Friar said, "The thing about Martin is, he always thought he'd be famous. That might be *all* he thought about. He thought he could do it by starting small here in Burnt River, and if he worked hard and kept his nose clean, Coke would take care of him. He's been working his ass off, driving that goddamned truck for ten years, and I'd have to say he ain't made much progress up the corporate ladder." He took a pull on the bottle, then added, "Such as the corporate ladder is around here."

"You think he could kill a guy?" Lucas asked.

"Nobody'll go huntin' with him," blue shirt said. "He likes them guns a little too much. One time this guy I know was walking in from his deer stand —"

Gold shirt jumped in. "Ray McDonald."

Blue shirt continued. "— and he bumps into Martin, and Martin goes, 'You smoke cigarettes and the deer'll smell it a mile away.' So Ray goes on home and he's laying in bed that night about to go to sleep, thinking about nothing, and then all of a sudden he realizes that he was about a half-mile away when he stripped that butt and threw it away."

Blue shirt looked at Lucas, Del, and the sheriff, a look that said, *This is of significance.* Lucas took a minute to decipher the look. "He'd

490

been watching him through his scope."

"Yup. Ray said he almost shit in his pants, laying there in bed. Martin Scott had been looking at him smoking, through a scope on that .300 Magnum."

"Didn't shoot him," Del said.

"But I bet he was thinking about it," blue shirt said. "Martin is fuckin' loony tunes, and he was a loony tunes when I met him in kindergarten."

Late that night, when Lucas and Del and a pensive Tom Olson were a hundred miles out of the Sheridan airport, on the way back to the Twin Cities, the sheriff called. "I got some sorta bad news," he said.

"Ah, God, I don't need any," Lucas said. "No time for it."

"We didn't find Scott, but we found his truck," the sheriff said. "It's parked next to the Coke truck, at the distribution center. We talked to Randy Waters again, and he said that Scott parks it there on nights he thinks will be extra cold, because his garage doesn't have heat."

"It's not gonna be that cold tonight," Lucas protested. "What's it gonna be?"

"Maybe ten below," the sheriff said.

"That's nothing," Lucas said. *"Nothing."*

"Yeah, I know. And we can't find Scott — I don't think he's in town. But even if he is in the Twin Cities, looking for his truck won't do you any good."

"Keep an eye out," Lucas said. "If we don't

find Scott, maybe he'll show up for work."

Lucas told Del, who shook his head. "Gotta be him, though," Del said. "You saw the room."

"But what do you think? He's hitchhiking down to the Cities?"

"No, he just got down somehow. Be nice to know the car, though."

Halfway back, Lucas said, "I just thought of something else. You know that Oriental chick at the Matrix? She saw the guy we think was the shooter — only for a second or two — but she thought it was the vending machine guy. She also thought he looked a little porky, and so did Jael, when a guy tried to break into her house that night. . . . But when St. Paul picked up the vending machine guy, he wasn't porky. He was skinny."

"Yeah?"

"I bet this asshole Martin Scott was wearing his Coke coveralls. One of those guys said he wore them twenty-four hours a day. I bet that's what this chick was reacting to — the coveralls, the kind a vending machine guy would wear."

"That's thin," Del said.

"But it's there," Lucas said.

"My ass is kicked," Del said, just before they landed. "You gonna drop me?"

"Yeah. But I'm gonna cruise up and take a look at Jael's place, make sure they've spread out that perimeter."

"I'll ride along for that," Del said.

They'd left Lucas's car at the motel, because it could only handle two, and had ridden over in Olson's rattletrap Volvo. "I'm going back to the valley," Olson said as he drove them back to the motel. "Back to Fargo. Tomorrow. Have somebody call me when you're gonna release the bodies. I'll come and bury them, but I won't wait here anymore. This place is a suburb of hell."

"Oh, bullshit. It's a pretty nice place," Del said irritably.

"Think about the last week," Olson said. His voice was mild, quiet. "Ten days ago, I had a family — now I don't. But it's not so much individual people who did this: They're just souls trying to get through life. It's the culture that does it. It's a death culture, and it's here, right now. It comes out of TV, it comes out of magazines, it comes out of the Internet, it comes out of video games. Look at that television set that poor Martin Scott had. The biggest, most expensive thing he owned, except for his truck. And all those video games. And he was a hardworking man; worked hard. But the culture burned him out, reached out through that satellite dish and grabbed him. We see it in Fargo, but you can still fight it there. Here . . . this place is gone. Too late for this place. Too late. You'll see."

"Shut the fuck up," Del said.

29

Sunday. Day nine.

Six o' clock in the morning.

Olson parked at the hotel and said, "Call me when the bodies are ready."

Lucas said he would.

As they got in Lucas's car, Del said, "He could still have a finger in it."

"Nah. There's no conspiracy here, Del. A bullshit drug murder and then a nutcase on the loose."

"Where do you think Scott is?"

"Here," Lucas said.

"In the suburb of hell?"

"Yup. Somewhere."

There were two guys in Jael's yard. "We get a car about once every five minutes," one of them said. "They're getting a little more traffic up at the Kinsley place, but man, there's just nothing going on."

"All right." They went inside, quietly as they could. A cop was sitting on an easy chair in a hallway, watching a TV on the floor. "We didn't want to get any TV flicker on the windows," he explained.

"Is Jael asleep?"

"Yeah."

"Where's the perimeter?"

"Two blocks out on every side; we got every street covered. He's gonna have to parachute in, if he's coming."

"What I'm worried about, if he comes, is a suicide run," Lucas said. "He's got that shot-gun."

"I just wish he'd come," the cop said. "This is boring my goddamned brains out."

Back in the car, Lucas said, "I'd like to go up to Kinsley's, if you don't mind. Take ten minutes, look around."

"It's all right with me."

Two blocks from Jael's, at a four-way stop, a crossing car paused as Lucas approached, then pulled slowly across the intersection. "Old goat," Del said.

"Yeah . . ." Lucas crossed the street, going straight ahead, then said, "Wait a minute." He swerved, did a quick U-turn, and said, urgently, "We're going after the goat. Get your goddamn pen out, write down the tag, number, call it in." They were back at the intersection, the old slow-moving GTO already at the end of the block. Lucas went after him.

The GTO paused at a stop sign; the driver seemed unsure of his destination, looked both ways. Lucas closed up behind, putting his headlights on the license plate of the other car. Del said, "Got it."

"Call it in, tell them we want an answer right fuckin' now."

"What . . . ?"

"Remember back in the motel, when we called in Lynn Olson's driver's license and asked them to run down his vehicle registrations? He had a Volvo, an Explorer, and an old collector GTO. I bet that fuckin' Scott parked his truck with the Coke truck and walked over to the Olsons' place and took the GTO. How many GTOs do you see around anymore — at six o'clock in the morning?"

Del was already talking on his cell phone, getting switched. Reading the number he'd written on his arm. The GTO went straight ahead. Lucas turned left, did another U-turn and switched off his lights, crept to the end of the block. The GTO took a left at the next corner. Lucas accelerated around the corner, lights off, ran as hard as he could almost to the end of the block, jammed on the brakes, and crept forward again.

The GTO was halfway down the block. At the end of the block, it stopped, then turned right. "He's just weaving around," Lucas said as he accelerated at the corner. "That's gotta be him."

Del was listening. "All right." He looked at Lucas. "It's him."

"Get everybody here. . . . Get everybody on the street."

They began vectoring squad cars toward the GTO, trying to stay out of sight. But four or five minutes after the cat-and-mouse game began, the driver of the GTO realized he was being tracked. Lucas again crept to the end of the block, and saw the GTO already turning the next corner. And when he got to that corner, and crept forward, the GTO was two blocks away and accelerating.

"Goddamnit, he must've seen us," Lucas said.

He jumped on the accelerator, and the Porsche whipped around the corner and they were flying along the narrow street; too fast to do it without lights, if anybody was out walking, and Lucas switched the lights on and up ahead, the GTO busted a stop sign and was out of sight and Del was screaming street names into the telephone; they made the corner and the GTO was already turning at a streetlight.

"West on Lake," Del shouted. "He's headed west on Lake Street." He stopped talking to brace himself as Lucas downshifted and the engine screamed, they drifted through the intersection, and Lucas began running up through the gears and Del started with the phone again. "He's at fifteenth ... fourteenth ... thirteenth ... twelfth ... Where is everybody?"

"Behind us," Lucas said. He could see flashing lights in the rearview mirror. No time for his flashers; he didn't even think about them. Then Del shouted, "He's making a turn under the interstate!"

"He goes on the interstate, we got him," Lucas said. "It's a concrete trough."

Del braced himself again as Lucas drifted the turn; they'd closed some distance on the GTO, which was now only a few hundred yards ahead. The GTO driver busted another traffic light, but Lucas was forced to slow and lost ground; and then the GTO was on the on-ramp and out of sight. Lucas accelerated after him, spotted him as they came off the ramp and started eating up the ground between them. Del stopped shouting into his phone long enough to ask, "What're we gonna do when we catch up with him?"

"I haven't figured that out yet," Lucas said. "Maybe . . . not pull up beside him."

"That would be a bad idea," Del said. "Unless you got your own shotgun hidden in this car somewhere."

"We'll just get on his ass and push him," Lucas said. "He'll either lose it, or we'll pen him."

There were four or five other cars on the roadway; there was still an hour before the morning traffic would start. After fifteen seconds, with the Porsche trailing by two hundred yards, the GTO crossed in front of a slower-moving Ford and swerved onto the shoulder lane. Immediately, the air was full of gravel; a small rock bounced off the Porsche's pristine hood, and Lucas groaned and said, "I'm gonna shoot your ass for that." He moved far left, and the GTO plowed along the shoulder lane for another ten seconds and then suddenly hooked into an upcoming exit.

Del had time to say "Jesus" before Lucas cut across the highway and barely made the ramp approach. At the top, the GTO was moving way too fast to make the corner; the driver tried, but the big car slid out of control, hit a curb while skidding backwards, bounced across a bus bench, and spun sideways into the pump pad of an Amoco station. Lucas had both the brakes and the clutch pinned to the floor, bounced across the intersection, narrowly missed a flying piece of bus bench, and finally stopped in time to see a man humping out of the GTO. He was carrying a long gun, and was headed for the gas station.

Lucas killed the engine, and he and Del were out on the street, Del still screaming into the phone. Through the plate-glass window of the station, they could see the GTO driver pointing his gun at a woman who had her hands over her head. But he was screaming at somebody else, and a moment later, the man inside the cashier's booth pushed the door open.

The driver pushed the woman inside the booth and closed the door behind them all.

In ten minutes, half of the on-duty Minneapolis police department was there. Lucas talked to the man in the booth by telephone: "We know who you are, Mr. Scott. You can't get out of there. I don't think you want to hurt yourself or those innocent people. That's not what you're all about."

"I don't want to talk to you," Scott said.

"We think it's best to keep the lines of communication open," Lucas began.

"I want to talk to your negotiator."

Lucas looked at the phone, unsure that he'd heard it right. But he had. "Whatever you say, Mr. Scott."

The negotiations began just before seven o'clock. Because of Scott's fixation on a woman, Alie'e, somebody decided that they should try a woman negotiator first. That seemed to work. The negotiator and Scott had a friendly chat to establish trust, and then Scott listed his demands: a Northwest Airlines jet at the airport with enough fuel to get them to Cuba, or he'd start killing his hostages.

"Aw, Jesus Christ," Lucas said. He went to look at the paint job on his Porsche.

The TV trucks began showing up at 7:10; Rose Marie was there at 7:12, with Lester two seconds behind. "That the guy?" Lester asked, looking toward the gas station.

"That's him," Lucas said. "You owe me some money for a Porsche paint job, by the way."

"How're we gonna get him out of there?" Rose Marie asked.

"I don't know," Lucas said. "He's locked in a bulletproof booth with about six hundred Cokes, a hundred pounds of corn chips and Hostess cupcakes, a thousand bucks' worth of cigarettes, and a TV."

"Sounds like a good weekend," Lester said.

"As long as he doesn't kill the hostages," Rose Marie said. She looked around at the line of TV trucks. "You think we could get any more coverage than this?"

"I don't know. We might be missing the Russians or the Chinese, but that's about it," Lucas said.

The negotiator was sweating. On the monitor, Scott was saying, "I know what you're doing. You're stalling. I'm not going to put up with it. I've seen this same deal twenty times; I know you're supposed to stall. But I'll tell you what: I know there are planes that fly out of here every day for Los Angeles and San Francisco and Hawaii, and any of those will get to Cuba. Don't give me any of that shit about reprogramming the computers or getting gas, let's just get me down to the airport and on the plane before I have to kill this lady here."

"I think we got a problem," the negotiator said to Rose Marie.

Del, standing next to Lucas, said, "More than one. Look at this."

Jael Corbeau, trailed by three unhappy cops, was marching down the street toward them. A cop at the perimeter moved to stop her, but she pointed at Lucas, and Lucas said, "Aw, jeez," and waved her through.

"That's him?" she asked. She was dressed in black from head to foot: a black woolen coat, black slacks, black boots, and small black pearls at her ears. She was luminous.

"That's him. He's a guy from Burnt River named —"

"Scott. Yeah, the guys told me. Martin Scott. So how're you gonna get him outa there?"

The negotiator said, "Listen, he's gonna set a deadline, and I wouldn't be surprised if he did it. Killed the hostages. If he's suicidal . . ."

"I don't think he's suicidal," Lucas said. "He's just nuts. He tried to cover his tracks on a couple of these things. . . . I don't think he wanted to be caught."

"Yeah, well, maybe. On the other hand, he may pop that woman," the negotiator said.

Rose Marie said, "What do we do?"

"Figure out some way to start him toward the airport? Maybe snipe him?" Lucas suggested.

She looked at Lester. "Where's that Iowa kid?" The Iowa kid was the department sniper.

"He's on his way."

"So let's set him up. If he gets a clear shot . . ." She looked at the negotiator. "We need some more time. Ask him how he wants to get to the airport, what will keep him safe."

"Aw, man," Lucas said.

"What?"

"I don't know. Look at this bullshit." He waved at the TV trucks; there were eight or nine of them. Four helicopters orbited overhead.

"Well, that's what it is," Rose Marie said. She looked at the negotiator. "Ask him how he wants to do it."

As the negotiator was talking, the mayor arrived. He looked at the gas station, then at Lucas. "How're you gonna get him outa there?"

An armored car.

"Aw, man," Lucas said.

"Will you shut up?" Rose Marie said.

"Can I talk to that guy? For just a minute?"

The negotiator looked at Lucas and said, "We have established an element of trust between us."

"Oh, bullshit, he sounds like he's making the moves before we are," Lucas said. "You trust him, he doesn't trust you. Let me talk to him."

Rose Marie looked at the mayor, who shrugged. "I'm no expert," he said.

"Go ahead," said Rose Marie.

Lucas took the phone. "This is Lucas Davenport. I'm the guy who chased you with the Porsche, and I want you to know you messed up a perfectly good paint job."

"Tough shit. What do you want?"

"I want to come up to the gas station door and talk to you, away from this crowd. You're up there in a bulletproof booth, I can't hurt you, you can't hurt me, and you got the hostages. I just want to talk to you away from this crowd."

"About what?"

"About TV."

"What?"

"About all this TV. Give me two minutes. I won't come inside, I'll just stick my head in the door."

After a moment: "If this is a trick, I'll kill this lady."

"This is no trick. I'm just tired of all the bullshit," Lucas said.

He walked up to the station with his hands open, held at armpit level, stopped at the door, pushed it slowly open, then leaned inside.

"How are ya?"

"What, you're doing a Henry Fonda impression?"

"No. I just don't want anybody to get killed. Especially me."

"What do you want?"

"To work a couple of things out with you. First of all, you don't want to go to Cuba. You know what they do to you in Cuba? They put you in prison. Forever. The last guy who hijacked a plane down there hasn't been seen since 1972. They might be Commies, but they don't like criminals. They'll stick you into a wet drippy dungeon with a bunch of rats, and you'll wind up looking like the Count of Monte Cristo. Stillwater prison is a goddamned garden spot next to anything you'll get in Cuba."

"Maybe I'll take that chance," Scott said. Being the hard man, Lucas thought. Lucas could see him clearly through the glass: a thatch of straw-colored hair, a heavy, ruddy face, plastic-framed glasses, and the Coke coveralls.

"Look, you see all those cameras out there? What if I walk one of those cameras up here and let you make a statement to the world about what you were doing for Alie'e. Then we cut out all this Cuba bullshit and killing innocent people in front of TV cameras so everybody'll know you're an asshole — and you just come in and tell us what happened to you. You'll have lawyers and everything. You'll be treated well."

"What channel?" Scott asked.

Lucas thought, *Gotcha,* and said, "Any channel you want. I'd recommend Channel Twenty-nine, because they play right into Fox, which has the best news department, as I'm sure you know."

"No, no. None of that Fox bullshit. Channel Three: that's CBS down here?" Scott asked.

"Yup."

"Let's talk to somebody from Channel Three, see what they say," Scott said.

Lucas walked back to the line.

"What's going on?" Rose Marie asked.

"We're talking," Lucas said. "I gotta go get some movie people."

He felt like he was plodding through knee-deep mud. He spotted Ginger House from Channel Three, with her cameraman, pointed at her, and gestured. She tapped herself on the chest, and Lucas nodded and shouted, "Bring your cameraman."

She trotted across the police line with the cameraman in tow, and other reporters began screaming in the background. Lucas said, "You will now owe me more than you can ever possibly repay."

"What?" She was a nice-looking redhead with freckles on her narrow nose.

"We're gonna walk up there, and the guy's gonna give us a statement, and then maybe something good'll happen."

"Is it dangerous?" she asked. She sounded reluctant.

"No, I don't think —"

"You know what's dangerous, Ginger?" the cameraman asked. "What's dangerous is, if you turn this down, I swear to God I'll go back to the truck, get out my gun, and shoot you in the forehead. Every goddamn person in the world is gonna see us do this. We do this, we're gonna be movie stars."

"Or I'll be dead," she said.

"Hell, you're a second-string reporter in Minneapolis. That's the same thing as being dead anyway," the cameraman said.

She thought about it for a second, then said, "Okay." As they walked up to the gas station, she said to Lucas, "I don't have to blow you or anything for doing this?"

"Well, yeah, that *is* part of the deal," Lucas said.

"Maybe I'll just describe what I would have done, and you can handle it yourself," she said, trying for a sweet smile; but she was shaking. "What do I say to him?"

"Fall back on your clichés," Lucas said.

Lucas pushed the door open, said, "This is Ginger House, from Channel Three." The cameraman focused on Scott. Ginger said, "I'll have to come in there to do the introduction. I don't have a gun or anything."

"Better not be a trick," Scott said. "We got a TV, and it's tuned to Channel Three." He nodded at a small four-inch television sitting on a shelf inside the booth.

"I'm too nervous for any tricks," Ginger said, and her voice carried conviction. She stepped through the door, and then turned to face the camera, with Scott looming behind her through the bulletproof glass. The cameraman refocused on her; he whispered, "You're live."

Ginger said, "This is Ginger House. We're standing in an Amoco station off I-35W in Minneapolis, where Mr. Martin Scott is holding two hostages. Mr. Scott is suspected by Minneapolis police of involvement in the murders done in revenge for the Alie'e Maison killing last week. Mr. Scott has agreed to be interviewed exclusively for the Channel Three *Good Morning* show. How are you, Mr. Scott?" Smiling, she pivoted toward Scott, who smiled and said, "Well, Ginger, I'm pretty busy this morning, as you can see. . . ."

"Aw, Jesus," Lucas muttered to himself. He turned and looked back toward the growing crowd. He could hear the howling of the other TV people from where he was standing. "Jesus H. Christ."

They talked for ten minutes; and Scott wasn't bad, Lucas thought. He explained the killings cogently, and justified them. Plain had exploited her death by selling pictures of her naked the same night she was murdered; her parents had gotten her involved in dope and deviant sexuality in the first place; Spooner, of course, had actually killed Alie'e.

At the end of the interview, Ginger asked, "Could we just ask a question or two of the hostages?"

"Sure, go ahead."

The woman was named Melody. "We've been treated very well, better than I expected. Mr. Scott has been a gentleman," she said, with a slight unidentifiable accent. Then she did a little finger wave at the camera. The other hostage, a dark-haired young man named Ralph, said, "I just want to get out of here. I've got classes this morning — we've got a quiz."

As Ginger and the cameraman walked back across the gas pad to the police lines, the howling of the press seemed to swell again. Lucas leaned in the door. "So now you've had your airtime. Now if you kill anyone, they'll figure everything else was bullshit, and you were a phony all the time."

"I'm thinking," Scott said.

And the woman, Melody, said to Lucas, "Please, please get me out of here." And to Scott: "Please, let me go."

"I can't yet," Scott said. He looked at Lucas. "There oughta be more than this."

"There *is* no more than this, Martin," Lucas

said. He gestured at the crowd, at the cameras. "You just spoke to the entire *world*."

"I don't know," he said. "There oughta be more."

Lucas sighed, looked around, then said, "All right. Maybe there is."

"What?"

"I'll be back."

He trudged back across the parking lot. Rose Marie said, "What?"

"We're getting there. It's like pulling a god-damn snail out of a shell." He spotted Jael and walked over to her. "I gotta ask you a favor."

They walked together toward the gas station, and Jael said, "I'm gonna wet my pants."

"That's good," Lucas said. "For six billion viewers, you're gonna wet your pants."

"Sort of a trip, isn't it?"

Lucas leaned in the door again. "Mr. Scott, I'm sure you know this young woman. You've been trying to kill her. She wants to apologize to you for any wrong she might have done to Alie'e, and in turn, she wants you to apologize for killing her brother, who she deeply loved."

Jael stepped just inside the door. Lucas had warned her to stay close so she could back off if Scott did anything crazy. "As long as he's *inside* the booth, you should be okay."

She began, "Mr. Scott, I am truly sorry . . ."

She did it almost perfectly, Lucas thought, fixing him with her eyes, letting him take in her torn-paper face. "I had a hard childhood. Look at my scars," she said. She touched her face. "I was in a car accident . . ."

They talked for a few minutes, then Scott shook his head as though dazed. "So what's the deal?" he asked Lucas.

Lucas said, "The deal is this: We go back to the lines, we get another camera of your choice. We come back here. You shuck all the shells out of your rifle — uh, where's the shotgun?"

"In the car. I couldn't reach it after the crash."

"All right. Anyway, you shuck all the shells out of the rifle, lay the rifle to the side. Then you open the booth, and you surrender to Jael — we're talking the world's biggest TV audience here — and then we all walk across the gas pad and you'll be taken into custody. With a lawyer right there."

"What channel?"

"Three? You want Ginger back?" Lucas asked.

"No. She was okay, but she was a little too . . . smooth. She didn't have that good jagged quality. How about . . . uh, what do you think?"

"Six. There's a woman with Six, sort of an understated beauty, if you know what I mean."

"Not Ellen?"

"Exactly. Ellen. She's out there, Martin."

He thought about it for a long beat. Then: "All right. Ellen."

Lucas went back, pointed at Ellen Goodrich, who raced out of the crowd, towing her camera. "Lucas . . . what can I say? And what're we doing?"

"We're gonna do the surrender."

"Aw, jeez, that's just . . . that's just . . ." He thought she might weep with gratitude, but she didn't.

"Let's go," Lucas said.

The surrender went well, to a point, Lucas thought.

Jael made a statement, a formal apology for any wrongs that had been done to Alie'e. Scott apologized for the killings, said he still felt that they were necessary — but that Jael through her gracious actions had made up for some of it.

Then, with the TV camera focusing on him, Scott jacked the slide on the Ruger until shells stopped popping out. He said, "I hereby surrender to Jael Corbeau, a brave woman."

He reached out and popped the lock on the door. As it opened, the dark-haired hostage, Ralph, screamed, "YOU COCKSUCKER." He snatched the small portable TV off the shelf, and as Scott turned, startled, Ralph hit him in the face with it.

Scott went down as though he'd been struck by a meteorite, and Lucas shouted, "Hey," and tried to get the door open, but the woman, Melody, began kicking at Scott, screaming

"SONABEECH" in an unexpected Mexican accent. Then she snatched a can of Pyroil starting fluid off the shelf and began hitting Scott in the back of the head, slicing off swaths of scalp.

Scott pushed up, tried to crawl through the rain of blows. Jael was there. Lucas tried to push past her, but she screamed, "You killed my brother, you motherfucker." Scott, stunned and bleeding, looked up, and she kicked him in the eye and he went down again.

The camera was crowding in, and Lucas swatted Jael to one side and tried to get at the dark-haired man, who was beating Scott with the remnants of the portable TV. Lucas grabbed him by the shirt, pulled him across Scott's body, and threw him into the cameraman; the cameraman, Ralph, and Ellen Goodrich all went down in a heap. Melody screamed, suddenly panic-stricken, and ran past. For a moment, Lucas and the stunned, bleeding Scott were behind the counter in a little pool of peace and privacy. Scott tried to push himself up, and Lucas whispered, "This is for Marcy, asshole," and hit him in the nose as hard as he could.

There was a satisfying crunch of bone, and Scott went down for the count.

An hour later, the mayor said, "I thought it went pretty well. You know, all things considered."

❧ 30 ❧

The media attention was intense through the morning, until football started. By nine that night, most of the out-of-towners were gone.

On Monday, Lucas, Rose Marie, Frank Lester, and the mayor met in Rose Marie's office. Rose Marie said, "We're getting a ton of stuff on Spooner. He was in it up to his neck. And the Ramsey ME's office is saying they're not so sure that Rodriguez was a suicide. They found residue of wood preservative in his hair."

"Told you," Lucas said comfortably. "He was hit with a goddamn two-by-four and dropped over the banister. By Spooner. Spooner not only killed Rodriguez, I bet he's the guy who leaked Rodriguez's name to *Spittle*. Set him up, made him the bad guy, killed him."

"Spooner had a safe-deposit box over in Hudson," Lester said. "There were some documents that say he made a personal loan to Rodriguez's company in Miami for half a million dollars. Then, the feebs say, there was a lien registered on the company's property with Dade County. Rodriguez couldn't sell the company without the lien being settled, which meant that Spooner had an alarm if Rodriguez tried to get out. Spooner had another hook, too. If Rodriguez tried to sell, he'd have to settle the mortgages, and as the loan officer at Atheneum, Spooner would have known."

"Where'd Spooner get the half-million for the personal loan?" the mayor asked.

"There was no half-million. It was a fictitious loan. That was Spooner's cut in the business," Lester said. "They put it on paper, and hid the paper. In fifteen years, with interest, Spooner's cut is maybe two million. And that way, Spooner always had a hold on the business, if he and Rodriguez had a personal falling-out. He could file suit down in Dade County, and nobody up here would ever know . . . and Rodriguez would have to settle."

"Still would have worked even after Rodriguez died," Lucas said. "If anybody even found out about the loan, they might have thought Spooner's investment was a little questionable — but hell, it'd be a minor thing. Especially if he trotted out all that bullshit about helping minorities and so on."

"Is anybody going to sue us?" the mayor asked.

"I don't know," Rose Marie said. "Spooner's wife might. She knows that Spooner's name was mentioned in our briefing of Olson, and that led indirectly to his death."

"That won't get her anywhere," the mayor

said. "I've done those kinds of suits, and she'd be lucky to get a buck and a half. *We* didn't kill her husband, his own greed killed him. Along with a nutcase."

"And then there's Al-Balah," Rose Marie said.

"He might not be around long enough to sue," Lucas said. "The guys from Narcotics said he went back on the street, but all of his old territory was under new ownership. The new owners don't want to give it back. There's gonna be trouble."

"That would clean things up nicely," the mayor said.

"What, a cocaine war?"

"Hey, dopers die. There's not a lot you can do about it," the mayor said. "It's a tragedy, of course. No man is an island, et cetera."

They all nodded.

When the mayor was gone, Rose Marie looked at Lester and Lucas and said, "We're good."

"I don't believe he bought the whole thing," Lucas said, meaning the mayor.

"He didn't. He knew there was some bullshit going on. But he was a very good lawyer. He knows there are times when you don't ask the obvious question."

"So we're good," Lucas said.

"By the skin of our teeth," Lester said.

"But we're still good," Rose Marie said. She stood up and did a heavy little hop-and-skip over to her window, not quite a jig. "All these other cities, all these big crimes, the media goes in, the controversy lasts for months. *We* have a big crime and *bang,* one killer's dead, and *bang,* the other guy confesses to a national audience. One week. The goddamn movie people think the sun shines out of our asses."

Lester seemed embarrassed. He said, "Yeah, but you know . . ."

"Don't say it," Rose Marie said. "Don't even think it."

"Can't help it," Lucas said. "A lot of things got fucked up this time around, and I personally fucked up most of them. I jumped all over Rodriguez. I bought Olson. I didn't think that the shooter could be using a rifle, because it was a .44. Dirty Harry's *pistol.* I didn't think about the way the word gets around in a small town. . . ."

"We've all got a little hubris in us," Rose Marie said.

"Yeah, yeah," Lucas said.

"You more than most," she added.

Tom Black said, "They took her up to a regular room."

"She's better," Lucas said.

"She's gonna make it," Black said.

"You gotta go get some sleep," Del told Black.

Marcy was awake.

"Don't do that pneumonia shit anymore," Lucas said.

She didn't smile. She whispered, "Hurts."

"I know, goddamnit."

"Hurts," she said again. She looked at Lucas as if he might be able to help. He sat helplessly with his hands in his lap. "I know it does. . . ."

Lucas hadn't seen Jael since the fight in the gas station, although she'd left a message. And he had a call-back slip from Catrin. Weather needed to talk to him: "About a frog," the message slip said.

He didn't quite know how to start. Instead of starting, instead of deciding anything, he went back to his office, put his feet in a desk drawer, leaned back in his chair, and tried to work it out. One thing was, he really wanted a couple of more days with Jael. Of course, Weather — the only woman he'd ever really loved. But remember the time that he and Catrin . . . Jeez. That thing with the Lady Remington, that he'd done with Jael on the phone — Catrin had *invented* that.

He smiled, remembering, and he'd almost fallen asleep when the phone rang.

He jumped, opened his eyes, picked it up.

A woman's voice said, "Lucas?"